PRAISE FOR AURORA AWARD-WINNING AUTHOR JULIE E. CZERNEDA'S WEB SHIFTERS SERIES:

"Julie Czerneda's novels ignite my sense of wonder, from the amazing worlds she creates, to the fully realized aliens and likable characters. I eagerly await her next." —Kristen Britain, author of *Green Rider*

"The plot of *Beholder's Eye* will strike chords with readers familiar with the work of C. J. Cherryh or Hal Clement, but Czerneda stamps this with her own style, proving that a story told from the viewpoint of an alien race is worth reading when properly handled." —*Starlog*

"It's all good fun, a great adventure following an engaging character across a divertingly varied series of worlds, with just a bit of unfulfilled romantic tension for spice." —*Locus*

"The unusual premise and excellent writing combine to make . . . a wonderfully entertaining book. Czerneda uses the opportunity to create widely different species, a far cry from the cookie-cutter critters found in so much science fiction." —*SF Site*

Julie E. Czerneda

HIDDEN IN SIGHT

DAW BOOKS, INC.

DONALD A. WOLLHEIM, FOUNDER

375 Hudson Street, New York, NY 10014

ELIZABETH R. WOLLHEIM
SHEILA E. GILBERT
PUBLISHERS

http://www.dawbooks.com

For Mistybrig's Kobayashi Maru

(March 12, 1989—November 11, 2002)

Hi Kobay. I know I'll reach down and expect to sink my fingers into your sun-warmed fur when I write by the pond next spring. You've snoozed beside me through all my books, after the required theatrical sigh whenever I appeared with paper in hand. I know I'll forget and call you when I'm heading for the garden. You were never convinced this was a reasonable activity, but would always try to help, as long as your paws stayed clean and no hose was in sight. I know above all I'll miss your beautiful face—how your eyes would light up when we asked you to do a trick ("Boulder!") or herd squirrels, and how you'd tilt your head just so when listening to us talk, quite willing and able to hum in answer.

In memory of long walks, Christmas presents, and soccer balls, to the best dog a family could love.

Go to bed, Kobay. Good boy.

And thank you.

ACKNOWLEDGMENTS

My seventh novel! My third about a certain blob's attempts to understand humanity. DAW's thirtieth anniversary and my fifth as one of their authors. Numbers are amazing things, especially when behind them stands the amount of support, enthusiasm, and friendship I've received while writing this book.

My thanks to Sheila Gilbert for "loving" the ending. I'm saving that message. I'd like to thank Kim McLean for her help causing mayhem with volcanic tubes and Dr. Isaac Szpindel for confirming some nose work. Thanks, Roxanne Hubbard, for speedy reading! And thank you, Luis Royo, for another stunning cover. I'd also like to acknowledge Wendy Cheatham (G'leep) for Z'ndraa, her wonderful alien and his music, and Saturne, for the poem which formed the lyrics.

Several kind folks lent their names to this story. As usual, there is no resemblance intended to the real owners of these names, although they are welcome to claim any nice bits. My thanks to Zoltan Duda (who I hear is a terrific pilot), Maren (Neram) Henry, Ruth Stuart, Susan Lehman, M.T. O'Shaughnessy (Uriel), and Pat Lundrigan (on behalf of his father, Alphonsus Lundrigan).

I do sneak in tributes to the work I love by other authors or filmmakers. This time, however, I would like to especially thank all those involved in making *Farscape*. You've set a new standard for storytelling in our genre, as well as inspired my own writing every week.

My sincere thanks to all those who hosted me at events this past year. While I can't mention them all, I must thank Donna Young and the staff of the Wright's Center, as well as Dr. Tom Easton and the enthusiastic educators who attended *Space Science XVII: Cosmology*. My thanks also to Rhonda Normore, Robin McQueen, and Vick Steel, as well as all the students and teachers in Fort McMurray, for valuing science fiction and my work.

Scott? Knowing you've been happy has been a tremendous help, believe me, as were your emails of encouragement. Jennifer? I hope you like this one too, and thank you for all the times you took over and looked after us while I was story-bound. Roger? I've no idea how you put up with me as I finish a story, but you always know what to do to make it easy. Thank you.

CONTENTS

Otherwhere

FINGERS stroked death. They ran lightly along its edge, explored its flawless surface, caressed its hilt. Finally, they opened. The knife fell on the tabletop with an angry ring of metal to stone. *Failure was inefficient.*

"I was expecting more—progress." The voice was like the knife, flawless, smooth, and as deadly.

The one bringing the report nodded. "As were we. There is an admirable level of paranoia in our subjects, Eminence." The Kraal touched the tattoos on both cheeks, bowing deeply. "We regret our lack of success."

"As do I." *Inconvenient, to find the Youngest this careful. Yet reassuring.*

Another sat at the stone table, reflected by its polished black surface; her hands, almost as dark as the stone, pressed themselves flat on the tabletop. Pa-Admiral Mocktap, tattoos glowing white against her skin, waited with unusual patience. Her ships did the same. The tattoos were marks of loyalty and obedience; the patience—perhaps—came from familiarity. Trust wasn't a word used by Kraal. *A comforting congruence.*

An ally of her own would be *expedient.* The trap into which foolish Esen had fallen—continued to fall.

She *would not make that mistake*

"Time to flush our prey from its lair," the deadly, flawless voice decided.

1: Cliffside Afternoon

"YOU made that up," I accused.

"It's the truth, Es. I swear on my father's grave."

I eyed my Human friend with deep suspicion, all too familiar with that too-innocent look. "Your father isn't dead," I reminded him.

"Picky, picky," he grinned. "Okay. I swear on my grandmother's grave. Noah and I really did swim in the Chidtik Ocean without suits."

"The body of your paternal grandmother was sent into the sun of her birth system, Hendrick," I countered. "That of your maternal grandmother was recycled, by her wish, into an exact replica of her favorite sofa. She is now gathering dust in your Uncle Sam's attic because no one in the family can bring themselves to sit on her. So you can't use their graves either." I paused to scowl. "No Human—even one so reckless as you seem to have been in your youth—would swim in the Chidtik without an environment suit."

The fine lines at the corners of Paul Cameron's eyes crinkled ever so slightly. "How do you remember all that trivia— No, stop. Dumb question. You remember everything." He leaned back, stretching his arms up to cushion his head against the stone. We were enjoying a rare moment of peaceful weather—in other words, the wind curling the clouds in front of our porch was whining instead of howling—and Paul was relishing every moment. Including this latest effort to persuade me of yet another impossible feat from his past. If he'd actually done all the things he claimed, it was quite remarkable he'd lived long enough to meet me, Esen-alit-Quar, Esen for short, Es in a hurry, or between dear friends.

"There may have been some mitigating circumstances," Paul ventured peacefully.

"Such as?" I rolled over on my stomach to better watch his face.

"A night of rain, a surfboard, and a keg of local beer." He paused, then nodded. "And some tall boots. I distinctly remember there were boots. I've no idea whose, but they did come in handy."

I was growing convinced despite my common sense, and shivered though the sun was warm on my shoulders and back. A temporary layer of fresh water on top of that caustic ocean, a board to keep most of his body from the depths, boots to protect his feet from the scalpel-sharp crystals that passed as beach sand to the unwary visitor. It was possible after all.

It was supremely stupid. "Was it worth it?" I asked him.

The Human's eyes gleamed. "Every minute. Even with my souvenir." He showed me the underside of his left arm. I'd noticed the faint swath of a scar there before, but had never asked about its origin. "Noah was a little drunker than I was and splashed me as we were coming out. I dodged most of it—but he had burns on his hand and wrist. Not that he remembers how he got them."

"I will never understand the ephemeral urge to risk shortening an already too-short life span by taking such risks," I said primly. "It is gratifying to know you grow out of it."

Paul chuckled. "Which is why I'm sunbathing on the side of a sheer cliff, my feet almost at the edge of this ledge, trading stories with a shapeshifting monster."

I didn't argue, although it was no accident I was stretched out between Paul and that edge. My Human form might be that of a slight young girl, but I would never let harm come to my friend. My Web.

"Speaking of trading stories, my ancient Blob, I've a request."

I raised an eyebrow. "Shall I describe the undersea ruins in the Chidtik, given you were so close to joining them?"

He wagged a finger at me admonishingly. "Not so fast. Yesterday you promised to tell me your very first memory, or did you forget?"

I'd hoped he had. Paul had an excellent mind, but I'd noticed if I left an idea alone long enough, or offered sufficient distraction, he would occasionally lose his train of thought. "Yours was far too interesting," I told him. "How could my earliest thoughts compare with your effort to fly from the roof of the family barn?"

I wasn't going to deflect him this time. I could tell by the gleam in his eye that Paul's curiosity was fully engaged. "C'mon, Es. What's the first thing stored in that perfect memory of yours? There has to be something at least a bit embarrassing in your youth. I've confessed my sins—what were yours? It's only fair, Fangface."

"My first memory," I repeated, giving in as always. There was no resisting my Human web-kin when he was this determined. I confessed curiosity. I hadn't thought back to that time since living it. Unlike my current form's sake, unlike Paul's, I had no need to reminisce over and over again to make my past permanent in my own mind.

I had no ability to change or romanticize my past either. Whatever I'd experienced, whatever I learned, became part of my flesh. The only way to lose a recollection was to lose part of my mass before I could withdraw the memories from it—a painful and highly disorienting experience I'd suffered only once.

"Well, Esen?"

I sat up, moving to lean shoulder to shoulder with Paul against our cliff, and stared out over plains and mountaintops of wind-tossed cloud, imagining the landscape beneath, the cluster of beings busy with their presents, their futures, their pasts.

"It was five hundred and fifty-three standard years ago, and a smattering of days . . ." I began.

Otherwhen

IMAGINE being a student not for ten orbits of a sun, or thirty, but over two hundred such journeys. Granted, I spent the first few decades doing what any newborn Lanivarian would do: eating, metabolizing, differentiating, growing, eating, metabolizing, differentiating, growing . . . I remember it as a time of restlessness, of an awareness I was more, but unable to express this other than to whimper and chew.

The day did arrive when I opened my mouth and something intelligible came out. I distinctly remember this something—web-beings being possessed of perfect memory—as a clear and succinct request for more jamble grapes. My birth-mother, Ansky, remembers it as an adorably incoherent babble that nonetheless signaled I was ready for the next phase of my existence. So she took me to Ersh, the Senior Assimilator and Eldest of our Web, who promptly grabbed me by the scruff of the neck and tossed me off her mountain.

While horrifying to any real Lanivarian mother—and likely any intelligent species with parental care—this was Ersh being efficient. I was thus encouraged to cycle into my web-self for the first time. It was that, or be shattered on a rock seven hundred and thirteen meters below. Instinct, as Ersh rather blithely assumed, won, and I landed on the surface of Picco's

Moon as a small, intensely blue, blob of web-mass. A somewhat flattened blob, but unharmed.

Unharmed, but I recalled being overwhelmed with foreign sensations as my universe widened along every imaginable axis. I floundered to make some sense of it all, until, suddenly, everything became *right*. I knew without being told this was my true self, that there was nothing unusual in losing touch, sound, sight, and smell while feeling the spin of stars and atoms, hearing harmony in the competing gravities of Picco and her Moon, seeing the structure of matter, and being perfectly able to distinguish what was appetizing from what was not.

Appetite. I formed a mouth, small and with only one sharp edge, then began scanning my new universe for something to bite. *There!*

Not knowing what it was, I ripped a mouthful from the edible mass so conveniently close.

Ersh-taste!

Ideas, not just nutrients, flooded my consciousness, new and nauseatingly complex. *Ersh-memory.* Even as I hastily oozed myself into the nearest dark and safe-looking crevice, I gained a word for what was happening to me. *Assimilation.* This was how webbeings exchanged information—by exchanging the memories stored within their flesh. *Our flesh.*

Exchange? I was mulling that over when a sharp, unexpected pain let me know I'd paid the price for my knowledge.

My studies had officially begun.

What followed were times of wonder and the expansion of my horizons . . . okay, what really followed were centuries of always being the last to assimilate anything and being convinced this was a plot to keep me stuck with one of my Elders at all times. In retrospect, it was probably more difficult for them. The ancient, wise beings who formed the Web of Ersh had made plans for their lives and research stretching over millennia and, as they routinely assured me, I hadn't been so much as imagined in any of them.

Maybe in Ansky's. Ansky's outstanding enthusiasm for interacting with the locals meant I wasn't her first offspring—just the first, and only, to taste of web-mass. The rest grew up clutched to what I fondly imagined were the loving teats, bosoms, or corresponding body parts of their respective species.

I was tossed off a mountain to prove I belonged here, with Ersh and whomever else of my Web happened to be in attendance. While they could have cycled into more nurturing species—the ability to manipulate our mass into that of other intelligent species being a key survival trait of my kind—I'm quite sure it didn't occur to any of them. I was not only Ansky's first, I was a first for the Web as well, having been born rather than split from Ersh's own flesh. This was a distinction that made at least some of my web-kin very uneasy. Mind you, they'd been virtually untouched by change since the Human species discovered feet, so my arrival came as something of a shock. Ansky was firmly reminded to be more careful in the future. Her Web, Ersh pronounced sternly, was large enough.

We were six: Ersh, Ansky, Lesy, Mixs, Skalet, and me, Esen-alit-Quar—Esen for short, Es in a hurry. Six who shared flesh and memories. Six given a goal and purpose in life by Ersh: to be a living repository of the biology and culture of all other, tragically short-lived intelligent species. It was an endless, grueling task that took years of living in secret on each world, ingesting and assimilating the biology of each ephemeral form, learning languages, arts, histories, beliefs, and sciences, all while traveling the limits of known space.

Not that I was ever allowed to go.

Ersh had dictated I was to stay on Picco's Moon until I was ready. *Ready?* I understood waiting until my body grew into its full web-size. After all, mass had to be considered when cycling into another form. It was wasteful, if entertaining, to gorge myself simply to cycle into something larger, then have to shed the excess as water anyway upon returning to web-form. Then there was the issue of learning to hold another form. The others presumed my staying Lanivarian from birth till impact meant I'd be able to distort my web-mass into any other I'd assimilated. They were wrong. While I could immediately return to my birth-form for a moment or two, after all this time, I still couldn't hold other forms for any duration. I might have done so faster, had Ersh chosen to teach me what I needed to know—and had the others refrained from terrifying hints I might explode if I wasn't careful—but Ersh had definite ideas of what and how I was to learn.

Which was the real reason I still wasn't "ready" after two hundred years. Ersh had insisted I be taught—by the others, as well as herself. Since this teaching could not be done by assimilation alone, and she found fault with almost everything I did learn—not surprising, considering I had four teachers who'd never taught before—"ready" seemed unlikely to occur within even a web-being's almost endless life span. I was stuck on Ersh's rock, safe and utterly bored.

It would have been nice if it had stayed that way.

"Esen!!!!!!"

My present ears were tall enough to extend past the top of the friendly boulder sheltering the rest of me. I swiveled them slightly to capture more nuance from the echoes ricocheting after that latest bellow from the window. It was important to gauge when Ersh was about to pass exasperation and head for all-out fury, if I wanted to avoid something thoroughly unpleasant in the way of consequences. The Eldest did occasionally give up before losing her temper. *Twice, maybe.*

"Are you going to answer, 'tween, or should I?" a velvet-coated voice from behind inquired, driving my ears flat against my skull.

Skalet? I didn't bother twisting my snout around to glare at her, too busy quelling this body's instinct to run from threat. I wasn't in any danger, except from heart palpitations at Skalet's bizarre sense of humor. She'd approached from downwind, naturally, having firsthand knowledge of my current form's sense of smell. Providing such unpleasant surprises was simply this web-kin's favorite game at my expense and quite the feat this time, considering she was supposed to be half the quadrant away.

However, Skalet was probably preparing to expose my hiding place to Ersh—her other favorite pastime. "I was just getting up," I told her, attempting to make this more casual than sullen. Skalet had no patience for what she called my "ephemeral moods."

When I finally looked at her, it was to affirm the voice matched the form I'd expected. I may have been the only "born" web-being, but that didn't mean the others were identical. Far from it. Even in web-form, they were distinct individuals, sending tastes as unique as themselves into the air, though this was usually only when they were sharing memories with one another. Revealing web-form to aliens was strictly forbidden, precaution as well as protection.

So normally, they chose another form, picked, my Elders informed me, for its appropriateness as camouflage and its convenience when using non-Web technology. I was reasonably sure their choices had more to do with personal preference, since if it was convenience alone, they'd all be Dokecian and have arms to spare—with a brain able to control all of them at once. Not that I'd been Dokeci any longer than it took to realize successful coordination required a certain level of maturity as well as a room without fragile objects.

Skalet managed to cause me enough grief with her present brain. She stood too close for comfort, straight and tall on two legs, dressed in a chrome-on-black uniform she likely considered subtle but which reflected glints of Picco's orange-stained light with each disapproving breath. *Kraal.* I replayed a portion of memory. Human subspecies. Not biologically distinct, though heading in that direction. Culturally so, definitely, with a closed society built around an elaborate internal hierarchy of family, clan, and tribe allegiance. New from her last trip was a tattoo from throat to behind her left ear marking a particular affiliation; she'd made sure to braid her thick hair to expose every line. I didn't bother reading it.

My obedient rise to my hind legs produced the expected ominous silence from the window and lit a triumphant gleam in Skalet's Human eyes. "What did you do this time, Youngest?" she asked as we walked together up the slope to Ersh's cliffside home. As we did, I could see Skalet's personal shuttle sitting on the landing pad. Shuttles to and from the shipcity on the other side of Picco's Moon were the only rapid means of travel across the tortured landscape. The native intelligent species, Tumblers, preferred to migrate slowly along the jagged valley floors, stopping for conversations that could last months. They had a time sense on a par with Ersh's, which I'd long ago decided was why she was usually a Tumbler herself. *Another difference between us.*

"Nothing," I said, quite truthfully. I was supposed to have finished repotting the duras seedlings in Ersh's

greenhouse this morning, making that "nothing" undoubtedly the cause of the bellowing. I hated plants.
They stank when healthy and reeked when ill. And
dirt. I hated dirt, too. Dry sand I quite liked. But no,
plants insisted on wet dirt that stuck to my paws and
got in my sensitive nose. It hadn't taken more than the
thought of coming outside to catch the monthly
Eclipse, an event I always missed because of some
task or other Ersh invented, to make me abandon the
trays.

"Ah," Skalet replied, as if my answer was more than
sufficient. "Neither did I," she said more quietly, her
steps slowing as if in thought. "Are the others here
yet?"

"What others?" I asked. "I didn't know you were
coming until now. Are the rest on the way?" My tail
gave a treacherous sideways drift before I could stop
it, tail-wagging being among those childish things I
was supposed to be long past. Lesy tended to bring
presents. To be honest, any of the web-kin did, in the
form of knowledge to be shared—even Skalet, though
hers often tasted more of conflict and politics than
wonder. Ersh sorted it all for me first, of course, as Senior Assimilator, but I could always tell the source.

"That's for Ersh to tell us," Skalet said brusquely,
our steps having reached the point of our approach
everyone knew marked where Ersh's sensitive Tumbler hearing must be taken into account.

Ersh had told us, all right. I gingerly pushed the
seedling into the revoltingly damp dirt with one extended toe. My Lanivarian hands were adept at such
fine maneuvers, if a misery to clean afterward. My
ears were cocked back, toward the kitchen, straining
to catch the mutterings of an argument which had
lasted longer than I'd thought possible.

No one countered Ersh's wishes. *Except me.* But

that was something my web-kin had come to expect. They all knew I'd give in, come home, do the job, and grovel appropriately. It was unthinkable to imagine otherwise, even for me at my most rebellious. Ersh was the center of our Web. Her word was Law.

Until today, when she'd stated her latest wish and Skalet had tried to refuse.

Another seedling went in, stubbornly crooked until I pressed the dirt to one side firmly with my thumb; I couldn't help humming happily to myself. Although it delayed supper and spoke volumes about my immaturity, the novelty of someone else taking the brunt of Ersh's ire was extraordinarily pleasant—not to mention I was on Skalet's side.

I most definitely didn't want her staying with me while Ersh left home for the first time in my memory.

That this arrangement was designed to punish both of us with Ersh's famed economy of effort was not lost on me, but what Skalet could have done to deserve it I didn't know. Nor wanted to.

Ersh should have told me.

"I've had enough of you."

My stylo halted its dive at the star chart and I peered up hopefully. "We're done for the day?" I asked.

A violent wave and: "Ssssh."

Skalet was using the com system. Again. As she had most of the morning since Ersh departed—in Skalet's own shuttle, something she'd known better than to protest.

I sighed and reapplied myself to the present lesson. Another three-dimensional strategy calculation, probably containing some unlikely ambush. Ersh must have removed more than usual from Skalet's latest memories of the Kraal before sharing them with me, for this made less sense to me than the last lesson.

Regardless, it would be my fault. I sighed once more, but to myself. Skalet was brilliant and, as a Kraal, had earned considerable acclaim within her chosen species as a strategist. Not an accomplishment she flaunted, given Ersh's obsession with keeping our natures and activities hidden, but there were no secrets in the Web. Well, technically there were any number of secrets held within Ersh's teardrop blue web-mass—most being kept from me—but none of us had that ability. And, when it suited her, or more truthfully, when Ersh was within earshot, Skalet could be a patient and interesting teacher. Otherwise, as now, she was maddeningly obscure yet somehow convinced I deliberately avoided what she saw as the clear, simple path to the right answer in order to waste her time.

Hardly. I was every bit as anxious to have this lesson done and be outside where I could observe the Eclipse. I wrinkled my snout at the problem before me, wondering if accidentally drooling on the plas sheet might somehow ruin it.

Skalet continued talking urgently into the com. "Listen, Uriel. Just bring it down here instead of where we arranged. That's the only change."

Maybe it was the lesson, with its layers of move and countermove, but I grew suddenly curious about Skalet's conversation with this mysterious "Uriel."

Of course, it's hard to be subtle with ears like mine. "Esen," Skalet said sharply, "if you can't concentrate on your work, go outside for a while."

Perversely, now that she told me to do what I'd wanted to do, I no longer wanted to do it. I glumly suspected this irrational reversal was another of those indications I wasn't ready to assume an adult's role within the Web. I opened my mouth to protest—and then closed it. Skalet had leaned back against the com unit, watching me with the obvious intention of not saying another word in my presence.

So I left.

Picco was a gas giant, her immense curve dominating a quarter of the horizon, reflecting, during her day, a vile combination of orange and purple over the landscape of her hapless Moon. During her night, Picco's silhouette occluded a chunk of the starry sky—the so-called Void. Early Tumbler civilizations had populated the Void with invisible demons. The belief continued to influence their behavior, so that modern Tumblers had a hearty dislike of moving about in the dark. As Ersh pointed out, this was a survival characteristic, given the fragile nature of an adult Tumbler's crystalline structure and the difficulty in finding any level ground on their home sphere. *Beliefs have value,* I could hear her repeating endlessly, *if not always that assumed by the believer.*

Picco's Moon did spin, luckily for those of us interested in a broader array of color, but with aggravating slowness. Once a moon week, Ersh's mountain faced away from Picco to bathe in the light of the system's star. This arrangement was called the Eclipse, Tumbler science persistent in its belief that Picco orbited her Moon and thus the shadow cast on the giant planet's surface mattered more than the arrival of true daylight. Legend said this was the time when the Void tried to drill a hole through Picco herself, only to be foiled by the magical strength of Picco's surface. Festivals and other entertainments were typically timed to climax at the end of the Eclipse as seen from the Picco-facing side of the Moon.

Other things were timed for sunlight. The sort of things I might accuse Ersh of deliberately keeping from me, except that I was afraid she'd chime agreement.

Sex wasn't the mystery. Ersh might presort the others' memories before sharing them with me, but biology didn't seem to be one of the taboos she enforced. On the contrary, we had many discussions, ranging from gruesome to merely nauseating, about the lengths to which species went in order to mix their genes. Oh, I knew all about Tumbler sex. Those individuals interested in procreation wandered about gleaning material from others of presumably attractive growth, incorporating each shard as it was received into their body matrix until they felt sufficiently endowed. There followed a rather orgasmic interlude of fragmentation, resulting in a smaller, presumably satiated adult, and a litter—literally—of tiny pre-Tumbler crystals dropped wherever that Tumbler had been roaming at the time. Somehow, during Eclipse on the sunside of Picco's Moon, those crystals were recovered by their proud parent and given the opportunity to grow.

Somehow. This was where Ersh grew annoyingly vague and, when pressed for details, had begun inconveniently timing my indoor tasks during the sunny side of Eclipse.

Skalet, however, didn't care what I learned, as long as she didn't have to teach me.

I bounded up the last, worn stone step to the top of Ersh's mountain and paused to pant a moment. Usually I avoided the place, unless it was one of those times Ersh insisted the sharing of the Web be done here, but there really was no better view. *Just in time.* The orange rim of Picco was disappearing behind the horizon, cut into a fanged grin by the distant range of mountains. Sunlight—real, full spectrum, right from the source light—poured over the surface, losing the struggle where Picco's reflection still ruled, but elsewhere striking the crystalline facets etched on every slope and valley in a display that explained quite clearly why this was a gem dealer's notion of paradise.

Gem dealers. I grinned, walking to the cliff's edge, stopping a comforting number of body lengths short. While Ersh disapproved of irony on general principle, given how often it involved disaster for the species involved in mutual misconception, I couldn't help but take special pleasure in this particular case. The most prized gems from Picco's Moon? Tumbler excretions. Those legitimate dealers—hired by the Tumblers for waste removal and treatment around their shipcity, the only densely populated area—did their utmost to regulate off-Moon availability and so keep up the price of the beautiful stones, but there was, naturally, a thriving black market fed by those fools willing to try landing where level merely implied nonperpendicular.

To their credit, the Tumblers were dismayed by this risky traffic in defecation and regularly tried to explain, but something kept being lost in the translation of their polite phrase: "ritual leavings."

I sat on my haunches, feeling the warmth of the Sun's rays on my back, and looked for Tumblers engaged in Eclipse activities, feeling deliciously naughty—especially with Skalet to take the blame when, not if, Ersh found out.

But what I saw was a midsized cargo shuttle with no markings, banking low in front of Ersh's mountain, heading to our landing pad.

If this wasn't Ersh returning too soon from her mysterious trip, or web-kin with a particularly large present, Skalet was going to be in more trouble than I'd hoped.

The advantage of a shared secret was a mutual desire to keep it. I had no doubt Skalet knew I was nearby, but also knew this time she wouldn't reveal my hiding place. Not to her guest.

A non-Web guest. Hair persisted in rising along my spine. *Alien*. Human.

And, most intriguing of all, male.

I held the genetic instructions for Human within my web-mass, along with all other species the Web had assimilated, but were I or any of my web-kin to take that form, we would be female. Cycling didn't change who we were—simply what we were. As a result, I'd never been this close to a male Human before.

Shared memory wasn't everything, I realized, aware this was something Ersh had despaired, loudly, I'd ever learn to appreciate.

He was as tall as Skalet, not as whipcord thin, but gracefully built. The wind picked up curly locks of black hair and tossed them in his face—surely distracting, but he didn't appear to notice. No tattoos. Perhaps not Kraal.

Or not wanting to appear Kraal, I thought abruptly, enjoying this live game of strategy far more than any of Skalet's simulations. Kraal didn't mix with other types of Humans, unless in formal groupings such as war or diplomacy. He could be—a spy!

Against us? My lips rolled back from my fangs despite common sense. With the exception of Ersh, none of us approached Skalet's paranoia about protecting our true nature. So, this Human wasn't a threat to Ersh or our home. *Then what was he?* I tilted my ears forward as the male began to speak.

"—nice spot, S'kal-ru. We should have used this from the first—"

His voice might have been pleasant, but Skalet's smooth alto made it sound like something from a machine. "This is not a secure location, Uriel. We have an access window sufficient to make the exchange, no more. You brought the grav-sled?" At his nod and gesture to the shuttle's sideport, she snapped: "Good. Then load it up. I'll bring the plants."

My plants?

This time when my lips curled back in threat, I left them there. What was Skalet planning? She had to mean the duras seedlings and the adult versions in Ersh's greenhouse—these were the only plants on Picco's Moon. While a constant source of drudgery for me, they were also the only source of living mass other than the local wildlife—and Tumblers—available to us.

That source of living mass was crucial. We could fuel and maintain our bodies by eating and metabolizing in another form. But it took a sacrifice of web-mass to energy to distort our molecular structure, to cycle and hold another form. To become anything larger meant assimilating living mass into more web-mass. To replace lost web-mass? The same. It was the fundamental hunger, the appetite we couldn't escape.

Skalet was robbing Ersh's supply? She must have her own source, not to mention plant life was hardly a rare commodity—anywhere but on this world. It didn't make sense.

Being without Ersh no longer seemed a holiday. I was faced with making a decision I shouldn't have had to make—whether to trust one of my own or not. I panted, knowing my emotional turmoil risked my form integrity and trying to dump excess energy as heat before I really did explode. Not as they'd teased me, but the exothermic result of changing back to web-form without control would be more than sufficient to catch the attention of the Human, in his shuttle or out.

I needed somewhere to think this through. Or explode. Either way, it couldn't be here. I crouched as low as possible, cursing the bright Eclipse sunlight, then eased back, paw by paw, ears and nose straining for any sign of Skalet, until it was safe to risk going to all fours.

Then I ran.

What life there is on Picco's Moon prefers to bask deep in the valleys girdling the equator. It's hot down there, for one thing, and the lowermost walls glisten with the steamy outflow of mineral-saturated water so important to the crystalline biology of everything native. Farther up, the walls are etched with pathways, aeons old, marking the migration of species to and from the drier, cooler surface for reasons that varied from escaping predation to a need to find the best conditions for facet cleaning. The annual plunge of the tendren herds over the rim of the Assansi Valley was, Ersh had assured me, one of the most dramatic events she'd ever seen. And she'd seen most.

I couldn't venture an opinion. Long before I joined Ersh on her Moon, the rim of the Assansi Valley had collapsed due to erosion, doubtless hurried along by thousands of impatient, diamond-sharp toes. Life here wasn't easy.

It wasn't easy for visitors either. Had I sought the depths of a valley, my Lanivarian-self wouldn't have survived an hour. As for forms that might, including Tumbler? I couldn't trust my ability to hold them.

So I avoided the Tumbler track leading to the nearest valley, the Edianti, and padded morosely around Ersh's mountain instead.

Not that I planned to go far. I might have Ersh's thorough knowledge of the place, but the Moon's geology was nothing if not active. Today's crevice was as likely tomorrow's upthrust, making any map based on memory alone unreliable.

I'd begun by scrambling up each rise, and slipping headlong down the inevitable slope, but calmed before doing myself any more harm than running out of

breath. I'd grown up here and knew the hazards—
evenly divided between those involving Ersh and
those involving slicing my footpads open on fresh
crystal. As for the utter unlikelihood of a Lanivarian
running around on Picco's Moon? The Tumblers who
climbed Ersh's mountain for conversation and trade
had long ago accepted her proclivity for alien house-
guests as a charming eccentricity and, given their in-
ability to tell carbon-based species apart, let alone
individuals, paid no attention to what kind they were.
Well, as long as they were tidy and didn't eat in public places—Tumblers being thoroughly offended by
the concept of body cavities and ingestion providing
too much evidence for comfort.

The plants. I had to do something. Skalet and this
Uriel were Human—at least one of them likely to remain so—and what did I know about the species
which could help? The flood of information on the
heels of the inadvertent thought brought me to a gasping standstill. I wasn't very good at assimilating the
larger chunks of information Ersh fed me.

A lie. I was very good at assimilating, just better at
resisting. New knowledge fascinated me—that wasn't
the problem. But each time I bit, chewed, and swallowed Ersh-mass, it seemed there was less of me, of
Esen.

The others didn't understand. Their personalities
were solid; they were *old.*

So when, as now, I needed information I'd shoved
aside in my mind, the assimilation happened suddenly, as if liquid poured into my mouth faster than I
could swallow, filling my stomach, rising back up my
throat until I couldn't breathe. I endured the sensation,
because I had to find a way to deal with this Uriel.

Ah. The turmoil subsided. I *understood* the species
as I hadn't dared before. Interesting. Complex as indi-

viduals, predictable en masse, amiable yet unusually curious in their interactions with other species.

And many cultures of Humans, including Kraal, valued gems.

I'd snuck back to the landing pad, keeping downwind in case Skalet was looking for me. I doubted it, feeling it more likely she was content to know I'd run and was out of her way. Something in the thought raised the hair between my shoulders.

Watching the two hadn't cleared up any of the mystery. Uriel had finished piling packing crates on a gravsled, lashing them together as though the cargo was fragile. I could smell wet dirt and bruised leaves, implying they'd been busy—and not particularly careful—putting duras plants into the shuttle. Mind you, Ersh was a little overprotective of the things. I knew from experience they survived being dropped quite nicely.

From what I'd overheard, Skalet was reassuringly adamant that the Human not enter Ersh's abode, insisting she'd move the cargo to a more secure location later. The Human, obviously not knowing Skalet as well as I, then argued he should accompany her. I'd waited for her to dismiss him, but she'd merely smiled and stroked his arm. They'd disappeared inside the shuttle for several minutes. Perhaps, I'd decided with some disgust, Skalet was following in Ansky's footsteps and experimenting with physical liaison. Ersh would not be impressed.

But Ersh must already know, I thought suddenly. Web-kin couldn't hide memory from her. This could be why Skalet had been left in charge of me—to punish this behavior while making it more difficult to accomplish.

As if that *had worked,* I said to myself, feeling wise beyond my years.

Their delay had given me time to put my own plan into action. I patted the bag against my haunch, its hard bulges a combination of luck and the now-helpful sunlight. Judging from the abundance of ritual leavings sparkling around the lower slope of the mountain, Ersh had had more Tumblers visiting than I knew. I'd worried unnecessarily about having to scout closer to Edianti's unstable rim.

"Aren't there any more, S'kal-ru?" Uriel's voice sent me ducking behind my boulder again. "These will barely suffice to start twenty cultures. Mocktap won't accept that as payment for what's in these containers—"

"These are enough. This strain of duras clones amazingly well, my friend, and grows even faster. We'll have plants for a hundred ships within months, providing both oxygen and—"

When her voice trailed away with suggestive triumph, I immediately filled in the gap. *Mass.* Ersh had modified these plants to produce the greatest possible amount of new mass in the shortest time. She'd picked duras over other species because they were hardy, thrived indoors, and, also importantly, were essentially inedible. No point sharing useful mass with other life. And, while the attraction was lost on me, Ersh confessed to finding their compact spirals of green leaves aesthetically pleasing. If Skalet was making sure her Kraal affiliates carried duras plants on their ships, it was for her own convenience as a web-being.

I was lost in admiration.

But what had convinced the Kraal? There were much easier botanicals to use as an oxygen supplement.

"The sap is even deadlier than you promised," the Human answered as if reading my thoughts. "And, thus far, completely undetectable."

Poison. I wrinkled my snout as if at a bad smell. The Web revered life, especially intelligent life, but Ersh hadn't spared me the realities of that life either. Most ephemeral species engaged in self-destructive behavior, including assassination and murder. The Kraal, for instance, granted exceptional status to those who managed to remove their rivals with the utmost finesse and mystery. A game, played with lives. I could see Skalet enjoying the strategy of it, the detached observer watching generations of Kraal worry and pick at their alliances, giving the odd push to a group that caught her interest, then abandoning them in another roll of the dice.

We had less in common than I'd thought.

My plan was simple and should have worked. There hadn't been any flaws I could see. Which had been the problem, really. Failing to see what was right in front of me all the time.

The Human, Uriel, had taken my bait. He'd helped Skalet move the grav-sled a considerable distance around Ersh's mountain, to the side that was more geologically stable, though still riddled with faults and caves. There, the two of them had off-loaded the sled, carrying each crate inside.

While they'd been out of sight, I'd slipped up to the sled and quickly pried open the nearest box. Packing material blossomed out at me and I'd fought to get it all back inside before they returned. But I'd had time to see what was so important: Kraal artifacts. Art. Trinkets. My web-kin accumulated and shared memories of such things, not the real objects. What would be the point? There wasn't enough room on Picco's Moon to house a comparably comprehensive collection from any one species, let alone from thousands. Then there was the risk inherent in storing such hard-to-hide treasures.

Treasure? Was that it? Had Skalet somehow become enamored of private wealth? Unlikely, since as a member of the Web she could access more than she could ever spend—Ersh having appreciated the value of economics well before Queebs could count.

There was another possibility. Ersh-memory, Skalet-flavored, floated up. A Kraal dynasty required not only a lineage, with the requisite ruthless progenitor, but the physical trappings of a House—the older and more bloodstained, the better. How long did Skalet plan to use this as her preferred public form? Human life spans were long, but that long? She was capable of such a plan, I knew. And would relish every aspect of it, including the cost.

If this bothered Ersh, something I couldn't predict, she could deal with our errant web-kin. I wanted my plants back in the greenhouse where they belonged. For that, I required the shuttle unloading to take a little longer.

Ears cocked for any sound they were returning, I began setting out my bait. Each crystal blazed in my paws, varied in color and hue, but all flawless, as if the facets had been cut with the skill of a lifetime. Biology was a wonderful thing.

One here. *So.* Two more there. The sunlight reflected so vividly the crystals might have been lit from within. This Uriel couldn't help but see them. Each was worth, conservatively, the price of his shuttle. *There for the taking.*

I backed down the path leading away from the landing pad, looking over my shoulder frequently to be sure I didn't step close to the sheer cliff which made this Ersh's preferred spot for flying lessons. I really wasn't fond of heights. *There.* I rounded an outcropping, intending to leave the last few less obviously in sight before running back to the shuttle, only to find myself surrounded.

Not that the Tumblers were interested in me. I froze, lowering my paw to the ground and letting the crystals fall discreetly behind, hopefully out of sight.

They were busy.

It was Eclipse, I remembered, drymouthed, and, of course, they were busy.

If I'd thought the crystals gorgeous, their makers were beyond description. Their towering bodies took the sunlight and fractured it into streams of color, flashing with their every movement against rock, ground, and one another until I squinted in order to make out what they were doing. They were picking up crystals with their trowellike hands and holding them up to the sunlight. I could hear a discordant chime, soft, repeated, as though they chanted to themselves.

Then a loud *Crack*!

I cried out as crystal shards peppered my snout and dodged behind the outcrop.

The Tumblers noticed me now. "Guest of Ershia," one chimed, the resonating crystals within its chest picking out a minor key of distress. "Are you harmed?"

Licking blood off my nose, I stepped out again and bowed. "I'm fine," I said, knowing there was no point explaining skin damage and blood loss to mineral beings. It would only upset them. "And you?"

One tilted forward, slowly, and gracefully tumbled closer. "In rapture, Guest of Ershia. Do you see it?" The Tumbler held up a crystal identical to those all around me, then placed it somewhere in the midst of its body. I couldn't make out exactly where in all the reflections. Then the Tumbler began to vibrate, its companions humming along, until my teeth felt loose in their sockets.

There were two possibilities. This was a group of crazed individuals, tumbling around looking for "ritual leavings" as part of a bizarre ceremony, or this was exactly what I'd hoped to find at the start of Eclipse—parental Tumblers hunting their offspring.

Which meant I'd been collecting children, not droppings. My tail slid between my legs.

However, this didn't explain the tiny fragments sticking out of my snout. Or why Ersh hadn't wanted me to see it.

Another Tumbler held up a crystal, identical, as far as my Lanivarian eyes could detect, to any of the others. The light bending through it must have meant something different to the Tumbler, however, for she gave a melancholy tone, deep and grief-stricken, then closed her hand.

I buried my face in my arms quickly enough to save my eyes, if not my shoulders and forearms, from the spray of fragments.

"Ah, you feel our sorrow, Ershia's Guest," this from another Tumbler, who graciously interpreted my yip of pain as sympathy.

I stammered something, hopefully polite, and hurried away. The hardest thing was to resist the urge to fill my bag and arms with all the crystals I could carry, to save them from this deadly sorting by light. No wonder Ersh had tried to keep me away from Eclipse. I struggled with the urge to cycle, focusing on that danger to block the sounds of more shattering from behind. *What if the Web had so judged me? What if I'd failed that day Ersh tossed me from her mountain?*

Different biologies. Different imperatives. Different truths. Different biologies—I ran the liturgy through my mind over and over as I fled home.

"Just a few more minutes, S'kal-ru! I see another one!"

The triumphant announcement brought me skidding to a halt and diving for cover again. Uriel! He was running down the path in my direction, pockets bulging, his face flushed with excitement.

I hated it when a plan worked too well.

I was out of options. The thought of going back to join the Tumblers horrified me, however natural their behavior. Cycling into that form was impossible—I needed mass, almost twice what I had, let alone what might happen if sunlight didn't travel through my crystal self in a way that enraptured the adults. I fought to stay calm, to think. Ersh had warned me a truly desperate web-being could instinctively cycle to match her surroundings—the oldest instinct. It would be the death of Esen-alit-Quar. Rock couldn't sustain thought.

"There's no time for this!" Skalet's voice in this form might be mellifluous, but it had no difficulty expressing fury. I could smell her approaching, but didn't dare look.

"It's the best so far," I heard her companion protest. "C'mon, S'kal-ru. What's a minute or two more? We'll be rich!"

"Only a minute?" my web-kin repeated, her voice calming deceptively even as it came closer. I shivered, knowing that tone. "Do you know how many moves can be made in a game of chess, in one minute?"

The sun was setting, sending a final wash of clean, white light over the mountainside, signaling the end of Eclipse. And more. There was a strangled sound, followed by a sequence of gradually quieter thuds, soft, as though the source moved away.

Or fell.

The seedling's tender white roots had been exposed. I took a handful of moist earth and sprinkled tiny flakes of it into the pot until satisfied. Most of the plants were unharmed. All were back where they belonged. It hadn't been me. I'd stayed hidden, afraid of the Tumblers, afraid of the darkness, afraid of letting Skalet know I'd been there.

I hadn't made it back to the shuttle before Skalet, but Ersh had. Apparently, she hadn't left—sending away Skalet's shuttle in some game of her own. Had Ersh set a trap? It paid to remember who had taught Skalet tactics and treachery.

What went on between the two of them, I didn't know or want to know. It was enough that there were lights in the windows and an open door when I'd finally dared return. The Kraal shuttle and Skalet were gone.

The plants, needing my care, were not.

Ersh, as usual, was in Tumbler form, magnificent and terrifying. I shivered when she rolled herself into the greenhouse. It was probably shock. I hadn't cleaned my cuts or fed. Those things didn't seem important.

Secrets. They were important.

"You went out in the Eclipse."

A transgression so mild-seeming now, I nodded and kept working.

"And learned what it means to the Tumblers."

I hadn't thought. To her Tumbler perceptions, I was covered in the glittering remains of children. My paws began to shake.

"Look up, Esen-alit-Quar, and learn what it means to be Web."

I didn't understand, but obeyed. Above me was the rock slab forming the ceiling, embedded with the lights that permitted the duras plants to grow. It needed frequent dusting, a job my Lanivarian-self found a struggle—then I *saw*.

Between the standard lighting fixtures were others. I'd never paid attention to them before, but now I saw those lights weren't lights at all. Well, they were, but only in the sense that, like a prism, their crystalline structure was being used to gather and funnel light from outside.

They were crystals. Tumbler crystals. *Children*.

"Like us, Tumblers are one from many," Ersh chimed beside me. "To grow into an adult, a Tumbler must accumulate others, each to fulfill a different part of the whole. The very youngest need help to begin formation and are collected for that reason. But Tumblers are wise beings and have learned to use the sun's light to find any young who are—incompatible. It is a fact of Tumbler life that some are born without a stable internal matrix. If they were left, they could be mistakenly accumulated into a new Tumbler only to eventually shatter—crippling or destroying that individual. It is a matter of survival, Youngest."

"You could have told me," I grumbled.

Ersh made a wind-over-sand sound. A sigh. "I was waiting for some sign you were mature enough not to take this personally. You think too much. Was I right?"

There must have been thousands of the small crystals dotting the ceiling. There was room for more. "You were right, Ersh," I admitted. "But . . . this?" I waved a dirty paw upward.

She hesitated. "Let's leave it that it seemed a waste to turn them into dust. Speaking of dust, go and clean yourself. That form takes time to heal."

I nodded and took a step away, when suddenly, I *felt* her cycle behind me and froze.

Ersh knew whatever Skalet knew.

She didn't know—yet—what I knew.

Suddenly, I wanted it to stay that way. I didn't want Ersh to taste that memory of hearing a murder and not lifting a paw to stop it. I didn't want Skalet, through Ersh, to ever learn I'd been there. I wanted it never to have happened. Which was impossible. So I wanted it *private*.

I didn't know if I could, but as I loosened my hold on

my Lanivarian-self, cycling into the relief of web-form, I shunted what must stay mine deep within, trying to guard it as I always tried to hold what was Esen alone safe during assimilation.

I formed a pseudopod of what I was willing to share, and offered it to Ersh's teeth.

I'd succeeded in the unimaginable, or Ersh deliberately refused to act on the event. Either satisfied me, considering I couldn't very well ask her. Her sharing was just as incomplete. There was nothing in her taste of Skalet's attempted theft or her plans for the Kraal. Or Uriel's existence. I supposed, from Ersh's point of view, one Human life didn't matter on a scale of millennia. I wondered if I'd ever grow that old.

Our lives returned to normal under Picco's orange glare, normal, that is, until the next Eclipse. Ersh went out in Tumbler form, with me by her side. There weren't many failed offspring this time, but those she found, we brought home to add to the ceiling. More prisms to light the greenhouse. I found a pleasing symmetry in the knowledge, a restoration of balance badly shaken.

Later that night, Ersh surprised me again. "I've had enough of you underfoot," she announced without warning. "Go visit Lesy."

Go? I blinked, waiting for the other side of this too-promising coin to show itself.

"Well, what are you waiting for? The shuttle's on its way. Don't bother to pack—no doubt Lesy went on a shopping spree the moment she knew you were coming. You'll be in a shipping crate, of course, since you can't hold anything but this birth-shape of yours long enough to get outsystem, let alone mingle with a crowd. And don't come out on your own. Lesy is expecting you."

Don'ts, Dos, and Details went flying past, none of

them important. "But I can come back . . ." I ventured, holding in a whine.

A low reverberation. Not quite a laugh. Not quite a growl. "Do you think you've learned everything you need to know, Youngest?"

My jaw dropped down with relief. "Of course not," I said happily.

Ersh came closer, lifting my jaw almost gently into place with her rock-hard fingers. "You aren't ready, Esen-alit-Quar," she told me in her blunt, no-nonsense voice, the one she used before inspecting anything I'd done. "But you have become—interesting. It's time you broadened your horizons."

I trembled in her hold. Did she know? Could she? Had I been wrong to believe I could, like Ersh, hide my memories? I drew a breath—to ask or blurt out a confession, I wasn't sure which—when she released me and turned away, saying only: "Don't worry about your plants, Youngest. Skalet's coming to tend the greenhouse. I think I'll have her dig out an extension while she's here—put some of that military training to use."

This time, I let my tail wag all it wanted.

I wasn't that old yet.

2: Cliffside Afternoon

OVER the years, I'd learned to edit my stories. Paul's eyes tended to glaze if I included such things as the composition of pavement where I'd walked, or the original source of various ornamental bulbs in a garden I'd passed. His passion was for language and culture—those details I could describe in any amount of depth and keep him fascinated.

When, as today, we exchanged stories about our separate pasts, I considered it a sharing and assimilation of a sort, so truth was important. Important to me, anyway, which was apparently why Paul found it so entertaining to exaggerate his exploits until I had to refuse to believe him. It was quite frustrating. But, over the years, I'd become used to it. This was the sharing I had, within our Web of two. It was, in its own way, gratifying.

However, some things, I'd decided long ago, should stay within me. It was my right and responsibility as Senior Assimilator—not to mention that it prevented embarrassment, something I managed sufficiently for any being without digging more from my past. So I'd edited some of the truths from this story, as well.

"Skalet," Paul murmured. "An interesting individual." He was a master of understatement. "Did she ever get her treasure from Ersh's mountain?"

I considered the question. "She didn't establish a House of her own among the Kraal." *That I knew*, I corrected to myself. Ersh hadn't shared such information with me, nor had I tasted it the one time Skalet and I had exchanged web-mass directly, without Ersh presorting her memories to those suitable for the Youngest of her Web.

I'd learned to be grateful for what I'd once considered Ersh's hoarding of secrets. Most of the things in my memory I preferred not to keep near the surface of my thoughts were Skalet's "gifts." Warfare: within a family or between worlds. Assassination and sabotage. Intrigue and lies. The cold assessment of everything in terms of expendability, risk, and gain. Curiosity without conscience. Passion without morals.

I might not care for these things, but they tried to surface even as I resisted. I wrapped my arms tightly around a body that Skalet-memory deemed too fragile and conspicuous. It was both, but it was a body I used only when I was with Paul, and this shaping of Esen was as much me as any other form I chose.

Well, to be honest, one other being knew this me. "Have you heard from Rudy lately?" I asked.

Paul accepted my blatant change of subject with good grace, doubtless aware Skalet's memories made me uneasy. He'd know more if I hadn't edited her murder of the Kraal, Uriel, from my storytelling.

There were, I thought comfortingly, *useful disadvantages to listening to a story rather than eating it.*

Otherwhere

A TUMBLER rolled its way along a mountaintop. This was perfectly normal behavior for a lifeform made from an aggregation of compatible crystals, if not a perfectly normal mountain.

This mountain was Forbidden.

Not that Tumblers paid attention to any prohibitions to their movement over Picco's Moon, especially during the bliss of procreation. They had no terms for property or trespass anyway. Up and down, yes. They had a plethora of words to describe slope, terrain, composition, the likelihood of finding scintillating conversation, and, most importantly, the predicted angle of the sun's rays during Eclipse at any one place.

Especially this mountain, of all places on Picco's Moon. In the past, many had sought it during bliss, believing offspring shed here were more likely to be perfect. Then, this mountain had been home to the strangest Tumbler of all, the Immutable One, a being older than memory, unchanged by time, and seemingly unaffected by mere biology, save for a compulsive curiosity about everything from Picco's orbit to the habits of those burdened by flesh. Over the millennia, it had become a pilgrimage of sorts to seek out the Immutable One, a memorable event to converse with a legend, especially one with such refined taste in rare mineral salts.

Especially one whose existence hinted at permanence.

A false promise. On a day that seemed like any other, Tumblers came to this mountain and found it empty. They mourned the passing of the one they'd thought indestructible, shedding diamond tears.

They declared this mountain Forbidden, in memory.

However, in every healthy species there exists variation. The Tumbler rolling over this mountain was, if one borrowed characteristics better applied to the flesh-burdened, more daring than most of its kind. Or more careless. The distinction depended on consequence.

This Tumbler was repeating a journey, in the way its kind had retraced their rolling paths since the dawn of time. One experienced bliss when and where it arrived.

It was, of course, necessary to retrieve the results.

The Tumbler slowed and stopped tumbling, having crossed the flat, worn peak of the mountain before finding what it sought. A litter of crystal was caught along the very edge. Some had surely dropped over the side. The Tumbler chimed distress at the accident, then forgot the lost ones, too intent on its task.

Over and over again, the being reached down, tenderly, and picked up one of the crystals lying before it. Each was held to the pure light of the sun; each accessed. Those worthy of further growth were accreted to the Tumbler's own body. Those unworthy were consigned to sparkling dust by the swift compression of a hand adapted to that purpose; a tone of grief struck each time, so they would know they were loved, if briefly.

The Tumbler was preoccupied with its labor, chased by the constraints of astronomy. Worlds turned, orbited, danced. The Tumbler needed the light of the sun to judge its offspring; needed the light reflected from

Picco herself to safely navigate the trip down the mountain.

The Tumbler had no attention to spare for concealed machines, busy at mysterious tasks. It had no time to waste on other trespassers.

As its body disintegrated into sparkling dust to join that of its flawed children, all it knew was that its killer wore flesh.

3: Office Morning;
Kitchen Afternoon

AMONG the thousands of living intelligent species, and the millions no longer with us, and probably, I told myself with disgust, the untold billions yet to come, Humans had to be the most obstinate.

And Paul Cameron was the worst of his kind. His fascination with the Ycl—obligate predators without any redeeming qualities, except their fortunate lack of the technology required to sample the multispecies' smorgasbord so temptingly beyond their world's orbit—boded well to give me ulcers in all five stomachs.

Not that such details mattered when my Human's mind was, as he put it, made up and his gray eyes had that dangerously determined glint. "We need to know more about them."

We were back at our offices, myself in Lishcyn form, which meant I could glare down at the Human over my ample—and very handsome—scaled snout. "You know all you need to know, " I reminded him. "The Ycl do not leave their planet. No one visits theirs. It seems an equitable arrangement, considering you or any other member of the Commonwealth would constitute a most welcome addition to the menu." At his scowl, I temporized: "Okay, so they wouldn't eat Tumblers—but Tumblers don't possess your fatal curiosity."

"Without your web-kin, Fangface," Paul countered, his

dark eyebrows meeting in a frown, "you must hunt for your own information. The Ycl is next on the list for an update."

"On your list." I struggled to keep my voice down, feeling my large ears flicking back and forth in an instinctive search for potential eavesdroppers although Paul was always careful where he spoke so plainly. "I know all I need to know about the form," I hissed. "I don't plan to socialize with other Ycl any time soon. Or at all, if I can help it." There'd been that episode with Ycl mating pheromones, for one thing. A most—embarrassing—episode. Perfectly remembered, of course.

Another story edited for my Human web-kin.

Of course this didn't convince him, but Paul was finally forced to stop badgering me as our moving argument brought us to the area of the building shared by our employees, none of whom were aware that their employers had other identities or ambitions to risk predation for the sake of a bit of chemical slang.

No, to them, Paul was Paul Cameron, a rather fussy but accomplished freight manager—not Paul Antoni Ragem, formerly Alien Language Specialist on a Commonwealth First Contact Team. Just as well, given that Ragem was officially listed as missing in action and presumed dead over fifty years ago.

Me? I was known to employees and customers of Cameron & Ki Exports as Esolesy Ki, Lishcyn, art appraiser and linguist; someone they treated with significantly less respect than they did Paul. Not that I minded. For one thing, it meant I was included in office gossip, much of it quite useful in forwarding my education into the social interaction of other species. Paul would not have been impressed—which likely explained why I was included and he was not.

They didn't know me as a web-being, last of her kind—at least in Commonwealth space—sought by some as a monster and by others as the possessor of secrets. Very few at all knew such beings existed—that I existed.

Yet even that few felt like far too many, particularly

today, when I floundered trying to communicate with the one alien I knew better than any other.

It had been our decision: to recruit a secret network of beings to feed us information. It had been Paul's, without my consent or knowledge, to recruit others, to make them aware of me, to be able to recognize me in several forms. My favorite forms, in fact. I might be polite about it—but Paul knew as well as I that I hadn't yet accepted this breach of trust from my first friend, no matter how impeccable his intentions.

My first friend. My best friend. But no longer my only one. I'd made another: Rudy Lefebvre—a fine and worthy being who was also Paul's cousin. Our paths had collided when Rudy chased rumors of Paul Ragem and found us both. We were neither the traitor nor monster he'd been led to believe, fortunately for all concerned. I had nothing but sincere respect for Rudy's ability to cause trouble, should he be so inclined.

He would have been a far more serious threat to our hidden lives than his superior, Lionel Kearn. Another who knew I existed. His feelings toward me were, at best, ambivalent—especially since our last encounter. Paul—well, I'd edited that story for his ears, too, on the logical assumption that if I didn't understand why I'd risked everything to contact Kearn, my web-kin wouldn't either. There might have been raised voices. There'd definitely be that look—the one which bore an uncanny resemblance to Ersh's expression whenever I'd apparently exceeded every imaginable means of causing her grief.

I shook off thoughts of those offworld, my concern here and now. A now in which Paul had evolved this ridiculous notion of somehow traveling to the Ycl system to observe firsthand the most deadly predators known to Ersh, a system definitely off-limits to any approach.

My Human had never truly appreciated the value of a dull life when protecting a secret.

Or, a sudden and highly alarming notion upset the contents of my delicate fifth stomach, *Paul was still looking for ways to risk his own.*

As usual, when Paul and I were in the midst of a disagreement, something put all arguments in perspective. This time, it was a message waiting at my desk.

I started reading it so I had an excuse to ignore whatever Paul began to say, rather vehemently, as he closed the door to gain privacy. As I reread it for the third time, for no reason whatsoever since the words were hardly likely to change in shape or meaning, I was aware on some level that he'd stopped arguing about the Ycl and now waited silently, in front of my desk.

Softly, for my sensitive ears only. "What's wrong?"

I ran my tongue tips over the inlaid gems of my right tusk, but the habit was no comfort. "There's been an incident," I said, doing my best not to crush the slip of plas in my four-fingered hand.

Behind me was a wall, decorated with artwork from our employees' offspring centered around an unlikely still-image of a Ganthor Matriarch in full battle gear accepting an artistic merit award from a stack of Noberan Iftsen. Like Paul and I—and the award, to be truthful—this wall was other than it seemed. Behind it was another room, much larger, filled with machines and communications systems tirelessly collecting and sorting a vast array of information.

Information like this.

"An incident? Where? What kind?"

I shook my huge head, knowing what he was likely thinking. "Nothing about another web-being. Or Kearn. But it's connected to me. There's a missing person—a Tumbler."

"Picco's Moon," he breathed, and sank into his chair, knowing as well as I that species was constrained by biology and temperament to one small hunk of orbiting stone.

Not just any hunk of orbiting stone. "Picco's Moon," I repeated, hearing the flatness of my own voice. "The Tumbler was last seen climbing Ersh's mountain. Given the fragility of the species, and the slopes involved, the authorities are treating this as an unfortunate accident. They probably won't search for a body. Tumblers," I paused, trying to be delicate, "tend to fracture."

"Why there? I thought Tumblers respected your property."

I sighed. "This was apparently a being after your own heart, Paul. A risk-taker. But there's more—" I handed him the slip. "The flyover the authorities conducted found something else."

He read quickly, then looked up with alarm. "Who the hell's mining your mountain?"

The operation wasn't legal, of course. Paul sent tracers through our system, tracers that multiplied outward, shunting through dozens of false origins before they converged like strands of a net over any com traffic in or out of Picco's Moon over the past year. There were reports of ships evading custom checks, an increase, it was thought, in the smuggling of Tumbler gems.

I hoped it would prove to be something so innocent.

I owned Ersh's mountain, an ownership part of me knew was foolishly dangerous, since it was a potential clue to any who sought a history to Esen-alit-Quar—not to mention the dozen forms of me registered as sharing that ownership. It had to be some ephemeral weakness; I had no other frame of reference for the compulsion I felt about the place.

But Paul knew I had no choice. All that remained of Ersh—Ersh herself—was that mountain. She'd chosen to spread her mass within its rock, to die in order to evade our Enemy. In some way, the mountain remembered being her.

So my Human watched without comment as I cued up the listings for travel to Picco's Moon—poring over schedules for something inconspicuously already in motion; failing that, hunting for ships currently assigned but whose captains might be persuaded to change their plans. I didn't have to look up to see his disapproval. The ears of this form were more than capable of detecting the deepening of each breath, the way he held it in, as if planning to burst out in argument—doubtless sensible in nature and one I'd totally ignore—and then released that breath with a low mutter.

We knew each other well.

"There are a couple of ships that might do," I said finally. "I can work something out, if you can look after that . . ." I paused to wave vaguely in the direction of the outer office.

"That." Paul lifted a brow. "Let me guess. You want me to find a logical reason to take a trip outsystem in the midst of our busiest shipping schedule ever, abandoning a dozen crucial negotiations and probably setting back the company by—conservatively—four years."

I shone a tusk at him. "Perceptive being, aren't you?"

"Es . . ." Whatever Paul wanted to say turned into a sigh of resignation.

"You know they'll believe you." They might have believed me, if it hadn't been for a few too many—creative—situations in the past. *None*, I thought rather wistfully, *were completely my fault*, but our staff typically failed to take that into consideration before hiding their keys, shaking their heads, then calling Paul for confirmation anyway.

"I'll do my best. Meanwhile, you keep out of trouble."

I made a great show of rearranging the piles of plas on my desk, saying virtuously: "I have work to do."

"Out of trouble. Please."

"Hadn't you better get busy inventing our excuse?" I said sweetly, resisting the impulse to stick the tips of my tongue out at him. "Sooner you do, sooner we can get to the bottom of this and be home again."

Had I known how wrong I was, I would have stopped Paul in his tracks.

Otherwhere

RUDY Lefebvre—former starship captain in the Commonwealth, former Botharan Patroller, former . . . well, his résumé made interesting, if unlikely, reading—knuckled the sleep from one eye, while keeping his other open and focused. The weariness of his body was nothing more than an aspect of his current job: spy.

Not that a Human back didn't complain after five standard hours spent crouched against a wall, positioned so a face could be pressed to a brick that hadn't been part of the original construction. Rudy tightened and eased various muscles along his spine automatically; never enough to stop the aches, but enough to prevent full cramping. He hoped.

He had devices installed elsewhere: worms inside comps, tattles leeched to com systems and their transmitters, sniffers dormant on ceilings until their targets arrived.

Rudy blinked both eyes and pressed closer, giving a silent grunt of satisfaction. *But nothing*, he thought, *matched seeing for yourself*.

The other side of the brick looked into one of Urgia Prime's ultra-private meeting rooms, the sort commonplace in most shipcities. They were leased by traders and others forced to negotiate in transit—particularly those who lacked the mutual trust involved in using a vid. Expensive place for a chat, unless you considered privacy to be more than a luxury. Rooms like this were regularly swept for any eavesdropping device and contained the latest in anti-snoop technology. Those using the rooms had to take written notes, if they wanted a record of their own. No other devices would function.

Rudy enjoyed the irony that the room's original designers hadn't considered the ultimate low-tech combination of patience, a good memory, and a willingness to share space with scurrying invertebrates. Perhaps one day he'd sell them the concept. Of course, had the designers been Kraal, rather than D'Dsellan, the space within the walls would have been laced with poison gas as well as dust. Some cultures were just too paranoid for anyone's good.

Meanwhile, the Human was content, if confined. The first three meetings he'd watched had been less than memorable—unless one fervently wished to corner the insignificant marfle iced tea market, cared passionately about an upcoming auction of Feneden artwork, or believed any prediction claiming interstellar commerce was on its last legs and it was time to buy dirtside storefronts before prices soared in response to the collapse of the economics of known space.

Ah, but the fourth meeting. That had been the reason for Rudy's giving up a perfectly lovely day's sailing for one spent as insulation. It wasn't for profit, though he knew information was more valuable than any real estate or fabric. Rudy was here at the request of a friend.

He could picture her now, as if his memory was as picture-perfect as any web-being's. Tousled auburn hair with hints of red, ancient eyes that couldn't decide if they were hazel or green, both belonging to a fragile wisp of a Human child who barely came up to his shoulder. A child who was not a child, with sufficient personality for six beings wrapped into one. Esen-alit-Quar.

Rudy grinned in the dark, knowing exactly how Es would react if she knew this remained his mental image of her. Not that he planned to ever say so, but he was reasonably sure Paul suspected. No harm done. He respected Esen for what she was, cherished her for what she did, and, like Paul, protected her in every way he could.

His grin became a smile, stretching dried lips. Another reason to endure imprisonment in plaster: Paul, Esen's first Human friend and her remaining family. Rudy's family, too, restored to him not only alive, but true to every memory and hope, despite the lies that had been spread about the Human "traitor" and his "monstrous" companion.

Well, not that Paul would approve of this particular activity, Rudy told himself ruefully.

Not that Paul would ever know, if Esen had her way. Rudy didn't enjoy being between them; he appreciated the necessity. Es was powerful, wealthy, and utterly vulnerable. Paul had tried to ensure she would be protected after he was gone by choosing others to share his knowledge of her, others who promised to keep faith, to become part of Esen's future.

Paul was an idiot. Rudy wished for room to shake his head. A noble, well-intentioned, blindly optimistic idiot. A harsh judgment, but relatives were expected to speak it as they believed. Sure, Paul could charm a Carasian out of its carapace. Beings wanted to rise to his level, to be what he saw in them.

Rudy did.

But once Paul left the room? Rudy rolled a hip joint to ease a growing stitch in his left side. Beings began thinking for themselves. Paul's trusted Group became no more than a collection of scattered individuals wondering what they'd agreed to do and why, worrying at a dangerous secret.

Esen had turned to him for help. She understood, as

Paul apparently didn't—or couldn't—how terrifying her species would seem to others. Semi-immortal shapeshifters known to have an appetite for intelligent life? Who could turn any living matter into more of their own mass with a touch? Who, though Esen denied she would, could travel through space as easily as the most advanced starship, not to mention rip apart the hull of that ship if the mood struck?

Rudy clung to his chosen image of Esen for good reason. Her frail Human-form was very reassuring.

Those he watched, however, didn't have that advantage.

The two met in what they assumed was guaranteed secrecy, from without and from recordings made by each other, that desire alone arousing Rudy's patroller instincts. He knew both, though they had made a modest attempt to disguise themselves by donning local clothing. It would have helped had either worn Urgian dress properly, starting with the sorpi. A sorpi was supposed to hang freely over the left shoulder and down the back, instead of being tied so each wore what appeared to be a ridiculous yellow-and-black-striped noose around his neck.

Maybe they knew they deserved one.

The first to enter the room had been the subject of Rudy's meticulous attention these past weeks. Esen had met this member of Paul's Group—part of her mission to reassure each of her peaceful nature. She'd come away uneasy for reasons she hadn't or couldn't explain. Not that Rudy needed details. If Esen felt Zoltan Duda couldn't be trusted, he would find out why for himself.

Slim, intense, with dark eyes and hair, given to gesturing with his hands during conversation, Zoltan was one of Paul's newer recruits, related in a murky way through Paul's father's third temp-contract, which had turned permanent. An illegally thorough dossier resided in Rudy's comp, containing such privileged information as the instructors' notes labeling Zoltan as a promising pilot and psych tech reports using words like: stable, methodical, and ambitious. Reading between the lines, Rudy imagined the shock of a multispecies' classroom on a youngster from Senigyl III, a predominantly Human planet, not to mention Zoltan's first roommate, who'd possessed a seemingly sentient parrot. Some situations altered lives.

Sure enough, halfway through his training, Zoltan had changed his mind about his future and unknowingly begun to retrace Paul Ragem's, enlisting in the Commonwealth military, selecting a specialty in alien cultures, outspokenly aiming to be a member of a First Contact Team.

To Paul, Zoltan must have seemed perfect—especially his youth. Many in the Group wouldn't naturally outlive Paul himself, a serious concern given Esen's virtual immortality, if she could keep out of trouble.

So, Zoltan, Rudy asked himself, *if you are so perfect, why doesn't the ever-trusting Esen-alit-Quar trust you? Could it have something to do with why you agreed to meet her newest Enemy in secret?*

Another intense Human. Another one remarkable for his ambition and interest in the unknown. Oh, Rudy knew Michael Cristoffen very well indeed.

Kearn's protégé.

Lionel Kearn. There was a résumé filled with contradictions. Senior Alien Culture Specialist on the Commonwealth starship *Rigus,* in charge of the First Contact Team and Paul Ragem's superior officer when a certain naïve shapeshifter had blundered on the scene. Forced to become Acting Captain when his own was murdered by a local population paranoid about aliens. An unhappy symmetry, as Kearn became equally paranoid about Esen-alit-Quar. In the years that followed, Kearn became Project Leader on the *Russell III*, in charge of a space-wide search for the Esen Monster, a threat Kearn refused to believe dead, despite Esen's valiant effort to leave that impression.

Rudy had joined Kearn's hunt for the web-being in its forty-eighth year. Kearn had worried his way through system after system, dedicated to his obsession, blind—perhaps willingly so—to how it turned his career into a mockery. He collected folklore about shapeshifters in every culture he contacted. "The enemy disguised as us." His frequent success didn't help him sleep nights. In a way, Rudy had been his mirror image—only he didn't believe in shapeshifting aliens and his nightmares were of betrayal and loss. Rudy's hunt had been for Paul Ragem, for evidence to prove his dead cousin's innocence—or guilt—once and for all.

Rudy had used Kearn for his own purposes. Most of Kearn's superiors had thought him a raving lunatic with a talent for collecting obscure data. Paul? He'd ensured Kearn's, and so Rudy's, hunt would be fruitless, using the resources of his Group to intercept any real clues, toss out false trails, and frustrate them from within.

Esen?

Other beings would have abandoned Kearn to inevitable failure and obscurity. Others might have done their utmost to hurry the process. But Esen, Rudy had learned, wasn't like other beings. Kearn's obsession, his fear, had made her deeply unhappy. She'd taken—steps.

Something else Paul didn't know. Rudy did, but not because Esen had confided her risk-taking in him either. No, he'd just happened to be there when Kearn arrived, babbling hysterically about Esen and how she'd revealed herself to Kearn—apparently to give him the key to critical negotiations between the Feneden and Iftsen.

Apparently, because to Rudy's way of thinking, a prudent, secretive being such as Esen could have easily found another, safer way. No, she'd shown herself to Kearn because she'd hoped to change his mind about her. A dangerous gamble.

Too dangerous. Rudy had done his best to convince the overwrought Kearn that he'd suffered a hallucination, that it was his own unappreciated genius coming to the forefront to solve the problem.

Kearn appeared to believe. He went on to avert catastrophe and become a hero, however briefly. The perfect moment to retire, to anyone less motivated.

But Kearn had no intention of abandoning his mission. His heroics unfortunately restored sufficient credibility with his superiors that he had no further problems obtaining support for his search for the Esen Monster.

Including being able to request any crew member he wanted, Rudy told himself glumly. Michael Cristoffen had been with Kearn since the Feneden/Iftsen negotiation, arriving shortly after Rudy's own departure. What Cristoffen thought of Esen was straightforward enough: she and her kind were deadly threats, to be hunted and destroyed.

What Kearn thought of Esen now was anyone's guess. Rudy sincerely hoped the web-being restrained her own curiosity in that regard, but nothing, he suspected, was beyond her. He was in no position to find out. He and Kearn had shared too many secrets about each other for comfort; distance seemed not only polite, but safer.

Paul? Rudy pushed aside thoughts of his cousin, especially the look he imagined on his cousin's expressive face should he ever learn how many secrets were growing around him. *Some things were best left unsaid.*

Such as the conversation in this room.

Zoltan had taken only a couple of strides into the room before saying: "Meeting here seems a bit extreme, Hom Cristoffen. Surely—"

"Forgive the theatrics, Hom Duda," the other said warmly. "Rest assured, anyone who sees us will think us simply traders, conducting business in the usual manner. I hardly wish to tip my hand to others about our—negotiations—before I have a chance to go over the details with you. I'm very pleased—very pleased— that you agreed to see me. Sit." Cristoffen obeyed his own command, then steepled his fingers as the other Human hesitated. "Come. Sit. What harm can it do?"

Inside a wall, their watcher tensed. *What harm, Zoltan Duda? If you plan to betray Esen or Paul?* He had the answer ready, strapped to his hip.

4: Kitchen Afternoon; Home Evening

ALTHOUGH Paul was exceptionally good at abusing the truth when the need arose—a skill honed by life with me, as he never failed to mention—that didn't mean he enjoyed it. I knew he'd come back from spreading the latest essential untruths around the office somewhat, well, bent.

There was no other word for it. The Human hated lying, which was why he preferred the gray areas that approached the line but didn't quite cross it: distraction, misdirection, confusion, and outright exaggeration. Whenever backed into the necessity—again, something he usually ascribed to me, which technically wasn't always true either—he'd grow quiet for a significant while afterward. It wasn't melancholy. It was as if Paul felt the need to remember who he really was, to return to his proper shape.

A not-unfamiliar feeling to a web-being, but the bent version of my friend was lousy company. And, to be honest, I felt some small guilt in the matter.

Which was why I was taking steps to hurry the unbending process before Paul arrived home. I wasn't much of a cook in any form, a lack I couldn't very well blame on my web-self's appetite for living matter. Ansky and my other web-kin would delve into assimilated memory, take over Ersh's kitchen for days, and create the most fabulous meals on a regular basis. Meals I'd enjoy, without doubt, but ones I found ridiculously time-consuming. Not to mention they'd make me wait for hours before allowing me to taste anything, then insist I clean up.

Now that I was Senior Assimilator of my own Web, I took full advantage of civilized conveniences such as synthesizers and restaurants. Not to mention delivery.

Paul liked to, as he put it, putter in the kitchen. He wasn't a great chef either, but every so often I'd hear him rise unreasonably early and start opening cupboards. I'd try burrowing my head deeper into the fragrant syntha-grass of my box, but it was hopeless. Not only did Paul make no effort whatsoever to be quiet, but I'd learned what such behavior meant. He'd be preparing more food than the two of us could possibly consume in a day, a clear signal he expected company. The Human had an instinct for when our peace was in jeopardy. Not that I minded visits; I just preferred more notice than an ovenful of delectable biscuits I was supposed to share.

Tonight, however, I was the one poking my paws into cupboards and drawers to assemble what I needed as cook. Between additions to my collection, I eyed the oven. It eyed me back, looking as innocent as any appliance could look that was capable of reducing a juicy piece of meat to crisped carbon without warning.

Not that I was working with anything so appetizing. No, what lay on the countertop was a bag of rock-hard noodles—the sort no restaurant would serve—and a swollen tube of a yellow-orange substance claimed by the lurid label to have once been cheese. From a mammal's milk.

I had my doubts.

Those didn't stop me from pouring the entire bag of noodles into the pot of boiling water, and setting the lurid tube close enough to warm and soften.

The next ingredient was harder to locate. Paul tended to hide his snacks, as if I'd eat them when he wasn't looking. There might have been one or two instances in which his suspicions were justified—after all, discovering fudge when one was looking for cleanser made it very difficult to re-

member the finer points of ownership—but this time I was
impatient with his secrecy. Fortunately, my present nostrils
were more than up to the task of locating an opened bag of
pickle chips.

I reached behind the D'Dsellan dictionary and grinned,
letting my tongue hang out one side of my jaw. Just
enough . . .

Just then, an alarming popping sound alerted me to the
peril of leaving any appliance unsupervised. I loped back to
the kitchen, chips in one paw, only to find the pot of noodles
had grown an intimidating mushroom of foam, fingers of it
dripping down to the hot surface to spatter, pop, and hiss. As
I hurried to contain the disaster, the tube of pseudo-cheese
ruptured with the heat and sprayed over the side of the pot,
forming a rapidly blackening crust. Some landed on my
snout and arm, repulsively sticky.

First things first. I grabbed the handles and yanked the
pot from the heat. The foam grumbled as it subsided, but no
longer threatened to spill over the entire kitchen. I remembered, belatedly, to turn off the unit, adding a tang of
scorched fur to the ambience as the attractive fringe under
my forearm failed to clear the heating surface. *Formerly attractive,* I whined to myself, using a damp towel to extin-
guish any still-smoldering hairs while assaying the damage.
I'd have to trim the rest to match. On both arms. I could hear
Ersh now: *A waste of good mass.*

Meanwhile, the pseudo-cheese had completed its escape
from the tube and formed a nauseating puddle on the countertop. And down the front. The resulting combination of
smells overpowered my presently sensitive nose. I cycled
reluctantly . . .

My Human-self didn't care for the smells of burned
starch, singed fur, and liberated cheese product either, but its
duller olfactory sense let me ignore the combination. However, this form wasn't as large or strong as my birth one.
Wiping droplets of water from my skin, I considered the
now ominously large pot of boiling water, noodles, and

dying foam. A little protection was probably in order before attempting the next stage.

After making sure everything but the empty oven was safely off, and damming the runaway pseudo-cheese behind a line of spice jars, I went to my room and pushed through the double row of silk caftans filling my closet. Behind was a wall, as one might expect, but unlike those at the back of most closets, mine was a second, concealed door. I keyed in the code, worrying what the pseudo-cheese was doing in my absence, and didn't delay any longer than it took to reach in somewhat blindly and grab some clothes suited to this form.

Back in my room, I realized I'd grabbed my winter coat and a pair of shorts, but had no time to pick anything else. Cooking was dangerous stuff.

For a wonder, the cheese had behaved. The noodles, however, were now a sullen mass at the bottom of the pot. I shoved my sleeves out of the way, already too warm in the coat, and stood on tiptoe to decant most of the water. Steam immediately billowed up from the sink and I blew frantically to keep my line of sight free. The noodles didn't budge, even when I shook the pot.

I wasn't going to be defeated by pasta. My steam-dampened hair trailed into my face as I heaved the pot down to the floor, somehow keeping it from crushing my toes. The noodles were too hot to touch. No problem. I found the utensil in one of the drawers that Paul used to pick up and turn animal parts on the grill. The toothed edges bit into the lumpy mass in a most satisfactory manner.

I was able to pry loose enough noodles to fill the bottom of the fluted Iftsen baking dish we'd been given by a grateful client. The rest appeared permanently attached to the pot and I wasn't about to argue. Outside it went. *Let's see how you like the weather,* I told it, only to discover conditions outside as close to balmy as Minas XII could provide. At least I could be sure that would change.

Meanwhile, the puddle of pseudo-cheese had cooled and thickened, but I scraped and pushed until most fell onto the noodles in the dish, forming little mountains of yellow-orange. The next step was, in my opinion, the only reason to make this particular meal. Making sure the top of the bag of chips was sealed, I put it on the floor, gathered myself, then leaped as high as I could before landing with both feet on the bag. It made a most pleasing sound.

I sprinkled some now-flattened chips on the noodles and cheese, then critically examined the result. It didn't look quite right. In fact, the bits of green between the yellow-orange looked more nauseating than food probably should. I poured chips over the dish until all the offending cheese was covered.

Into the oven. Which I planned to watch very carefully indeed.

I dropped into the nearest chair, postponing the need to deal with the devastation around me for a moment. Cleaning the kitchen was going to take more energy than cooking, and I'd have to be done before Paul arrived home. Done, and with the revolting dish on the table. I shrugged off the winter coat and sagged a little more.

Would it work? I'd watched Paul make this before. More to the point, I'd seen when he made this. Humans had a term for it: comfort food. Paul's was this—he called it Auntie Ruth's Quick Macaroni, and claimed a distant cousin named Susan had added chips to the treasured recipe.

I didn't consider the concoction remotely edible, regardless of how many talented Ragems had contributed to its creation. Yet I'd seen how any tension eased from my Human's face and shoulders when he pulled it from the oven, how his eyes crinkled at the corners as if he was holding in a laugh. He'd offer me a share, almost apologetically, then be quite visibly pleased when I refused.

I nibbled on a fingernail—a habit appropriate to my birth-form and less so to this one—and pondered being Human. This reaction to a particular meal was not something I understood. As Ersh would doubtless remind me, I was probably too young.

Whether I understood it or not, I was counting on it. Paul was web-kin and friend. He needed unbending. *And,* I sighed to myself, *it went a little distance toward an apology for making him lie—again—for me.*

Keeping an eye on the seemingly cooperative oven, I went in search of a mop.

My offering went well, though Paul insisted we retrieve the pot. I'd hoped he'd let it sit outside until the next sandstorm, which would either scour it clean or remove it altogether, but had to concede his point. It wasn't nice to add flying kitchenware to the navigation hazards facing our visitors. Minas XII was challenging enough for those who dared her skies without the risk of dead noodles soaring through the clouds.

"So, Old Blob," Paul said peacefully, leaning in the doorway to watch me chip away at the mess. "Any problems arranging our passage to Picco's Moon?"

"None," I said, grunting as I worked.

"Ah," he said. "You called Joel." I swiveled my head so I could glance over my shoulder at him, amazed.

Then I lowered my ears. "Bah. You've been eavesdropping." The Human had become quite adept at avoiding observation; I'd long suspected that sort of expertise went both ways. He certainly knew whenever I'd had a misadventure and thus had to courier myself home in a box, no matter how circumspect I'd been. *Not that those incidents were as frequent lately,* I told myself, having learned the hard way to arrange a source of extra mass near me at all times. Our clients assumed the multitude of potted plants in my office meant I'd prefer those as holiday gifts. *Fudge. I really preferred fudge.*

Paul's laugh rumbled in his chest. He came away from the door to join me at the sink. "Here," he said, nudging me aside with his shoulder and hip. "Let it soak a while." As he filled the pot with hot suds, he continued: "I don't need to eavesdrop, Old Girl. You are a little predictable when it comes to asking for help. And we both know Joel can't say no to your charming, tusky self."

"Or to you," I countered, happily abandoning the pot to chemistry in order to follow Paul into our main living area.

This was my favorite part of our home, cheerfully crowded by chairs of varying size and shape—supposedly as a courtesy to any nonhumanoid guests, but in reality to provide comfort to any nonhumanoid me. Paul had arranged them to offer a choice of view. Either window overlooked the front of our home, which as often as not meant staring at the massive shutters saving those windows from Minas XII's hyperactive weather. The other focal point was the fireplace, with its stone mantel host to my collection of images of Paul's offspring sitting on my broad Lishcyn knees at several pivotal moments of their growth, nestled around a set of large, never-used gift candles whose fragrance made both of us sneeze, and, newest addition, a three-dimensional close-up of a truly stunning tusk inlay I desperately wanted but Paul considered a bit extreme for the office.

I was wearing him down.

There were shelves loaded with readers, vids, and puzzles. A tall stand in one corner sprouted chilled bottles of wine and beer instead of vegetation. And somewhere, on the floor, I distinctly remembered we'd put down some expensive and colorful Whirtle carpets a while ago—now lost beneath what was a cozy, albeit crowded, place meant for living.

There were no secrets here, no dictionaries for languages unknown to the Human Commonwealth, no collections of information that would be impossible for Cameron or Ki to explain. Such wealth was safely stored within my mass; any I'd shared with Paul locked either in his memory or in our hidden machines. Yet, given enough wine or a melancholy mood—or both—my Human would talk to me for hours about the library we could build, if we dared. At such times, I believed he truly understood how incomplete my life sometimes felt, without the sharing and assimilation of mass.

Not that it felt that way now, I thought contentedly, heading for the waiting chessboard. But Paul didn't take his seat, as I'd expected. Instead, he went straight to the closet beside the fireplace and pulled out our carrysacks, tossing one in my direction. "Packing," I objected firmly, "gives me indigestion."

"Being awake gives you indigestion."

Possibly true, but hardly polite. "Fine." Perhaps if I gave in to his efficiency, we'd have time for a game. "Pass out my other sack."

"One is all you'll need."

"One!" I sputtered indignantly. *"One??* I'll need at least two. Maybe," I scowled, "three."

Paul shook his head, grinning at my outrage. "We'll be in one of Largas' freighters or climbing rocks for the entire trip. Not to mention we'll be carrying our own baggage, Fem Ki, which means you'll be carrying yours. I presume you'll want one hand free in case it's night when we disembark?"

My shudder wasn't completely theatrical. My Lishcynself, having no night sight worth mentioning—unless one wished to say something derogatory to an otherwise peaceloving being covered in tough hairy scales and possessed of a body that could splinter most furniture just by accident—had a healthy aversion to dim light, let alone full darkness. Paul was right, as usual. I must be able to carry my lamp. "One sack," I sighed. Then brightened. "But I'll have to go shopping. For the return trip."

His lips twitched. "On Picco's Moon?"

I'd already thought of that. "The freighter makes another stop on the way home. Urgia Prime!" *Low standards, great shopping.* Despite my anxiety about what was happening on Ersh's mountain, I showed Paul both tusks. "Might as well enjoy ourselves." The first thing I'd buy, I promised myself, would be a new set of matched luggage. Ready-to-fill luggage.

Apparently Paul didn't share my enthusiasm. His grin faded and a look of growing suspicion was wiping any remaining humor from his eyes. "Let me get this straight, Esen," he said in *that* voice. "You asked Joel to not only find you a ship to Picco's Moon, but arrange a stopover—there of all places? How did you manage that?"

"I said you'd been working very hard," I said defensively. "You needed a vacation. Joel agreed with me. That's all."

My Human sat down on the couch. His eyes didn't leave mine for an instant. "What else did he say?"

My third stomach lurched slightly as I perceived I may have been a little quick to assume Human responses would match my own in this instance.

As I hesitated, Paul added firmly: "Exactly."

Exactly? I cleared the contents of the unruly stomach, shunting them into my fourth with a gulp I was reasonably sure even a Human could hear, and sat as well. "Which 'exactly' do you mean? We talked about a few things." Relationships between ephemerals were such complex and tricky things. I'd had some problems in this area before. But I really couldn't see what I'd done wrong this time. Joel was our friend.

And more. Joel Largas was the recently retired founder of Largas Freight, which owned most of the starships worth using on Minas XII or anywhere in this part of the Fringe. By any reasonable measure, he still ran the company—it just looked as though his plentiful offspring were in charge. In practical terms, this made Joel Largas almost a partner in Cameron & Ki Exports, since we relied on his ships above all others. A powerful being, by Minas XII thinking. It was a fairly common belief that what Joel Largas didn't know wasn't worth knowing.

As that included the truth about us, I heartily agreed. Joel Largas, his family, and friends had escaped the destruction of their homeworld only to be attacked by Death, a web-being with a taste for intelligent flesh. Their survival and new life here owed everything to Joel's grim determination to make them a new, safer home.

That his daughter, Char Largas, had found Paul Cameron in that home, and together they'd added two grandchildren to the Largas' dynasty, simply reinforced the need for secrecy. Easily done—refugees understood a desire to look ahead rather than to the past. Joel had welcomed Paul into his extended family with a keen appreciation of my Human's sterling qualities, taking me as part of the package. Over the years, we'd come to enjoy one another's company in the way of old friends who find the rest of the universe occasionally perplexing. He was the one being I could talk to when Paul and I disagreed. To Joel, I was never so much in trouble as troubled—a refreshing attitude I valued highly.

"Esen. What did Joel say about our leaving, now, during all these negotiations?"

I hunted for something neutral. "He was sure you knew what you were doing."

Paul ran both hands through his hair, leaving it more disheveled than usual. "Dare I ask what you told him that was?"

"Well, I couldn't, could I?" I said primly. "You were the one making the excuses at the office."

"So what did you say?"

I noticed the edge to his voice, but for some reason I went on happily, much the way migrating tendren once plunged over the walls of the Assansi Valley: "Oh, you know Joel. He agreed family always comes first."

"Pardon?" Paul, like Ersh, could instill one word with a positive wealth of consequences. *Negative consequences.*

I cycled before my stomachs could embarrass me completely, leaving warm damp spots on the furniture and floor as I shed both excess heat and mass. *Better than the alternative.* "I might have hinted you planned to visit the twins," I admitted in a voice made higher in pitch and softer by virtue of a smaller set of lungs, snatching enough of the woven blanket from the back of my chair to cover most of my now-shivering self.

Paul ground the heels of his hands into his eyes, surely an uncomfortable procedure, then glared at me. "We agreed long ago there would—*never*—be lies about my family. Esen. You promised."

"I didn't lie," I protested, confused by his distress. "I only hinted. I said it had been too long since we'd seen Luara and Tomas. That's true—it has been years. And their ship does the Urgia run from Omacron—you told me that. I'd like to see them, too. They're so much older now—they must be different. I thought . . ." Something quite desperate in his face stopped the words in my throat. I swallowed, hard, knowing what I hadn't until now. "You don't want to see your offspring again."

My web-kin turned over one empty hand; his eyes seemed just as hollow. "I said good-bye, Esen, when they left home. That wasn't for a week, or a year, or a handful of years. It was forever."

"Why?" Aghast, I stood up, clutching the blanket because my Human-self needed the comfort, trying to make some sense of what Paul was saying. I'd helped raise the twins—a very pleasant series of memories. And more. "How can you say that?" I heard my voice cracking. "You love them—I love them! Why?"

"I have my reasons, Es," Paul said heavily, getting to his feet. "I'm going to pack."

A younger me would have let him leave, afraid of the truth. I counted it as the penalty of maturity that I reached for his arm and grabbed it with my too-small hand, that I looked up into his troubled gray eyes and insisted: "Why?"

"Because—" Paul hesitated, studying my face—a version he could read all too easily—before coming to a decision. "I don't mean to upset you, Es," he said in a low voice. "But it's because when they left, they were beginning to ask questions. Questions I couldn't answer."

There was such a thing as too much truth. I dropped my hand and backed away, but my Human continued as if he hadn't noticed, or as if he felt further mercy unnecessary to us both: "It's bad enough I lie to everyone else. Did you think I could bear to lie to my own children?"

"About—me." This Esen had an annoying habit of leaking fluid from her eyes. And hiccuping.

"No, Es," Paul said very gently, though his face had grown pale and stern. "About me. They wanted to know my past. It's what Humans do, at the age when we start to contemplate our own futures. It gives us continuity . . . and a way to measure our own accomplishments. We talk to the older members of our family, gather the threads of their lives, make sense of our place in its history. But Paul Cameron has no past. I couldn't, for their own safety, give them Paul Ragem's." He drew in a deep, shuddering breath, then said, almost lightly. "For all my practice with lies, I couldn't utter one to answer them."

"Paul, I—"

"It's all right," he interrupted, as if it was his turn to fear what I'd say. "I keep track: where they are, how they are doing. It isn't hard. They've become good, strong people, busy with their own successes. I've simply—faded—from their lives. It's all right," he repeated, more quietly. "They have their mother's heritage. That's something to be proud of, being a Largas."

I considered this from every angle, then made a rude noise. "So you have no past—many of your kind are orphaned. It's you they deserve to know, foolish Human; you, they should measure themselves against. How can you possibly fail to see that?" I repeated the rude noise, seeing the truth quite clearly. *Ephemerals.*

Paul shook his head, whether at what I said or the noise I couldn't be sure, but his eyes had warmed. "Esen-alit-Quar," he said fondly. "Just when I forget how fortunate I am, you remind me." He opened his arms in invitation and, after an instant's consideration, I stepped awkwardly into his embrace. He laid his cheek on top of my head and we stood like that for a long time. I was content, if this comforted him, though I couldn't see how.

What I also couldn't see, yet, was how I could alter this terrible choice Paul had made. I might be Youngest in our Web, but I knew he was wrong.

A shame he was also the most obstinate of beings, I thought, remembering our argument about the Ycl. *This wasn't going to be easy.*

Otherwhere

THE crisp, clean bite to the air, the glow of the sunrise, were Urgia Prime's promises of a day perfect for any outside activity—particularly those involving large muscle movements. Instead, here he was, once more packed inside the wall, barely able to scratch his nose. *They could have picked another meeting place*, Rudy grumbled to himself.

Not that he was complaining. Another location might have been more difficult to infiltrate or, worse, been in public where he'd risk being seen. Cristoffen had complete access to ship's records—Rudy's face was one of those he'd memorize. The *Russell's* former captain had left soon after Kearn's almost successful monster chase. A success that wasn't—and was. Rudy felt truly sorry for Kearn sometimes.

Zoltan Duda and Cristoffen must have arranged to arrive separately. The officer was unexpectedly late, judging by the frequency with which Zoltan had checked the time since entering. He didn't sit, pacing around the room as if he'd come to some important decision and was impatient to act on it.

The meeting room's protections might scramble recording devices, but Rudy had no trouble remembering the salient parts of their previous conversation. Not that it mattered, since what they hadn't said seemed more telling than they had. No word of Esen.

No whisper that a web-being might still be alive and at large within Commonwealth space.

Instead, and with impressive gall—assuming Cristoffen knew exactly with whom he was dealing—Kearn's protégé had attempted to recruit Zoltan for the crew of the *Russell III*. Rudy had almost choked. Cristoffen had claimed Zoltan could complete his remaining courses while acting as a research assistant to Project Leader Kearn himself. He spoke persuasively about Kearn's groundbreaking work. He blithely described one aspect of this research—the legends describing mysterious shapeshifters—and Zoltan hadn't so much as blinked.

The second was true, as far as it went, but Rudy knew how well Kearn guarded his work from outside eyes. Kearn might appear to share his research with academics, accept speaking engagements on the cross-species' commonality of myth, but he never shared what lay at its core. He would never allow a complete stranger to work with his data. More to the point, he'd never allow a subordinate to bring a stranger on board. Kearn might be a fool about many things, but that lesson he'd learned.

So Cristoffen lied.

Rudy couldn't imagine what excuse the officer had made for meeting in secrecy to make his outrageous offer, but Rudy suspected Zoltan had been easily convinced. Every member of the Group had a vested interest in secrecy, especially about this particular topic. Zoltan would have recognized Cristoffen before any introduction—all of the Group had received information about Kearn's crew at Esen's insistence. As she'd put it: *best to know who not to invite for dinner.*

A warning Zoltan hadn't taken to heart. Or, Rudy thought, studying the younger Human's back, *he'd decided to act on his own. But for or against Esen and Paul?* The jury—himself—was still out on that one.

Zoltan had acted every bit the interested and flattered candidate to Cristoffen's offer, stopping short of committing himself, but apparently eager to meet again.

Cristoffen, unfortunately for them all, was no fool. Rudy knew Paul considered the Human a serious threat. Oddly, Esen didn't, claiming—even more mysteriously—that Kearn would keep him in line. *Ineffectual Kearn, controlling this passionate and determined individual?* Rudy's mind wouldn't wrap around the concept.

The door opened, startling Rudy as much as Zoltan, who immediately confronted the new arrival with an angry-sounding: "You're late."

Cristoffen's eyes were strangely bright; he was breathing rapidly and lightly through his nostrils. *Now what's got you all excited?* Rudy wondered, pressing his face closer to the brick.

The officer hadn't bothered with much of a disguise today, tossing aside the cloak he'd thrown over his uniform as he strode into the meeting room, his other hand closing the door behind him. "And for good reason, Hom Duda," he crowed. "Look what I have here!"

With a flourish, Cristoffen produced a data cube from his pocket.

Zoltan looked at the cube as if it had teeth. "What is it?"

"Proof." The other dropped into a chair, grinning broadly. He tossed the cube onto the table, where it bounced twice, then slid to a stop near the center. It was impossible not to stare at the tiny thing, alone on the polished surface.

Rudy felt as though ice settled into every bone of his spine. *Proof of what?*

"Proof of what, Hom Cristoffen?" Zoltan echoed, seeming to have regained his composure. He took up the opposing seat. "More about your offer to conduct research? I have to say—"

Cristoffen reached out his hand and flicked the cube toward Zoltan with a finger. "Proof your Esen wasn't the only shapeshifter to invade our space. Proof another monster has been here even longer." He leaned back, eyes glistening and spots of red on his otherwise pale face. "And is still here."

"I've no idea what you—"

Cristoffen surged from his seat, pounding both fists on the tabletop. "Shut up! Shut up!"

Zoltan obeyed, his face showing nothing more than dignified affront as he waved an impatient hand for the other to continue. *Perhaps his cousin had chosen well after all,* Rudy thought, impressed.

Cristoffen took a deep breath, his face relaxing almost too quickly, as if his outburst had been a feint. "Top of your class in alien cultural studies," he said, putting a strange twist to each word, as if they left a foul taste in his mouth. "You know exactly what I'm talking about, Hom Duda. You know I didn't arrange our meetings to discuss some ridiculous academic study. You know I contacted you because you are one of Them—one of those misguided fools protecting the Esen Monster."

Later, Rudy would play this scene over and over in his mind, trying out different possible outcomes based on things he might have done.

Zoltan shrugged. Rudy could see his face, but couldn't understand its expression of calm confidence. Personally, he counted himself doing well to be still inside the wall and not out there, with one hand around Cristoffen's thin neck and the other aiming a biodisrupter at Zoltan's head. "Say, for the sake of discussion, I do understand you. If I'm who you think, why bring me this—proof?"

"Because you need to know—you all do." Words tumbled out of Cristoffen's mouth as if a dam had burst. "You're wrong—misled. These creatures are abominations. They hide among us—as us! It's all here." He snatched up the cube and brandished the fist holding it. "This is only one more. How many others wait in their perfect camouflage, ready to strike without warning? We must find and destroy them all, before they destroy more of us! You can help. You can lead me to the Esen Monster. We'll make her lead us to the rest of her kind—"

Regret could be distilled and poured into a voice. Zoltan's was the purest Rudy had ever heard. It brought up the hairs on the back of his neck, and froze Cristoffen in his seat, mid-tirade. "To my everlasting shame, I would have agreed with you once, Hom Cristoffen," that voice said. "Then I met Esen for myself. Not a monster. Not a danger. Just the most amazing and gentle of beings, intending no harm to you or anyone, wanting only to be left in peace. And she is alone, whatever old trail you think you've uncovered. More alone than any of us can possibly imagine.

"You and those like you won't ever understand her. I know it. Others know it. But Esen-alit-Quar isn't wired to accept that—she'd keep trying to win you over." Zoltan glanced toward the ceiling, as if looking for someone. "Part of her charm, you could say. Which is why I agreed to meet with you, Hom Cristoffen. Oh, don't look so surprised. Several of us were—prepared—to take you up on your offer." He looked down at Cristoffen, still apparently transfixed by the unexpected—a reaction Rudy sympathized with completely—and drew a blaster from the pocket of his coat. It was a smooth, practiced move that left the weapon aimed directly at the other's head. "All swore you would no longer be a threat."

At that distance, Rudy thought with a strange detachment, *aim hardly mattered.*

Cristoffen lifted his arms. "Kill me, then."

It might not be the wisest choice, but Rudy couldn't

stay imprisoned in the wall while these two played at murder. Even if he'd been able to fight his own instincts, he knew full well Paul and Esen would count on him to intervene before things became worse. *If he could.* He squirmed frantically, having planned a stealthy exit outside, not to burst into the room.

The drill he wriggled from his hip pocket was servo-controlled, smart enough to know the difference between flesh and wallboard, and able to respond to whispered commands as well as its preprogramming. Once activated, it would recarve a body-sized exit for him through the outer wall into the alley behind the meeting room, where a groundcar waited. Since he knew he'd be stiff after his sojourn in plaster, and had to consider the possibility of discovery and pursuit, the groundcar had its own servo-control. When it detected the drill activating, it would retract its roof so Rudy could drop inside, then would, unless countermanded, immediately move away at a discreet yet rapid pace.

Now he had a new plan, to force an opening into the room quickly enough to avoid being shot himself. The drill had never been designed to cut at speed through brick. It muttered a machine protest, showering him with dust. He covered his eyes with both hands and waited.

Then a fierce concussion drove pieces of plas and stone into every exposed bit of Rudy's flesh.

Silence. Rudy ordered the drill to stop, doing his best to wipe blood and dust from his eyes and the bricks. His heart pounded in his ears. When he'd cleared his view into the room, it took him an instant to process what he was seeing.

Cristoffen sat, untouched, his arms still up in mock surrender, a smile twisting his lips.

Zoltan Duda, or what remained of so promising a being, lay across the scorched table, wisps of smoke trailing upward from charred flesh and bone as the ventilation system responded to the need to freshen the air. The scorching ended in a perfect half circle in front of Cristoffen, a line of bubbled black he followed with one finger, careful to avoid soiling its tip.

Rudy stared. He'd heard rumors the Kraal elite were developing an anti-assassin shield to reflect weapons fire at close range. If true, such a device would be restricted to the highest family affiliates, its secret zealously guarded. No one stole that level of technology from the Kraal and lived to use it.

Which meant it had been given to this young Human of unremarkable past, a former station steward turned Esen Hunter.

Forget Esen's secrecy. Paul had to know about this.

"I'm grateful, Hom Duda." Rudy stopped trying to free himself at the startling sound of Cristoffen's voice, feathered around the edges by adrenaline. *Or was it triumph?* "Yes. Most grateful. Here. A gift." Cristoffen callously flipped the remains of the data cube to join Zoltan's ashes. He stood, then bowed to the corpse. "After all, thanks to you, I know my caution in dealing with you fools was justified. Thanks to you, I need only retrace your movements to learn where you met with the Monster. And, thanks to you, indeed, I'm sure that's all I'll need to find—Esen."

He then strode from the room.

Rudy writhed in his tomb, digging his fingers into the plaster in a futile attempt to push his way out. Dust filled his mouth and stung his eyes, stuck to the blood on his face and neck. He gagged, then forced away his rage and fear, fighting for calm instead of freedom. He counted under his breath to three hundred, giving Cristoffen time to clear the building.

Then, Rudy ordered the drill to free him from the wall. *It was going to be a race.*

At least he knew how to find the finish line.

5: Office Morning; Starship Afternoon

"OH, the easy part's done. The Tik-shi Matrimonial Knives are back in the warehouse vault, Fem Ki. However, the second authentication?" A pause. Meony-ro, dour at the best of times, looked positively funereal. Mind you, it was a fairly common look for the former Kraal turned office staffer/chauffeur, especially since a memorable interlude that saw his bosses kidnapped, tortured, then ambushed within the same vacation. I think he'd hoped to retire from the military a little more peacefully when he picked this Fringe colony.

He did liven up at parties—well-lubricated parties. Meony-ro may have sensed my attention wandering, for he tapped the offending memo. "Do you have any remotely conceivable reason I can attach to the request?" he demanded. "Ramirez and company will not be happy."

"Double his usual fee. As long as the authentication is made by three Hisnath Priests," I decided, a spur-of-the-moment improvisation. Paul bit his lower lip. "I've a client insisting—a client with religious interests."

"Hisnath?" Meony-ro's eyes widened. The imperceptible tracery of the tattoos removed years ago from the skin of his neck, jaw, and cheeks grew almost legible again as he paled. "Fem Ki! Be reasonable! There probably aren't two Hisnath who agree on the time of day. How do you expect Ramirez to find three?" I glowered, something my Lishcyn-self did rather well. The Kraal waved his hands in surrender. "Fine, fine. Double the fee for the impossible."

"It's not as though there's a rush on it," I assured him. "The *Vegas Lass* will be occupied with an urgent—courier job in the meantime. Hom Cameron did brief you?"

Hom Cameron seemed to be developing a cough, but Meony-ro didn't look away from me. He appeared relieved. In fact, he began to grin—an expression I found oddly alarming on the sober version of this Human. "The Largas' ship, *Vegas Lass*?" he repeated, as though to confirm something delightful. "Can't say I envy you traveling with Hom Wolla."

Meony-ro went on as if unaware he'd dropped a conversational blast globe. "I'll let Ramirez know he has some time, Fem Ki."

I wasn't letting him get away that easily. "Traveling with whom?" I demanded.

"Hom Wolla—a pleasant being, of course, but hardly the easiest to . . ." The Kraal's voice trailed away as he went back to frowning at me. *Yet another employee who lacked any respect*, I thought fatalistically. "The '*Lass* is taking him home, right? Joel Largas gave me—I mean, gave Hom Wolla—his word: the next of his ships leaving Minas XII, no matter what."

I felt my scales swelling in an automatic defensive reaction. The last thing we needed was a passenger; the last thing we had was choice in the matter, if Joel had promised. Cameron & Ki kept a credibly modest budget—like everyone else, we relied on local operators such as Largas Freight. Flashing too much wealth on Minas XII was like sending unwary tourists for a stroll along the beach—the predators would be on us just as quickly. We didn't dare run out and buy anything as ostentatious as a private starship. "Surely there's another ship—" I began weakly. *Who was this Wolla anyway?*

It was the Kraal's turn to look alarmed. "None ready to lift. Fem Ki. Please. You can't leave Hom Wolla here. I can't share my quarters with him a day longer." At my doubtlessly blank look, given the Kraal was notoriously private, he explained: "I only took him in as a favor to Aeryn Largas. She needed him to stay long enough to fix the tug pads. Well, he did—over a week ago. I can't get rid of him. He's—he's—ruining my furniture!"

From the sounds of air strangling in his throat, Paul should be rushed to the med techs. I refused to elevate his playacting with so much as a glance. "Fine, fine," I grumbled. "Contact this Hom Wolla and have him meet us at the *'Lass*. Promptly and with his belongings."

Meony-ro, as if his sole desire for the day was to find as many problems for me as possible, shook his head. "Wolla isn't where we can call him. He's down in the Dump."

"The Dump," I repeated numbly, then did look at my Human partner. Paul was attempting to look back with polite interest and nothing more. My upcurled lip was just as sincere. "You aren't surprised," I accused.

"I am acquainted with the being," Paul admitted. "It's become Hom Wolla's—habit—in the afternoon. Every afternoon."

If there had been any other ship I could commandeer without question—or, for that matter, any other with a captain and crew willing to do what we asked without unreasonable questions—and for only a mildly exorbitant fee—I would have used it. But the *'Lass*, and her promised passenger were necessary.

If I was to reach my mountain as soon as possible.

And what it concealed.

I bowed, with a nonvocal snarl, to the fates. "Paul—"

"I'll get him," he told me, suddenly and reassuringly all business, collecting Meony-ro from his desk with a nod. The Kraal was a comfort. He didn't know my true nature. He didn't need to—his loyalty was to Paul Cameron. I needn't worry that Paul would be unguarded in the Dump.

I should have remembered that Kraal loyalties were tattooed into their flesh for a reason.

* * *

I had our carrysacks moved into a cabin on the '*Lass* and joined them as soon as possible. Paul had covered our business lives with as many delays and confusions as he could imagine—a busy office being the best deterrent to curiosity in our employees. To avoid causing confusion of a highly suspicious nature, I decided to stay out of range of questions.

An ephemeral lack of patience had nothing to do with it, I assured myself as I paced in very small, concentric circles. *Exercise was important to any form.* Well, there were some sessile forms where exercise was primarily a matter of constricting internal organs at the appropriate moments, but my Lishcyn-self could use a little more than that.

But after an hour of such pacing, I was faced with an unpleasant truth.

Paul and Wolla should have arrived by now.

Punching in the com, I asked, nonchalantly enough: "Any word from Hom Cameron or Meony-ro?"

"No, Fem Ki." I knew the voice: Silv Largas—prone, as most newly minted captains, to forget he paid his crew for such menial tasks as answering the com. Then again, he was a being who tended to anxiety of his own. *He didn't need mine.*

"Thank you." I hit the com button again. I'd planned it to be a controlled movement, but my strong Lishcyn fingers crumbled the outer casing. I'd have to make sure I compensated Largas for the damage.

Inane thought. It was better than any alternative, starting with the one that I'd let Paul run a potentially dangerous errand because of my impatience.

Ersh would have bitten a strip off me for such carelessness.

Had I thought it would feel more painful, I would have done the same to myself.

Otherwhere

WEATHER on Picco's Moon was a rare occurrence, unless one counted the daily fingering of valley rims by mineral-laden mist. There was the occasional breeze as cooling air sank down shadowed slopes. With almost no moisture outside the valleys, such breezes did little more than moan through cracks and crevices, a dirge taught to young Tumblers as the signal they were out too late for safety and must remain stationary until dawn relit the perils of the surface.

This Tumbler heard the sigh of night air through the rocks' wounds but didn't dare stop. The Elders no longer understood their world; there was no longer safety in stillness.

It tumbled a familiar path that soon became strange with shadow, each roll as slow as possible, each second a greater risk. It was brave, if such a term had meaning for the crystalline folk. It was determined to succeed, where others had not.

There had been a message received, a request invoking the mighty name of Ershia, the Once Immutable. There was no doubt they would comply; no questions need be asked.

There was no doubt the task was dangerous. This Tumbler, healthy and strong, was the fifth to be entrusted.

It stopped, having heard a sound other than the wail of the coming night.

There were trespassers on Ershia's Mountain. The Tumbler had seen for itself the machines of the flesh-burdened, done its best to notice what might help identify those ravaging the peak. They moved by shifting two pillarlike structures, but so did many who came and went through Picco's shipcity. Other body parts appeared to flap loosely, as if about to drop to the ground. Like many who were soft, they scampered about with unsettling speed and in erratic directions.

They took from the ground.

At the memory, the Tumbler chimed to itself, a single note of dismay. This was not the foolish trade in ritual leavings. These flesh-burdened used their machines to rip apart the living mountain, throwing what they stole into the maw of a starship somehow fastened to the cliffside. What rock they didn't choose to keep was carelessly dumped over the side, a growing talus of desecration.

The sound seemed closer. The Tumbler's instinct was to freeze in place, to meld into the strength and power of the rock on all sides. But rock could no longer save itself. Somehow, the Tumbler forced itself to lean forward and roll away, not knowing what lay ahead in the path . . .

But knowing death lay behind.

6: Dump Afternoon

"SO pay attention next time," I muttered under my breath, wrestling the aircar back into its lane. I could see the driver of the other aircar making a very rude and improbable gesture at me through what remained of his forward windshield.

I wasn't fond of flying. Not like this, anyway, strapped into a machine inclined to overreact to the simplest commands. But I hadn't been in the mood to explain to anyone who might drive for me why I wanted to go to the Dump, nor why I had to go immediately.

There were enough lies floating around already.

Which had meant taking myself, at an admitted risk to the rest of the flying public. *A minor and mutual risk*, I assured myself. I'd worry about repairing the bottom front shielding of the *'Lass'* aircar later. Not that anyone would ask for an explanation; I'd acquired an unfortunate reputation with moving vehicles over the years.

Before and after the mishap, I was on course straight to the heart of Fishertown, the area that had once been its shipcity and was now something else entirely. The Dump.

As landscapes went, this one lied more than most. In the Dump, grounded starships pretended to be buildings. Roadways concealed themselves under roofs. The very flatness of the scene misled, for the lava that had poured into this irregular valley, smoothing it with pillows of shiny black and red at the shoreline, raising the rest above sea level for the first time in aeons, was rotten to its core. Each outflow had added its own deceptively smooth and fragile crust, the result riddled with tunnels and hollow spaces where one expected strength. Sensible beings wouldn't have built anything more than a road over it. Better yet, a bridge.

It was, I'd told Paul more than once, simply another good reason not to linger when visiting the Dump.

But ephemeral beings, seemingly incapable of leaving behind either dead ships or dreams, lingered their entire lives here, no matter the risk. Humans, as always, had the temerity to nickname the occasional failure of a lava tube—and inevitable collapse of any buildings above, with loss of life and livelihood—a "dive."

Dives occurred at least once a year, most often during the monsoon season, when the tunnels filled with runoff and already brittle walls were scoured thinner by sharp gravel washed from the heights. Starship captains, grounded or otherwise, appeared oblivious to such facts of nature.

Perhaps, I decided, it was more that they chose to believe their ships would someday fly, preferring to be oblivious to reality itself.

As for reality, I knew where Paul had expected to find Hom Wolla. I'd asked the crew member who'd prepared the aircar. I seemed to be the only being on Minas XII who didn't know the Iedemad was addicted to salt. Mind you, I'd never have guessed it in a sluglike creature who required an osmo-suit to function in anything other than water-saturated air.

I did know there was only one place in the Dump with enough salt on hand and a clientele who wouldn't object to slobber or slime, being prone to it themselves.

Dribble's Trough. A popular watering hole for Ganthor, as well as our missing Iedemad.

Paul was probably happily practicing his clickspeak with whichever herd was presently lurking around. He could lose hours that way.

I certainly hoped so.

*   *   *

Landing was a skill I'd made some effort to acquire, hauling Meony-ro to the rooftops on his mornings off. He seemed bemused by the entire exercise—though that could have been due to his frequent hangovers—but was an excellent teacher nonetheless. It was in my flesh to respect the knowledge of relatively older beings, so I did pay attention. It didn't hurt that landing was patently more useful than lane holding or traffic regulations, particularly to my Lishcyn-self, which wasn't fond of heights—or landings, for that matter.

This time, my approach and touchdown were textbook perfection, something guaranteed by the total lack of an audience. *No doubt any innocent passersby heard I was coming,* I grumbled to myself, taking a moment to set the auto-sentry. Copious signs in a variety of languages, all equally misspelled and all having been used for target practice of some type, served as ample reminder the Dump wasn't a place to leave things unguarded.

The parking lot for Dribble's was on its roof. Or rather, was the roof. I climbed out of the aircar and put my foot down as though about to step on a relative's eggs. My previous experience with the construction of such things in the Dump was, to put it mildly, memorable. This time, the roof held, accepting my other foot and full weight without so much as creaking. Well, it vibrated, but that seemed to be a feature of the building. I smoothed the silks of my third-favorite caftan over my ample thighs, settled my least-favorite beaded bag on my chest, and ran one fork of my tongue over my tusks for a final polish before taking the lift to street level. Dribble's might be a seedy, disgusting bar where only the dregs of Dump society gathered, but it was a public place. My Lishcyn-self cared about appearances.

Humans weren't the only species with a predilection for gathering in noisy, inebriated groups—just among the more docile. Their bars thus tended to remain intact over the years, begrimed by memories of the stickier sort and any scars lovingly cherished as souvenirs of brawls some patrons claimed to remember later. This probably explained why Human-run establishments gradually spread throughout shipcities where Humans prowled in any numbers at all. It wasn't that they were more successful barkeeps—their buildings simply out-survived more challenged establishments.

Dribble's, for example, wasn't run by Humans. For that reason, among others, it was presently in its fifteenth incarnation, judging by the number of shiny "Open Since . . ." plaques hammered into its somewhat cockeyed doorframe. The number of partial restorations would be much higher but such wouldn't rate the pride of an opening ceremony. Rrhysers were a species who knew how to throw a party. And furniture. And customers.

Things seemed reasonably peaceful this afternoon: no stretchers or repair crews in sight. I did watch where I put my feet as I negotiated the stairs. This wasn't an unusual caution—my Lishcyn-self had rather generous feet—however, in this instance, my somewhat obsessive attention to the footing had more to do with what lay, squirmed, and otherwise coated most of the steps leading down to the main entrance. Rrhysers let their offspring play anywhere they chose.

Offspring with very pointy teeth.

Child safety was one reason for the Dribble's location. The Dump might lie within the boundaries of Fishertown, but the city administration kept hoping if they ignored it, it would go away. So there were no servo street sweepers or disposal collectors to mistake a young Rrhyser for litter.

Customers, I groused, forced to stretch precariously over the second-to-last step to miss a pair playing squirm-and-go-seek, evading a quick snap in my direction, *fended for themselves.*

No children on the floor inside, which was just as well. They'd probably get lost in the debris. The bar must have enjoyed a rare amount of peace and tranquillity lately. I dropped a handful of chits into the waiting hand of the bouncer, who didn't look up from whatever she was reading but, to her credit, did lift an older model weapon scanner vaguely in my direction. I wasn't armed, but the thing couldn't go off in any case—I could see its power pack on the floor beside her seat. More to the point, I'd seen the Rrhyser's broad nostrils open and close, checking me for any illicit substance. You weren't allowed to bring your own.

Proprieties observed, I headed through the entrance to the bar itself.

I'd unconsciously kept my hand on the bag around my neck, ready to snatch out the powerful lamp I carried with me whenever there was a chance of entering a room with lighting designed by beings with superior night vision than my present self's. The old joke about losing a Lishcyn in a closet by closing the door was regrettably accurate. But Dribble's was very well lit, even by my standards—a wise precaution in an establishment where blundering into someone in the dark could mean being mistaken for an appetizer.

Well lit, but crowded. I was taller than some here, especially the nonbipedal, but it didn't help. I tried to filter the din for Paul's voice, but my exquisitely sensitive ears kept flattening against my skull in a futile attempt to protect themselves.

The place was more a broad hallway than a room, with openings on either side. There was a bar at one end—at least, I assumed the lineup in front of me was for drinks—and musicians on an overhead scaffolding were pounding out the latest Rrhyser dance rhythms, explaining the vibration I'd felt on the roof.

I made my way through the crowd, surprised by the number of species represented here. The Circle Club, Fishertown's most successful multispecies' restaurant, could hardly boast such variety—except on all-you-can-ingest nights. *Maybe it was the music?* I was no judge in this form. My Lishcyn ears were tone-deaf. I did know it was loud.

The openings from the main room were large three-sided chambers; each was similar in size and shape to the others, but differed in their dècor. Perhaps the Rrhyser had rebuilt those portions of Dribble's at different times—or under the influence of different substances. The one to my left was an eye-damaging fluorescent orange, from wall hangings to blocklike seating; ahead to my right was another furnished with what appeared to be rotting wood, piled into irregular platforms. Regardless, the result was a sequence of drinking areas that appealed more to certain species than others. I shook off the uncharitable image of a zoo where the inhabitants paid the keepers for beer.

I eased out of range of the pair of Rrhyser waiters arguing over which of them had seen me first. The adults might seem fairly standard tripeds, soft-voiced and peaceful, but their tempers were infamous. I had no time to be distracted by the thumping of chest plates, ritual or otherwise.

I was here to find my Human.

Of course, there were Humans to be found. Predictably, they weren't conveniently all in one place, but instead had scattered like spilled noodles throughout gatherings of other species. *When I was in a hurry, nothing was ever,* I thought with growing disgust, *ever easy.*

However, I didn't need to look for Paul—one humanoid among the hordes. I should find him wherever this Wolla was sloshing about in salt, which meant a pool or tub large enough for an Iedemad. I kept moving among the semi-drunk—the truly drunk apparently favoring the security of an inclined posture—and those attempting to join them. Since the means of achieving this blissful state differed with biology, I had to watch for errant puffs of intoxicating vapor as well as overfilled containers. My Lishcyn-self was reasonably invulnerable, unless there was a tub of steaming, bubbling water involved.

The mere thought inspired a lengthy contemplation of blissful and rather naughty ideas, during which I likely stepped on a few limbs.

Enough of that! I scolded myself. In another form, I would have blushed at those vivid memories, all stemming back to that embarrassing incident on D'Dsell. My Lishcynself fought the urge to flash a lecherous tusk or two.

I continued forcing my conveniently large and robust self through the throng, muttering a running commentary that went something like: "Sorry. Excuse me. Not interested. Isn't that your mate over there? Oh. Still not interested. Excuse me. Was that your—appendage? Sorry."

The sound of splashing brought up my ears. *There.* After struggling past another pair of trenchant, chest-thumping waiters—sharing of any sort, including tips, never having been a successful strategy in Rrhyser society—and the thirsty patrons awaiting the outcome, I found myself standing triumphantly by a pool. A round, raised, and very dark pool. With rows of gleaming black eyeballs floating on top. All looking at me.

"My mistake," I said, backing away slowly in case this wasn't a male-only party of Carasians.

I had no time for this, I complained to myself, then looked at the situation more rationally. If I was having trouble finding this Wolla, so would Paul and Meony-ro—not to mention what they faced trying to pry the being from his salt supply. If the Iedemad was thoroughly osmofied, it was unlikely he'd grasp the concept of a planet, let alone a ship leaving one.

My ship. Which was waiting to take me to Picco's Moon and Ersh's Mountain. My impatience and worry took a distinct turn toward irritation. *How had I let Meony-ro talk us into this?*

I knew the answer. Guilt. The other side of secrets.

"Es? What in the— What are you doing here?"

I flicked both ears forward and open to capture every nuance of that most welcome sound: Paul yelling at me.

He was safe!

Then my now-opened ears picked up furious clickspeech

from behind Paul. That was alarming, but not as much as the even more furious answer from behind me.

I might have jumped to the conclusion about safety a little too soon.

I didn't need Skalet-memory to tell me the last place to be caught by surprise was between two herds of unhappy Ganthor.

Otherwhere

THEIR precision was pleasing.

As was action after years of observation. This move had been planned and practiced, with variants calculated around setting and time—elements beyond control, but always offering unique advantages. The figure watching at the console nodded with satisfaction. This was better than anticipated.

Efficient.

She traced the edges of the display lightly, with one finger, interpreting the multiple feeds as if they were extensions of her own senses, all the while effortlessly predicting the next move by each of the individuals they represented. So far, she hadn't intervened; not for their pride's sake, but because it hadn't been necessary. She'd trained them, after all.

Her finger paused over a small square of yellow, then covered it for a moment.

Time to grow up, Youngest.

7: Dump Afternoon; Tunnel Afternoon

THERE were moments I could swear I didn't just remember Ersh, but could hear her voice ringing in my head. An ephemeral conceit, perhaps. Right now, that voice, imagined or not, was loud and aggrieved: *And* this *is how you remain inconspicuous?*

Since I was presently diving for cover along with a barful of drunken beings, or those still conscious, while trying to keep my eyes and ears fixed on Paul as he did the same, I thought it a bit much to have my subconscious scold me for the effort. But I conceded the point. There wasn't much inconspicuous about a huge lump of Lishcyn crashing through furniture in search of a hiding place. It might have helped had there been another Lishcyn within three systems.

The Rrhysers, waiters and all, were remarkable in their absence, obviously conceding Dribble's Trough was due for thorough reconstruction. The Ganthor were still talking, though with the amount of steamy mucus being flung about, it seemed unlikely they'd restrain themselves for long.

"It seems to be a case of *Herd-theft!*" Paul shouted and clicked, having made his way to where I crouched.

"Where's Meony-ro?"

"With Hom Wolla." His arm shot past my snout to point at the end of the main room, where what appeared to be a large chartreuse bag was draped across part of the bar, displacing the arrangement of varied consumables in large bowls. I could just make out a Humanish figure beside it. Ah. Our missing Kraal.

No wonder I hadn't found the Iedemad, I thought with disgust. He was still in his osmo-suit. Wolla must be one of the semi-insane and understandably rare salt addicts who preferred to take his fix through his digestive tract. *Ersh.*

"We can't stay here," Paul insisted, reasonably. As if knowing reason wasn't enough, he was also pulling at my arm. I didn't budge. "Esen, let's go!"

"Just a moment," I requested, studying the Herds. *Something wasn't right.*

The Herd which must have entered Dribble's right behind me consisted of a Matriarch, her Second, and three others. All were heavily armed, with ammunition-filled bandoliers crisscrossing their chests. Mercenaries.

Fine-looking ones at that. Successful, by the investment they carried on their bodies and the healthy rolls of fat rippling beneath their hides. The Matriarch, though scarred around her snout and over both shoulders, was of magnificent size. All five held their right hands curled before their chests, horned digits from that hoof ready to click. That they'd stopped clicking was ominous. Mucus bubbled from every snout as they strained information about one another from the polluted air of the bar.

I looked at the second Herd. No doubt as to the culprits in the *Herd-theft!* A dozen individuals: another Matriarch, two Seconds, underlings busy pushing at one another but staying in a protective circle. A poorer Herd: armed with secondhand gear; members thin, pockmarked, and, in one case, missing an arm that should have been replaced. No wonder they'd stolen their prize.

The object of dispute and desire stood in the center of their circle, taller than the others, a strapping, unscarred youth in his early prime. Without smelling him, I couldn't be sure, but his body posture seemed confused. He should be accepting his new Herd or struggling to return to what must be his own; instead, he rocked slowly from one foot to the other, snout aimed downward. He wasn't even smelling the air.

"He's been drugged," I said to Paul, suddenly sure. Not a Ganthor tactic. The oddness of his behavior was the key here, unsettling both his kidnappers and rescuers. Neither knew what to do beyond click insults at one another. For now.

Unsettled Ganthor were the deadly kind. What should be resolved by a bit of bump and bruise, followed by snouts deep in beer and sly liaisons between the higher ranks, could well turn into a firefight—especially between Herds with sufficient ordnance to level this part of the Dump. While that might not be a waste, in terms of urban renewal, it definitely wasn't something to stay around and watch. My usually shaggy scales began to swell and close, an admirable defense against bug bites and surly relatives, if ridiculously ineffective against disrupter or blast globe.

Paul obviously agreed, having continued to tug at me, now digging in his feet and using both hands. "Let's get out of here, Esen. Now!"

Finally, I let him pull us into the general stampede for the main doors. It didn't get very far. There was an obstruction—something happening at the entrance. I was tall enough to make out what appeared to be a scuffle. Several Rrhysers were trying to prevent Humans in black battle gear from entering. The authorities? In the Dump? Whoever they were, the patrons of Dribble's able to see these new arrivals reacted with predictable paranoia, cursing as they turned and began pushing back toward us. Which meant toward the enraged Ganthor.

Somehow I held onto my Lishcyn-form as well as Paul, frantically dumping heat as I fought the instinct to cycle into something better able to struggle to safety through the now-panicked crowd. My broad, semiwebbed feet probably crushed as many toes as stepped on mine. I gave up trying to apologize.

"This way." Somehow I heard Paul's calm voice through

the bedlam. He was taking us into one of the chambers, the one decorated in lurid orange.

I protested: "The roof—I brought an aircar—"

"Too late. They'll be—" I missed all but: "—take the lava tubes."

Then Paul was torn from my grip.

I cleared my line of sight by the simple expedient of picking up the being closest to me and flinging him, with another apology, into the group of Humans blocking my view. They went down in a heap.

Meony-ro! I sagged with relief, now able to see the Kraal hurrying Paul through a previously hidden door—explaining the former location of a large and truly vile wall hanging. That must be the way into the underground tubes and tunnels. No sign of Hom Wolla; likely the blissed Iedemad hadn't noticed the impending riot.

Now a war. My famed hearing caught the unmistakable whine of a disruptor charging to fire. I flung myself on top of the groaning Humans as some tried to rise, quite sure they'd thank me later. Better bruises and a temporary loss of lung capacity than Ganthor cross fire. I covered my ears, grateful Paul and Meony-ro were safe.

Wishing I was.

Otherwhere

A TRUE believer . . .

. . . was all Lionel Kearn had wanted from life, not so long ago. To hear that someone believed him, to have someone share his fear of the Esen Monster and the terrible danger she and her predatory kind—Shifters— were to intelligent life. To see his commitment to end that threat reflected in another's eyes.

Now he had all this, plus the respect and support he'd needed so desperately all these years.

His hands, soft and pale, clenched around one another until his nails left bright red marks in the skin.

What had he done?

Under his hands was a report, as precise and wordy as any of the academic papers filling Kearn's shelves and piled by his desk. A report from his new assistant, Michael Cristoffen.

Assistant? Kearn's hands flew apart and rubbed over his shiny scalp. *Disciple. Goad. Nightmare.*

The report outlined actions taken, meetings held, next steps. Kearn's eyes squeezed shut as if he could erase the truth between those sickening layers of euphemism.

His fawning, talented protégé had committed murder and would expect him to be pleased.

Oh, not that Cristoffen could be accused or convicted. It had been self-defense. No doubt Zoltan Duda had threatened, then fired a weapon. Cristoffen had appended the Port Authority findings concerning the event, having quite properly, if anonymously, alerted them.

Nothing on the plas pages on Kearn's desk suggested Cristoffen had gone to that meeting hoping for exactly that outcome, had orchestrated Zoltan's death before leaving the *Russell III*, had committed the perfect murder.

But Kearn feared it was so.

He forced his hands from his head, hopefully before the rubbing inflamed the rashes on his scalp again. A new cream was helping, but only when he could control the nervous habit. *Given Cristoffen's presence on board,* Kearn sighed, *it was likely to get worse.*

The Human stood, turning away from his desk, and stared at himself in the mirror, wondering why the changes there hadn't changed anything else. The ill-fitting uniform he'd worn every day for fifty years was gone, replaced by dark blue tunic and pants of Iftsen-weave, the plain fabric pleasingly soft. He stood straighter and ran one hand down his chest and belly, feeling the firmness there; drew a breath, and felt the smooth movement of air through lungs that served him well during his runs with Timri, when only a year ago he'd had trouble lasting minutes. His face?

Kearn scowled and watched the expression wipe the haunted weariness from his eyes, tuck away the new lines around his mouth, and fail to make him look the least bit intimidating.

Nothing really changes, he told himself, letting the scowl fade to confusion. He still needed to fear and suspect the goals of everyone around him.

Including his own.

8: Tunnel Afternoon

THE Humans hadn't thanked me. Not that I cared. *I had more to worry about.*

I was in Paul's tunnel. I hadn't found Paul, or Meony-ro, or even the reprehensible Wolla—a being I chose to blame for everything happening around me. *A target made muttering more satisfying.* The tunnel had been the easy part, since most of the occupants of Dribble's not involved in fighting with one another or dodging battle-mad Ganthor had run, leaped, hopped, slithered, or bulled their way into it.

I'd only to follow along.

The famished darkness pushed my shoulders, trying to slow me down.

I'd followed, wedged between a singing Ervickian and a sullen, limping Human, down crude stairs that showed all the design foresight of an accident, into this maze. Behind us, the sounds of what should have been a more-or-less friendly barroom brawl began to include screaming as well as concussive explosions.

The wicked darkness grabbed my feet, trying to make me fall.

I should have cycled into anything but this form before coming to Dribble's; I should have listened when Paul wanted to leave in the first place; I should have— I focused on the beam of light as it fought its way along the floor. Floor? It was a pool of stygian black, slick and deadly cold beneath my feet. I—

Ersh, I pleaded inwardly, as if she could hear me—or

would do anything but chime her scorn if she did—*let me hold myself together for another minute.*

I'd found it wise not to ask for too much at once.

My ears flicked back and forth constantly. It wasn't all terror at the darkness on every side, at what lurked there—though my night-blind Lishcyn-self knew beyond doubt that anything dimmer than twilight held creatures with teeth: hungry, Lishcyn-eating creatures, with long, needlelike teeth. Venom-oozing fangs were always a distinct possibility. No, I listened to more than my imagination and the roiling sounds of my stomachs. I listened to my train of followers. Having the only light—and refusing to surrender it in no uncertain terms—had put me in charge.

I could really learn to detest that slug of an Iedemad.

By such careful listening, in the rare moments when someone wasn't snarling threats, ejecting bodily fluids intentionally or otherwise, or singing in complete oblivion to danger, I'd determined I was now escorting eight soggy drunks beneath the Dump.

The impatient darkness snatched the air from my nostrils, trying to smother me.

Coms didn't work down here; whether jammed deliberately by those in the buildings over our heads or by nature, didn't matter. Fortunately for the eight, and unfortunately for me, I did know where I was going. These tubes ran parallel to one another, more or less, having formed as lava poured down the seaward slope of the valley floor. The outer shell of lava had cooled first, while the inner stream kept flowing through and past, leaving these hollow cavities behind. The intersecting tunnels we kept passing had nothing to do with volcanism, being dug by those who thought they'd found the perfect hiding place or, more likely, escape routes.

Adding random tunneling to the recorded tendency of this roof to join the floor? I steadied the lamp in my hand and tried not to think in terms of stability and structural strength. After all, the Dump itself was an exercise in building by what remained standing, so one could hardly expect better in its basement.

Basement? An unmarked, deliberately deceitful labyrinth. At least my gaggle of inebriants could follow me to safety. My Human had detailed maps of the maze. He judged them reliable, though the source was one of Diale's cronies and I had serious reservations about anyone who'd claim that lawless and quite impolite tech dealer as friend. Paul, however, had an obsession for escape routes and insisted I look at the maps. For a web-being of perfect memory, once seen was enough.

This way, I decided, would take us to the nearest surface exit to Cameron & Ki. We were already walking slightly uphill.

Unfortunately for me, I couldn't abandon the others, tempting as the thought grew each time one of them started arguing about the direction, or ejected more bodily fluids. But Paul would not approve.

The treacherous darkness swallowed the beam from my lamp, trying to make me lose my way.

Eventually, they quieted, though I could still count eight sets of respiratory organs at work over the flapping of my feet and rather pronounced complaints of my fourth stomach; I surmised walking in the cold, damp air had its sobering effect on these species. Or perhaps they, too, felt the darkness as a living force, a threat to survival kept at bay only by the pathetic sword of light I wielded in one hand. One very tightly gripping hand, with a strap attached to the lamp fastened around the wrist. *Ersh*, I told myself firmly, *hadn't raised a fool.*

I thought she'd be proud of me, successfully fighting every inclination of this form in order to keep and use it, to hide my true nature. *Or maybe not.* Ersh had expected such things. Paul would understand, though. He'd appreciate the effort I'd made, if not how.

I could always, I told myself in much the way Humans whistled when afraid, *count on Paul.*

He would be waiting for me at the office. We would find out who had drugged the poor young Ganthor in order to start a fight in a bar. A bar where we both happened to be, exactly when we were both there.

As Skalet-memory insisted: *there were no coincidences.*

"We're being followed."

I started at this reminder I wasn't alone in the dark, a reflex that sent the beam careening alarmingly along the walls and ceiling, sparking uselessly dim patches of fluorescence where fungi had taken hold. Then I aimed it at the face of the being who'd spoken, dipping it to the floor again as the Human threw up an arm to protect his eyes. "I only hear you," I said reasonably, though my stomachs abruptly remembered they existed to cause me grief. "I have excellent hearing."

Apparently the Human wasn't relying on senses, mine or his own. His hand appeared in the beam, showing all of us the small device in its palm. "Sniffer," he explained, sounding much more sober than I'd expected. "I dropped the other half behind us, in case those were Port Jellies. Not that I'm a runner, you see, but I'm not lookin' for trouble either. Several someones just tripped it."

I was filled with admiration—and a healthy dose of dread. "Did anyone see Port Authority badges?" I asked.

A chorus of negatives followed, along with one completely irrelevant comment about sugar. Ervickians stayed drunk longer than most species.

It wasn't Paul. My Human was too careful to trip any spy device this crude. More significantly, I'd seen Meony-ro lead him into the tubes ahead of us, not behind. I would never have left Dribble's if I'd imagined he might still be in there. Hom Wolla, yes. My first and best friend—no.

I considered what I'd seen of the black battle gear. Too nondescript to identify with certainty. Kraal perhaps, but they sold their military tech to many systems and species.

Another image floated up: faded tattoos. We'd been at Dribble's because of Meony-ro.

The untrustworthy darkness gibbered and plucked at my ears, trying to confuse me.

I refused to become paranoid. "I'm sure we aren't the only ones using these tubes," I said firmly, swinging the light forward again.

Keeping one ear aimed behind.

I learned the reward for remaining my Lishcyn-self when willing hands and rumps shoved aside the storm grate that served as a doorway from the lava tube to the real world. Light flooded my eyes, painful, wonderful, safe light that vanquished dangerous shadows once and for all. I felt a joy so visceral I had to shunt what remained in my third stomach to my fourth to contain it.

The implacable darkness behind grabbed me, trying to keep me inside.

I rushed into the open. I wasn't alone, my compatriots from the tube hurried with me, but none of them had my combination of inertia and motivation. As a result, I was in the middle of the roadway dodging a groundcar before I could stop myself.

I grinned, shining both tusks at the flustered driver, who may not have taken my expression exactly as intended, given his speed leaving my vicinity. *No matter! We were out of the dark.* For a change, Minas XII wasn't raining, hailing, or otherwise trying to obliterate us from its surface.

But it seemed memorizing a map wasn't quite the same as following one. I lost my smile as I looked up. In fact, I lost my jaw as it unhinged in shock and dropped to my chest. The Sweet Sisters, a set of seven ominous volcanoes marking the northern end of the shipcity itself, should have been far to my left. They loomed out of storm clouds straight ahead.

Not to mention they were towering over the now-smoldering roof of what remained of Dribble's.

I'd led us out of the Dump, all right, and back in again.

Oh, dear. I took a moment to snick my jaw back into place.

Surprisingly unconcerned, my former tunnel mates scattered in all directions, save one. "Are you all right, Fem Ki?" His voice sounded more impatient than concerned—the Human with the 'sniffer. He was by himself now, standing safely out of the flow of traffic. The others were flagging down for-hires, arguing loudly where two tried for the same conveyance. The Ervickian was singing to a lamppost.

There was no sign of black-garbed Humans, though a few Ganthor milled around in the wreckage, exchanging rather incredible boasts from what I could hear of their cheerful clinking as they hunted for unexploded, and hence still useful, globes. "Can you help me arrange transport?" I asked the Human, feeling somewhat overwhelmed by this evidence of normalcy returning. "I want to go home."

An ephemeral saying, I told myself, that suited the moment perfectly. I wanted my rooms, my bright, safe lighting, my own walls around me.

I should have remembered who and what I was.

Otherwhere

DRIP. Drip. Drip. The valley wall gleamed with wetness; the ramplike road braiding its slope was etched with channels of steaming liquid. Even the air lipping at the road's sheer edge was heavy with mist. Water was the bringer of life, carrier of all things mineral. Water was the agent of death, returning living matter to the rock from whence it came.

The Tumbler scraped its trowellike fingers along the wall, collecting what drops it could. There was no time to linger within the seeping of the Edianti's famed springs, to recrystallize the gifts of the earth along every facet of its body. Despite its ordeal, this rash, hurried feeding had to be enough.

This road was old and unfamiliar; its crumbling steepness a hazard best avoided. The Tumbler had been forced to it by those terrifying sounds in the dark, an unnaturally regular repetition of something falling to the ground, as if it were being pursued by an avalanche able to move along the surface.

Drip. Drip. Splash.

They were behind it still, as they had been night and day, through the revealing truth of Eclipse, to true day again. The Tumbler had led its pursuers away from the innocent, done its utmost to lose them in the tears and wounds of the Moon herself. Nothing had stopped the sounds from behind.

It wasn't self-preservation. There was danger to

more than itself here. Flesh-burdened who would chase one Tumbler across Picco's Moon? Who dared trespass here? The Elders must know.

The Tumbler chimed a troubled minor as it rolled down the road. The lawlessness of the flesh-burdened ignored the treaties that welcomed them only to the shipcity and the heights. Elders of the Assansi had granted permission for a group of their scientists to enter a living valley, but that had been long before this Tumbler had been accumulated.

The flesh-burdened had never been invited to the Edianti. They never would be.

Drip. Splash, splash, splash!

The mist thickened with every roll and slide downward, growing sweet with acid and filling with the tastes of home.

Home. And they followed still.

The Tumbler slowed to a stop and straightened. If words such as desperation and courage applied to a being made of stone, it knew both as it turned to face upslope. Condensation trickled along its every edge, as if water already knew what must happen and was greedy for the result.

The Tumbler put its back to the wall, leaned forward, and gracefully rolled off the road's edge.

Let them follow now, it thought as it plunged through the mist.

9: Cliffside Afternoon; Greenhouse Night

HOME, for a web-being, was wherever her Web gathered. For me, it was Minas XII, a world on the Fringe. *Well, some part of it, anyway.* The part with Paul in it. But I'd learned other habits over the past decades. Since my Human persisted in calling the stone-walled structure where we lived "home," I'd begun thinking of it that way myself.

And now? It was gone. I pressed my snout against the aircar's windshield, the plas creaking a protest. The rumblings of all my stomachs was louder, and just as unimportant.

Had Paul been there?

I stared into the deeply shadowed crater that was supposed to be home, Skalet-memory automatically hunting and deciphering clues, Esen-memory helplessly recording and remembering. The amount of explosive used: excessive, even against a semi-fortress built to be snug and cozy through winter's hellish storms. Likely method of delivery: by remote, a piece of aircar undercarriage was embedded into what had been the landing pad out front, where Paul had first arrived, ending my loneliness. The reason?

No clues to that lay seared into the rock.

"Fem Ki."

Words that made no sense. *Esolesy Ki did not exist.* I kept form by instinct, not will.

Had Paul been there?

"Fem Ki."

There could be a host of reasons he wasn't answering to the com, starting with being too busy.

"Please. Fem Ki, we should get back to Fishertown. The wind's picking up." The note of anxiety in the driver's voice reached me if not the meaning of his words.

I could go down there, cycle into web-form, taste the debris—and find out.

Had Paul been there?

The view disappeared behind what was left of my lunch, breakfast, and last night's indulgence of fudge. I tapped the driver's shoulder in mute apology. He took it as a signal to send the aircar careening down the cliff face, back to the Port City and its lights; by his speed, I presumed he hoped to arrive before further interior decorating.

I didn't bother telling him that all of my stomachs were quite empty. Nor did I argue with his decision. To go into the burning hole that had been our home, hunting for Paul, was to admit the unthinkable.

Something I couldn't do.

We couldn't land at the office itself. The driver might be a licensed for-hire and so presumably somewhat law-abiding, but this was Minas XII. He didn't need me to tell him to slow and turn away when we saw what waited for us. The landing pad on the roof of Cameron & Ki Exports was crammed with aircars—highly official-looking aircars, with all the potential for delays and questions those implied. I had a sudden happy image of Paul, looking his usual imperturbable and vastly respectable self, answering those questions with the truth, or suitable facsimile, removing suspicion and concern as deftly as he would offer a sample of the latest Inhaven wine. Not as a bribe, but as a signal of how he valued the time of his visitors. My Human could work magic with bureaucrats.

He might be demanding answers himself—answers

about the wanton destruction of the wine cellar and home of decent, tax-paying beings such as ourselves.

In either case, Paul did not need a starving Lishcyn coated in multicolored bile to waltz in the door. I'd done that before and Humans really didn't react well. *Weak-stomached creatures in their own way.*

"Over there, please," I shouted to the driver, pointing over his shoulder at the long building next to the office. I had to shout. He'd lowered the roof and opened all the side-ports for some reason, despite the hail starting to pepper us both. I couldn't hear what he said in return, having replaced my hands over my suffering ears, but the aircar obediently swerved left toward the warehouse.

I was trembling by the time we landed, and hurried to key in payment plus tip. Despite my somewhat soggy and distinctly odorous state, the driver helped me climb out. I took a good look at his face for the first time, seeing the lineage he probably didn't know. Human. Garson's World. Refugee. A typical Minas XII import on the surface, but one with eye-folds and cheekbones linking this individual incarnation of humanity to one group of ancestors, to one part of that world where his species had evolved. Warmed by Ersh-memories of fireworks and five-fingered dragons, I grasped tightly at that sense of past retained, as much a comfort to me as the anchor of his strong arm.

He wouldn't leave until I stood in the lift and waved good-bye. *Extraordinary courtesy*, I decided, sagging against the wall the moment the door closed. My lip struggled to lift over a tusk in a smile as I imagined his expression when he saw his tip. *It seemed only fair to replace the aircar I'd so abundantly christened.* One bright spot in a day that I sincerely hoped couldn't get worse.

Of course, I reminded myself, *that kind of hope usually gained me nothing but a chuckle from the Cosmic Gods.* Once I knew Paul was safe, they could laugh all they wanted.

The lift could take me to the warehouse floor, but I'd

pressed a sequence of buttons known only to myself, Paul, and a handful of our closest associates. This stopped the lift much sooner than would seem reasonable from the outside. The door opened, and I drew the reason in through my every pore, feeling the scales of my hide finally shrinking to normal.

Minas XII boasted some trees, waist-high to a Human but only knee-high to a Screed, and a few genera of grasses and moss. Its plant life had struggled onto land, only to be beaten into sullen toughness by the extremes of weather the Humans so enjoyed complaining about. But here?

I stepped into a jungle, my shoulders stroked by fronds of lush purple-green, my eyes soaking in the bright colors on every side, crisscrossed by sunbeams drawn inward by concealed collectors. My wide, webbed feet left no lasting impressions on the moist turf that made up much of the floor at this end of my greenhouse. My sanctuary.

My safe and secret place, where I could recover my poise while waiting for Paul. My stomachs growled in sequence, from first to fifth, reminding me of the other very good reason to be here. It might seem I'd chosen the plants by their appearance, but most, if not all, had other uses. *Aha.* I plucked a nicely ripe cluster of liliming nuts, tossing them to the back of my mouth and unhinging my jaw so my rearmost teeth could crack their shells. A quick swallow moved them into my first stomach, already grinding in anticipation. Another cluster beckoned and I made equally swift work of it.

"Esolesy Ki!" That voice, with its rich depth and warmth, was as nourishing to my spirit as the nuts now in my second stomach.

I swallowed more quickly, and rehinged my jaw. "Joel. Have you heard from Paul?"

"He told me to watch for you." The Human abandoned the trimmer he'd been guiding through the shrubbery to hurry up to me, hands outstretched. He stopped short of touching me, which was probably wise. "What have you done now?" This with the confident suspicion of someone who knew me well indeed.

Joel Largas. Second only to Paul as a dear friend. Grandfather to Paul's twins. A thoroughly admirable being who had built a life on one world, seen it destroyed, then stubbornly gone on to build what boded to be a lasting dynasty on a new one. As he stood there fussing over my disheveled and smelly self, scolding me on general principle, I shone my tusks at him happily, sure everything would now be right with the world.

I should have been listening for laughter.

"Paul's on his way." Joel delivered this welcome news with a straight face, then chuckled, his eyes twinkling. "I told him to hurry if he wanted to catch you in there. You're a sight, Es, you really are. I should take a vid for the twins."

Between full stomachs and the reassuring news that Paul and Meony-ro had arrived safely at the office, knew everything, and were dealing with it, I merely lifted a tusk and rolled on my stomach within the mud wallow, another delightful aspect of this sanctuary. It wasn't dirty mud. This was a warm concoction of pink-hued sand and fragrant oils, with a hint of naughty carbonation. Warmer than usual—I'd needed to release some of my built-up tension as heat, since cycling was out of the question. Joel, grimly aware of what had happened at the bar—and to our home—hadn't stayed with me out of a wish for companionship. Paul had asked him to watch for me, a job Joel took as meaning watch over me as well.

And if there was anyone who must never see me as anything but Lishcyn, it was this Human. Joel Largas had witnessed the slaughter of friends and family in the jaws of a Web-being, unable to do anything but watch as ships were breached, lives stolen. He'd come away as scarred by that attack as if Death's teeth had ripped his own flesh.

Worse, as if that were conceivable, my mindless kin had already incited the obliteration of Garson's World by the

Tly, the act which had turned the Largas clan into homeless refugees.

A terrible debt, I and my kind owed this forthright and capable being. My friendship couldn't begin to repay it, not that Joel would ever know.

I shook off the past, then flattened my ears, closed my eyelids, and shoved my entire head beneath the surface, feeling no guilt whatsoever at the soothing luxury of sand rubbing away the last evidence of my dreadful day. I'd share, but Humans developed unpleasant rashes. The time I'd pushed Paul in—well, suffice it to say even Ersh hadn't made me feel quite that much remorse.

Good to know he was finally coming. Paul had been stuck at the office past the supper hour, fending off apologetic officials and newsmag writers. Not much happened outside the Dump on Minas XII, missing tourists being too common for a headline. There had been a pair of opportunistic contractors—Fringe worlds were well-endowed with those looking for profit in tragedy. Not to forget the lawyer—Paul had refused to press a suit against the Ganthor for willful endangerment.

Joel had relayed the last with a disgusted look, the lawyer being one of his many younger relations, a being obviously possessed of more enthusiasm than sense. I imagined she'd get an earful from the family patriarch over supper. No one sued Ganthor. As well sue the windstorm now rattling the warehouse roof plates.

Our home wouldn't have rattled.

I resurfaced and began skimming the oily sand from my scales with the rubbery paddle Joel passed me, finding it impossible to grasp what had happened no matter how perfect the image in memory. *It was a sign*, I told myself with significant self-pity, *that I'd grown too ephemeral in my way of thinking*. But it was hard for my Lishcyn-self to stop grieving over those lovely silk caftans, with matching beaded bags, all reduced to sooty bits in the wind.

My true self, Esen-alit-Quar, had no need for possessions. I'd collected the odd trinket over the years. *But I didn't need them*, I thought, skimming my left arm, something that was probably fortunate under the circumstances. Paul? Since our new life together, he'd avoided acquiring what might have to be abandoned with a zeal worthy of Ersh herself.

I didn't know how he felt about needing a new wardrobe, but my own mood began to improve dramatically at the thought of shopping.

"Excuse me," I warned Joel, turning my head politely to one side before violently blowing the last trace of sand from my nostrils. Stepping over the tiled side of the wallow, I reached for a strap of polishing leather and began rubbing my scales. The front was easy, but my thick arms and reinforced joints made doing a thorough job on my back a definite struggle.

"Here, let me." Joel took the leather and began burnishing my shoulders, stopping now and then to shake accumulated sand from the strap. I poked my toe into the growing pile of pink and eyed the nearest duras plant. Before I could succumb to temptation, Joel snapped the leather against my backside. "Don't go sticking leaves in yourself—you're finally clean," he chided, as he would to any of his grandchildren or their offspring.

My backside was quite invulnerable to leather, but my sensitive ears flattened at the snapping sound. "I wasn't going—" The completely insincere protest faded as I spotted the figure pushing through a grove of fine-needled trees toward us. Paul! I showed both tusks.

More rattling. I'd thought it had been the wind, but as I brought up my ears to better hear Paul's approach, I swiveled them uneasily, puzzling at an odd echo to his steps. There, to the left, where vines trailed from the ceiling in a curtain of flower-encrusted green. No, there, to the right, behind the tiled depression of the wallow, where ranks of fystia bushes impersonated amber flame.

Humans might have relatively impoverished hearing, but

Joel Largas was no fool. One hard look at me, and he had a disrupter in his gnarled fist. Where he'd hidden it until now I couldn't begin to guess.

Paul began to run toward us, silently, desperately, thrusting plants out of his way. As if that had been a signal, every leaf started to shake. The surface of the mud wallow developed ripples even as I felt the heavy vibration through my feet.

These were impressions I sorted out later, overwhelmed by sound. Breathing: heavy, fast, irregular, on all sides. The breaking of stems, the sick wet sound of ruined flowers as bodies came crashing toward us through the growth. How they'd been so silent before I couldn't guess. Now, I could hear what had to be dozens approaching.

"Es!" Paul reached my side, his eyes wild, a weapon free in his own hand. Perhaps he said something more to me, made some foolish request for me to leave. I ignored him.

Besides, it was too late to run.

We were surrounded by figures in black armor, identical to that worn by those who had tried to enter Dribble's. And probably to that worn by those who had destroyed our home, so I would come here, where Paul would follow.

Skalet-memory was right. There was no such thing as co-incidence.

Otherwhere

"YES, sir. It's all in my report."

Cristoffen sat the way he wrote. His feet, not that Kearn could see them from his side of the desk, were always aligned; his knees would be together; and his back? Ramrod straight, as though bending his spine might be grounds for dismissal.

By the book. Kearn tapped his fingers soundlessly and considered the sad truth that, once upon a time, he'd longed for crew members as precise and committed to regulations as this one. He'd judged Ragem and Lefebvre insubordinate louts at best, dangerous mutineers at worst.

But regardless of whether he'd agreed with their motivations or not, both considered the consequences of their actions before they acted. He could have ordered them to do anything, without fear they'd actually do it.

"Sir?"

For a horrible moment, Kearn thought he'd spoken out loud, then realized Cristoffen was, as usual, impatient. This time he had cause. Kearn had delayed this meeting as long as he could, unable to decide what to do. Finally, he'd run out of excuses.

Kearn coughed before saying, in his most stern voice: "I'm concerned about what isn't in your report, Ensign."

"Sir?" Cristoffen's dark eyes widened. "Everything's—"

"I am not a fool," Kearn said, ruffling the document with what he hoped seemed offended dignity and not dread. "You were shot at with a blaster, point-blank, no farther away from your assailant than you are from me now. Putting aside, for the moment, why you were there in the first place to risk such an attack—without consulting me, your superior officer, before taking such rash action—I want to know how you survived. Do you expect me to believe you not only had the foresight to purchase and wear a personal shield, but that his weapon misfired? I am not a fool," Kearn repeated, a firm believer in emphasizing the key parts of any speech.

"I have the highest respect for you, Project Leader Kearn. You know that." Cristoffen's skin was like transparent porcelain, flawless but quick to suffuse with blood. "That's what happened, sir. I was lucky."

Kearn pursed his lips. He'd given a copy of the Port Authority analysis to Comp-tech Timri. He loathed the necessity, but needed someone with the expertise to understand it. He trusted Timri more than anyone else on board, which was barely, but she'd been trusted by Lefebvre, who'd never been a fool. Kearn didn't want to know if Timri, in turn, sought other help among the crew. He did want to know what she had to say before disputing Cristoffen's earnestness.

"You must be more cautious in future," Kearn told his assistant, watching how the suggestion pleased Cristoffen. Not that he'd found such suggestions were ever followed by anyone under his command. He pretended to relax, flipping the pages, aware Cristoffen flinched whenever one was creased by his fingers. *Something in here is dangerous*, Kearn decided, wondering glumly if he really wanted to find out what. He'd had so few months to enjoy the peaceful life of a researcher, taking the *Russell III*—now fully provisioned and funded—wherever whim struck him; being welcomed with open arms—or whatever limbs were appropriate—by academics of every species. There had been luncheons.

Until Michael Cristoffen had begun pushing his notions of where to look for shapeshifter folklore, becoming so insistent Kearn had had no choice but to give in, notions that sent them traveling from place to place seemingly at random, without so much as time for civil conversation. If Lefebvre had still been captain, well, things would have been different. *Rudy wouldn't have stood for such nonsense,* Kearn thought wistfully, *even from him.* But the Commonwealth had installed replacement after replacement, each less content than the one before to stay on such an erratic ship. Hardly a situation to instill command presence on the bridge. Kearn hadn't bothered to meet the latest one, leaving such things to Timri.

"Was there anything else, sir?"

Kearn rubbed one hand over his face. "Yes, of course, there is." He scowled at Cristoffen. "Why did you go to such lengths to meet this—Zoltan Duda? He was just a student. What possible connection to our work did he have?"

For the first time, Kearn thought he saw a hint of fear in Cristoffen's eyes. "It's in my report—"

"Yes." The Project Leader made a show of flipping pages, then stopped at one. It was at random, but he covered the document with both hands so the other wouldn't be able to tell. "You cross-referenced several interesting factors here, starting with any connection to Paul Ragem before he—died. Not matter how remote. It must have been helpful to find that list in the *Russell*'s comp."

"Yes, sir." Confidence. Perhaps Cristoffen felt he was about to be praised.

"And these other factors. Quite the selection." Kearn pretended to consult the report; he knew the disturbing list by heart. "You specifically looked for Humans, without close family, healthy, who regularly traveled from their systems on business, who spoke one or more non-Human languages as well as comspeak, and—now this is particularly insightful—who had received highly illegal anti-truth drug treatments." Kearn looked up. "And you found ten names?"

"Yes, sir. I've listed them—"

"I see that." Kearn dropped his gaze to his desk, then pressed his lips together. *He could do this.* He lifted his head to stare directly at Cristoffen. "What I don't see is someone capable of performing this level of analysis or of obtaining restricted data." Kearn was faintly surprised by the firmness of his own voice, and continued before he lost it. "Who gave you these names? And why?"

Cristoffen had half-risen from his chair, hands clamped to the armrests. He hung there as if Kearn's question had pinned him in place. "No one gave them to me, Project Leader. I found them—"

"Am I a fool, Ensign?"

"No, sir! You're the hero of Iftsen Secundus—the Shifter Hunter of the Feneden—Project Leader. You—" Cristoffen seemed to run out of titles and sank back into his seat, looking, Kearn thought without pity, very young indeed.

"Let me take a guess, Ensign." Kearn stood up and walked around the desk, leaning against it. He'd tried propping himself on one hip, the way Lefebvre used to, but his legs were too short. "You've been receiving messages from an unknown informant who shares our goal of gathering information about the Shifter species. Detailed, credible, very helpful messages. You've been told—" Kearn put up his hand when Cristoffen made to speak. The other closed his mouth, his eyes wide and astonished. "—told that if you reveal the existence of these messages, they will stop."

"How did you—"

Kearn scowled again, his most reliable command expression. His face wanted to collapse in dismay. Oh, he'd received similar messages, messages that had led him perilously close to Paul—to the Monster. *From a Kraal.* "It doesn't matter how I know. What matters is what you've been told about these ten Humans." *And why you wanted to kill one*, Kearn added to himself.

"It's too dangerous for you to know, Project Leader Kearn. I can't let you risk your life." The younger Human had the gall to look smug at this, as though he'd found the ultimate argument.

And, not so long ago, he might have.

But Kearn didn't think very much about his own life, these days. And he'd acquired, if not courage itself, then a hearty dislike for the way things happened around him when lives were endangered. "Tell me," he snapped. "Or spend what little time you'll have left on this ship confined to your quarters. Am I clear?"

"Yes, sir!" The admiration on Cristoffen's face at the rebuke was vaguely offensive, like the salivating of a hungry Ervickian on the footwear of anyone with credit. "According to my—informant, they are part of a secret organization formed by Paul Ragem before he was killed. Their purpose is to protect the Esen Monster and her kind. As you saw in my report, they are willing to use any means to that end, including murdering Commonwealth personnel. I can't imagine what they seek to gain—unless it's their own safety from attack when the multitudes of Shifters invade this part of space."

Kearn walked around his desk and sank into his chair, feeling somewhat short of breath. "Multitudes," he repeated.

Cristoffen's face took on a fanatic's glow. "The Esen

Monster isn't the only one here. She and others—they've been scouting our weaknesses, locating the best sources of—of food. More of their kind are on the way. It's only a matter of when—and if we're ready to defend ourselves."

"Your informant told you all of this?"

"There was no need. I've known about the threat of invasion since I first heard about the Monster and your brave hunt. Why do you think I was so eager to join you, Project Leader Kearn?"

A true believer. Kearn began gathering pages, scooping up Cristoffen's report in the process. "That will be all for now," he said with the air of distracted purpose he'd perfected years ago. "I trust you will keep this to yourself?"

"I—yes, sir." Cristoffen leaped to his feet and saluted, an unwelcome gesture Kearn acknowledged with the briefest of nods.

When the door closed, Kearn stopped fussing with plas sheets. He stared at nothing, seeing everything.

Of course Paul Ragem had arranged for help.

He should have guessed, should have known. Ragem had had friends and family, not to mention an uncanny ability to gain the trust of strangers, regardless of species. Kearn had seen him do it. Tough, determined Rudy Lefebvre, who'd poured years into their search for the Monster, had cheerfully abandoned a promising career—and Kearn—when he'd found Ragem alive.

Lefebvre, Kearn nodded to himself, *was probably one of Ragem's Group by now. Maybe leading it.*

At what terrible risk? No one in their right mind would accept treatment against truth drugs, unless willing to die for a cause. Because of his deluded assistant, someone had already paid that price for Ragem's desperate secret.

A secret Kearn had spent fifty years trying to expose.

Her secret.

Kearn dropped his face into his hands. "Esen," he whispered, "what have we done?"

10: Greenhouse Night

WHEN confronted by a superior force, and running or hiding, always preferable, weren't viable options, I had my own, non-Skalet, approach.

As now.

I drew myself to my not-inconsiderable size; though completely naked, I had the confidence of being remarkably clean. My swollen scales covered any biologically curious parts anyway. "Look what you've done! Who is in charge here?" I said as fiercely as possible. My left ear caught the absence of an expected breath as Paul held his. I raised my hand to point, a movement that swiveled twenty-three muzzle tips in my direction, and indicated what remained of my fystias. "You realize these are virtually irreplaceable. I had to order them three years in advance, then wait while the rootstocks went through their preliminary fermentation. Now look at them! Crushed. Every stem! And who let you in here anyway?"

My right ear detected the slightest movement of Joel's fingers on his weapon, still in his hand, though aimed downward. I flicked the ear furiously, as if to dislodge an insect, hoping he'd pay attention. We couldn't win a fight. My only problem was credibility. Joel didn't know me as "Esen the Wise and Intrepid Adventurer." He only knew me as "Esolesy Ki the Well-Meaning Importer," who took pink mud baths, generally caused more trouble than she avoided, and never forgot his birthday.

Whether or not my warning was understood, the lack of

further finger shifting let me turn my full attention to those surrounding us.

Humans. An educated guess, though that body form was common enough to have spawned cross-species' fashion trends. To my trained eye, there was something telling about how they stood, how their arms bent. Bent arms with weapons at the holding end. Nasty, highly sophisticated energy rifles. *Unnecessary in a greenhouse at any time.*

They were uncharacteristically identical in dress and size: heads covered in elaborate hoods that doubtless contained sensing equipment; ammunition, equipment, and ropes hanging where such things traditionally hung. I supposed there weren't too many options that left joints free to move, unless you were Carasian and could bolt your gear wherever you chose on your carapace, preferably in jaunty patterns.

Identical Humans in disguise, interchangeable until one spoke, a male voice, distorted through a mechanical interface. I glumly suspected surveillance vids would record neither image nor sound from our "guests."

"You won't need to replace the plants," the invader said. A gloved hand produced a bone-white tube, etched with designs—a pretty little thing Skalet-memory informed me was a Kraal remote control. Usually the remote part was a large and unpretty container of explosives. Or tubes of poison gas. Or boxes set to release sharp objects. Or . . .

I stopped remembering her list. "What do you have against plants?" I asked reasonably enough, doing my utmost to hold shape.

"Es—" Paul protested almost under his breath.

Not quietly enough. The one who'd spoken turned in his direction. "You are Paul Cameron." A squeaking distracted me as Largas tightened his grip, preparing to raise his weapon. I flapped my ears again, forcefully enough to make it seem I was trying to fly. "I was told to relay a message to you."

I approved of conversation in general, especially instead

of shooting. I hoped Largas felt the same way. Paul's answer was steady and cool. "A message from whom?"

"You do not need to know."

One dark brow lifted. "What's the message?"

"Good-bye, Paul Ragem." With those words, every weapon turned on my friend.

There was no time to consider, weigh odds, or think. Ersh, for all her aeons of life and experience, hadn't prepared me for split-second decisions. She'd done all she could to train me not to react quickly.

I hadn't always paid attention.

Regardless of the consequence, I took the only action I could. As they prepared to fire, I surrendered my hold on my Lishcyn-form with what I trusted would be a blinding flash of exothermic energy, even as I launched myself in front of Paul.

It certainly felt wonderful.

Web-form. Blind and deaf. The core of Minas XII had more substance to this Esen than the beings standing near me, though I tasted their organics in the atmosphere pressed against my surface. As my true self, I was a being more energy than matter, and capable of manipulating both. So when five bolts of searing energy converged on what would have been Paul, but was now a teardrop of web-mass, I absorbed the death they aimed at him, changing it into more innocuous forms I could release without harm to anyone.

Had all twenty-three fired at once, I might not have succeeded. Had they used projectiles or simply jumped on Paul with shovels, I couldn't have stopped every attacker in time. It was as well for my peace of mind there hadn't been time to think of such potential problems with my plan. I'd acted.

Had I succeeded? Regardless of risk, I had to know. I shed mass in a spray of newly formed water, gaining eyes, ears, and an elegant muzzle.

And stood in the midst of destruction. Flames were failing to take hold among the too-moist remains of my garden. Between the stench of scorched earth and bruised leaves, spices from hundreds of different plants, different worlds, my sensitive nose was thoroughly offended. I blinked at the irritation. The tiles had cracked from the heat and telltale lines of soot from my uncontrolled cycling led outward from my paws.

What I didn't see was anyone else.

Oh, dear.

No bodies. No one. Without taking time to worry why our attackers had left so abruptly, except to hope it didn't involve clearing the way for something worse, such as a remote-controlled something, I began hunting Paul and Joel.

A groan from beneath a deep coil of fallen vines led me to the former. I pulled frantically at the mass of vegetation. "Paul! Paul!"

To my relief, his head and shoulders appeared almost like magic. After a quick look around to assess the situation, a look that ended in an expression of stunned surprise that probably mirrored my own, Paul heaved his way free of the vines. My Human seemed none the worse for wear, I decided, studying his face.

"You've been practicing," he said with a nod at the mess, the words a little shaky, as if he'd only just regained his breath.

Humor? Not being equipped to deal with life-threatening situations with a smile and wink, I ignored this in favor of a more pressing question: "Who were—"

Paul's eyes slid past me and suddenly widened. With no more warning than that, he thrust me violently to one side, shouting hoarsely: "No, Largas!"

A crackle of energy discharge passed through the air where we'd both stood the instant before. I whirled in time to see Paul tackle the older Human, pinning him to the floor. He seized Joel's weapon and tossed it into my wallow. Perhaps it sank in the pink sand. I didn't watch, my eyes on the two who had been family—before I revealed who and what I was.

I'd seen that look, the one on Joel Largas' face as he lay

panting at Paul's feet, the one he was giving me. The fear pulling his lips from his teeth in a dreadful parody of a smile. I'd never forget that look; knowing it, I felt my tail slide between my legs.

But the hate in his eyes was a brand new horror. For both of us.

Paul took a step away, then another—staggering, drunken steps, as though Largas' blast had managed to wound him after all. I squeezed my eyes shut for an instant, unable to bear the sight of my friend's grief, then opened them.

This was my doing.

"I am still Es," I told Joel Largas, doing my utmost to keep my voice from a whine. "In this form, Esen-alit-Quar, Esen for short, Es–Es to my friends."

Joel Largas' mouth lost its rictus to spit at my feet.

"Let's go." At first, I didn't recognize the thickened voice as Paul's. He put his hand on my shoulder. I don't think he was aware of pressing down so heavily I had to brace myself.

Meanwhile, Joel was struggling to get to his feet, trying and failing. For the first time since I'd met him, he moved like someone very old, in large awkward sweeps of arm and leg as if his joints no longer understood him. Paul didn't offer to help. Instead he used his grip to jerk me back a step, setting his body between us as though Joel could somehow still be a threat.

I didn't see how.

"Go. Run." Joel's harsh words were said to us both, but I thought he meant them more for Paul, the father of his grandchildren, contract husband of his favorite daughter, business associate—friend. Human bindings, now cut. "It won't matter." Joel finally reached his feet, wavering but steady enough. What he lacked in coordination, he made up for in sheer determination. "I'll find you wherever you hide."

Cords stood out on the sides of Paul's neck, as if he'd

fought to keep himself from helping the other being. "You have to leave, too," he told Largas, his voice flat and hard. "They've probably left explosives. You know what they did to our house."

"Oh, you'll let me leave?" Joel's face twisted. "But haven't I seen too much? And isn't—It—hungry?" The last words were coated in the venom of decades spent waiting for revenge.

I leaned past Paul, the words pouring out in a torrent I could no more stop than I could change my true nature. "Joel. That wasn't me. It was another of my kind, yes, I admit it, but a mindless monster. You know me—"

"I don't know you. I don't know either of you! Did you think you could simply lie to me all this time, call yourselves friends—" He spat again, as if the word seared his mouth. "Did you think you could insinuate yourselves into my family? Do you dare believe I won't kill you for this?"

Well, yes, I had hoped for better, I sighed to myself, but there was nothing to reason with in his contorted face.

If I was babbling in my distress, Paul might have turned to ice, unmoving and silent. I couldn't tell if he breathed. Had he'd lived out this scene so many times in his imagination nothing Largas said now could touch him? Or was he mesmerized by the hate in the other Human's eyes?

It didn't matter. We couldn't stay here. Paul was right. Only fools would waste the chance to escape whatever doom our attackers planned. But we stood, frozen, as if the binding of betrayal was somehow stronger than that of love.

I should have known Paul would break free first. Muttering curses, no few involving blue blobs and empty brain-cases, my Human took Largas' arm in a grip from which the other couldn't fight free, using that hold to pull his protesting father-in-law over the vines and toward the back wall.

I loped behind, hopping over damaged vegetation and shattered pots without a word, knowing where Paul was taking us. He'd insisted on hidden exits in our office and home. Here, as well, there was a doorway leading to a secret passage, with a fueled and ready aircar concealed at its end. Where he thought we'd go after that, I didn't know. No where on Minas XII—not any more. This world belonged to Joel Largas and his kin.

When we stopped for Paul to enter the codes releasing the camouflaged section of wall and opening the revealed door, I moved to one side and cycled, flowing among my wounded plants, assimilating any still-living cells into more of myself. When I had enough, I cycled . . .

. . . and, under the hate-filled gaze of her dear friend, Joel Largas, Esolesy Ki sat on the floor and proceeded to tuck bits and pieces of dying leaves between her scales, one at a time.

It seemed, I sighed to myself, *as fitting a way to say good-bye to my greenhouse, this form, and this life as any.*

Otherwhere

"THEY must have died in the explosion, Eminence."

The figure in black and chrome raised a brow and waited.

The Kraal officer standing before her shivered. Her quarters were set several degrees below ship norm. *Convenient.* In this instance, however, she judged his reaction to be other than physical. "We will scour the wreckage of all three buildings again, Eminence, look for any trace—"

"No." Pa-Admiral Mocktap tapped the tabletop dismissively. "Port Authority will be watching each incursion site. The risk of exposure has grown unacceptably high. If you concur, Your Eminence," she added more temperately, as if realizing speaking out of turn at this table was unwise.

The figure nodded, once, then spoke, her voice velvet over steel: "A search for remains serves no purpose. Their deaths were not part of my strategy."

The Kraal officer did his best to hold his face expressionless, but the tattoos curling over his forehead compressed. The beginning of a disapproving frown.

"You doubt me?" The steel more prominent.

Another officer, standing to one side and behind, dared take a step to bring himself level with the one being questioned. A request. She raised her brow again, this time in invitation. "What is it?"

"Your pardon, Eminence, but our orders did include the execution of Paul Ragem."

Thin lips stretched in what might have been the faintest of smiles. "Did they?"

"I swear it."

"Did you succeed?" At his flush, she lifted a finger dismissively. *Offended pride was tiresome.* "They've left the system sometime in the last few hours. A report on all outbound traffic, immediately." The two officers touched fingertips to their tattooed cheeks and left the room.

"Minas XII is a busy port." Mocktap commented dryly. The Kraal leaned back in her chair, abandoning her rigid posture now that subordinates of indirect affiliation were no longer present to notice and report. *Ephemerals—pathetically worried about the signs of age and its consequence.* The previous Mocktap to hold the rank of Admiral had been the same, until assassination ended her concerns. "I've checked the time frame," Mocktap continued. "Over seventy departures were listed with Fishertown Port Authority. Let alone what's not on that list. This is a Fringe system, after all." An unspoken, possibly automatic challenge. Kraal nobility expected results and detested failure. *Irrelevant.*

Where will you run, Youngest? Not home. I haven't left you that option. "Make sure our list is complete. When I see the destinations of those ships, I will know where they have fled."

11: Freighter Night

THERE had been times, innumerable ones at that, during which I was convinced my reason for being was merely to provide a hearty laugh for the Cosmic Gods, should such deities exist. At others, I'd been just as sure they ignored me completely. *Esen who?*

Both were the misconceptions of youth, I decided, spitting a morose bubble from my swim sacs and watching it float by my oculars. Whatever forces shaped this particular universe were neither ignoring me nor amused.

They were out to get me.

"Esippet."

It had been so peaceful while he was pacing around the compartment. I twitched a forelimb—hopefully sufficient reaction to reassure Paul about his flawless pronunciation of my formsake's name without encouraging conversation. It wasn't. "Don't you ignore me, Es! Where in the Sixty Frozen Hells of Urgia are we going?"

While it was gratifying on some level to have my friend and partner finally take an active interest in events, since that implied he might also take responsibility for doing something about them, shouting at me was hardly necessary. I turned color, knowing the e-suit would express the purple hues of dignified displeasure quite efficiently, if with less than perfect tonal accuracy. One could only do so much with plas, syntha-cable, and a color wheel.

My Human wasn't color-blind, just persistent. "You aren't the only one less than happy at the moment, Fangface," the Human reminded me, crouching for a better look inside my helmet. *As if he could read an expression from folded mouthparts and a rosette of shiny oculars.* "It isn't helping having you wait it out as—as seafood."

My purple morphed to a furious red without any conscious thought on my part. "That's disgusting," I informed him, feeling the translator in my e-suit turn the vibrations from my pre-gills into something Paul could hear. "I am not food of any sort!" Well, perhaps the Ycl and multiple denizens of this form's home planet might argue that point, but the Human was being deliberately offensive. The Oieta was a fine form, dignified and expressive. Well, to be honest, the suit diminished those characteristics somewhat. But it did enhance others.

For instance, my present self, Esippet Darnelli Swashbuckly—the latter two names being those Lesy had picked for me from her favorite Oietae novel during my first excursion to the oceans of Oietai Tierce—gained significant stature from the suit. I was the same height, standing, as Paul, though more slender. Inside the suit, my Oieta-self was no more similar to his preferred seafood, Mendley Shrimp, than the Human was to a Terran platypus.

I supposed there were some similarities in design. My tender body was protected along back and sides by a flexible segmented shell, though mine was encased within a thick, soft integument studded with chromatophores and bioluminescent glands, as one would expect in a species reliant on visual signals.

I possessed delicate, long antennae and twenty-three sets of gill-fringed legs, the first eighteen being swimmerets while the lattermost and larger pairs were for walking. Preceding them all were several highly functional appendages: three pairs of specialized arms, each with a comb on the inner surface of their second joint so I could groom any part of me that required it. Handsome, fastidious beings, the Oietae. The combs were also very useful when it came to urging delectable living things toward the filtering brushes lining my mouthparts.

From the outside, thanks to the suit, I appeared to be something significantly different—almost humanoid, if you overlooked a few oddities. There was that smooth bulge where a spine should be and my wonderful antennae, presently imprisoned down my back in long, immobile tubes. The suit did a better job of accommodating my arms, having supple sleeves fitted to my clawtips. All three pairs of arms. There was, however, a distinctive flare of material, forward-directed, extending from under my lowermost arms, down both sides of my slim torso, to the bottom of the suit. My remaining appendages had to be fitted in somehow, with room to move. The swimmerets needed to keep beating—the suit recycled water over my gills, so there was no need to augment the mechanics, but it felt more natural to breathe on my own.

Moving I couldn't do on my own, being completely adapted to a marine lifestyle. So any independently mobile Oieta-suit came with an antigrav unit, allowing me to float a very small amount above any surface. The sleeves covering my lowermost and strongest pair of arms ended in telescoping poles that I could use to push myself along.

Or to poke an obnoxious Human in the ribs. "Not seafood," I stated firmly. "And we're going to Prumbinat. I told you before we boarded."

"You didn't tell me why."

Another advantage of the suit was being able to magnify the images reaching my oculars. Too much! I hastened to reduce my view to a close look at Paul's face, rather than into his pores. "You're still upset about having to squeeze into one of these, aren't you?" I'd considered it a very clever idea—two suited Oietae casually boarding a freighter. What could be less like a Human and Lishcyn fleeing for their lives?

He ran one hand through his hair, as if I needed him to point out the streaks of bright yellow-green now lacing its black. At least his skin had kept its light tan color—where it wasn't pink from scrubbing. "Be grateful you can't smell," Paul said, mildly enough. Our present accommodations didn't include luxuries like 'fresher stalls. The Human had compulsively rinsed himself and his clothes using the outlet for drinking water. Several times, in fact.

I still thought it had been a brilliant plan. Paul had worn an artificial gill, so his lungs could exchange gases with the fluid inside the suit. But there had been one, small miscalculation. That fluid, though vital and pleasantly tasteful to my Oieta-self, had turned out to react in various unfortunate ways with Human physiology. *And so quickly, too.* "Well, you've stopped vomiting," I offered helpfully.

He gave me that look. "Esen. Please. I didn't argue your choice of transport, or the suit—"

"Because I was right," I said, wishing I could preen myself properly with one of my lower arms. "Right, right, right."

For some reason, Paul ran one hand over his face. Perhaps he felt an urge to preen for me. "How long are you planning to use this form?" he surprised me by asking.

I blew another bubble and watched it float by my face. Maybe he'd be quiet if I ignored him.

"Esippet?"

Or maybe not. "Yes, Paul?" I asked.

"Damn it, Esen-alit-Quar!" His voice was inconsiderately loud. "I need you. Do you understand me? You can't be like this. You can't—" The Human's lips shut tight and he seemed to study me. Something in his expression changed. I didn't bother trying to interpret it. "Maybe you have to be. At least for now. Forget I asked."

"Of course," I agreed, going back to semi-morose bubble gazing while contemplating the Cosmic Gods, aware but not acknowledging that Paul had returned to pacing our compartment.

As long as he left me in peace, he could do as he pleased.

*   *   *

Our escape from the greenhouse was well-timed. A series of
explosions ripped the warehouse apart moments after Paul
piloted the aircar out of its hidden hangar. As we sped away,
my Human glanced at me and shook his head once, eyes
somber. I understood. The explosions were too well-timed.
They'd wanted us out and on the run, not dead. Whoever
they were.

My scales became swollen and refused to relax again.

We couldn't discuss our next move, not in front of our
passenger, bound and silent behind us, his eyes boring holes
into our backs. *Not that there was much to discuss,* I
thought. I could call up the list of ships fin-down, legally
and otherwise, from memory, and saw only one choice. I
couldn't go home, if the word applied to Picco's Moon and
Ersh's corpse. Largas knew we'd planned to go there. Paul
couldn't go home, if the word still applied to Botharis and
the family who thought him dead. Kearn knew he lived, and
we couldn't know if he watched for Paul's return.

Above all, we couldn't risk any ship controlled directly,
or indirectly, by Largas Freight.

Last, but not least, I wouldn't go to any system containing a member of Paul's Group. Something I hadn't told my
Human yet. I didn't expect him to be happy about it, especially when he knew why.

I finally believed in the Prime Law. *No one outside our
Web could be trusted.* Ersh would have been proud.

I didn't like remembering. I liked watching bubbles released
from my swim sacs as they floated past my oculars. I didn't
like the pensive glances Paul gave me. I liked it much better
when he stretched out on the floor to sleep. Or pretend to
sleep—it didn't matter to me which, as long as he refrained
from conversation.

I very much liked my suit. It made me tall and graceful.
It protected me from the filth of this cargo compartment. It
nourished and cleaned me.

Paul should have endured his. Then he'd be safe from all

harm. To be safe meant to stay hidden. I knew what mattered. Stay hidden; stay safe. If we were hidden, everything would be fine again. In the suit, no one would be able to see what he was or know his name. *He should try again.*

I couldn't disturb his sleep. Sleep was important. I'd been trying to sleep since the freighter went translight. I'd found a spot between a rack and a pair of tables, where I could lean my lovely suit against the former, and push with my poles against the latter. Oietae are rocked to sleep by the waves of their home ocean—well, those who did wilderness swims were. Urban dwellers managed nicely by clinging to the vibrating rope of their choice.

No matter how I tried, the rocking was never right, either too rough or too frequent or too . . . I was growing exhausted. It was most annoying.

I'd been wrong. *How odd.* Paul wasn't asleep. He was standing in front of me, a lump of netting in his hands. His face was weathered ice, chipped into a down-turned mouth and grieving eyes. He didn't speak, becoming busy with the net and some cable, so I kept trying to rock myself.

Then I wasn't rocking—I was rising in a most alarming manner. Before I could do more than flail my poles and flash red with indignation, the Human deposited me into his net. The last desperate movements of my arms tangled me in the dreadful device. I gave up and lay still, peering up at him. "I'm sorry you vomited in your suit," I said very clearly. "But that's no reason to take your revenge on me."

"Shhh." He shoved the mass of net and suit that was me away from him. I swung toward the ceiling, slowed, then swung down and past him, the water in my suit sloshing as inertia fought momentum. He gave me another, gentler push, let me pass, then another, even gentler.

"This is nice," I admitted, fading to amber.

"I've had practice," he said quietly. "Now, shhh. You're so tired I'm afraid you'll blow a hole in the deck soon."

I clenched my swimmerets, courses of yellows playing

over the suit. Laughter. "Silly Paul. I won't do that. I'm safe now."

"How so?" Softer still.

"I'm hidden—right here. Look. You can't see, see—" for some reason I was finding it hard to concentrate. "Me. You can't see me, can you?"

Push and swing. "Does that make a difference?"

"Yes. No. Yes." I would have kept this going but lost track with the next upswing. "You should put on your suit. I like my suit."

"The suit keeps you hidden," he repeated cooperatively.

I flashed a contented amber. "Oh, the suit does much more than that, silly old Human. Put yours on—it's so much better in the suit."

"What's better, Es?" I cringed at his tone, its bright edge of suspicion. *Ersh used it too.*

This body wanted to curl up suddenly. I tried not to let it, to keep relaxed and enjoy the motion. I could fall asleep so easily, if he'd stop talking.

I thought he had, and let myself drift. The swinging slowed without Paul pushing, but continued to soothe.

Until the swinging stopped with a jerk. I focused on the Human, now leaning over me. His suit trailed from his hand. "Oh," I said happily. "You're going to put it back on."

"I think one of us blissed out of our gills is enough." His voice was an odd mix of frustration and pity. I didn't like the sound of it at all. I didn't like stopping either, and tried to get the net swinging again by wriggling. He tossed his suit behind him and reached for mine. "Hold still, Es. I've figured out the adjustments from mine—"

If I hadn't been wrapped in the net, I would have been able to defend myself. As it was, I made Paul's misguided attempt to sabotage my suit as difficult as possible, managing to hit him with my head twice, the second time drawing a pained, "Oof! Es, will you stop that!" from the Human.

But it didn't stop him.

* * *

There was no way around it. We had to leave Joel somewhere. It didn't help that Minas XII was showing her finest fall colors, namely the black of storm clouds and the white of a too-early snow. I waited for Paul, not knowing what to do, not knowing what a Human as old and angry as Joel could withstand.

I did know how dangerous he would be to us both, now. It made me wish for a form that could weep.

The storm was moderate by local standards, meaning you were judged moderately insane to be flying in it. Couriers stayed in the air, for-hires did not. Port Authority would play it safe. I didn't think our attackers would.

It made for scarce traffic. A good thing, given the view out any port was of complex whorls of suicidal snowflakes all heading straight for us, despite physics. Paul would be relying on scanners. He had, I'd noticed with a thrill of fear, disengaged the automatics. I understood why. The nav system was interactive with the mains at Port Authority. Fishertown didn't have much in the way of flight control, but it did provide a navigation grid. If Paul linked us to it, we could be followed by those with the right equipment—and motivation.

It seemed we'd joined that category of inhabitant who couldn't afford safety.

"Don't drop me near any of the family," Joel said, his voice strained but calm. "And not in the ocean. Leave them a body to space, if you have any feelings for them at all."

A muscle jumped along Paul's jaw, nothing more.

I levered my jaw over my shoulder so I could stare at Largas in horror. "We would never hurt you, Joel."

"Don't use my name." He squirmed like a trussed bird of prey, unable to believe its wings were tied, frantic for freedom. "Don't use it! I don't want it in your monster's mouth."

"Leave her alone."

I couldn't bear Paul trying to protect me from Joel's honest hate. "I won't use it again," I promised. "But we mean no harm to you or anyone."

"If you meant no harm, why did you follow us here? Hadn't you done enough to us? And him—" words seemed to fail the older Human as he glared at Paul's back.

I opened my mouth, then saw my Human shake his head very slightly. He was right, of course. There was nothing I could say that Joel Largas would believe, nothing he'd want to hear.

Especially from the mouth of a monster. The window nearest me was fogged despite the efforts of the internal ventilation system. It was my fault. I was dumping heat to hold this form, and the warmer, moist air near me was condensing on the frozen plas. I rubbed it clear with one hand.

The aircar dropped. As we passed through an eddy in the snow, I spotted the lights of a familiar landmark.

Paul was taking us to Joel's house.

I hoped my Human knew what he was doing. The home of the Largas' patriarch was not only filled to bursting with hardened spacers at any given time, those spacers owed their lives to our new and deadliest enemy.

There was something wrong. An imbalance grated along every nerve fiber I possessed; the way the universe tilted made my head float. Perhaps my swim sacs were infected again. The feeling had been similar. Lesy had kept an ointment in her cupboard that was most effective, if one could get past the unpleasant part of having to squirt it between one's fifteenth and sixteenth segments . . .

Lesy was gone. I'd tasted her despair and death. Ersh— was I losing my mind?

"It's a hangover."

The sound vibrations initiated a wave of fire down my body, colored white with pain. I tried to remember how to cover my ears, then couldn't remember where they were. Or if I had any. *I must,* I thought, feeling clever, *if I could hear Paul.*

Paul?

*   *   *

"Paul?"

His answer dropped into the silk covering my lap: a tiny vial of powder and a knife. I stared at them, my hands retreating to clench at my sides. Skalet-memory recognized the vial. It would deliver its contents—poison, disease, drug—into the face of a victim, to be absorbed through whatever structures were sufficiently open to air. Well suited to Human anatomy, with its porous skin and the moist linings of mouth, eyes, and nose.

The knife? Skalet-memory knew too many knives.

I looked up at my Human.

There's no other way, that flash of gray eyes meant.

I'd seen Paul like this before. I judged it a Human trait, that such a gentle being could turn dark and dangerous, could become something far more perilous than a hungry Ycl or rampaging Ganthor. They, at least, were following the passions of their nature. Paul, at such moments, abandoned his, as if the contradiction between what he was and what he might have to do was unendurable.

The aircar was circling, bouncing as Paul fought gusts that threatened from one side, then the other, as if Minas XII couldn't decide how best to knock us from the sky. I couldn't bring myself to touch either vial or knife, not even for him. He shot another glance at me, then said curtly: "Take the controls."

I'd barely gripped the bar in my hands, feeling how the aircar battled any correction and reasonably sure we would now crash so all other concerns were unimportant, when Paul swept the vial from my lap and aimed it over my shoulder. He sat back down and took the controls, relieving me of responsibility for our lives. "Cut him free and hide the bindings. Quickly. We can't stay up here much longer. It will look suspicious."

Without knowing if I'd have a source of mass, I couldn't cycle from this form, so it served Paul right that my spacious hips required most of the front seat—both front seats—in order for me to turn and reach where Joel Largas lay. I sighed with relief. He was breathing. Unconscious and flushed, but breathing.

Paul might not have my hearing, but he couldn't very well miss a sigh rumbling millimeters from his ear, especially a sigh through lungs the size of my present ones. "You thought I'd killed him," he accused. "Damn it, Esen, you know me better than that!"

"Of course I do," I told him, more than willing to lie for friendship's sake. "I'm—It's not been a good day, Paul." *For us,* I thought darkly, imagining a celebration of sorts probably underway among the Humans in black.

The bindings cut easily. I shoved the pieces and the knife into one of the rear cupboards, then straightened Joel's arms and legs, relying on form-memory to choose the most comfortable positioning. *There.* If I didn't know better, I'd assume Joel was sleeping off one of his famed visits to the Circle Club. His face even had the same mottled flush.

I struggled into my seat as the aircar entered the shelter between buildings, nodding as Paul said: "Let me do the talking."

I didn't know what to say. *Doubtless, Ersh would have found that a pleasant change.* What Paul thought, I couldn't imagine. He was resting, having spent the past hours defending me from the suit I'd so loved, making sure I was no longer harming myself. *No longer hiding from myself.*

During those hours, he'd talked until his voice was hoarse, nonsense mainly, anything to keep me awake as my mind cleared. I remembered only fragments: children's rhymes, imperfect verb forms, a price list for tea, a prayer.

It hadn't been a drug. I couldn't decide if I'd unconsciously reset my suit's environmental controls to circulate an excess of aldehydes, or missed some improper adjustment when I'd first cycled into the form. I hoped, for pride's sake, it was the latter, then realized that only made it worse. Paul had been made ill by his Oieta-made suit; under some conditions, that illness might have harmed or killed him.

If I'd reset the controls myself? I'd remember, wouldn't I? Could my perfect memory be flawed? Green, the color of shame, stained the ventral surface of my suit and spread up my sides. Several aldehydes were potent intoxicants to this form. Paul had called me "blissed out of my gills." Another day or two of such detached contentment and I might have stayed mindless. Or died. As it was, I recovered slowly, prone to violent tremors, as if my nervous system was relearning itself. The water inside my suit didn't taste as it should.

Paul had assured me, and I think himself, that the suit was now set to its default parameters, optimum for an active Oieta. More reassuring than any gauge was the rising flood of emotion and memory. I was Esen again.

Whether I wanted to be, or not.

There'd been a fuss in the Largas' household when we arrived, of course. Offspring and their allies had boiled from every door like so many insects, Joel had been carried inside, a pair of cousins with medical training summoned from their kitchen duties, and we'd been treated with every kindness.

After all, hadn't Cameron & Ki been the subject of an unprovoked assault? Hadn't we lost our home and warehouse? How fortunate, became the theme, that our office had been unscathed.

The office, this new, untrusting Esen thought, *where Meony-ro would have been during the attacks. And others.*

Their kindness made it difficult to make the quick exit we'd hoped. Paul and I managed to refuse to go farther into the house than the front entrance, but a group of seven Humans, of varying ages, stayed to offer their interpretation of events. We knew them all. The youngest, John, had come to the greenhouse with his great grandfather earlier in the week. He leaned against me now, one hand gripping the silks on my leg, the other with thumb firmly embedded in his mouth as he watched with larger-than-normal eyes.

All I could think about was Joel's reaction if he woke and saw the child with his monster.

"He's going to be fine," Aeryn Largas announced loudly, passing on a message received via a com held to her ear. Common practice—continued additions to the original building had produced a sprawling complex in which I tended to be lost more than found. "They say he should wake up on his own soon." I watched the round of relieved expressions, including the surreptitious wiping of tears. Two of those who hugged at the news had been contracted wives, here to visit their former spouse while their ships were on Minas XII. Age hadn't tarnished Joel Largas' charm to any extent I'd seen.

"Good," Paul said, then bent to pry my silk from John's fingers. "We have to get back. The Port Jellies should have answers for us by now."

"Thank you for bringing Joel home first." This from Aeryn. She'd been a baby on one of the ships threatened by Death. Now, she oversaw engine maintenance for Largas Freight. There was a self-portrait, complete with chubby cheeks and curls, in my office. A gift, for my birthday.

A gift I couldn't keep.

Conveniently—for the first time in recent memory—my third stomach rumbled, causing those near me to edge away and Paul to take my arm. "We'd better get you out of here," he said, managing to make it sound amused.

Since only we knew it was good-bye, they merely waved. A supper invitation for later in the day was noticeably lacking, but there wasn't a Largas on this world who didn't appreciate the hazards of hosting an upset Lishcyn.

The storm hadn't abated so much as it had decided on a direction from which to pummel the valley. Paul selected a course into the wind, then set the controls and turned to me.

"Well, Old Blob," he said, brushing his hair back from his forehead and letting his expression settle into a bruised weariness. "What now?"

There was comfort in being able to quote Ersh. "Our Web must be safe. It must be hidden."

One eyebrow lifted. "I'm all for a strategic retreat, Es, as long as it's quick. If they let Joel sleep off the sedative, we have six hours. If they wake him—" Paul shrugged then winced. Feeling the effects of being too close to an exploding Esen, I decided.

"Joel isn't the worst problem we have," I reminded him, keeping one hand under my jaw as a precaution.

His mouth tightened into a grim line of agreement. "The trap at Dribble's—I know. I don't think that part went as planned. What did was their little stage play in the greenhouse."

"Stage play?" I was glad of my hand. "They were going to kill you!"

Paul leaned forward, eyes intent. "And maybe they believed that. But I think whoever sent them knows you, Esen, well enough to appreciate what a web-being could do against blasters—well enough to know you'd cycle to save my life."

"All that just to make me reveal what I am?" I blinked. "Why? And why let us go?"

My Human nodded slowly. "It makes sense, Es. Joel Largas is the one person who can force us off this planet, make sure we aren't safe anywhere in the Fringe. By turning Joel against us," he halted, as if his throat closed over the words. "With one stroke," he went on, "we're adrift and friendless in this part of space." Paul put his hand on my knee. "We haven't been let go, Esen. This someone is driving us in a specific direction. I'll bet we find our choices at the shipcity are pretty limited."

"More than you know, my friend," I told him. "We can't—"

"Go near any of the Group?" I stared at him and he patted my knee. "I thought of that too, Es. We can't risk exposing them." Paul paused and his voice became a growl worthy of my Lanivarian self. "And we can't know for sure one or more weren't behind this attack."

"Well, Old Blob?"

I used one pole to push, the other to hold, the result being a graceful swing to face the owner of that voice. "Do you mean, have I recovered?" A quick inward assessment. We were getting ready to disembark on Prumbinat—or rather to sneak off the freighter as she refueled—and I knew I could ease at least one of Paul's concerns. "Yes. All of Esippet Darnelli Swashbuckly present and accounted for—" I paused. "Have you picked a name?"

We'd spent our final day translight talking about the future and avoiding the past. Our strategic retreat, as Paul called it, would be temporary, to gather resources and plan how to find whoever had destroyed the comfortable lives of Cameron & Ki. Unstated? We needed time as well, having neither healed nor fully comprehended what had happened. *Prumbinat,* I recalled fondly, *was the ultimate hiding place.*

Paul shrugged our belongings over his shoulder, tied together in a bag made from the blanket he'd used. All we now had, but all we'd need. The few supplies we'd had waiting in the aircar, among the more important being credit chits under various names and species. "How about Paul Antoni Ragem?"

I checked the aldehyde balance in my suit. *Nominal.* "It's a good name," I said weakly, broadcasting an alarmed beige and white.

He laughed. I didn't find it a happy sound. "Don't look so worried, Esippet. I've chosen something suitable for our new life. Paul Gast. Like it?"

Names anchored history; they came with their own. I watched a bubble float past my oculars and didn't need to tell Paul I understood his choice. He would know.

Gast. In the language of his distant ancestors, the original word for that which neither lived, nor had substance in the real world.

A ghost.

Otherwhere

DONE. For whatever good it would do.

Rudy ejected his chit from the com terminal. He flipped it into the air with a casual whistle, then reinserted it, counting under his breath. *Five, four, three . . .* He ejected the chit again at . . . *one.*

The worm he'd just released would tunnel through the translight data streams, destroying any records of the messages he'd sent.

As an afterthought, he tucked a tiny globe of acid with a timer inside the casing. No point taking chances.

The recipients of his warnings should be equally careful, given their chosen calling. Rudy shrugged. *Their problem, not his,* he reminded himself. As was how seriously any in Paul's Group would take an anonymous warning about Cristoffen. He'd debated with himself during the past three days about offering the warning at all, but it was hardly a level playing field if Cristoffen had gained a Kraal backer.

He'd sent the warning to everyone but Paul, who didn't yet know his cousin possessed detailed information about his little organization. *Interesting how secrets grew on each other, like layers of mold,* Rudy thought.

He joined the throng of tourists admiring the view from the balustrade, another Human of less than average height and wider than average build, complete with distance lens and vid camera around his neck.

Even his face helped him fade from notice: blunt-featured, almost coarse, the sum forgettable.

When he chose, Rudy could transform his face with a broad, careless smile into that of an easy mark, the sort who carried unsecured credit and lusted after the seedier type of local entertainment, if only he knew where to find it. The former patroller had used his appearance to advantage many times. It wasn't his fault if others underestimated the speed with which he could move, or the power in his well-muscled frame. It wasn't his fault if they failed to recognize the scorn in his eyes.

If they chose to make assumptions, Rudy was always happy to correct them.

He could have used such a distraction today, as he waited for Esen. He'd left the innocent message they'd agreed upon, the one meaning she must find a way to contact him as soon as possible. How and when depended on Esen's resourcefulness. She'd find a way to avoid Paul and reach him. She had before.

All he had to do was wait where she could find him.

Rudy played tourist until sunset, a spectacle producing exclamations of awe and delight from those unaware that the Urgians paid to have the horizon outside their largest Port City appropriately tinted, being a businesslike species who refused to allow the unreliability of nature to disrupt their trade. Then he'd caught the next transport to the Casselman Hotel Complex, confident a message would be waiting.

There wasn't.

"Would you please look again?" Rudy kept it casual, as though this wasn't his fourth unsuccessful trip down to the desk tonight.

He was eyes to eye with the night clerk, an Urgian sitting on the counter, its present morph state discreetly hidden beneath a series of veils, presumably lest she/he/it distract the other staff. The being's eyelid lowered slightly, lending it a remarkably bored expression. It sang and whistled, the sounds reemanating from a filigreed box on its lap in soprano comspeak. "There is nothing for me to look for, Hom Leslie. As I've explained, on several occasions, any and all communications would be directed to your room immediately. There is no need to check here."

Rudy put his foot on the rail and got comfortable. "And as I've explained, the message I'm expecting may come by unconventional means. My business associate tends to be creative."

The eyelid rose, exposing the delicate tracery of pink blood vessels surrounding a limpid pool of reflective, emerald green. By Urgian standards, an eye of stunning beauty. Rudy wondered how his compared. "An artist?" she/he/it asked, the whistle tremulous, as though the words held more meaning than the translator could express.

Rudy didn't hesitate. "An artist," he agreed, pushing the limits of the definition to include being able to trace around one's fingers with charcoal on a wall. Esen might be a knowledgeable appraiser and lover of art in all its varied forms. She'd be the first to admit she owned no creativity whatsoever. "You know how they are," he continued, "always trying to find new means of self-expression. I'm never sure what she's going to send me next." *That much was the truth,* he grinned to himself.

"You are so fortunate to benefit directly from a creative mind. How wonderful! I wish you'd told me this sooner." The tip of a white tentacle, coated in tiny iridescent scales, slipped from under the veils to depress a gilded button on the counter. "I have summoned my assistant. An artist? This is most gratifying, Hom Leslie." The Urgian clerk was vibrating.

Rudy wondered if this was at the prospect of seeing Esen's latest creation and felt a twinge of guilt.

A servo rattled through the door behind the counter, its torso bedecked with laundry. Only one ocular showed. If it was an attempt to disguise what was patently a Human-built mechanism, it must fool only the Urgians. Rudy was careful not to smile as the night clerk sang and whistled a series of commands, while two of her tentacles danced over a control panel she may have thought out of his line of sight. The servo responded with a series of tenor hoots and a squawk.

"I'm sorry, Hom Leslie. Roams tells me everything left with us for guests today has been sent to their rooms. But I will keep my eye watching for you—that is the Human expression, isn't it?"

"Close enough. Thank you."

The Casselman catered to tourists and business travelers on a budget, which explained the air of reassuring sameness that promised exactly what you paid whether in this hotel or in its mates over half of the quadrant. At the same time, almost apologetically, the Casselman possessed a surprising amount of local charm, being distant enough from the shipcity to attract Urgian guests. The main lobby thus had low, white cushions on the floor, set between couches more suited to swallowing Human-sized posteriors. The walls of each lift were ribbed so Urgians could avoid the peril of sharing limited floor space with heavier, footed species. They needed only two arms to climb vertical surfaces, leaving the others free to hold luggage or wave in conversation.

Urgians. The species made Rudy feel like a tree taking root, an old, gnarled tree at that. As a younger fool, he'd imagined himself something of a poet, writing mountains of verse to various young ladies, publishing a few whenever verse outlasted passion. Then

Paul, with the best of intentions, had brought Rudy a collection of Urgian love sonnets. Rudy had wept as he read; he hadn't written since.

This late at night, he rode a lift free of boneless white poets or other guests, glad of the solitude to think. Cristoffen had left Urgia Prime immediately, rejoining Kearn on the *Russell III*. The ship had been scheduled to launch. *Coincidence or collusion?* Rudy frowned as he stood at the door to his room, pausing with his hand on the lock plate. *Kearn?* He shook his head and opened the door. His former commander might be incompetent and weak, but that was a long way from being an accomplice to cold-blooded murder.

Still, Rudy knew better than to rule out any suspect. No matter what he believed about Kearn, the *Russ'* had full access to Commonwealth records. If Cristoffen had Kearn's authorization—or his codes—he could abuse that access to trace Zoltan's past movements. *He had to warn Esen.*

No rest for the weary. Rudy stripped on his way to the 'fresher, leaving a trail of clothing from door to stall. Once inside, yawning, he set the water for needle-sharp and cold. He exhaled and plunged his head into the spray, tensing every muscle against the urge to shiver. When instinct tried to force him to breathe, he ignored it. His feet and hands grew numb. It was his choice when to toss his head free of the spray to draw breath in through his nostrils, a breath he took slowly, down the back of his throat, feeling every part of the passage of cool air into his body.

Under control, no matter how his lungs ached to be filled.

Rudy turned off the spray, then shook himself like some beast roused from hibernation, his skin raised in gooseflesh. There was nothing careless about his smile now that he was alone. *Like old times alone on patrol,* he reminded himself, when succumbing to sleep might have cost him his quarry. Or his life.

Alert and fully awake, he headed for the com terminal by the bed, not bothering to dry off. *Cristoffen wasn't sitting around waiting; why should he?*

Rudy knew what troubled him: Esen was more resourceful than this. Only once before had Rudy waited more than a standard day for her reply, a delay Esen had explained, rather mysteriously, as due to her being held up in shipping, but he shouldn't worry because everything had been fine once she'd been delivered.

He might have a suspicious nature to begin with, and a professional career that had encouraged paranoia, but three days? *Something was wrong.* If so, this was no time to knock on the front door.

There were other options.

For instance, Cameron & Ki Exports had a representative here, on Urgia Prime, a broker they shared with other small companies. *A suitably coded message should catch Esen's attention,* Rudy decided. An order for rostra sprouts would do. He'd never met any being but Esen who was fond of the poisonous stuff. If Paul noticed first, well, he'd deal with that if it happened. Rudy dried his hands on the cover of his bed and keyed in the request.

"Hello?"

At this hour, the last thing Rudy expected was a living voice, especially one sounding Human, young, and anxious. He scowled at the ornate box housing the com. "I want to place an order with Cameron & Ki Exports—"

"You can't," the voice informed him. Rudy's eyes narrowed. No doubt about the anxiety.

"Have I keyed in the wrong code?"

"No, Hom. But—I suppose it's no secret. Cameron

& Ki has gone out of business. For good. I can recommend another shipper for you—"

"What do you mean, 'gone out of business'?" *Cristoffen couldn't have found them so soon.* Rudy assumed his best captain's tone: "I place orders with them on a regular basis. I would have been informed. You must be mistaken."

"Oh, it's been a shock to us, too. One day they're up and running normally—the next? We've had to scramble to get shipments rearranged—overtime for everyone, believe me." The young Human warmed to his topic. "Cameron & Ki weren't a big part of our warehousing, you realize, but some of their specialty goods were perishable. There were these insect cocoons for Inhaven I thought were going to hatch yesterday and who knows—"

Rudy interrupted: "What's happened to Cameron & Ki?"

"Your guess is as good as mine. All I know is what's going around. Some kind of trouble on Minas XII. A criminal investigation. Would you believe it? And no one can find the owners—" the voice broke off.

A new, harsher one took its place. "This is Captain Silv Largas, of the *Vegas Lass.* Who is this? Identify yourself! Answer me—"

Rudy silenced the com, resting his hand on the control.

He recognized Silv's voice well enough, if not this sharp, angry version. The two of them had done their best to finish a keg of beer during his last stopover on Minas XII, celebrating Silv's assignment to the *'Lass.* Access to Joel's well-stocked cellar was one of the perks of being a regular guest in the Largas' home, a guest Joel outspokenly courted to captain one of his ships. The courting was real. Only Rudy was not.

Largas' interest in his skills, his friendship, gave Rudy an excuse for his infrequent stops at Minas XII;

otherwise he risked drawing the attention of watchers like Cristoffen to Paul and Esen. But when he was there, Rudy paid the price of sharing Esen's secret: he couldn't let down his guard, even when celebrating; he couldn't acknowledge Paul as kin; and he couldn't allow a closer connection than casual friendship, however tempting Joel's offer of a future.

Hardest of all, he had to endure the nights when too much celebrating rolled Joel's mind into the past, and his deep, gravelly voice would tell of the flight from Garson's World and the arrival of Death. Others who remembered would gather close and avoid each other's eyes; those who'd been too young would start at shadows and shiver. The room would fill with silent, attentive forms as the Largas clan relived their darkest hour. Joel would stop, abruptly, as if surprised to see his family, then wander off to bed. The rest would exchange looks, then do the same.

Esen was wise to guard her secret from such friends as these.

Silv Largas, a proud new captain, intercepting calls for Cameron & Ki. In the middle of the night. On Urgia Prime.

Rudy drew his hand back slowly, watched it tremble, watched it clench into a fist, watched how the trembling didn't stop until he drove the fist into the com and shattered it, blood mixing with white splinters of delicately filigreed wood. *Answer Silv Largas?* Not until he had proof the Largas clan hadn't been involved in whatever had transpired on Minas XII.

Rudy could guess part of it. He knew the measure of his cousin. Under any circumstances, even if Joel himself stood in the way, Paul would make sure Esen escaped. That didn't guarantee anyone's safety. Or that things hadn't been ugly.

Time to make a discreet exit. Rudy pulled on a pair

of used spacer coveralls, pausing only to wrap his scraped knuckles. He picked what he'd take with him, packing quickly but surely. The stunner on his hip was for show. He secured a blister stick up his left sleeve; its mate rode his calf. The closetful of low-budget tourist clothing could stay, as could the cases of clever, invasive devices sure to worry hotel staff. He'd already sent whatever recordings he'd acquired off-world. What he needed now was speed, not subtlety.

The scorched data cube, likely worthless, he taped to the skin beneath his ribs.

The door chimed.

Esen's message? A shame he'd broken the com terminal—the night clerk must have had to slither her way up to this floor.

If *it was the Urgian, or her servo assistant.*

Rudy checked the impulse to answer, instead taking a soundless step to move out of alignment with the door. He'd used an alias to book this room, but hadn't bothered to disguise his appearance or hide the source of tonight's call to the broker. Regrettable lapses. He really must be more careful in future.

A second chime.

He made up his mind. *No taking chances.* Sweeping up his bag, Rudy went to the door that connected his room to its neighbor, opening it with care before slipping through into darkness, finding his way past furniture conveniently in the same location as the room he'd left. No worries of disturbing a sleeping occupant—booking the adjoining room under another name had been a reasonable precaution, in his line of work.

Before he could take another step, lights turned on as if to prove his point.

So much for worrying about the door chime, Rudy thought, smiling his broad, careless smile. In case that might be insufficient reassurance for the six overly-armed figures in black Kraal military gear waiting for him, he dropped his bag and made sure his arms were the appropriate distance from his sides.

Cristoffen's Kraal backer and a scorched data cube taped to his skin. *This could,* Rudy decided grimly, *get interesting.*

It was definitely going to delay his search for Paul and Esen.

12: Cove Morning

FROM the air, Mouda Cove took a significant bite out of the eastern shore of the peninsula, spitting out a chain of rocky islands that simultaneously protected its deep, tranquil waters and threatened attempts to seek that tranquillity. A crust of bright yellow warn-off stations could be seen on the ocean side of each, several bent and twisted, as if klaxons and lights weren't always enough to deter the truly obsessed boater.

Had this been an ocean traveled by boats, that is. I'd peered out my window port as the aircar approached for landing, my suit the blue of calm and attentive interest, admiring the cheery twinkling of light reflected from the water's surface even more for knowing the darkness beneath. Prumbinat's single ocean was, to put it mildly, a little deeper than most and far more secretive than any my Human companion had yet experienced. I was looking forward to his reaction.

Other than its unusual depth and paranoid hazard markers, Mouda Cove might have been any semitropical paradise. *Well,* I squinted as I looked around, *it could have used some vegetation closer to the shoreline than fifty meters, but overgrazing was always an issue at this latitude.* The few trees and shrubs that managed height were perched atop isolated towers of dead coral. They looked down on the lovely beach like castle dwellers under siege.

The Prumbins had, of course, kept the center aisle of the beach free of anything crushable. Common sense, given the nocturnal wanderings of their Drossy herds—gentle creatures, if ungainly on land. Washed-pink buildings lined the outer arms of the cove; awnings of purple, yellow, and red flapped gently in the wind to offer welcome shade, bordered with more of the brilliant yellow warn-offs. The ocean might have been at our feet, but even as a Lishcyn I couldn't have heard the tiny waves kissing the white sand. Marashaci music thumped from every patio, despite the lack of conscious dancers at this early hour. Prumbins, like their livestock, were most active at night. *Such wonderfully tropical music,* I thought, humming to myself. Steamy melody with a sting of metallic percussion. It translated nicely.

"So, Es, where's the transport?" Paul's eyes blinked at me, magnified by the domelike lenses of his goggles into black-centered whorls of gray, rimmed in bloodshot white. They looked, I decided, somewhat like owlish fruit. Or stale hors d'oeuvres. "You said it would be waiting—and we don't have much time."

He was covered from eyeball to toes in a gaudy green e-suit we'd bought at a stand beside the main wharf. Paul had insisted on something made for humanoids, so we'd had to take the only one available. Had my Human been a lesser being, I would have suspected him of being quite satisfied by the color, knowing it signaled humiliation and despair to my present form. I refused to believe he'd deliberately distress me. He did need a new one. We hadn't been able to clean his Oieta-suit, a thankless task we'd left for the freighter's crew should they want to salvage the valuable garment.

The Prumbin who'd sold us this suit hadn't budged an appendage to help me squeeze Paul into the ill-fitting thing. Its reluctance could have simply been a species-specific desire to remain as inactive as possible while the sun was up, but there could have been another reason. I'd seen its row of nostrils snap shut as we approached, despite this lending a nasal pitch to its voice. While I couldn't detect any odor, unless the substance was dissolved in the fluid circulating over my body, Paul had assured me that he smelled worse after our journey in the freighter—and his misadventure—than the occasional carcass being torn apart by crustaceans along the waterline. He'd done this to clarify why our aircar pilot had insisted we sit in the back of her vehicle. And kept her window open.

Even if Paul hadn't smelled like something overdue for burial, the Prumbin had no need to be pleasant. It was the only e-suit dealer within sight and knew full well what my dear web-kin didn't. Yet.

Other than the aircar returning to the Port City, a suit was Paul's only way to leave Mouda Cove.

"A modicum of patience, Human," I told him. It was probably less than mature of me to have enjoyed stuffing my friend back into this corresponding garment, but at least he didn't have to endure having his antennae bent.

The thought made my entire body itch. It wasn't so much that I was uncomfortable—my current form would have been flopping on the sand in agonized death throes by now if exposed to air—but I was missing most of my sensory perceptions. Tasting the water recycling around myself, however artificially fragrant, was no substitute for the ocean so close. I held this form simply by promising myself I'd be out of the suit in a few moments.

Paul might beat me to it. He'd put down the piece of luggage we'd bought—too big for our few belongings, but I hoped to remedy that—and was tugging at his neck fasteners again, even though I knew they were as well-fitted as possible. "Patient!" he grumbled—words and tone quite nicely transferred into pulses against the tympana lining my lower arms. "I should never have let you talk me into this—this sightseeing excursion! In case you forget, Old Hound, we aren't exactly safe here."

"Where would we be safe, Paul?" I fluttered a gesture of *sorrow* with my pre-gills; the suit turned a mournful gray in translation. Then I saw the water just offshore heave itself into a round smoothness as something began rising to the wharf. "There!" I said in triumph, bobbing up and down with excitement. "Our transport!"

"Esen . . ." My name seemed to dissolve as Paul's magnified eyes blinked and blinked again.

"Isn't this a sight worth seeing?" I asked.

The wharf, its pylons set deep into the sloping beach, extended from where we stood to a considerable distance into the middle of Mouda Cove. The reason for its length was now apparent, as our transport calmly docked alongside, stern hanging beyond the wharf and bow grinding gently toward us on the sand until sighing to a stop.

We had to look up.

And up. I bobbed almost constantly, colored bright yellow with delight by Paul's frozen posture. *Ha! Thought he'd seen everything by now, did he?*

There were bigger things in Prumbinat's ocean, but a Busfish was the largest I'd be willing to stand beside.

I should have expected Paul could take a Busfish in stride. After all, he'd lived with me for over fifty years. Still, even he took a moment to stare at what was, to Ersh's knowledge, the largest sea-dwelling creature to be domesticated. There were other partnerships between the small-scale smart and larger-scale not-so, including the living—and mobile—moss cities of the Ycl, but the Busfish reigned supreme in terms of harnessed biological power.

Size aside, it was a remarkably ordinary creature; Ersh-memory gave it an amusing resemblance to the cod which had been so pivotal in early Human history. Its tall, thin dorsal fin flopped untidily in the air, having temporarily lost the support of water. Antennae and other rigging were leeched to the thickened scales of its back, just in front of the fin. Its eyes were protected by goggles, while its gills were covered by plas domes, much the way a respirator would seal over the mouth slit of a humanoid. The plas on the wharf-side gill-cover was scratched and dented, explaining some of the corresponding damage to the wood. Any metal and the older of its blue-yellow scales were coated in a crust of tyr-barnacles or showed white remnants of glue where previous hitchhikers had been scraped free. My Oieta-self itched with sympathy.

Boarding wasn't for the weak of circulatory pumps. I led the way, having experience in the matter—if not previously in a form that would actually be a food item for a wild Busfish, which I suddenly discovered added a significant level of apprehension. It wasn't exactly panic, but I might not have poled myself down the ramp as swiftly if it hadn't been for a shove from behind. I flashed an indignant red.

Paul chuckled. I thought various dire thoughts about when best to shove him into something's mouth, but didn't slow down again.

The ramp met another which protruded like a tongue from the Busfish's now gaping mouth. Green-tinged seawater trailing lines of froth poured over and around it as the mouth emptied, revealing dripping platforms built over the lower tooth ridge. The upper tooth ridge had been removed—a safety precaution of which I highly approved. My shell would have been no protection whatsoever—and a fleshy being such as Paul? I shuddered, sending a curtain of tiny bubbles rippling past my oculars so I could hardly see where I was poling.

Someone, I assumed my Human, grabbed my suit's upper arms and stopped my forward motion. Just as well, since when the bubbles cleared I was hanging half over the side of the ramp, looking down at the churning waves being forced between fish and wharf. I waved a pole in what I hoped was a carefree and reassuring manner, then poled myself the rest of the way down the center of the ramp.

Only to wind up teetering on a wet, spongy surface that I wasn't going to think about. A surface with taste buds and mucous glands, and no doubt a dangerous enzyme or two in the puddles filling every dimple.

A mouth easily twenty of Paul's strides wide and three times that in length. A removable ceramic mesh covered the hall-like opening to the throat, looking dangerously flimsy for something intended to guarantee the Busfish didn't digest paying customers. Figures in suits similar to Paul's were either clamped in seats on the platforms or moving between them. A few were a reassuring blue, a color my Oietaself interpreted as calm professionalism. *Attendants.*

One of the latter approached me as I teetered—a Prumbin, I assumed, though there were few other clues from the suit beyond that balloonlike width around what would correspond to Paul's waist, hips, and thighs. This close, the suit lost some of its blue under algae stains and glasslike fragments of Busfish scale. "Please turn off your antigrav. Do you want closed or open?" The words were in a monotone that suggested boredom rather than a pattern of speech.

Ah. The moment I'd been waiting for, I thought. Then I stared up at the pinky-white irregular surface my mind said was the roof of a reliable means of transportation, and my instincts screamed was the roof of a hungry mouth—the inside part, no less. "Closed," I whimpered, turning beige, white, and gray as if my natural camouflage could possibly help. The fluid in my suit warmed as I dumped heat.

The Prumbin didn't comment, just waited for me to signal my antigrav was off before picking me up and tossing me toward the nearer arc of the platform. There, two other suited figures ignored my worried coloration and started to tie me to a most uncomfortable seat. A humanoid shape in vile green climbed up beside me, seeming to have little problem with either tongue or ridge, and waved them aside. "I'll look after her."

"Don't you dare say a word about food," I told my Human as he fastened my safety harness as deftly as if he routinely did such things inside a giant fish. "Not one word."

I didn't need to see Paul's face to know he was grinning as he fastened himself in beside me.

Next down the ramp was a trio of Oietae—likely spawnsibs. They paid no attention to me or any of the other passengers, obviously eager to accept the "open" option. Their attendant pulled them to one side, then used a hooked pole to pry up the tongue along that edge. Beneath, a long puddle of seawater beckoned, appealing even with its telltale gleam of fish mucus. The Oietae slithered out of their suits and into this pond, their shells blazing an almost orgasmic orange as they sank beneath the surface.

I envied their pleasure, but not enough to make me play morsel-in-the-maw.

It wasn't long before the Busfish prepared to leave, having consumed its passengers, their luggage, and an awkward though functional pallet stacked with containers of varied size. The Prumbins had eventually wedged the pallet along the back left of the tooth ridge using what appeared a tried-and-true technique of ramming themselves against one side until some containers toppled sideways and lodged under the ridge itself. I hope the contents survived the process, but this cavalier treatment didn't appear to bother the Busfish, which was becoming alarmingly lively as it must have sensed it would soon be submerging.

"This is certainly different."

"What?" I twisted within my suit so I could focus on Paul. "Oh. Yes."

"Will you tell me now?"

"Tell you what?" *The Human must be trying to distract himself,* I decided. After all, this had to be an alarming, possibly terrifying experience. Especially as the attendants had started knocking down the braces holding the mouth open and you could almost feel how anxious the Busfish was to slam its mouth shut on those inside—

"Fem Swashbuckly. Esippet. You promised to tell me where you were taking me. I think now's a good time, don't you?"

"Now?" I repeated, torn between looking at Paul, which was polite, or checking the rate at which the braces were being removed, which seemed prudent.

"Now, Esippet. Es!"

Paul's sharpening voice reached me when probably nothing else could have, given Ersh was now part of her mountain. I unlocked my swimmerets, which had somehow taken a death grip on one another, seriously hampering my breathing, and focused on my green-suited Human as though he was the anchor to my part of the universe. "I'm a little nervous," I confessed.

"I can see that. And it's perfectly reasonable," he said soothingly. "Keep talking to me. Don't!" This as I craned around to see the last brace dropping onto the tongue, right beside the tips of my poles. "Try not to pay attention to anything else for a minute, Old Blob. Switch to suit-to-suit and we'll check if the com works. No guarantees on privacy, remember?"

I flashed a wan yellow down my sides.

"Good. Here goes." Paul made the adjustment with his chin; I echoed it with my mandibles. "Can you hear me, Esippet?"

There was no difference in tone or quality I could detect, which made sense: our suits still had to translate sound through both air and water, simply those media were now within rather than without. But his warning about potential eavesdroppers chilled my circulatory pumps; the old familiar cautions had new significance. "Yes, I hear you. How do I sound?"

"Sweet as ever," he said.

"Silly Human. It's not even my real voice," I chided, but resolutely kept my oculars from the slowly disappearing beach, wishing I could see more of his dear face than the distorted image of his eyes through the suit's goggles. "I know you are a resilient species, but how can you take this so calmly?"

A kind laugh. "Let's leave it that my biological heritage worries more about the dark."

"There are interior lights," I promised.

"Good to know." A pause. "Feeling any better?"

I tested myself by glancing around the inside of the Busfish before answering. The mouth was closing, no doubt of that. The view beyond was now restricted to the bottoms of buildings, sand, and the retreating ramp. But the movement downward was so gradual as to be almost imperceptible.

I ignored the regrettable conclusion that this gave beings a final chance to jump for their lives.

"Better," I said with determination.

A well-trained creature, this Busfish, obedient to its handlers now seated before a tiny console I hadn't noticed before. The controls would be relatively simple. Open, close. Up, down. Port, starboard. Fast, slow. The Busfish could do the "how" of each by itself. It could even find its way home.

Ah, the advantages of biology over tech.

Mind you, that home wouldn't be anywhere my Human could survive without his suit. *Petty detail.*

A spasm, like some Busfish-quake, signaled our transport was starting to wriggle itself into deeper water. The straps held us in place, but those who'd chosen the "open" option were sliding along the tongue. From their actions, I concluded they were either writhing in agony or having fun. Since the attendants ignored them, it had to be the latter, although I couldn't fathom the "fun" in living out one's worst nightmare.

Then, we were under the surface, smoothly, quickly, with all the grace of living flight and all the power of surf rushing to fill the mouth over and between the gaps in its rock hard lips. The covers over the gills must have been retracted, as the inflowing water went down the throat but didn't return. Sunbeams stroked their way past just outside, then faded, then were gone. As I'd promised, the interior of the mouth began to glow—not only with the lights beading each suit, but also those growing on the ceiling and along the platforms, natural symbionts of the Busfish who normally lured their host's prey in to its doom and now reassured its passengers.

Meanwhile, the mouth closed as much as it could. Ocean stopped beating against our suits and teased at them instead, making me long to tear off mine. It didn't help when two of the Oietae scooted past me, still that wanton orange but now with telltale mottlings of aroused black, mingling their swim-merets in what I was shocked to realize was reasonably ad-vanced foreplay. The third flicked his antennae in a debauched manner along my side before following the rest up to the lights. Not spawn-sibs after all. A mating group.

I turned to face Paul, trying and failing to keep my suit from displaying my humiliation with a green matched to his.

"Well. You are cute," the Human observed, after a long pause. *He'd probably struggled not to laugh at me,* I thought rather glumly.

"I'm not—" the green deepened. "You know what I mean."

"Old enough?" He reached out and patted the ridge of suit over my lower left limb. "You will be, one day. Don't mind them. Honeymooners. They can hardly tell your age while you're in the suit, can they? An honest mistake."

I wasn't sure if I was offended or reassured.

Paul, as befitted the father of two grown offspring, changed the subject. "So, Esippet Darnelli Swashbuckly. Anything you'd care to reveal about our destination, now that I most definitely can't refuse to go?"

I managed a flash of happier amber. "The Nirvana Abyss."

"What?" The com picked up the sound of his swallow. "I thought the Abyss was only a rumor—a myth!"

I had him. I could tell by the tone of his voice as it trans-lated into vibration against my membranes. Paul was feeling the thrill of curiosity again.

"No rumor," I told him. We were forced back against the straps with all the rest as the Busfish made a sudden turn. Passing out of Mouda Cove, I surmised. I hoped this partic-ular Busfish hadn't been responsible for damaging the haz-ard markers. The Oietae cheerfully ricocheted from one side of the mouth to the other, doing a few unnecessarily intimate spins as they went.

"You've been there?"

Maybe a little too much curiosity for an open com. I tapped his leg with my pole. "I'm much too young to have been here before. One of the founders of my cluster has leased chambers on the Brim. I've tasted— I've seen images. I believe you will be impressed."

"The Nirvana Abyss." Paul stretched out the name, as if he could taste the memories in it for himself. "It's legendary! I can't believe you never told me it was real until now."

"I was saving it for a—" I couldn't utter another word. My suit saturated with black and red. *Despair.* Everything came smashing down again, my mind reeling with perfect recollection: the chase, the crater that had been our home, the attack in the greenhouse, the dreadful look on Joel's face—on Paul's—our flight here. We weren't safe— My left mid-arm floated to the control of my suit before I considered what I intended, caught and stopped by Paul's quicker hand.

"You were saving it for when we needed it," he finished for me. "Which is today." There was nothing more than a pleased anticipation in his voice.

But my web-kin, whose memories were the same as mine, kept hold of my arm.

Otherwhere

THEY found what remained lying on the eastern slope of the Edianti, cracked but not shattered beyond coherence. What remained conveyed a warning, passed along the dreadful truths discovered on the heights. Then, having completed its duty, what remained fractured along the cleavages of its kind for the next night and true day, the sequence as old as rock itself, becoming a glittering powder that was ceremoniously delivered into the boiling waters of the Geyser of Rebirth.

When the ceremony was complete, the message began.

The initial chimes were dissonant and sorrowful, with undertones of fear. Tumblers who heard took the sounds inward for consideration, then chimed the message onward. The alarm spread along the floor of the Edianti and into the smaller valleys that cut into its crystal walls; it traveled up and over the valley rims to the Assansi and plunged downward again. In this way, it swept across Picco's Moon, slower than any com signal yet more profound, as every listener added both reaction and decision to the message.

By the time it had returned to its source, the message had become answer: *The flesh-burdened were no longer welcome on Picco's Moon.*

13: Mouth Afternoon

"WAKE up!" I poked Paul's suit-encased ribs with my left-hand pole. "We're here."

"I wasn't asleep," he muttered. *He wasn't awake either.* My Human was capable of remarkably lucid conversation in this semicomatose state, something he denied when fully conscious. Adamantly. Along with any recollection of what had been said. It had taken seven years and some months for me to become convinced this wasn't a trick; once I was, it was hard to resist the temptation to play some of my own. But his memory might improve with age and I was usually in enough trouble without trying for more. *Not that I deserved it,* I reminded myself. *Not all, anyway.*

Poke. Poke.

"Es!"

I pulled my pole from his outraged grab for it, my swimmerets trying their best to move me around inside my suit. "We're here," I repeated. "Finally!"

He stretched, then pretended to consult a wrist chrono. "It's been less than four standard hours, of which you've only let me have one for a nap."

"Well, it felt longer than the trip from Minas XII," I grumbled, then flattened my pre-gills as I heard what I'd said, my happy amber stained with green.

The silence between us had a shape, as amorphous as my memory of those three days, as impossible to ignore.

"Understandably." No condemnation in his voice. *There didn't need to be.*

Before I could become more embarrassed—and green—
if that were possible, a Prumbin attendant swam up to us.
"Brim administration requires a suit check before passengers may disembark."

A standard, if somewhat meaningless precaution. The
mouth wasn't sealed against the outside. The Busfish would
suffocate, if it were. My suit, unlike Paul's, didn't resist the
growing pressure or cold. I'd felt my swim sacs compress-
ing as we traveled deeper and deeper, their contents more ni-
trogen than oxygen by now as my circulation took over
resupply to maintain volume. It was wasteful as well as
more difficult to make bubbles for my mandibles to play
with—adding to the boredom of the last hour. Which Paul
had slept through.

I could see the Prumbins' side of this, however. Those
running the underwater resort wanted some assurance they
weren't going to lose new guests in a messy and difficult-to-
retrieve-for-relatives' manner. The fact that it was too late by
the time those guests arrived spoke volumes about the similarity of insurers of every species.

*There was that expression concerning locked doors and
escaped livestock.*

I endured the Prumbin's inspection, with its finale of a
sharp tug on each of my poles, as if trying to take them from
me. They were, of course, affixed to the material covering
my arms. Had my poles been loose, the attendant would
have tied them on the pallet, hopefully near the bag of our
belongings already so secured.

Satisfied, the would-be pole thief went to check Paul's
suit. When done, instead of leaving Paul and going to the
next passenger on the platform, the Prumbins came back to
me. Its goggle-enlarged eyes, vertically-pupilled and bloodshot, peered into my helmet. "Sure you want to stay closed,
Little Oieta?" it asked, seeming concerned I wasn't enjoying
myself like the others.

It probably was. In one of those ironies Ersh had found
meaningful and I found frustrating, Oietae considered the

Prumbins to be stoic bores at best, while the Prumbin word for my form's species translated, literally, as "gorgeous dimwits." No gathering at the Abyss was considered complete without colorful Oietae swimming about. There were transparent, water-filled corridors in every Prumbin building in Nirvana—a feature Oietae tour guides extolled to their travel-loving culture. Would they, if they knew the corridors had been designed to allow the Prumbins to view Oietae at whim?

My Oieta-self seemed to have no problems being displayed as living art. *I did,* I thought, suddenly even more nervous. Camouflage beige threatened to climb up my back.

"Go ahead, Esippet." An annoyingly awake Paul poked me in exactly the spot where the suit chafed my antennae. "Your frisky friends are buckled in anyway."

I knew that, having been fascinated by the efforts of the slower-moving Prumbins to net and tie down the cavorting Oietae nearby. It hadn't taken them long—something, I thought, that implied a disquieting skill at fishing.

Perhaps the Human sensed my hesitation. *More likely,* I told myself much later, *he'd learned to distrust my desire to stay inside what could be a self-serve bar.*

Regardless, I was as shocked as the Prumbin when Paul reached over and hit the auto-release on my suit. I hadn't realized there was such a dreadfully unsafe control within reach of others. As alarms went off, mine as well as the suit's, I started composing a letter of complaint to the manufacturer, along with dire plans for my so-helpful friend.

Then, the sea herself entered my gills.

I remember this, I realized with urgent joy, pushing and squirming my way out, as this form would have freed its way from the confines of its egg. Information flooded my senses: the Busfish, our neighbors in its mouth, the steady current of replacement ocean flowing between gaps in its lips, the rush of oxygen toward its gills—passing mine first.

And fresh food. The suit may have sustained me, but nothing compared to the way the constant flutter of my swimmerets and arm combs pushed the life-rich ocean through the fine hairs lining my mandibles, the way tasty, tiny morsels collected there, the way my mandibles automatically swept this harvest into my mouth.

There was something to be said for eating at all times, I decided, blissfully amber, even as I continued to struggle from the suit.

But the instant every limb was free, something grabbed my lowermost appendages and hauled me backward. I struggled helplessly as a net imprisoned my newly outstretched antennae.

In final insult, the other Oietae were laughing at me, bodies bright yellow. The vibrations they sent tickled my entire surface, let alone my tympana.

Not only their vibrations. Paul was trying to say something using the external speaker on his suit. Sound traveled exceedingly well through water—even random noise, which was about all I could gather from his Human sounds. I worked my antennae through holes in the netting before aiming my oculars at him. The noise stopped as Paul doubtless remembered that without my suit, my tympana couldn't translate his vocalizations into understandable speech.

Twenty-three pairs of appendages allowed me to shrug expressively and with just a touch of satisfaction. *This wasn't my fault.* Then I relented and flashed a calm, forgiving blue, the true color, no longer approximated by technology.

In answer, my perceptive Human held up his thumb.

His wasn't the only reassurance. True speech, bubbling with laughter, played along my sensitive membranes ::Won't be long, Too-Young::

I was unsure if the older Oieta meant my maturation time or our mutual wait to be released from net and mouth. It might have been both. This was a species fond of double meanings.

Playing it safe, I answered with the courtesy due an elder ::I value your counsel, Old-Enough-for-Joy:: The appellation was required and appropriate; I blushed anyway, feeling the stripe of green flaring down my dorsal surface.

More laughter from all three, but kind. They'd been netted into a happy mass of limbs, antennae, and segmented body parts. If I hadn't known there were three, I'd have estimated more—or less—individuals. One was expected to acknowledge such a tight group. ::Greetings, Joyous-Ones,:: I vibrated, settling into a chaste if envious amber in contrast to their glowing orange. ::I am Esippet Darnelli Swashbuckly. My Soft Companion is Paul Gast::

This was, I thought, *the cleverest part of my planning thus far.* Oietae preferred to travel with a Soft Companion, if they could afford it: a nonaquatic someone to stand in lineups, handle luggage, and look after the myriad tasks that being in a suit made awkward, if not dangerous for the species on land. Humans were most commonly hired, being adaptable and about the same body mass. The latter was a practical concern, since shared seating was more economical. There was, of course, certain status gained by traveling with more challenging species, as exemplified by the brief trendiness of Ganthor as Soft Companions. Since the only solitary Ganthor were rutting males or insane, such partnerships had cut short several tourist excursions.

The Oietae's names arrived as nonsense, confused by interfering currents as all the Prumbins began lifting braces into position around the tongue at once. I felt another laugh, then, more clearly: ::Well met, Swashbuckly! Our Soft Companions left our service when the starship docked.:: A tint of pink on all three—remembered annoyance. I imagined they'd flashed quite another color on being abandoned mid-vacation. ::The tour guide arranged this one. She is called—:: a pause during which body parts were rearranged. *I hoped they were conversing.* ::She is called Wendy Cheatham.:: Three antennae merged to point at a hunched figure on the opposite platform, seated slightly apart from what I took to be a family of three, probably also Human given the attention paid to the smallest member throughout the journey. ::Would you care to trade? Yours seems more fun. Ours hasn't moved since the mouth shut. Dull, dull, dull::

Fun? Given the frenzied activity of this group throughout the trip—and the work looking after not one, but three Oietae entailed? Unlikely they'd have noticed if their Soft Companion expired from exhaustion, although I hoped the Prumbin attendant would. I gave their poor Human a glance of sympathy and resolved to be nicer to Paul.

::Maybe another time, Joyous-Ones:: I told them.

::There's time at the Abyss! No one should ever miss . . .:: This being only the first lines of a long and bawdy song, I resigned myself to having to feel the entire thing, sung in an enthusiastic three-part harmony, interspersed with giggles. Elder Oietae were notoriously fond of embarrassing younger ones in public.

As if to spare my tender tympana from such abuse, the Prumbins chose that moment to begin ramming their braces into the roof, a clear sign that we'd arrived at the Nirvana Abyss and the Busfish was about to open its mouth.

So we weren't to be Busfish entrées, I sighed happily to myself, twitching my freed antennae, glowing amber.

It hadn't been a completely rational fear, but which ones are?

Otherwhere

"DID you fear my people were thieves and murderers, Hom Leslie?"

As this neatly summed up Rudy's initial assessment of the black-garbed figures who'd ambushed him, and his likely fate at their hands, he grinned. "Something like that. More wine, Sybil?"

"Please." The Human female sitting across the table held her refilled glass closer to the candle, her eyes squinting as she examined the color. "An engaging Merlot, wouldn't you agree? A touch—rustic—but with promise. Such a shame."

Rudy raised his own glass and took a careless swallow. He'd recognized the bottle: a match for the few remaining in the Largas' cellar—the treasured final vintage from Garson's World. The former patroller refused to ask if his tablemate spoke not of the wine, but its source.

A Kraal game within a game. He played it to the hilt, having no other option. Kraal left the cradle knowing survival and success depended on affiliation, and affiliations were forged by actions taken in secret, using every advantage to elevate those stronger or bring down those weaker. Professional paranoids, with a fondness for vendetta and assassination, they were most deadly if exposed, but unpredictably dangerous at all times.

Those who'd waited in ambush for him had been

courteous but firm, saying only that his presence was requested. Rudy had hardly been in a position to refuse.

In truth, he was curious. "Sybil. An unusual name, is it not?" And the only one she'd offered since he arrived.

They'd brought him here, to a darkened room of astonishing luxury, considering they'd only gone up three floors within the Casselman. He'd entered on carpeting that rippled beneath his feet, inhaled the scent of half-seen flowers, imagined rich furnishings barely catching the light. That light had come solely from a candle in the mouth of a jewel-eyed reptile, rearing in surprise from the center of a table set with a platter of delicate appetizers and a pair of tall, crystal glasses. A chair had waited for him, across from this woman. The guards had left them alone.

By the whisper of lines at mouth and eyes, Sybil could be old enough to be his grandmother, yet sat as straight and strong as any of her guards. Hers, for Rudy had no doubt this was their commander, despite the heavy veils of flame-red and silver covering her from head to toe. Only her face, throat, and hands were exposed to view, their surface a maze of white tattooing on dark skin, a bewilderingly complex record of affiliations and loyalties, both hers and those she could claim. A person of power and influence, among the Kraal.

And as such, completely untrustworthy, Rudy reminded himself.

"Sybil was once a name of great favor in the lineage of he who sired my mother's mother," Sybil answered readily enough. "I use it when it pleases me. And your name, Hom Leslie. One you use when it pleases you?"

They hadn't disarmed him. They hadn't touched him or searched his bag. But Rudy was under no illusions his concealed weaponry would do him any good here.

Old or young, a Kraal noble like Sybil needed no line of guards to protect her. Had she dismissed them for privacy or sent her guards to kidnap her next guest? He bowed slightly, conceding what they both knew. "Rudy Leslie Lefebvre, at your service."

Her lips thinned in a smile. "Captain, was it not? Under the Famous Fool."

"Under Project Leader Lionel Kearn," he countered, matching her smile. Never diminish your affiliations in front of a Kraal.

"Kearn," she echoed, dark eyes reflecting the candle's flame. "How fares Kearn's quest, former Captain Lefebvre? Has he found his Monster?"

Rudy put down his wineglass, acknowledging the end of courtesies. *A Kraal in a hurry,* he decided. The table loaded with the food and drink—"essentials" of polite Kraal discourse, as well as a mutually convenient way to administer poison—had lent an appearance of normalcy to their conversation, but Rudy was willing to bet it was intended for her guards, not him. He doubted she'd expect him to feel alarmed by her failure to provide a second round of food and drink before moving on to their business, or be insulted by the use of wine, regardless of pedigree, instead of ceremonial serpitay.

Of course, he wasn't Kraal, to be treated as such. Or Sybil wasn't in the mood to be polite. *Either,* he reassured himself, *were more logical reasons to be abrupt than a need to question him before he died of some offering at her table.* He hoped.

"I don't keep in touch with my former shipmates, or Kearn," Rudy informed her, glad his voice was steady. "Nor was I convinced by incredible stories of a shapeshifting creature. I was captain of the *Russell III,* nothing more."

"Really?" Another glint from those otherwise expressionless eyes. The eyes of a killer, Rudy judged, or of someone who ordered murder without compunction. "What I've learned of you suggests a great deal more, Rudy. May I call you Rudy? You have an unusual range of skills for a simple starship captain, some better suited to the other side of those laws you once protected. Burrowing within walls, for one."

So Cristoffen's meeting with Zoltan had been a trap for him as well. Rudy accepted the premise, controlling his anger, knowing the fear at its core: *had they detected him or had he been followed?* The former? He'd better seriously brush up on his technique before spying on anyone with Kraal tech. The latter? Rudy went cold. Had he made a mistake that exposed Esen and Paul? Perhaps even been responsible in some way for their disappearance from Minas XII?

One thing he saw as clearly as if written in the tattoos masking the Kraal's face. If he failed to impress her, or gave any wrong answer, he wouldn't survive. They might let him leave this room, but she would have placed a precautionary poison in the wine, or along the rim of the glass, or in the lightly scented smoke drifting between them. The jeweled eyes of the lizard shone red.

With a nonchalance that made his stomach twist with effort, Rudy leaned back and smiled. "Let's say I can do what needs to be done without attracting attention. Unlike some."

"A laudable quality." Sybil pursed her thin lips. "Among many. Still, I have heard the strangest thing about you. You have a reputation as an honest being. Surely your former employers knew better."

This, from a member of a race that rewarded deception? Rudy shrugged, giving her his best grin. "Former employers," he said, emphasizing the first word.

"Ah." A satisfied sound. "Then you are available to take a contract?"

Rudy fought to keep his face unchanged, although

this was hardly what he'd expected. *Another trap?* "I wasn't aware Kraal hired outside their affiliation."

If the shift in tattoos near her eyes could be taken as clues to her expression, Rudy thought Sybil looked smug. "We prefer that others believe so," she said calmly. "It keeps away unsought solicitations." Fabric hissed as her arm stretched toward him, her hand, pressed flat to the table, coming to rest close enough to touch. She kept it there while looking straight into his eyes. "If wealth matters to you, Rudy Lefebvre, fulfilling this contract for me will bring you all you could require for a new life. If affiliation matters, success will bring you within the orbit of my House." Her lips twisted. Amusement. "Which may or may not survive that success, but we take our turns on Fate's Rack."

Her hand, more shadow than flesh, lifted. Beneath it lay a blade. Its ornate etching fractured the candlelight into lines of twisting flame. The hilt was carved as well, in designs so intricate that the eye was initially fooled into judging them simple. The knife was too large to have been concealed beneath her hand. Yet here it was. The impossible made real.

In more ways than one, Rudy thought. A knife had been a gift to Kearn from his mysterious Kraal backer, the same backer who had urged Kearn to keep hunting Esen and Paul all those years, feeding him information that kept the hunt alive. When Kearn had had enough of the Kraal, he'd given the knife to Rudy. Timri had found a tracking device hidden in its hilt and destroyed the weapon.

Twin to one now pointing at his heart.

14: Brim Night

IN common with most creatures domesticated and trained as beasts of burden, a Busfish possessed an exquisitely-tuned ability to sense when the end of its labors drew near. The calmest, most disciplined Busfish would make its final approach to Nirvana as though pursued by a school of famished Gigamouths. Younger individuals had been known to crash right through their docking yokes and head to the stable without pausing to disgorge passengers at all.

Rather than fight this instinct, had it been remotely feasible to do so, the Prumbins took the safer course of protecting their charges—hence the securing of loose passengers and their belongings in case of collision. They'd also come to grips with the reality of having the Busfish carry what would otherwise be lunch in its mouth. A Busfish wouldn't snap and swallow while it swam, but once stopped, and the mouth open, the reflex was occasionally irresistible—hence the braces to prevent complete and regrettable closure.

I hadn't bothered telling Paul about the early days of Busfish travel. It wasn't dishonesty so much as what Ersh used to call "appropriate timing," something that had applied regularly to my own education. After leaving the 'fish, I could show my Human the Prumbin monument to those gobbled on duty.

The other aspect of working with living things was offering them gratification. Since nibbling snacks was out of the question, the Prumbins had decided to allow the Busfish to spit. This likely had a great deal to do with the difficulty of training any creature not to violently rid its mouth of inedible debris, but the Prumbins preferred to believe the Busfish enjoyed the process.

I certainly did.

When I felt the inflow through the lips slow and stop, I nudged Paul with an antenna, lacking any other way to prepare him. Any moment now, water would surge back up the throat, propelled by gill flaps and stomach muscle—gill flaps three times taller than Paul and a stomach typically fifteen times the volume of the mouth. Five Prumbins, roped together, were standing by the lips, ready to be disgorged first. From the casual way they stood talking to one another, I assumed they were old hands and inured to the process.

I, on the other hand, flared almost orange with anticipation.

Paul turned to aim his begoggled eyes at me. I was quite sure the ensuing series of muddied vibrations I felt coming from him was a variant of: "Is there something you aren't telling me, Es?" He often asked such a question, even when he knew the answer was yes.

I waved my arms cheerfully, as best I could within their fastenings, then mimed holding on tight. *Appropriate timing, indeed,* I thought, as what felt like a wall of Busfish-flavored ocean tried to expel us out the now gaping mouth.

I extended all my appendages to enjoy the flow and became completely orange.

What a rush!

The Prumbins released us in time to join the third group spat out by the Busfish. I'd hoped to be last, but there was no point in being greedy. It was a quick, tumultuous exit, ending in a sudden stop as nets ensured we'd stay safely within the yoke instead of zooming out over the Abyss. The stop left a minor dent in the sleeve of one of my lowermost segments. Paul didn't make any unusual sounds, such as yelling, which might have implied a connection between my dent and the new one on his helmet.

Dents aside, it had been fun. Well, I knew one of us thought so.

Our net swung down and away from the mouth as another rose to take its place, a wise precaution so subsequent mouthfuls of passengers wouldn't be plastered over the previous ones. One set of Prumbin attendants freed us from the mesh, then others pushed us toward the nearest of the funnel-mouthed corridors leading away from the yoke. It wasn't necessary to swim; suction within the corridors produced currents to sweep us away, timed so passengers from our Busfish didn't collide with those from others.

I kept Paul in sight. He was highly adaptable, even for his kind, but there had been that incident with the suit in the freighter. It wasn't hard to spot him ahead of me. The revolting green of his suit stood out among the myriad shades and shapes of others, not to mention distinguished him from the fortunate nonsuited passengers such as myself. I sculled along, but kept my speed politely down to that of the current. There were, however, those impatient with our progress. Several Jylnics surged past me, knocking me to one side. I corrected with a twist of my abdomen, not bothering to paddle.

The Jylnics passed others, causing similar disturbance, then came close to Paul, who tumbled and overcorrected in their wake. My Oieta-self had trouble deciding if the way he continued to roll uncontrollably in the current would make a Human queasy. Ansky-memory assured me that the Prumbins took better care of alien guests than leaving them to choke within their suits; unfortunately, the same source was sure Prumbins didn't know much about Humans, since that species rarely stayed long at the Abyss. And no blue-suited figure was heading for my Human.

Before I could take action myself, Paul's outflung arm was snagged by a neighbor, stopping his roll. Another Human perhaps, though they all looked the same to me in those vile suits. *Someone should send a memo*, I grumbled to myself, in spite of knowing my distaste was Oieta-based.

Still, I thought even Prumbins should have noticed the color wasn't popular with their favorite tourists by now.

The two stayed in contact long enough for Paul to stretch himself into something almost hydrodynamic, then his rescuer released him.

I relaxed, and flipped a swimmeret to enjoy some rolling of my own.

All corridors from the yokes flowed to the main processing area, a dimly lit and cavernous space enclosed within an opaque dome. Not surprisingly, the literal translation of the Prumbin name for it was "Dull Place to Wait a Long Time." Incoming currents were dampened by immense, slow-moving paddles rising from the floor, which also served as map displays and advertising for various hotels and recreational opportunities. There were, of course, frequent and exaggerated depictions of emaciated Prumbins toiling on land—sponsored, I presumed, by the various time-share companies eager to find new victims. It was a rare Prumbin indeed who left Nirvana without putting its smudge on a contract.

Here, the water entering my gills was stale and uninteresting, despite the efforts of the Prumbins to enhance its flavor. Not only was that water doubtless passing through more than its share of gills, given the proportion of unsuited species, but Essence of Sun-Kissed Algae just wasn't the same when one was sculling to hold a place in a queue. For almost a standard hour.

Bored, I waved at Paul again. He was leaning against a rail, waiting for our luggage. He waved back, but remained preoccupied talking to the other Human. *Humans bonded almost as quickly as Whirtles on a cruise.* At least I'd be able to talk to him myself, soon.

If this line would move. I fastened my oculars on the Jylnics ahead of me, longing for a form that could scowl. In an intimidating manner. *Or*, I thought wistfully, *at all*.

::What are you doing here, Too-Young? This is the line for com attachments.::

Startled, I bent to orient my oculars upward and found an Oieta approaching me rapidly. I was relieved to see she was a passive blue with spots of determined, businesslike brown. A kite tail of necessities was attached to her mid-arm: ident, credit chit, com, a mesh bag bulging with tools. *A Greeter*. The Oietae equivalent of a Human ambassador, med-tech, and building superintendent. ::My Soft Companion is Human, Gracious-One:: I explained, inclining one antenna in Paul's direction. ::I need to communicate with him.::

::Why? You will not need his services again until you leave Nirvana:: A hint of disapproving purple. I tasted impatience. ::Do you see any other Oietae purchasing such devices? They are expensive, uncomfortable, and unattractive.::

Hard to argue with such a sensible being, I decided. She was right in every respect, even without mentioning the distressing part about applying glue to my shell for a firm fit near my pre-gills. But I needed to talk to Paul, something she couldn't possibly understand. *Or could she?* I thought, having a wonderful idea.

I chose to ignore the immediate echo of Ersh-memory that wanted to list the regrettable instances which had involved my coupling of the term "wonderful" with "idea."

With a flick of my antennae, I invited the Greeter to approach and entwine, a courtesy rarely offered between strangers.

She complied. Our antennae wrapped around one another, guided by stiff hairs into a perfect alignment of our corresponding sensory pores, from those responsive to electrical current, and thus excellent indicators of mood, to those capable of detecting the slightest trace of key pheromones. It was said among the Oietae, quite literally, that one tasted the truth of another.

We stayed in contact as long as it took us both to turn a pleased amber, then moved apart. ::I am Neram Marenelli Holdswisely:: she introduced herself, flashing back to a more neutral blue. ::Welcome to Nirvana . . .:: she paused.

::Esippet Darnelli Swashbuckly, Greeter Holdswisely. My cluster instructed me to—::

Her vibrations cut across mine, though soft in their feel against my tympana. ::Please, Esippet. No need to explain. You were handling yourself so capably in line, I had no idea you were freshly hatched. Of course your family wishes you to be able to communicate with your Soft Companion. Until they arrive, I trust?:: An opinionated mauve began to creep across her sturdy segments. ::Perhaps you should come with me until then.::

So much for my great idea to be rid of her, I thought with disgust. The Oietae weren't as parentally-obsessed as mammals like Humans, but I should have remembered they would keep better track of pre-spawning offspring than letting them visit a multispecies' resort without a family member nearby.

Just then, fortune smiled on me. *Or,* I grinned to myself, *one of those ironies of misunderstanding was about to work in my favor for once.* I stabbed an antenna toward Paul again. My Human was now in the midst of a tumbling group of three orange-and-black Oietae. *Familiar Oietae.* That made Paul's newfound friend the Soft Companion who'd been so weary in the Busfish. I presumed the Oietae were harassing her about their luggage.

The why of their presence didn't matter to me, only the pure convenience of it. ::Oh, I'm not alone:: I assured the Greeter with a pert vibration of my pre-gills. ::There's my family now.:: I waved madly and wasn't at all surprised when all three Joyous-Ones waved back.

Her purple deepened. *Ersh,* I grumbled to myself, *what did I do to deserve an official who'd worry about a child in the care of distracted elders?* It had never bothered my web-kin. Before Neram could voice her doubtless valid objections, I gave her a flare of sincere blue and the truth. ::My Soft Companion will take good care of me. He's been with the family for years. And—:: I added as an afterthought,

pleased to use Paul's own praise for a babysitter he'd hired
::—he doesn't let me get away with anything.::

Greeter Holdswisely didn't need to know Paul had been
praising that babysitter for not letting a certain doting and
scaly Aunt indulge his offspring with unapproved treats. I'd
objected later, in private and strenuously, at the injustice of
being bossed by someone younger than I was by close to six
centuries. *Paul*, I remembered, *had laughed.*

The Greeter wasn't completely convinced. I kept myself
that polite, calm blue, moving only as much as required to
breathe and not drift from my place behind the Jylnics. If the
organs along my dorsal ridge could sense the impatient
thrumming of the Nimmeries in line after me—a species the
Oietae had seriously considered eradicating from the oceans
of their colonies during various border disputes—so could
hers.

Whether she felt their impatience, or cared a whit about
it, what the Oieta did next took me by complete surprise.
She took what looked like a miniature pair of grips from her
mesh bag. Before I guessed what she intended—and could
avoid it—she'd snapped them closed over the edge of one of
my middle segments. *Hard enough to hurt.* I bent my oculars down in alarm and saw my segment whitening with
pain—and, as she undid the grips, could see the neat, little
imprint pressed into my shell. It was her address on the
Brim. ::In case you need someone more reliable:: Neram
said gruffly.

Not knowing what to say that wouldn't include something bitter about the sanctity of one's shell, even for the
freshly hatched, I kept my pre-gills still.

It will be, I promised myself with significant self-pity, *so
nice to grow up.*

There were stunning accomplishments of sentient life held
within my flesh—soaring leaps of intellect, projects that
consumed generations and altered worlds; there were simpler achievements as well—a new and biologically unlikely

ending to a drinking song, a safer way to cook rostra sprouts, a law that banned cruelty. They were equal in that they had been conceived and acted upon by those now gone. They wouldn't be forgotten, so long as I endured.

Yet among them all, the Nirvana Abyss stood apart. I floated at Paul's side, overjoyed to be free of queues and alone with my Web, happily struggling to comprehend why this was so. *Perhaps*, I could hear Ersh now, *I was being ephemeral enough to be impressed by messy geology.* Certainly she'd see little to revere in a gash in the ocean floor, especially one that would be erased by upwelling magma before I could approach her years.

I'd have defended my better judgment, if Ersh would have listened. She'd never been prone to giving me a fair share of time in what weren't really debates. But I didn't believe it was the plunging rift that made me feel the closest to awe I'd ever experienced—well, there had been a time or ten when I'd been just as awestruck by the cataclysmic results of some inadvertent and completely innocent mistake on my part, but that was to be expected in a past like mine.

No, I decided. What held me mute with admiration was the stubborn will of the Prumbins. No other species in web-memory had learned to warp the universe to suit themselves quite this well. It was, frankly, inspiring. Or alarming. It depended on how you felt about the ramifications of enjoying the afterlife in the present one.

The Prumbins weren't native to this world, though they'd named it. They weren't in the least aquatic, needing the suits for survival as much as Paul. But the otherwise unimaginative and unremarkable Prumbin had taken this ocean as the personification of their paradise, and had built a living Nirvana so they could dwell in it. The result sprawled along and over the Brim of the deepest abyssal depth of this world.

And, I reminded myself with a hint of yellow, *it was a great place for parties.*

Paul drifted closer to the lip of the viewing balcony, presumably for a better look. I scrambled to keep up to him. *Lit-*

erally. My Oieta-self was a capable swimmer, if you were among those life-forms who counted the well-timed thrashing of limbs as good technique. I could, if pressed, cover a short distance in a straight line and at considerable speed by adding the flex of my lowermost segments. It would be backward, but that was usually a preferable direction anyway if confronted by an obnoxious relative or salesbeing.

I was, however, perfectly comfortable beneath a column of seawater that would have flattened the lungs or simpler gas bladders of those less well-adapted. Comfortable and, I paused to swallow the latest accumulation of delectable *petites* offered by my mandibles, continuously well fed.

Stunningly illuminated, too, I thought, twisting around to admire myself. Blue luminescence shimmered in the soft creases of every contentedly amber-tinged segment, with glowing egg-shaped dots along both sides of my nethermost five. The dots, called oiesies, indicated my feminine nature. *Oh, dear.* I stared at them. They should have been glowing, advertising my sexual state to anything sufficiently attractive with oculars. My amber streaked with blue-blue as I realized my oiesies were masked by a layer of translucent keratin—a holdover from my last molt.

Woeful adolescence was my lot in most forms.

My Human, being restricted to head and wrist lamps, wasn't as brilliant or beautiful; he was as comfortable, thanks to Prumbin technology. His suit could protect him from the pressure even at the bottom of the Abyss. It wouldn't protect him from the searing temperatures farther down, hence the servo propulsion system which would bring any suit—with willing or unwilling inhabitant—back to safer zones should its wearer be so reckless.

And I was here.

The companionway into the Brim itself was widest along this spot, built out over the Abyss so those arriving could answer the natural inclination to stop and gaze into Nirvana from any of a series of balconies. Fortunately for those reliant on the electromagnetic spectrum, the Prumbins had installed, hung, and otherwise suspended immense floodlights to show off the more spectacular features of the chasm. Those beings able to ignore how the Abyss and surrounding ocean swallowed those lights in every direction probably found the view charming.

Below where Paul and I stood was a balcony for arriving Prumbins, allowing them separate space to gasp, faint, worship, or point out the best restaurants, depending on how many times they'd visited. An attendant, one of the largest Prumbins I'd ever seen, sat in mammoth splendor on a raised dais in the middle, ready to sell permanent accommodations to any of its kind ready to end the toil of life on land—if they could afford the price. Ansky had told me it was the single best advertising ploy she'd ever seen. For Prumbins, size was success.

The com patches affixed to my tympana vibrated. Words. "So this is their idea of heaven."

I settled so I was dorsal-down in front of my Human, keeping in place with a gentle sculling of six pairs of swimmerets. "You sound doubtful," I commented, having made sure the balloonlike device over my pre-gills was in the right spot to transfer my vocalizations to his suit. The appliances, like everything that had to be brought down to the Brim, had cost a small fortune; it didn't guarantee a perfect fit. *Hence the distressingly large amount of glue*—which I'd have to reapply if I cycled. "Why?"

"I thought you told me most agrarian societies constructed their notions of paradise around an absence of toil, fields of plenty, with sunshine and an abundance of beer." One magnified eye closed and opened. A wink.

"There's beer," I assured him, now aware I was being teased. "And the Prumbins' view of the afterlife specifically includes not just the end of toil, but being able to move without effort." Paul knew as well as I that Prumbins accumulated body mass with age, which had made evolutionary sense for the species until they developed medical techniques to extend their life span past a magnificently solid—

and predator-proof—maturity. Now, a Prumbin living on land died not of old age, but when its bones finally shattered under the strain. They could have retired to live more comfortably in deep space, like the Dokecians who lost muscle tone with age. They liked the dark, too. However, space wasn't an option for Prumbins; its lack of life caused them fundamental distress. The species were farmers for a reason. They needed to be part of a network of other organisms, to feel connected to a viable ecosystem. Here in the Abyss, though the life and ecosystem were as alien as imaginable, any Prumbin could float about in a toil-free paradise within their lifetimes.

And, not insignificantly, grow larger than any Prumbins before them.

"Paradise," my Human repeated, staring up into the black of what I calculated wasn't a night sky at all, given Prumbinat's spin, despite the occasional starlike twinkling as a Busfish or other transport moved within visual range. "Is that why you brought us here?"

Anger? Perhaps my receiver was failing to convey his tone properly. His suit didn't help—no subtleties of body language, no expression. If anything, its repugnant green made me judge him suicidal. I paddled myself into a position that more or less corresponded to standing beside the Human. I didn't bother saying: *I wanted you to see this.* Instead, I said: "We needed to hide."

"And you think being at the bottom of an ocean is good enough?" No mistaking the anger now. "If we can get here, Es, anyone can. You should have listened to me. We should have hopped another freighter from the shipcity, started to confuse our trail. Worst of all, you've trapped me in this—" I was impressed with the suppleness of his suit. Paul could swing his arms in fury despite the water pressure.

"Paul—" I stopped and waited as another group of Busfish passengers either swam or walked by where we stood. Ansky-memory didn't overwhelm me the way Ersh's could, but I drew upon her pleasure in this place, her fondness for its inhabitants, in order to stay calm myself. It wasn't easy. If I hadn't been blissed most of the trip here, I'd have seen what I only now realized.

Paul's anger wasn't at being confined to the suit or where I'd taken us. It wasn't so new. This was how he'd felt every moment since we were attacked in the greenhouse.

Why?

We were alone again. I turned a confused and unhappy blue-blue. "Are you angry with me?"

"I—" he seemed to hesitate. "I'm sorry. I didn't mean to yell at you, Esippet. I'm filthy. I'm tired to my very bones—that's all. I trust your judgment. And you did promise there would be a bed, a nice, Human-suited bed." This last sounded charmingly wistful.

I wasn't fooled. "You're angry at what happened on Minas XII. So you are angry with me."

Paul held out his hands. So invited, I let four of my dainty clawtips grip the fabric of his gloves, using the contact to anchor me in place. It had the feel of maturity, to be stilled despite the drift of current. Yet all that held me here, in this moment, was this Human and his boots, designed to grip the balcony flooring. "Don't mistake the two, Esen," he said. "Yes, I'm angry. It's a natural Human reaction to being betrayed, to being attacked, to being forced to abandon everything and run like this. But not at you. For you. I'm angry for us both."

As a denial, it left much to interpretation. My integument settled into an eloquent, if motley, combination of lilac with beige patches: anxious confusion. *Sometimes,* I thought with disgust, *a form could be a little too revealing.* "We have rooms waiting," I promised, deciding to avoid the topic of Human anger and its potential targets for now.

Although I knew enough about this particular Human to realize it couldn't be avoided forever.

Otherwhere

"WHEN were you going to tell me?"

Kearn blinked at the onslaught of light as much as at the low, angry voice. "Timri? Tell you what?" He levered himself on his elbow and squinted reproachfully at his door. *Which seemed*, he sighed, *only effectively locked when he was outside and had forgotten the latest code.*

She was crouched at the side of his bed, hands gripping the blankets as though planning to toss them—and him—out an air lock. "About Cristoffen working with the Kraal."

He laid back and closed his eyes. *Of course, she'd overheard.* They maintained a polite fiction on board the *Russell III*, one in which he was in command and no one spied on his every move. *He must*, Kearn supposed, *hold up his end.* Or things would change. He didn't like change. "How did you know?"

"You gave me that report to read. Didn't you think I'd figure it out? He had to be using their stinking tech." Smooth and without hesitation. *Years of practice*, he thought. The mattress shifted violently. "Don't you think of going back to sleep on me, Lionel. I'm not leaving until we talk about this."

"I know." Kearn opened his eyes to gaze up at his comp-tech and second-in-command. He almost smiled, which wouldn't have helped her temper. But her fine-boned face—with its high glowing cheeks and elongated eyes, expressive mouth and rich dark skin—

had become endlessly fascinating to him, whether impatient, puzzled, or, most typically, completely unaware of him. *Even when brimming with fury at him*, he decided, *it was a face worth watching*.

Timri gave him room to slide out of bed and stand. Kearn pulled a robe over his shoulders and tied it around his waist—not that she'd notice if he'd been naked.

"Brandy?" he asked, heading for the cupboard. Taking silence for a no, he poured himself a small glass, pausing to stare into the amber liquid and remember another late night visit. Then, he'd been the one seeking answers. *Now?* "I don't know all the answers," Kearn said evenly, turning to face Timri. "But you're right. He admitted it to me yesterday, when we discussed his report."

She sat on the end of his bed, hands precisely folded together on her lap, fury replaced by something darker. "What are we going to do about it?"

Action was her way, he thought, knowing it wasn't his. His strength, if he had one, was patience, the ability to keep his goal in view for a lifetime if necessary. Kearn took a swallow, feeling the smooth burn of the liquor down his throat, the warmth in his stomach. He'd learned not to cough. "Do you have a suggestion?" As Timri leaned forward eagerly, he held up a hand. "A suggestion that won't alert the Kraal or involve Cristoffen's disappearance."

Her lips twisted as if on something sour. "He killed Zoltan Duda."

"You're sure. You finished your analysis—"

She snorted. "Didn't take long. The Port Jellies on Urgia Prime came to the very convenient conclusion that Duda's weapon misfired in a robbery attempt. Case closed. Oh, they'd like to talk to the intended victim, but they respect that being's right to private commerce. So they won't be looking."

"But you don't think it was a misfire."

"According to the technical evidence in the report? Not a chance. Incompetent fools or well-paid ones, makes no difference. That weapon fired properly— then every bit of its energy was reflected back at Duda. You know what that means. Cristoffen must have been wearing a shield. A very special one."

Kearn took another, larger swallow. "So, it was self-defense."

"I'm not absolving the dead," Timri countered. "They both intended murder that day. But you can't call it self-defense simply because Cristoffen succeeded."

"No." Kearn sank into a chair, careful not to disturb the stack of abstracts he'd left on the arm last night, reading material that wasn't about death. "I believe Cristoffen went into that room knowing he'd survive and Zoltan Duda would die. Something we'll never be able to prove."

"What are we going to do?" Timri repeated. "Don't you tell me to wait while Cristoffen meets his next victim—did you know he's set us on course for Picco's Moon already? That dolt of a captain didn't so much as blink."

"I didn't know," Kearn admitted. "But I'm not surprised." *Fourth down on Cristoffen's list*, he thought. *Alphonsus Lundrigan.*

They were close enough that Timri could rest her hand on Kearn's knee. "Lionel. I've never pried into your—dealings—with the Kraal. I've never asked about that time. But—do you think they ordered Zoltan's death? Were you ever told to–to—"

"Kill someone for them? No!" Kearn shoved his chair back to stand and move away, his reports tumbling to the floor in protest. Timri stood also, forcing him to look up to meet her level gaze.

"We all have secrets," she said, her voice harsher

than he'd ever heard. "We're all capable of terrible things."

Kearn stiffened. "You think I'm capable of murder?"

"Did you think it of Cristoffen, before you gave him virtual control of this ship?"

"He wasn't my friend."

His unthought protest, half wish and half plea, hung between them. Kearn sat back down and poured himself another drink, pretending he hadn't seen her sudden confusion, pretending she couldn't see how his hand shook. "We'll go to Picco's Moon," he told the glass. "But not directly. Relay my order to Captain What's-his-name to take us to Sacriss XIII first. If he objects, tell him I want to exchange information with the local universities. Buys us time."

Very quietly. "Time for what, sir?"

"Time for you to send tracers through the logs of Cristoffen's communications since coming aboard. Use my authorization code and go deep."

"What about his comp? I could get into his files. He'd never know—"

"No," Kearn said firmly, hiding his panic at the mere thought of her being more involved. "His 'friends' are very careful, even if he's not. Stay clear. But make up some excuse to keep Cristoffen from sending any new messages—wreck the com system if you must. I'm sure Resdick would be glad to help. He's been bored lately."

"Lionel. What I said. I was only—"

Kearn didn't look up. "I don't trust any translight com from this ship, my office, or the bridge, not with Kraal involved. When we reach Sacriss, I'll need access to a secure system there, no questions asked." A long pause. Kearn waited until he heard her indrawn breath, then added: "I know you can arrange such things, Timri. I know you have your own 'friends' and resources."

He cradled his glass in both hands, refusing to rub his scalp, refusing to learn what expression filled the face he so loved to watch. "I'm only a fool sometimes."

"I—"

"Dismissed."

15: Abyss Afternoon;
Happy House Night

"I TOLD you. I really don't care where we stay, Es, as long as I'm out of this as soon as possible." Paul was either gritting his teeth or one of our coms had some static. The "this" to which he referred was his suit. It wasn't the quality of the Prumbin garment that so perturbed my Human. He appeared to have reached some limit of tolerance for his own odor—or his suit's air scrubber had given up. Though a peaceful being, I was reasonably sure he entertained thoughts of violence if he didn't get into a 'fresher soon.

"Patience," I told him, finding it odd to be the one using the word. "It's not far now. We must stay at Anienka's Happy House. I promised my cluster."

It wasn't quite a lie, since Ansky—technically my mother—had insisted I stay with her on each of my visits to Prumbinat. She owned a piece of property of the sort commonly referred to as "unique." As one might expect, this meant a place where no sane being would choose to build a permanent structure, although if one could . . .

. . . and Ansky, in her Prumbin persona of Anienka, had. Mind you, she'd had some help. Mixs had been intrigued by the challenge presented by our web-kin and spent several years on the project.

We were approaching the result on a towsled, the Prumbin version of an underwater aircar. It was, as the name stated, a flat sled with hand/claw/sucker holds on its dorsal surface—

presently being used by myself, Paul, and thirty-seven members of varied species—towed by Busfish fry. Since the fry were too young to have lost their urge to school, the Prumbin driver used reins connected to the harness of an individual swimming in the midst of the others. The rest of the fry were harnessed directly to the sled. The result wasn't particularly straight travel, but speed made up the difference.

A pretty, if intimidating means of locomotion, I thought, watching the flickers of bioluminescence coming from the mouths of our Human-sized fry as they lured close any unfortunate creatures swimming along our path, then snapped them up.

A dangerous place to swim no matter where one looked. Our sled was among hundreds moving along the Brim, a sight that mimicked the appearance of the small shoals which seemed to fly above a reef. Just replace the varied colors of coral with the gemlike lighting from the Prumbins' city, and move the source of all this life into the Abyss.

Our sled veered out, as if following my thoughts. I swung over the side to admire the depths, holding on with all six arms as I passed outside the shelter of the coning plas and faced the substantial current being produced by our passage. Except where massive, down-directed lights from the Brim painted the walls in drifts of grayed sediment and black rock, vision was of no use here. But my Oieta-self could taste the richness of the life below, however strange its chemistry compared to that where a sun could reach. Here, the planet's core heat started the binding of energy within molecules.

And, as Ersh would have said, life always took advantage.

"Is that it?" Paul asked.

I was about to answer, having stayed hanging over the side to enjoy the suspended smorgasbord being delivered to my mouth, when Ersh-memory surged through me and I saw where we were going . . .

*   *   *

. . . through multiple eyes, each so exquisitely sensitive starlight would burn. No light here. Muscles shudder as they are pushed past fatigue. No rest here. Danger follows, its taste contaminating above and ahead. Only the depths remain free of the taint. For now.

There.

A glow only these eyes could see marks home. *Triumph!* A final drive forward—

Pain! A stab through scale and muscle tissue that becomes a grip, a pull. *Upward to the danger.*

Cunning serves better than anger. Ersh/I recognize the harpoon's barb shaft, understand its purpose, know the three-fingered hands at the other end of the line. We've seen the newcomers who hunt this ocean.

Rise, slowly, offering no resistance. When there's enough slack, whirl with mouth gaping and sever the line tied to the fish-riders, a motion that continues with a fluid dive into the safe dark of the abyss.

Listen, taste, feel for signs of pursuit. The depth the air-breathers have already come in their pursuit is unprecedented. The new is dangerous.

There! Turn, a move so powerful and swift it drives a wake against the wall of the abyss, disturbing ancient clouds of what had once been the shells of green and dancing life. Slip through the clouds into a fissure unseen from above, a cavernous hiding place large enough for a dozen more of her/my kind.

Except that her/my kind was as alien to this ocean as those left to hunt in vain above . . . *Amusement* . . .

. . . I came out of Ersh-memory to find myself shocked. While the bits of Ersh I'd consumed years ago often had that effect on me, being prone to arriving when least expected and always containing what I couldn't imagine, this time was different. I'd never felt her amused before. *For all I knew,* I thought with some distress, *there could be memories of Ersh laughing buried in my mass.*

I wasn't ready for such disturbing revelations about the founder of my first Web. Shuddering, I climbed back up beside Paul. "Sorry," I mumbled, gesturing further apology with my swimmerets. "Old memory."

"I hope it was a good one." He might be angry, smelly, and very tired, but I had no doubt of the sharpness of Paul's mind under any circumstances. He knew what I meant.

"Nothing to worry about," I assured him. Although the upwellings of Ersh-memory came less often, I shared any new knowledge with Paul, my web-kin, immediately. *Or fairly soon*, I told myself, then added a more honest *eventually*. At least the important—must be shared or there could be a huge misunderstanding later to the lasting detriment of a young web-being—bits of Ersh-memory. The rest I tended to store away, on the basis that Paul hardly needed to know more about another web-being when, as he frequently told me, he was doing his utmost to keep up with one. *How*, I reasoned, *would it help him to know more about Ersh?* She and I had been as different as two individuals could be, and still claim the same biology.

I gazed out at our destination as our school of young Busfish zigzagged closer. The fissure that rent the side of the Abyss was no longer dark but webbed with colored light, as if filled by a whisper-thin cocoon, in turn filled by the half-seen form of a winged insect about to emerge in all its glory. As we moved nearer still, my Oieta-oculars could distinguish the individual strands crisscrossing the fissure from side to side. Each appeared deceptively thin, given these were enclosed corridors, and beaded along their length. The beads were rooms of various sizes, some in combination, others alone.

I put my mid-arm around the shoulders of Paul's suit. "Welcome to Anienka's Happy House."

Ersh-memory overlay past and present, discovery and result. I found myself believing I'd done the right thing after all—something I usually postponed until the distant future, when there was some hope of evidence to prove it. "Remind me, Paul," I said, "once you've washed and eaten, and we've both slept, to tell you the legend of Etienka the Fisher and the Guardian of the Abyss."

I was sure the Human would enjoy the tale of how Etienka, revered as the discoverer of the Nirvana Abyss, had been guided through the depths by a vision of the largest Prumbin of them all—a saintly figure who had magically disappeared within the Abyss after showing Etienka the way.

Funny how the legend, so rich in detail, completely missed the part about the harpoon.

I had a feeling Ersh had been amused by that nugget of irony, too.

I slept our first night in Nirvana cradled in a watery bed, caressed by exactly the right amount of current to make my Oieta-self perfectly comfortable. It was a complete waste of luxury, since I was exhausted to the point where I could probably have rocked myself to sleep with one suit pole. I wasn't the only one. When I checked on Paul before bed, I found him asleep inside the 'fresher, leaning into the spray. It had taken considerable thumping from my side of the ceiling to rouse him. From what I'd seen through the mist—an unsettling phenomenon to my Oieta-self, given it was just enough moisture so one died slowly rather than quickly—his skin had already pruned.

Perhaps it hadn't been exhaustion alone that finally made us let down our guard enough for sleep. The Human hadn't told me if he'd been concerned about my remaining an obligate aquatic, but I thought his first sight of Anienka's Happy Home must have reassured him. Water and air competed for visual space in every direction. It was less a building than an exercise in interactive plumbing. *Mixs*, I thought, *had done the Web proud.*

Take our suite of rooms. Paul's door from the wet corridor—Prumbins were fond of the obvious in naming—was an air lock, complete with storage for his suit; mine was a simple door. Our doors to the dry corridor? The mirror image, with my room opening through a wet lock. His side of our suite, or rather its lower floor, was dry and filled with what appeared to be species-appropriate furnishings. I'd been too tired for an inventory. Mine was a lovely series of concurrent bubbles, shaped by a force mesh; predators were an unspoken natural hazard. There was no weather in the Abyss—another feature the Prumbins found heavenly. *Well,* I corrected to myself, discreetly cleaning my filters of nonconsumables with the brushes on the inner surface of my arms, *there was always detritus.* But the rain of solids through this watery sky never varied enough to be worth forecasting.

If I preferred, I could invoke the exclusion casing over the mesh and use the House's internal water supply; even, had I wished, selected an optimum temperature and pressure, since not all aquatic life-forms enjoyed the physical environment of the Abyss as much as the Oietae. Any water entering my rooms would be rich with life—room service took on an entirely new meaning when it came to filter feeders.

There were sections of the Happy House where any distinction between ocean and air blurred, corridors half-flooded, rooms that were pools with islands in their midst. You could wade, float, or swim, depending on physical ability or preferred technology, all at a temperature and pressure suited to your species' optimum. I supposed even flying species could have managed, if they could fit inside a suit for the trip down. To the best of my, and Ansky's, recollections, none had been tempted. *Perhaps sky dwellers weren't interested in a paradise without one.*

Most importantly, however, my floor was Paul's ceiling, made from a transparent, membranelike material the Prumbins had discovered, called "clearfoil." Clearfoil resisted pressure, becoming stronger as more was applied to it. It was thus, unsurprisingly, the perfect building material for the Brim. From Paul's side, there was a control to invoke a privacy mode, temporarily opaqueing the clearfoil. I didn't have that option, but any aquatics choosing this particular accommodation knew they were on display. Most, like real Oietae, wouldn't be bothered at all. Best of all, our suites contained a com system that allowed us to freely converse—or listen to the same music—through our respective media.

The almost intimate arrangement of living quarters between species who couldn't survive one another's natural environment unprotected was all Ansky's doing. Before falling to sleep, I remembered hoping I wasn't going to have to explain "why" to Paul.

When I awoke and looked around myself for the first time, I realized it was likely too late. The lowermost walls of my room were a ring of interesting objects. *Oieta objects*. I bent my oculars into my ventral surface, as if that would help. When I dared look again, the interesting objects were still there. When Ansky was running the place, such things had at least been discreetly inside an orange-and-black trunk. *And what was that?* I sculled into an upside-down position to try and comprehend the use of one I'd never seen before. It had these twisty fibers . . .

"Good morning! Or is it night?"

I scooted backward so quickly my dorsal ridge hit the mesh and I rebounded into the center of my bubble. "G–good morning," I ventured, peering down at Paul.

Clean, dressed, and smiling. Amazing recuperative powers, Humans. *And already busy*, I noted with satisfaction. Paul may have greeted me, but he was occupied with what he'd probably planned to do before falling asleep in the 'fresher—scouring his room for listening devices.

"You don't need to do that here," I told him rather smugly. *Esen the Clever.* "The Brim takes privacy very seriously. Snoops and other devices are illegal."

He grunted and climbed on the oversized bed to check behind a painting. "They usually are. Doesn't seem to matter."

"Then what might is that the Prumbin screen all incoming luggage—and bodies—in the processing area for anything that could be used to spy or record. Not to mention Ansky and Mixs took special care here, when they built the Happy

House. Ansky wanted to be sure no other owner would be able to modify her building to eavesdrop on her guests."

"Why—" Paul began, then appeared to really look at the painting in front of him. I sculled closer to the floor to see him better. "Oh," he said.

"She was interested in relationships," I said defensively.

He tilted his head to one side and continued to study the painting. "I see that."

"She enjoyed her work," I added, then blushed so dark a green I might have been black. "What I meant—"

Paul looked up at me. His lips quirked and there might have been a twinkle in his eyes. "I did meet her, as you recall. A being of rare charm and warmth."

Since he could equally well have said: of rare appetite and boundless enthusiasm, and, from his apparent mood, probably would say that—or worse—if I let him continue, I quickly changed the subject: "There is room service, if you're hungry."

"I'd rather go exploring."

Any remnants of green were swept from my shell by pleased amber and yellow. "Wonderful! This is a—"

"On my own."

Ersh. I burped a bubble from my swim sac and settled to the floor, trying in vain to keep my shell from turning a confused mix of red and gray. *I might as well hold up a sign*, I scolded myself, imagining it saying: See Esen's feelings! Now showing: resentful hurt.

Still standing on the bed, Paul stretched up to press his hand against the ceiling under my limp arms. I thought I felt its warmth and rolled my oculars so I could see his face. "You are a goose," the Human said inaccurately, but in that calm, gentle voice that implied he understood something I didn't. *Wouldn't be the first time.* "I only meant I want a chance to scout without attracting attention. Your idea of a Soft Companion was very clever, Esippet, but anyone hunting us will be looking for a Human paired with an alien. We're conspicuous together."

"Not here," I mumbled, flashing green again.

A dark eyebrow lifted. Paul opened his mouth as if to speak, then seemed to notice my color. He lowered his hand and rubbed his lean jaw, a habit when mulling over a new thought.

I sighed and rose from the floor to a more dignified posture. It didn't help, but I went on anyway, carefully not looking at Paul or the devices in my own room. "Ansky built this place for members of different species who wish to—experiment with their biological urges—but had—" if I'd had teeth, I would have gritted them myself here, "—technical difficulties. The Happy House is quite—renowned—in some circles for the capabilities of its staff." Though not as much as it would have been if Ansky had permitted word to spread. She'd relied on the Prumbins' desire to keep their undersea paradise from being overrun by air-breathing tourists. No one was ever turned away, but, to be blunt, Nirvana wasn't on any maps.

Lesy, the only one of my web-kin who'd been prone to giggle at the universe, had explained to me that it wasn't so much that the Prumbins made an effort to keep the Abyss secret, as that other sentients tended to be confused by the entire concept of paying to tour Prumbin Heaven.

One-way pilgrimage and interspecies' confusion aside, Nirvana and the Brim had become popular destinations for the handful of adventurous and colorful aquatics like the Oietae who enjoyed the rarity of decent accommodations at abyssal depths. They didn't appear to care that the Prumbin offered discounts for beauty—or that the Happy House offered them for ardor. Not that those individuals of varied species aware of the special opportunities offered by Anienka's establishment were prone to discuss them with the uninformed. They were—too busy.

It was, I realized, *an apt name for a place where one being's pleasure was literally another being's joy. Or more.* There were larger suites.

"Oh," Paul said finally, instilling the sound with a wealth

of meaning. "Well, that does help explain the activity last night in the front lobby. I'd wondered if I was seeing things."

"They were after the group rate," I mumbled. There was something else he should know. I sculled myself around to look down at him. "You don't have to wish interaction to stay here," I said, now well past embarrassment. "It is a hotel. But there are those who come here alone in search of—interested—partners of other species."

"So that's why the Jylnic behind us kept slipping his tentacle around my feet?"

"What?" I flared brilliant red from antennae to telson until Paul grinned and I knew he was teasing me. Subsiding to annoyed pink, I said with what I considered admirable restraint: "You are an attractive being. For a Human. Roaming about on your own will doubtless have you being accosted improperly—by Jylnics as well as who knows what. As long as I'm with you, this won't happen. As often," I amended, having surveyed my friend critically during this little speech and realizing, to my dismay, that Paul Ragem was probably more attractive now than at any stage in his life. I wasn't counting those early months when, as a baby, he doubtless melted Human hearts at a considerable distance, given those eyes and thick lashes.

Now, as he ran one hand through his tousled black hair and gave me another "Esen is a goose" look, I paid attention to the graceful strength shaped by bone and muscle, the intelligence and compassion molded by an expressive face, the unconscious nobility of every move and word . . .

And was trapped by the mute vulnerability of grief-bruised eyes—which could probably melt a Prumbin's sturdy hearts.

We were in trouble, I thought with sudden and complete conviction, hearing Cosmic laughter already.

So much for this plan.

Otherwhere

THE ribbon was the width of a finger and finer than a hair. She anchored the end of the first piece between her toes and began to wrap it around foot, then ankle, then calf, overlapping the edges with absolute precision. The material formed to her skin. As each new section warmed, it seemed to melt and re-form as skin. *Satisfaction.*

The other leg, both arms, fingers, hands. There was no pause, no hesitation, as if she knew her body so well there could be no wasted motion.

Torso, shoulders were sheathed in ribbon, skin replacing skin.

She stood at this point and sought a mirror. Not because she couldn't do this last step by touch alone, but because she wanted to see if the results matched the claims. *If they didn't,* she thought calmly, *someone would die.*

Encased fingers laid a strip along the rise of throat, over the line of jaw, up the hollows of cheek and brow to lie over the scalp.

Within a breath, it was as though a knife of flawless cream had slashed across her face, severing the marks of affiliation and trust.

How—appropriate.

16: Happy House Morning

I'D underestimated my Human. *Not for the first time.* While there were a few incidents during our initial stroll through the corridors of Happy House, he managed to deflect would-be suitors before most did more than take notice. Being an expert in alien cultures did help, I supposed. He knew better than to ignore the batting eye covers of the Heezle, since inattention was a common "follow me" signal and we definitely didn't want a hopeful pillar of ooze sloshing behind us all day. And I had to admit his strategy during our encounter with the Jylnic worked remarkably well. A pair had approached with their usual reckless speed through the wet corridor, quite rudely shoving me out of their way in their eagerness to check out the new arrival. Paul had lifted one arm, pretended it was a tentacle, then used the bend in his elbow to pantomime it being broken.

They'd actually offered him condolences and the name of a reliable medic, before dashing away again.

Through me.

When I stopped spinning on my long axis, I swam back to Paul's side. The illusion of walking together was almost perfect, thanks to the clearfoil between us, except for the fact that other pedestrian traffic affected only one of us at a time and I tended to bob. "You lied to those poor creatures," I commented.

"I waved."

Good point.

We were finishing our first quick circuit of the facilities.

The Happy House was a manageable size, despite its appearance on approach. New arrivals were given suites along the same thread of corridors, allowing the operators to shut down power to any unoccupied threads. Our arrival, luckily, had come during a typically slow season—harvest time for the major growing area on the surface, requiring all available Prumbins of manageable size to participate. As they were too busy for pleasure, they assumed—like many other species—that everyone else was too busy as well. So fewer Busfish were swimming their loads up and down and the Prumbinat shipcities were choked with freighters loading produce.

I, for one, was pleased with our timing. Paul wasn't, since he'd hoped for more opportunities to leave the planet at our own convenience. *Wait until tomorrow*, I sighed. *Mind you, nothing seemed to please him today.* I rolled an ocular his way. He'd ordered new clothes through room service, entailing a three-way battle between his desire for subdued and inconspicuous, my insistence that he at least look like a joyous being on vacation, and the choices available. The result, a classic black tunic and pants on which he somewhat defiantly displayed the silver pendant I'd given him, was not helping him avoid attention.

But where another being might see an attractive Human out for a walk, I saw a being on a mission. He was hunting for something, and the number of closed corridors didn't seem to be helping.

I'd have helped, if he'd told me what he wanted. Hinting hadn't worked. I presumed my Human viewed my assertion that we were safe from being overheard here as something not worth testing.

Another good point.

A call from behind us interrupted my thoughts. "Hom Gast?" *Behind Paul*, I corrected as I spun around to see a figure walking quickly in his direction.

Paul smiled before he turned as though he recognized the voice. "Fem Cheatham."

"Wendy, please." The figure arrived, holding out her hands

which, I noted, Paul didn't hesitate to take in his own in a warm greeting.

While I stared at this apparition.

I'd expect any being to look better outside those vile green suits the Prumbins inflicted on unknowing guests, but I hadn't expected the Oietae's Soft Companion to look this much better. Granted, I'd only seen her hunched over with exhaustion or surrounded by her charges in a lineup.

Now? She was definitely no longer hunched. This version stood as tall as my Human and was as slender, though curved in those places appropriate for the other gender. I didn't have to guess. She was clothed from neck to toe in a tight wrapping of gauze-thin white ribbon, overlaid by a transparent sheath of pale blue-silver that just happened to cling to those curves with every movement. Including breathing. Her face appeared to have the requisite features: flawless skin, expressive dark brows, bright green eyes. Braids of red and black streamed to her waist, flowing over her shoulders and back.

The colors of rage.

I distrusted her on sight.

"Have you eaten?" she asked, her voice annoyingly high-pitched and soft. "I was on my way to lunch."

"I do not require intermittent feedings," I informed her, trying not to extend any bristles, somehow staying a proper, if dull, blue.

Paul didn't bother glancing at me. "Wendy, I'd like you to meet Esippet Darnelli Swashbuckly. My Shelled Companion."

She turned to face me through the clearfoil. Her eyes went to the com attachment over my pre-gills and then rose to my oculars. "How odd. Usually Soft Companions don't continue to provide service on the Brim. Unless—" One elegant brow rose. "But no. This Oieta is too young to have any more—interesting—requirements." She glanced at Paul, then smiled.

The next time I chose a form, I fumed to myself, *it would be one where I didn't turn a demeaning mix of red and green.*

If I had to reveal my reactions, I'd prefer to inflate a poison bladder or at least raise spines.

And there was nothing wrong with a good snarl.

"I promised to keep an eye on Esippet until her family arrives," Paul explained, releasing her hands as if he'd forgotten they were still in his.

"You are very kind." Her hand strayed as if to touch the pendant. "Must your responsibilities as a babysitter preclude lunch with me?"

"Babysitter!"

Before Paul could intercede—most likely to scold me for losing my temper rather than to scold her for being insufferably rude—Wendy bowed in my direction. "My apologies, Fem Swashbuckly," she said graciously. "I've had a difficult experience with the Oietae recently in my care, exhausting in fact, and, well," she shrugged, which happened to send braids cascading over one shoulder. "I'm probably a little overprotective of other Soft Companions right now."

Now Paul did look at me. My first eight swimmerets drooped a little as I read in his face what he wasn't about to say out loud.

Who is the more civilized being here, Esen-alit-Quar?

"No apology necessary, Fem Cheatham," I said as politely as I could. "It is not my intention to monopolize the time of my Soft Companion." I decided to impress Paul with my magnanimity. "I have some errands to swim. Paul? I'll see you back in our rooms later."

At the same time, I forced my color into a mottled beige and white, the camouflage hardly functional in a coral-free corridor, but a display with specific meaning to other Oietae depending on the situation. Self-effacement and concern, always. But I hoped Paul remembered what this color pattern conveyed, when used between equals encountering a stranger: *caution.*

I'd found I could release a bubble, if sufficiently coated in saliva, that would last long enough to almost reach the uppermost ceiling of my suite, before Paul returned from his lunch. I listened to his footsteps approaching as I watched my latest tiny globe struggle its way past the first inward curve, then the next.

"Es."

It might have traveled free and clear, but I must have made some involuntary movement, however small, that sent a wave following the bubble. It lodged against the force mesh of the near wall, as if trying to find its way to the open ocean, then was gone.

"I don't believe it. You're sulking. Of all the juvenile—"

"I'm not." *Well, I might have been, but that was hardly the issue.* I sculled upright, then drifted to the floor where I could see him. Paul was staring up at me, his face stern and pale except for a flush over each cheek, proving that Humans had rudimentary color signaling of their own. "We are hiding," I reminded him. "She is a stranger. It was too dangerous."

"You of all beings know Humans are social," he snapped. "Nothing would be more suspicious than my refusing a friendly invitation to lunch, especially from the only other Human here doing the same work."

"You refused other friendly invitations."

He ran a hand over his face. "This wasn't the same."

I bobbed up and down. "True. The Heezle was far more attractive."

Paul tried to keep looking angry, then his lips twitched. "I'm sure it takes another Heezle to appreciate that."

"You'd be surprised," I said primly, turning a little more amber myself.

"I don't really want to know, thank you." My Human sat on his bed, then lay back, hands behind his head, in order to gaze up at me in comfort. "Before you ask, yes, Wendy was a charming lunch companion and I enjoyed her company. And, yes, given our present circumstances, I spent the entire meal worrying what trouble you could stuff yourself into while I was gone." He grinned, as if this was humor, but I was fairly sure Paul had done exactly that. *I didn't,* I sighed to myself, *have the most enviable record.* "Of course I'd rather have stayed with you. Happier?"

A rhetorical question, since I was by now bright amber. "I have never begrudged you time with your own species, Paul."

"And that's the truth, Fangface." Lightly, as we both shied away from the past. "At least Wendy introduced me to a new dish."

I turned an anxious beige. It wasn't so much that my Oieta-self had minor difficulties with the concept of eating at specific moments in time and serious difficulties with the concept of cooking—which it did—as that I was concerned over what exactly had been in that dish.

Paul laughed, stretching arms back to snag a pillow for his head. "Silly Esippet. Do you really think I'd indulge in seafood while you're so shrimply? It wouldn't be the same. But it was delicious. You should try it—next time you have a mouth."

I flashed a faint yellow, oddly relieved by this return to insufferable behavior, including his obvious effort to tweak my curiosity. I'd have ignored the latter and gone on to more important topics, but, after all, I wouldn't stay in this form—and on this side of the menu—forever. "So tell me about this delicious new dish."

"Erpic Shell Soup. A most intriguing blend of flavors." He closed his eyes, as though to better remember the taste. "Not to mention more colorful than your stunning self—although I admit having bright blue bits of shell suddenly pop up through the yellow broth is startling at first. A shame you can't try it."

Automatically careful of secrets, I didn't simply say "I have." But it wasn't a meal I'd had for a century. Or one I would willingly have again.

Erpic Shell Soup was a typical Kraal delicacy. Eating it was a measure of trust in one's host—or in that host's cooking staff, since preparation involved several complex steps to remove the natural toxins from the animal's shell. Naturally,

Skalet had chosen to serve it when the Web had gathered in a system near her space. Her way of showing courtesy to those who had traveled farthest.

We'd been in various forms, with Ersh's permission. Only Skalet and Lesy had been Human. I'd taken my first mouthful, unsure if one should swallow the hard pieces or chew them—a risky procedure without fully closing lips—when Ersh had suddenly flipped over her bowl. She'd extended her claws into the table, roaring with rage while I'd frozen in my seat, wondering what I'd done now.

But it was at Skalet that Ersh had stared, her eyes dilated in unmistakable predator-fix on our web-kin.

"How dare you try ephemeral tricks on me!" Ersh had growled, the sound from deep in her mammoth chest. "How dare you risk your own flesh!"

Skalet had known better than to move—or even breathe. I remembered watching her Human skin lose all its color beneath its tattoos. I remembered being amazed that Skalet, the most careful of us all, couldn't make soup.

Then, when Ersh hadn't immediately launched herself over the table at her throat, Skalet had taken a cautious breath to answer: "An accident, Eldest. I've been adding trace amounts of duras to my meals—to increase this form's immunity. It didn't occur to me to check which soup stock I used today." There'd been a flash of rebellion in her eyes. "Not all of us are free to cycle on the spot to remove ingested toxins." Something three of our web-kin had already done.

Skalet had continued to hold form in defiance, I'd been too shocked to react, and—I decided sometime after the fact—Ersh had preferred remaining something that could snarl and potentially flay skin from the target of her rage.

She hadn't, of course. *Well, there'd been snarling.* Once sure I'd be ignored by both, I'd cycled into something small that could evacuate the room, removing the duras extract from my system in the process, and awaited the outcome with Ansky. My web-kin had been horrified. I'd huddled around my secret, understanding Skalet as never before. She must have managed to get duras plants to the Kraal after all . . .

And then had to fear her own poison.

"Es?"

Nothing more than coincidence, I told myself, angry at being distracted by my own memory. *Ersh's was bad enough.* I unlocked the deaths' grip my limbs had taken on one another and didn't quite lie to my friend: "I'm sorry, Paul, but the subject of—lunch—seems to upset this me. Could we talk about something else?"

"Of course." Paul frowned slightly. He held a hand to one ear and raised his brows in question. *Ah.* My careful Human wished me to confirm our privacy first.

I sampled the water slipping over my gills—ocean-wild and full of food—and felt the connection to the Abyss and Prumbinat's wide-open seas. "My rooms are open to the world. Yours are not. The difference? Clearfoil." I tapped the slender tip of one antenna gently against the material separating our worlds.

The controls to invoke the exclusion casing were embedded throughout the floor. It was a simple matter of keying in my room code. Paul and I watched as red streaks of clearfoil grew across the force mesh, blended into a smooth membrane, then disappeared. There might be nothing separating me from the Abyss, except that the water inside my room became more civilized to my senses—though still swarming with tasty bits.

I continued: "If you try to use certain equipment within clearfoil, it produces an interfering resonance that scrambles the information contained in recordings or transmissions. The clearfoil itself clouds permanently and must be replaced—an expensive nuisance. The Prumbins almost stopped using it for construction, until someone developed a com system that included the clearfoil itself to communicate between physically connected rooms. That system is licensed for use only here." I waved two pairs of arms. "An old acquaintance of mine was involved." Mixs hadn't bragged, but even Ersh had been impressed. "You did notice most suites do not touch each other; they don't, unless that's requested by all parties."

"I'd wondered," Paul said, sitting up as if knowing we were safe to be ourselves had energized him. "So we can talk freely?"

"One more thing, first." I turned a thoughtful blue as I stroked the clearfoil with both antennae, learning nothing except it had a slightly salty taste and felt as impenetrable as the metal hull of a starship. "There's another unique property of clearfoil. I haven't actually tried this myself . . ."

But the mere thought was enough to lose my hold on this form, I cycled . . .

. . . feeling almost delirious relief as I became myself and could feel the drumming of the impatient magma below, sense its tides and movements, know the tension building within the solid crust of the Brim had enough energy to shoulder continents aside. The press of water on my every surface refined my shape into a perfect sphere rather than a teardrop. I quite liked it.

Before I became too entranced with the comfort of my new shape, the thrill of hearing gravity sing, or the exhilaration of being so close to shifting magnetism, I tightened my attention to the room . . .

And its floor, through which I should be able to pass without risking Paul's only protection from the pressure, water, and cold of the Abyss. *Or risking me.*

To my web-self, clearfoil was almost kin—a mutable form of matter I understood on an instinctive level. I'd never interacted with it before, having caught a good dose of caution from an argument I'd overheard between my elders. Mixs had been expressing a scientific curiosity about whether I'd become stuck permanently if I attempted the passage; Ansky had rebutted that she wouldn't be the first to share with Ersh if I did. Terrified, I'd vowed I'd never let Mixs coax me into trying anything so dangerous. She'd been disappointed when I refused, but I wouldn't tell her why.

I wondered suddenly: *Had my Elders been so callous — or had I been tricked?* In retrospect, this seemed all too similar to an argument between Char and Paul about whether they should let the twins use the stove, an argument staged when I'd cued their parents that I'd heard the excited breathing of two hidden children. To my knowledge, neither Luara nor Tomas had made further attempts to melt their toys in the appliance.

Cheered by the novel idea that I might have had some parental care after all, albeit of the "hope you survive" kind, I prepared to join Paul. First, I gathered mass from the living things surrounding me on every side, stopping when I'd assimilated what I would need on the other side of the clearfoil. The clearfoil itself was appetizing, but was definitely off limits.

The Prumbins used the wet corridors to circulate their internal supply of seawater between suites, just as they used the dry ones to recirculate air. My surface absorbed chemical information from the current flowing through my room, including some complex proteins that I identified as excess pheromones from someone else's moment of joy. But I couldn't sense Paul as anything but a source of heat below me.

It would be wise if he wasn't right below. In fact, it would be entirely more sensible if the Human took shelter inside his air lock before I tried penetrating the clearfoil. *Why*, I thought with some aggravation, *did I always think of such things after losing the ability to speak?* My com attachments were floating about somewhere in my room. I'd have to reglue them when I returned to my Oieta-self.

Enough delay, I could hear Ersh now. *You'll survive.* Mixs and Ansky had done this all the time. I drew upon their memories of the process and lost my apprehension in the wonder of it.

The clearfoil didn't live, as the Web defined life, but it listened. I concentrated on focusing my web-mass to a point, then extended that point to barely touch the clearfoil that made the floor. Other extensions of me went to the walls, to counter any tendency to float out of position. *Neutral buoyancy was highly overrated.* Then, I vibrated the point of me in contact with the floor, as had my web-kin.

No response. Before I could register disappointment or plan to try again, I felt a strangeness in the room around me. As if part of me understood before the rest, my point was allowed through the clearfoil.

Instantly, I could taste the air in Paul's room, and sense his accelerated breathing in the carbon dioxide against my surface. *Perhaps*, I thought, *he wasn't sure if the blue pouring from his ceiling was me or the beginning of a flood.*

The blue was me, of course, or rather a tube made of me. Having "talked" my way through the clearfoil, I was using the narrow space to funnel most of my mass through. It was a race as the portion of my outer surface in contact with the clearfoil had already been assimilated into more of it; that change was spreading like a stain.

Ersh, it was fast! While this was no time to be thinking, I understood now why this experience would have been dangerous for a younger Esen. This me could ignore the horror of sacrificing web-mass, having survived worse, and I'd made sure the outer rim of me contained no memories to lose. In a final effort, my insides surged through the tube and plopped onto Paul's bed, abandoning the smallest amount of me possible.

I cycled quickly enough to see what appeared to be a lumpy blue patch in the clearfoil give up its identity and become clear itself.

"I may leave through the door," I said, feeling somewhat subdued.

My Human didn't give me time to say more than that, pulling me off his bed into one of those too-tight and anatomically-inconvenient hugs he appeared to find necessary after a long separation. *Perhaps this one was more necessary than others*, I thought, disturbed to feel him shake. Rather than squirming free, which I usually did, I patted him a couple of times on the back.

The shaking abruptly grew worse, as if my gesture had harmed him. "Are you ill?" I demanded, pushing him away so I could see his dear face.

Paul's eyes were spilling liquid. Some had landed on my fur, but I decided not to complain until he was calmer. Instead, I used my paws on his shoulders to guide him to one of the two oversized couches in the room, pushing him into its softness before crouching in front.

My Human ignored the moisture on his face. His mouth worked for a moment without words coming out, then he said in a very odd voice: "I'll be all right, Es. Give me a minute." He ran one trembling hand along my damp shoulder and down my arm, as if he'd forgotten this shape of me. I held myself steady, not understanding anything but that I'd somehow caused him pain by appearing like this.

"I'm sorry—" I started to say, a whine under the words.

"None of it is your fault. None of it." His hand went to my shoulder again, stroked downward. It trembled less, I thought, which was just as well since I was beginning to shake with the urge to leap up and run. He felt it and stopped, bringing his hand back into his lap, then said, more quietly, but with no less anguish: "Forgive me, Esen. I didn't realize how alone I've felt since leaving Minas XII. Touch is—a Human need."

I lunged up to give his cheek a quick lick, tasting salt and Paul, then sat at his feet. I rested my chin on his hand so I could see his expressions. He wasn't asking me to become Human, but to understand Human. *It was never easy*, I sighed to myself, and resolutely prepared to try. "You are upset," I said carefully. "Why? Is it still your anger at what happened or are you grieving for what has been lost? You told me you were prepared for anything, that you could walk away from your life on Minas XII as easily as you did your life on your ship."

"I did, didn't I?" His eyelids closed tightly, squeezing free a runnel of new moisture. When they opened again, I whined at the bleak look in his eyes. "Then consider it poetic justice, Old Blob, that I finally know, here—" for some reason he put his hand over his heart, "—how you must have felt all this time. Must still feel. To be the only one of your kind. To be so terribly alone—"

"I am not alone. You are not alone. You are of the Web of Esen," I protested, quite alarmed by all this. "We are one."

Paul lifted the pendant in his hand, my gift to him of web-mass, cryo-preserved. I could have sensed its life, this close, had I remained in web-form. "We are friends, dear friends," he said, as if correcting me. "Family."

Confused, I wrinkled my snout at him. "The meanings are compatible. Aren't they?"

He opened his mouth as though to say something, then hesitated. His eyes no longer leaked. "Of course they are," he said very gently.

"And you are my web-kin," I said, wanting some things very clear.

The hint of a smile. "Web-kin, indeed. As you are my family."

Though it was a gesture foreign to a body that preferred the camaraderie of a good bump at hip and shoulder, or the friendly chewing of an ear, I put my paws over Paul's hands for a moment. "We are safe here. We have friends still. Rudy. Once we learn who is behind this, we will find a way to be safe everywhere. I—"

Paul tilted his head when I paused. "I'm enjoying this list of yours. What's next?"

"I want dessert," I stated. "I just noticed this form hasn't eaten."

I didn't want to tell him the truth, not with the sadness still haunting his eyes, for me, for himself. I was no longer as Young as I'd been.

I understood what Paul hadn't said and why.

A future, even safety, could never replace what—who— we'd both lost.

Otherwhere

"SACRISS XIII, it is."

Rudy picked up the Kraal blade, turning it over and over in his strong, scarred hands. Sybil had given him this token, plus a pouchful of data cubes containing bureaucratic mundania: shipping records, genealogies, tax rolls, property transfers, military records. As the names had been replaced with codes, the former patroller did wonder how she expected him to ferret out her traitor. Especially with only these clues.

He'd scanned much of it, his attention caught by two items that likely didn't tell him anything about Sybil's target, but did reveal more about the Kraal. First had been a newsmag report describing a fabulous find: a household's-worth of artifacts, hundreds of years old, recovered from an Ervickian warehouse on Dranaris, several months ago, presumably without the new owner's approval. The artifacts would remain in a communal vault while the varied claimants sorted out ownership. From what Rudy knew of the Kraal and their obsession with family history, that translated as a flood of attempted thefts and assassinations, probably enough to lock entire Tribes in bitter and violent dispute for another few generations, and possibly sufficient to redefine affiliations—the equivalent of toppling governments. *Some treasures*, he thought, *were better left unfound.*

More telling were the criminal records: remarkably

few for a Human culture, unless Sybil had been selective. Rudy didn't think so. To his understanding, very little was illegal among Kraal. However, what was tended to be punishable by loss of life or, what was essentially the same, loss of affiliation. Without affiliation, an individual became a legitimate target for any and all Kraal, whether the intent was theft or simply to test the potency of a new weapon before buying it. Without affiliation, that individual's family lost status with every day of his or her continued existence, making suicide the preferred means of removing such contamination from the family line.

Which meant the Kraal living on Minas XII, Meonyro, either retained his affiliations despite the effort to remove his tattoos, or was not only a lawbreaker, but a dishonorable one. *Interesting.* Rudy tapped the knife blade against the scorched data cube in front of him, included with the others now that he was safely on his own. Having spent a considerable portion of his adult life pretending to be what he was not, Rudy was willing to gamble the Kraal could be as well. *A spy within arm's reach of Paul and Esen.*

The knife began to shake in his hand. Rudy carefully put it aside, as carefully as he put aside any emotion that might distract him. The weapon had been sealed against contamination when he received it. He'd already extracted fingerprints, protein and heat signatures, and DNA. There'd even been a trace of dried blood on the tip.

Before being sealed, the knife had been handled by only one individual: a Human female, presumably Kraal, approximately middle-aged, give or take a decade. No genetic disorders or diseases detected, so his comp had generated an image based on optimum health. Tall, long-boned, strong featured. If athletic, the musculature would be rope-thin and wiry rather than tend to bulk. Thin lips. Eyes wide-set and slanted slightly upward under a high brow, their irises so dark a blue as to appear black. The type of eyes that saw distance and kept secrets. Pale blond, fair-skinned— relatively rare traits, the easiest to alter.

Rudy had memorized the face and form, then erased all data from his system. The image wouldn't be enough to identify her, not if she'd made any effort to change her appearance, not if her life had taken a different path. He could imagine a hundred ways that same face could alter over time. The tattooing of a Kraal was only one.

Why hadn't Sybil simply told him her enemy's name, since she obviously knew it? Why hire him to find her, instead of using her own guards?

Rudy picked up the scorched cube. He didn't believe in coincidence.

It was time to talk to Michael Cristoffen.

And he wasn't at all surprised that the supposedly confidential flight itinerary for the Commonwealth Research Ship *Russell III* was one of Sybil's "gifts."

17: Happy House Afternoon

I STRETCHED my tongue to its utmost, reaching almost to the outer corner of my left eye, and was rewarded with what had to be the last speck of syrup on my muzzle. What that said about my eating habits, I didn't want to know. But once the syrup was removed from my fur—a tasty bit of grooming—I looked at the remaining tower of dessert and sagged back in my chair, admitting defeat. "There is something to be said for intermittent meals," I told my companion, who'd given up some time earlier in favor of watching me attempt to conquer our plate. *Mind you, he'd had lunch.*

"I was thinking there was something to be said for never being hungry," Paul said, glancing meaningfully at the ceiling.

I shuddered. "And miss chocolate?"

"You have me there." A long, comfortable pause. "That was quite the brownie."

We spent a reverent moment contemplating the remains, our spoons sticking upright from the topmost layer as if we'd planted flags. Or, more accurately, climbing poles. "Do you think they always make it that size?" I asked at last. "Or was this an aberration?"

Paul gave a short laugh. "I dare you to order another one tomorrow."

Tomorrow. The word was a thief, stealing the ease of the moment. My ears drooped for all I tried to keep them up. Yet, I had to think about the future, make plans to keep our Web safe. . . .

"We have to make plans, Es."

I should have known Paul would be thinking the same. "Ansky—Anienka—made provision for any web-kin who might stay here," I assured him. "I used her code to check in. It lets us stay indefinitely without questions, buries information about our being here so it can't be accessed even by staff. Our room service is paid through a series of blind, unrelated accounts. We're safe here."

My Human was shaking his head before I'd finished, a lock of hair tumbling into his eyes that he raked back impatiently. "Doesn't matter. We have to go."

"No—" I started to object, then read something in his face that changed it to: "Why?" If there was a hint of a whine beneath, he did me the courtesy of ignoring it.

"Wendy told me she had to leave tomorrow because it would be the last regularly scheduled Busfish to the surface. After that, there are only emergency and supply runs for three weeks. We'll be trapped here."

I didn't need to search my memory for the Prumbin calendar. "Hops Fest," I nodded, dropping my lower jaw in a satisfied grin. "There won't be any new arrivals either."

He gave me that look. "You knew?"

Given his reaction, this seemed one of those questions unlikely to have a right answer. I closed my jaw and gazed back at him in silence.

Paul gently pushed the table aside, then moved his chair so close to mine I could easily have licked his ear—or bitten his nose. "Esen," he began in a low voice, "I know you are upset—that your instincts tell you we must hide. But unless we can get access to a secure translight com down here, we have to leave. It's very—" He suddenly broke off and stared at me. "There isn't one, is there? That's why you picked Prumbinat and dropped us at the bottom of its ocean."

"Why would I do that?" I said, trying and likely failing to keep my tone light. *Was it my fault that the Prumbins had very firm ideas about how one interacted with their para-*

dise? And one of those was that all communications must be part of a physical pilgrimage in the mouth of a fish?

"You'd do it to keep me from contacting any of the Group. But I don't understand. Don't you see? We have to warn them—"

"Why?" I snapped.

"They could be in danger—"

My lips curled back from my teeth in threat, but not at Paul. "Or they could be the danger!"

"Ah." Instead of looking angry, Paul pursed his lips and eyed me thoughtfully. Finally, he said: "We need to know, don't we?"

I fought the urge to leap up and pace—the Lanivarian response to stress being an often inconvenient urge to chase down prey—by pressing one foot over the tip of my tail. *Hard.* "How? Scour their communications and credit ratings? Trace their movements? Find out who they've met? We've lost the comps and library. Where would we start?"

Counted against the loss of home and family, our hidden machines and their capabilities hadn't seemed to matter until now. But I had no doubt why our home and warehouse had been targets, but not our office. Our assailants understood as well as any web-being the value of stored information. *They were welcome to whatever they found,* I thought, wrinkling my snout. Paul had installed devices to melt the interior of every comp and auxiliary, including data storage, in the event of any flesh but ours entering that secret room, or any voices but ours entering the codes. I'd worried at first if even this would be sufficient protection, in part because he'd bought the equipment for this destruction from Diale the impolite and never-trusted-by-Esen tech dealer. But Paul had reassured me: he'd had Rudy add his own touches during one of his infrequent visits.

So if anyone had found our secret room, it would be empty of all but hollow cases and barren shelves. "We have no resources," I finished.

"That's not entirely true, Old Blob."

I gave him my own version of that look. "If you think I'll be spending the next hundred years or so dictating everything I remember from our files—" I knew Paul cared deeply about the data we'd collected over the past fifty years about other species, but there was a limit.

"Thank you, but that won't be necessary."

There were moments when I floundered in my efforts to understand my Human, and felt a deep frustration; there were others when I understood him completely, and felt exactly the same way. "You could have told me you made a copy," I growled, "and saved me worrying about your precious lost data—"

"You weren't exactly open to the idea, as I recall."

For what it was worth now, I could recite every word and nuance of our argument over whether it was safer to keep those revealing records in paw's reach or permit a duplicate set to exist beyond our control. *I'd thought I'd won it.*

"So I'm not always right." As his lips quirked at what was a grand understatement, I went on: "Where is it?"

"Well," Paul hesitated and had the grace to look a little uncomfortable. "There's more than one. And before you blow up—" interpreting my sudden and noisy panting correctly, "—the data's secure. I arranged for host systems, each twinned separately with ours on Minas XII so that every bit of information we received was archived by all. But only our system could access the data. Feel better? I can get another up and running, whichever one we choose, by sending a code via translight com. Then we can start hunting for a change."

I ignored how the word "hunting" lifted the hair along my spine and filled my mouth with saliva; Paul was shamelessly using my form's nature to divert me from a key point. "How many choices do we have, Paul? Where are they?"

I was right. My Human's face took on that guarded look, the one he used when considering the possible consequences of telling me something. "One hundred and ten."

"The Group." I decided to pace. *It was more civilized*

than biting. He watched me, not denying it, perhaps giving me time to think it through.

I knew his first motivation for sharing knowledge of my existence with these other Humans: Paul accepted his nature as an ephemeral being. He wanted to ensure I had companionship and help after he was gone. Care for such continuity mattered to Humans; I no longer tried to argue the point that I'd outlive them, too. His other motivation? To protect Humans from me or my kind. I never doubted Paul's friendship; I never doubted his species' loyalty. I would never betray either, but I knew, better than any of them, how dangerous my kind could be.

I could follow Paul's reasoning now, and lost the reflex to snarl. His friends were among those who added information to our system—and, because of their understanding, even I had to admit their information was superior to any other source. Who else could appreciate my real need for details on Dokecian art trends or Poptian slang, as well as reports of overdue starships along the Fringe?

Who else would appreciate Paul's need to preserve what he'd learned?

Even if Paul didn't share my compulsion to secrecy, he did share my fierce protectiveness of knowledge. In me, it was a treasuring of mass. I was, in a sense, what I knew. The knowledge Paul treasured was in those machines. I shouldn't be surprised he'd found a way to protect it.

Or that he'd find a way to turn that to our advantage.

"How—no, that doesn't matter." I sank back down on my haunches, pretending I didn't see the relief on his face. "Although please tell me Timri's isn't on Kearn's ship."

Paul raised one brow. "I said one hundred and ten. Timri doesn't have one in her care. It seemed wise to have a system outside the Group. So Rudy has one."

Somehow, I didn't laugh. Poor Rudy, beset with secrets from both of us. *He must wonder if we ever told each other the truth.* "Knowing your cousin, I don't want to know where he put it," I said, glad my Lanivarian face was less readable than the Human version.

"Ah, but you have to know this, Droolycheeks." Paul tapped me lightly on the muzzle, as if claiming my full attention. "A signal from either of us will erase the data from any or all the systems. I'll give you the code. And they'll self-destruct if no data is accessed in a year."

The tip of my tail thumped on the carpet. "Use them or lose them." *My clever Human.*

"I try."

"So we have one hundred and ten duplicate machines, waiting to help us make sense of the universe. Not a coincidence, is it, that those machines are the best way for us to find out if their owners betrayed us?" I considered the concept and wrinkled my snout. "I do believe even Skalet would have approved. You are a devious being, Human."

"Me?" The flash of a grin. "Just trying to be ready for anything, although you do make that difficult, Old Blob. Life with you is—well, it's never dull."

"And I suppose you'd prefer boring and predictable?" I teased, then regretted the words immediately.

Paul merely lifted his hand and measured a small distance with his finger and thumb. "I could use a smidge," he confessed.

I pretended I'd found room for more of the brownie. "I'll see what I can do," I promised my first friend, doing my best to force down the mouthful I truly hadn't needed. "We'll rest here for a few weeks, then surface and get to a translight com. You can start investigating—"

Paul reached over and ruffled the hair behind my right ear. "Web-thinking," he said in a light voice, but his gray eyes were serious. "Ephemeral trails grow cold much faster, Esen. We act more quickly, too. Days may count, if we need to be warning those in danger. I don't think either of us wants safety at the expense of others."

Well, I thought morosely, *one of us might give it serious consideration.* "Tomorrow, then." I leaned into his hand as he switched to my left ear. "As long as all this isn't just to spend more time with that female. You did say she'll be taking that Busfish. I," I reminded him virtuously, "have a perfect memory."

Paul grinned. "Unnecessary. We're meeting for supper—hey, don't bite!"

As I'd only sat up quickly, with my mouth firmly closed, I thought this admonishment uncalled for and didn't dignify it with a response.

Otherwhere

THE trouble with being a law-abiding, peaceful species was the difficulty convincing others of your intention to act in a lawless and forceful manner.

The Tumblers sent what they considered an intimidating ultimatum to all flesh-burdened aliens on their world, stating, in no uncertain terms and three hundred pages of comscript, that "the climactic moment of departure will echo in a pleasing and memorable harmony for which all Tumblers shall be forever grateful."

Most aliens filed it under religious dogma, though there was some amused debate about rocks and sexual cycles among the Ervickians. A trio of Human traders, having overheard this debate—being at the same bar and, while not as affected by juice, definitely not tracking on all channels—paid for translight transmission of the ultimatum to several pharmaceutical companies, hoping to be first to corner the market for gem dust aphrodisiacs.

Frustrated, the Tumblers sent a delegation of Elders to chime in ominous and telling discord around the shipcity.

There was an undignified rush of the flesh-burdened from their ships to follow the delegation and collect their ritual leavings, followed by notes professing gratitude and hoping for a similar delegation every day.

The unauthorized throwing of ritual leavings at the flesh-burdened by younger Tumblers only produced more messages of goodwill and happiness. There was also a flood of outgoing coded messages similar in tone to that from a Largas freighter captain, exhorting friends and relatives to hurry and join the rush. As a result, not only did every ship remain, but more arrived every day.

Distraught, the Tumblers leaned to necessity and decided to do what so many misunderstood and distressed species had done before them: fight fire with fire.

Or, in this case, call for Ganthor.

18: Restaurant Night; Happy House Night

I WASN'T behaving well.

It hadn't required the memory of Ersh's disapproval or of Paul's reproachful gray eyes from similar occasions to make me aware. This time, I knew my transgression well beforehand.

And didn't care.

Sculling more with my left set of swimmerets than my right aimed me at a pair of suited Prumbins. By their substantial waistlines, these were permanent residents enjoying a well-planned and vigorous retirement. They probably never used the dry corridors, where they'd have to attempt to walk for themselves, and stayed in the pond-style suites where they could float without need of suits. I spared a moment to wonder if elderly Prumbins ever missed the sun, or if it was such a relief to be able to move they were willing to pay that price.

The issue of cost was something on my mind a great deal lately. The cost of friendship; the cost of trust. *What was it about this female that made Paul willing to risk such things again?*

It wasn't attraction. Not that my Human was immune to seduction, but he was too wise to fall into that particular trap. I'd learned that to my chagrin when I'd tried to "help" him resist the infamous Janet Chase.

No, Paul sought this Wendy Cheatham's company—or allowed her to seek his—in order to learn something.

Which meant I needed to learn it, too.

The Prumbins moved more slowly than I'd have liked, but their bulk provided admirable cover as the current swept us all closer to the restaurant where Paul and this female were dining. There was nothing more I could do to disguise myself. I'd looked for other Oietae, hoping to avoid Paul's notice in a crowd, but so far I'd found only mating groups uninterested in anyone Too-Young. Plus, form-memory had reproduced the Greeter's address on my shell in demeaning detail. I might as well carry a sign saying: Runaway Child—take me home!

I wanted home. Home was my web-kin, or as close as I could possibly get to Paul without being caught.

I was, I feared, *acting precisely my age.*

I sculled faster to keep up as my Prumbins began to hurry, perhaps sensing they were close to a source of more mass to accumulate. It didn't help me escape my conscience, but I was used to ignoring it.

No matter where you were, restaurants for airbreathers seemed to contain plant growth as well as pillars or archways. I remained uncertain how the combination helped the digestion of anything but a herbivore fearing aerial predation, but was grateful this one followed tradition, since I hoped either pillar or plant might hide one small Oieta from view. It was a new section of the Happy House; the Grub Grotto wasn't a name Ansky would have chosen for a dining area—another indication, had I needed it, that this restaurant had been added by its Prumbin caretakers after my birth-mother had died as an Artican.

Skalet had judged Ansky's death proof of the folly of interacting with ephemerals, and had dared threaten Paul. *The only argument I'd ever won with my web-kin had to be moments before her own death.* Yet, I thought, because of Paul, I alone had survived.

Despite its pragmatic Prumbin name, the Grub Grotto deserved its billing as the most sophisticated and elegant dining establishment along the Brim. Its ceiling was deeply concave; the floor bubbled up in the center as if eager to meet it. Both were clearfoil, opaqued only where tables and chairs ringed the floor—presumably so those seated could find their napkins when they dropped. *Mine always did.* The plunging sides of the fissure beneath the restaurant were bathed in gentle ultraviolet light, so diners could gaze down at the luminescent wildlife of the Abyss as it dined as well. Few bothered, because by looking up at the ceiling one could gaze into an area where brilliantly orange- and-black Oietae were, well, not dining.

From the wet corridor that circled the restaurant and led to its several air locks, I could see very well for myself that they weren't dining—not one of what could be over a hundred individuals, depending on when you looked.

Technically, they were eating. I ate with every pulse of water directed past my mandibles. *What else could you expect from filter-feeders?* These Oietae, however, also were busily engaged in the most sensual aquatic ballet imaginable. I'd have turned orange myself just from watching, if I hadn't had other things on my mind. As it was, I stared long enough to lose my Prumbin escort and had to swim furiously to catch up to a sled of luggage being towed by an attendant.

There! I did my best to stop quickly, which isn't easy when you are in a current to start with and that current is filled with other beings using it to move around you as quickly as possible.

Paul and his companion weren't hard to spot. Both were tall and, I had to admit, admirable specimens for their species. They were also the only Humans in the Grub Grotto, something, I also had to admit, that made the task of finding them easier.

As I'd hoped, their table was partially and conveniently screened from the wet corridor by a fystia bush—a specimen with a highly unlikely number of blossoms. I supposed the Prumbins tied on extra blooms so their deep, dark paradise gave visitors the requisite aura of plenty. Still, the plant was more than large enough to hide one Oieta—given I could reach it without being noticed, and resist the current in order to keep in place once I did.

The luggage sled served the first task admirably, although the Prumbin towing it had begun to look over its shoulder at me as if growing worried about my intentions.

It might have worried more, had it realized what I was doing while alongside.

I'd found very few advantages to being young in form, while mature in mind. Put another way, few forms allowed me to interact with other adults as the adult I was. *Or would be soon,* I added, inclined to self-honesty. Rarest of all was a form where being young was to my advantage, as now.

Newly-hatched Oietae were sessile creatures, staying glued to their original kin cluster for several molts. Old Oietae retired to this peaceful lifestyle, although they then had to suffer the attachment and attitude of every new generation until calcification. I was young enough to have the remnants of my holdfast under my second-to-last segment. By scraping away the accumulated keratin, which I managed to do while swimming with the luggage—*multiple limbs came in handy*—I was able to expose some of its sticky surface.

Ready, I waited until the current brought luggage, sled, Prumbin, and me opposite the fystia bush, then launched myself at the clearfoil between us, bottom-first.

There were times I knew the Cosmic Gods paid profound attention to me.

It did work. The current tugged at me, but I was firmly glued to the clearfoil and not going anywhere.

Unfortunately, I'd missed the bush entirely and was now glued, head down, mid-limbs widespread, and antennae flailing, ocular-to-eyeball with Paul.

I didn't think being as green as the bush was going to help.

*   *   *

The Prumbins had, eventually and painfully, managed to scrape my nether end off the outside wall of their restaurant. Naturally, they'd ignored everything I said and proceeded to escort me to the office of Greeter Neram Marenelli Holdswisely, since her stamp showed so marvelously well against the glowing green of my humiliation.

Paul and his companion had been given another table. The only reaction from my Human had been to cover his mouth with one hand, quickly. I presumed he'd stifled a laugh; I didn't expect to find him still amused when I returned to our suite.

The Greeter hadn't been amused at all. She'd flared a solid crimson as the Prumbins had explained the situation and apparently intended to remain that color for the rest of the night. In its way, the red was every bit as intimidating as one of Ersh's famed silences while deciding what to do with me.

At least the water let me dump heat without any problems, though I had to be careful to stay down current from the Greeter. As this was only polite, given the situation, I felt in no danger of being exposed as anything but an utter disgrace to the Oietae species.

"If you were that interested in watching others mate," Greeter Holdswisely said, for the seventh time, "you could have gone to the upper level and joined the other aquatics in the wet half of the restaurant, sparing us this embarrassment."

"Yes, Greeter." I found it amusing the Oieta hadn't considered for a moment that I might have been more interested in watching a pair of air-breathers, mating or otherwise, but kept the reaction to myself. *It never paid to show you were entertained by those scolding you, especially if the scolding was for your own good.*

"However," she continued furiously, "such interest is completely unseemly in the Too-Young. You should still be attached to your cluster!"

"Yes, Greeter."

"You know what this means, I trust?"

I couldn't help a little blue of curiosity. *Finally, something new.* "What does it mean?"

Her red sides flushed with the purple of authority. "You will be sent home on the next Busfish. Fortunately, there is one leaving tomorrow. Your Soft Companion has been notified, in case you think you can avoid this penalty."

This didn't have quite the impact it might have had, given Paul would doubtless be satisfied with that decision.

"Yes, Greeter," I said dutifully, turning myself a doleful beige.

I managed to elude the Prumbin assigned to return me to my room by the simple, if impolite, strategy of swimming just fast enough to make keeping up with me a significant effort. It had finally waved me on in disgust, veering away into the current of the next wet corridor. Doubtless another green smudge on my record—not that it mattered, now that I was being expelled from the Happy House.

Which, I thought with a twinge of irreverent pride, *could be a first.* Certainly Ansky had accepted a broad range of questionable behavior from her guests, so long as no one else was damaged. Paul might not approve of my achievement; Rudy would. I'd noticed the younger Human possessed a more liberal view of what was acceptable.

I let myself into my room and looked down for Paul in his, only to discover what I considered completely unacceptable.

He wasn't alone.

The Human female, Wendy Cheatham, was sitting on the black syntha-hide couch, legs outstretched and crossed at the ankles. Her footwear was on the floor. My arrival coincided with her tossing her head back in a laugh at something Paul had said. He was on the other couch, sitting forward, eyes intent on his guest.

Only for an instant. Those eyes shifted upward, as though

he had the ability to sense when I was nearby. *Ersh had had the same uncomfortable gift.*

I worked so hard to keep from turning green again that I ended up a disgusting mottled brown with pink streaks, all the while scooting backward until I reached the force mesh defining the topmost bubble of my suite. There I stayed, appendages dangling.

My effort to become inconspicuous wasn't a success. I couldn't opaque the floor and Paul had stood to stare up at me. *But I could,* I decided, *refuse to move.*

"Esippet, were you hurt?" His question, warm with concern, didn't help. I went completely green.

"Don't embarrass the child," Wendy chided, coming to stand beside Paul but looking at him, rather than at me. "I'm sure it's nothing time won't heal."

Paul didn't appear convinced, so I flailed my limbs at him as proof all of Esippet Darnelli Swashbuckly was present and accounted for, managing to add a wan: "I'll be fine." *In about a hundred years,* I added to myself glumly. Or as soon as he removed our unwelcome guest.

We thought alike. My Human turned to her with that regretful smile I'd heard had made more than a few staff members of Cameron & Ki feel faint. "I'm afraid our evening's come to an end, Wendy," he began graciously. "Thank you for your company."

She placed one hand on Paul's chest, the other reaching playfully for the silver pendant he wore. "Are you quite sure?" she asked, running the chain through her fingers.

This was completely inappropriate behavior, I fumed to myself. Well, it actually wasn't, considering our location and the graphic paintings of physical encounters on the walls—not to mention the abundance of floor space—but my muddy brown began to assume a significantly rosy hue as I let myself sink downward.

Paul ran a finger along the braids tumbling past her cheek and shook his head. "Quite sure," he told her in that low, gentle voice that probably made such females rethink their plans for the future. "I'm sorry."

"In that case—" Wendy wrapped her hand around the pendant and ripped it free, stepping back in the same smooth motion. I flared pure red in shock and outrage.

Paul reached after it, then stopped short, holding himself so still I could barely see the movement of his chest as he breathed. "What do you want?"

Instead of answering, Wendy put two fingers inside her mouth and drew out a small black oval, like a seed. She flicked it aside, then held up the slender fist holding the pendant. "What I want . . . I have," she told him in a new voice, a new voice that was an old voice, a voice like the rich velvet used to polish a blade.

A dead voice.

I pressed myself to the floor between us, turning white even as Paul named the impossible without hesitation.

"Skalet."

Otherwhere

ON entering the Sacriss System, with its fifteen inhabited planets and busy intrasolar traffic, one had the impression of a highly technological culture. Negotiating with the various levels of authority, from the ubiquitous Port Jellies to local jurisdictions that were in many instances one building in size, gave the impression of dealing with an insanely bureaucratic one. Walking around the subequatorial Port City of Nastarsila, on Sacriss XIII, Rudy decided, was the fastest way to learn both were wrong.

This place had never experienced technology or organized government.

Rudy wiped sweat from his forehead and neck, tucking the already soggy cloth into a handy pocket, and consulted the city map. Nastarsila, like every Sacrissee city, was a maze of tiled walls peppered with tiny round windows and archways of various sizes. You could glimpse the buildings behind the walls only if you stood before the correct arch, at the correct time of day. There were no signs or streetlights; no aircars or ground vehicles competed with foot traffic and grav carts. If Rudy closed his eyes, the sweet tang to the air reminded him of standing outside a stable, early in the morning, after fresh straw and hay had been laid in every stall.

If he opened them, and looked behind, he'd see the spires of the starships forming the shipcity that sprawled, wall-less, noisy, and changeable, outside the city gates. The *Russell III* was one of them. He'd avoided the temptation to take a look at his former command. Time for that later, when he found a way to get on board.

The ancestral Sacrissee had been cautious, solitary herbivores, low-built and slender, to better lurk in the safety of dense underbrush; with huge eyes and ears, to detect any potential threat before coming out to graze; swift and agile, in case both eyes and ears failed. They'd maintained exclusive territories, except during the rut, marking boundaries with a variety of bodily excretions and rebuffing intruders of their own kind with a whiplike tail capable of cracking ribs.

As Esen was fond of saying, Rudy remembered, the evolution of sentience changed the world more than the species. *For better or worse.* The modern version of the Sacrissee remained cautious and solitary, attractive to Human sensibilities, and tended to rebuff visitors—usually without recourse to their still-dangerous tails, but not always. Sacriss XIII wasn't the biological home of the species—that honor belonged to Sacriss VII—but its inhabitants had carved it into a copy distinguished from that home only by the shape of its land masses and the length of its calendar.

The Sacrissee had found a way to compromise between an economy that required an increasing population and a biology that demanded isolation. Evidence from early civilizations suggested individual Sacrissee had surrounded their crops and lairs with walls of brush and thorn, keeping the walls well-marked with fluids. To save effort and materials, walls were shared by adjacent individuals. Over time, these villages developed into cities as densely populated as any D'Dsellan hive, structured so the inhabitants could live almost entirely—and happily—as hermits.

Rudy consulted his map again, then counted the

number of archways he'd passed since turning onto this street. *Should be the place,* he decided, stepping into the shadow of a generously-sized arch on the opposite side. Cooler, out of the sun, but not empty. The rapid scurrying of feet, along with a Sacrissee "hufff" of displeasure, meant he'd disturbed a resident—likely one taking a peek at the outside world before deciding to risk a venture to the market.

Cluttered along both sides with crates and barrels, the archway penetrated a wall several meters thick, itself hollowed into more dwellings. Servants, artisans, and shopkeepers lived within the walls themselves, occasionally renting rooms to offworlders. If he squinted, Rudy could make out the building protected by the wall, but it was difficult to see details. At this time of day, the sun reflected a fierce abstract rainbow from the building's tiled surface. The Sacrissee would have peepholes everywhere possible to be able to admire the mosaic without having to admire one another.

There were peepholes lining the archway as well, their darkness glinting with shy, curious eyes. Rudy considerately avoided looking directly into any as he made himself comfortable on a barrel. *It shouldn't be long now.*

Naturally, it was longer than Rudy'd hoped before his quarry appeared. He eased himself from the barrel, sure the manufacturer's symbol was now a permanent imprint, as Michael Cristoffen walked into view. Rudy stepped closer to the archway opening, not making a sound. In spite of his care, peepholes cleared of their occupants with a series of breathless "hufff, hufffs."

The cobblestone was a warm gold where the late afternoon sunlight brushed it. Elsewhere, shadows surrounded archways like tongues licking after scraps. When they filled the roadway, Sacrissee would start to emerge from their homes. They'd slip by taller, more social aliens with anxious little "hufff, huffs," more like desperately preoccupied accountants than ghosts, despite moving like spirits. Sometimes all one really saw was a length of tail lying outside a dark archway, where its owner had paused to look over its shoulder and forgotten part of its anatomy remained in view.

Once in a while, a rude—or curious—offworlder would catch a local in a beam of light. The Sacrissee, creamy fur dappled across shoulders and back with leaflike brown, would crouch in the glare, huge slit pupils constricting, long fingers stroking dark trails of fluid from the glands lining arms and neck as if its assailant could smell its outrage as other than a pleasant mint. The tail would twitch along its length, though the gentle Sacrissee were patient with offworlders as a rule. It took a too-close approach by one of their own to send tails lashing outward, the bones of the tip thickened to withstand the resulting force. There were nicks shoulder-high in wall tiles along the street, the marks of carefully timed but daunting near-misses.

Most considered the species harmless; some enjoyed doing business with partners who loathed meetings. But Cristoffen flinched as a Sacrissee ran past, seeking the anonymity of the next shadow.

Or was he afraid of something else?

The archway filled with another round of "hufff, huffs."

Something—someone—behind him.

Rudy shook the blister stick down from its holster into his palm, feeling its eager vibration as he wheeled around. Even as his eyes sought a target, his other hand reached for the barrel beside him, ready to fling it in the path of a pursuer.

Then he stopped moving, which seemed the safest course of action when staring down the glittering edge of a very low-tech knife, its point pressed to his throat.

Eyes reappeared in peepholes. The eyes regarding

him over the knife were equally dark and liquid, if set into a Human face. *A familiar one.* Rudy didn't quite relax, but he did venture an opinion. "There are other ways to say hello, Timri."

Unsmiling, the *Russell III's* comp-tech sheathed her knife and pulled him deeper into the archway. The Sacrissee "hufff, hufffed" and disappeared again. "Be grateful I waited to see a face first. What are you doing here, Rudy?"

Rudy tucked away his now-quiet blister stick, a non-lethal, intimidating, and thoroughly nasty weapon, usually favored by thieves. He preferred it to those which left gaping wounds; he wasn't surprised to find Timri felt the opposite. "I'm here because he's here. Your busy Mr. Cristoffen." *No point denying the obvious.*

"So you know."

"Know what? That he believes every word of Kearn's blather—or that Cristoffen is playing fast and loose with the Kraal?"

Timri shut her eyes briefly, as though holding in some emotion. "Both—and worse, much worse, Rudy. Thank goodness you've come," she told him. "I didn't know where to turn once I learned Cristoffen's hunting us—Paul's and Esen's friends. He's . . . he's killed one already." Her words began spurting out, faster and faster, like blood from an artery. "I overheard him bragging to Kearn. He has a list, Rudy. Not of all of us. My name's not on it—not yet. But it's only a matter of time before he tracks us down. I don't know if Paul's getting my messages—he hasn't answered. I don't dare—"

"These walls have ears, Timri," he cautioned her, now thoroughly alarmed. Of all the people who might panic, he would never have picked Timri, who'd successfully spied on Kearn for fifty years, sabotaging his search for Esen from the beginning—sabotaging Rudy's own, until he'd confronted her with evidence of her tampering. Other than Paul and Esen, she was the only one who knew Rudy shared their secret. If anything, Rudy would have thought her more likely to simply slit Cristoffen's throat. *Then again, with Kraal involved, that might not be enough.*

"You're right, of course. I'm sorry." She took a deep steadying breath, then looked past him at the street. He heard a frown in the change of her voice. "He's gone inside. I've been following him from the shipcity. How did you know to wait for him here? What is that place?"

"Trust me, our Michael will be in there a while. I'll tell you why later. It's more important that I get a look inside the *Russ'* before he gets back. Let's go." Rudy waved his hand. The ensuing "hufff, hufffs" as their fascinated audience withdrew again made his point.

As they left, Rudy glanced at the archway Cristoffen had taken. Its Sacrissee peepholes had been filled with plaster, doubtless annoying the locals. Within the arch, a pair of Human-shaped figures stood watching the street. He couldn't see the building they were guarding, but he didn't need to—he knew quite well what it was.

A Kraal weapons' dealer ran a legitimate business, at least on Sacriss XIII, albeit not one you'd want next door. This address, and Cristoffen's newly-made appointment, had been among Sybil's "gifts."

On the way here, Rudy had made inquiries of his own. This particular dealer was of the sort the Kraal referred to as exclusive, specializing in fulfilling unusual requirements. They were rumored to offer experimental tech for sale, if you were among those desperate enough to play with untested means of dealing death.

Kearn had used such technology against Esen.

As Rudy walked beside Timri, he kept a smile on his face and made meaningless conversation about the local sights. Inside, his thoughts grew darker and darker, until he wished he'd brought something more permanent than blister sticks.

The pieces were coming together, thanks to Sybil's search for her traitor. The result wasn't pretty, but had the feel of truth.

Kearn, bringing his ship here so his protégé could visit a Kraal contact—a contact capable of supplying more than an assassin shield. Kearn, already prepping the *Russell III* for the hop to Picco's Moon, where another of Paul's Group could be a target. Kearn, who'd once come perilously close to believing Paul Cameron to be Paul Ragem, and Esolesy-ki to be Esen-alit-Quar.

Paul and Esen, on the run, *betrayed by Kearn?*

"Slow down," Timri hissed. "You look as though someone's chasing you."

Startled, Rudy obeyed so abruptly he collided with the Sacrissee trying to sneak around him. The smaller being let out a shrill "Sssshuppptt!" that was taken up by what sounded like every other of its kind in the city, even as the creature ran up Rudy's back and leaped off into the safety of the crowd.

"You're not very good at being inconspicuous, are you?" his companion said, smiling until she caught a glimpse of his face.

"Tell me how our friend Lionel has been, Timri," Rudy said grimly.

Sybil's traitor would have to wait while he dealt with one of his own.

19: Abyss Night

ONE word rewrote the universe—and the last fifty years I'd spent in it.

Skalet?

"Stay as you are. Meet us in my rooms," she ordered me, those wrong green eyes never leaving Paul, only the voice as I remembered. *It wasn't her.*

The floor became opaque, cutting me off.

Was it?

I scooted backward to the door with every bit of speed in this form, not daring to cycle, not daring to delay.

Skalet?

I tasted her memories, filled with misdirection, distraction, and disguise, her love of games and strategy, her lack of conscience. She'd hidden from me; now she showed herself. Why? Part of me feared for Paul's safety, for my own.

Part of me knew nothing but the flesh-deep need to rejoin the Web of Ersh—to share and assimilate what had been learned by each of us. *As if that would be pleasant.* There was no memory of mine I'd willingly give her; none of hers I'd want to know. It didn't take the exchange of web-mass to tell me who had been Kearn's mysterious Kraal backer—or who had destroyed our new lives.

Still. I longed to cycle to web-form, to satisfy the craving. To be myself again.

I feared that desire most of all.

*   *   *

The way wasn't in Skalet- or Ersh-memory. It lay within the giggles of Lesy-memory, the strangest web-kin of all. She'd liked secrets for the fun of discovering them, and found Skalet's seriousness on the subject the perfect excuse to play spy. I'd enjoyed assimilating her single-minded efforts to ruin Skalet's privacy, not that those had been the parts of Lesy-memory Ersh particularly wanted me to have. In her hunts, Lesy would find the most extraordinary vantage points; those, Ersh had deemed useful for me to know.

The looks on Skalet's various faces when Lesy uncovered her hiding places had been the bonus.

The Happy House hadn't been a challenge to a being of Lesy's exuberant determination. She'd happily spent months as a Jylnic, pretending to have been hired to adjust force mesh from the outside, all the while peering into each and every transparent bubble. Most of what she'd seen clearly demonstrated the hazards of being interrupted by a curious spectator during cross-species' sex, wet or dry.

But she'd found Skalet's lair in the underbelly of the fissure, a series of interconnected bubbles unlike the others, linked to the rest of the complex by only one set of corridors. Our web-kin had insisted on autonomy; Mixs had never argued with Skalet.

So, thanks to Lesy, I knew the way. Straight down, if I'd dared go outside, but I was well aware my tender Oieta-self would be no more than a tasty nibble for an assortment of less-educated Abyss dwellers. Inside was hardly safer. The Prumbin authorities expected Fem Swashbuckly to cooperate and remain in her room until leaving tomorrow. They would not be pleased to find me swimming through this series of agonizingly indirect corridors like a pheromone-crazed Jylnic. Busy, transparent corridors, at that.

Maybe everyone official would find their own emergency, somewhere distant. I did my utmost to avoid bumping into elderly beings and causing any such emergencies along my route, sculling around the slower floaters, unable to keep my integument from a desperate black and red. Any Oietae I passed flared a startled black in answer, then returned to their previous color, likely assuming I was fleeing a scolding from my elders.

Instead, I was swimming to one. I had time to think—between almost dislocating my swimmerets trying to gesture apology for those unavoidable near misses—time enough to realize Skalet had planned this, too. She would have been impatient with any juvenile outpouring of emotion, disdainful of either anger or joy as irrelevant to our Web. To her way of thinking, this journey gave me time to compose myself properly.

Ersh could have told her it wouldn't work. In fact, I was becoming less composed every minute.

Over to the junction, down to another corridor, follow that one to a sharp bend—too sharp, as a sled of luggage was being held by the current against the far wall, pinning a large, protesting Prumbin. I went up and over both. *It had been too long since I'd thought as Esen-alit-Quar*, I realized with despair. *Too long since I'd interacted with others of my kind.* I dredged up memory after memory even as I used my normally useless walking legs to propel me around the next corner, using the abdomen of a slower moving Human as a handy spring-off point. It had nothing to do with my formself's instinctive reaction to another of those shameful green suits. *Well, not much.*

Skalet and I had never shared similar thought patterns, but we'd been of the same Web. We'd shared more than thought; our mass, through Ersh, had been that of one being, serving the same purpose, obeying Ersh's Laws.

But now? I'd lived as a scaly Lishcyn, with a Human web-kin to teach me ephemeral ways.

Ersh was rock.

And I was quite sure Skalet no longer served Ersh's purpose or followed her Laws.

She had taken Paul.

I found I could swim a little faster.

*   *   *

Skalet's wet lock was standard fare, containing an emergency all-species' bag instead of a suit. I closed the outer door, thinking various dark things I didn't bother muttering out loud. Then I noticed the water was draining out of the wet lock faster than I could possibly slither my Oieta-self into the bag.

Skalet at her best, I said to myself, as if the impossible were true. I was forced to cycle well before the floor was dry. *She knew I hated wet fur.* I tucked my com attachments into a holder along one wall, determined to make my own decision on the form I'd wear next.

There was sufficient delay before the inner door opened for me to worry that she planned to flood the wet lock again, just for the fun of seeing what that form might be, considering I had little extra mass.

But I was spared further indignity as the door opened. I hopped out quickly, just in case.

I entered a room surely unique to the Happy House. Its walls were squared at the corners, every surface opaqued for privacy—as they'd probably been ever since Lesy peeked inside. Animal pelts from a dozen worlds fanned in a circle on the burnished stone floor, surrounding a table of the same substance, itself centered under a chandelier elaborate enough to have come from a battle cruiser. *And probably had.* The table was set for three, a chair in front of each collection of wineglass, plate, and other Kraal nonsense.

I could almost hear Ersh's sneer: *ephemeral trappings.* I agreed, but wouldn't make the mistake of underestimating them.

The Human female I was to believe was Skalet sat there, Paul to her left. I guessed they'd arrived ahead of me by several minutes. Mixs had undoubtedly been asked to design shortcuts for our web-kin's amusement.

First things first. "Are you all right?" I asked my Human. The briefest of nods. She'd returned his pendant, I noticed. *More theatrics.*

"What about me, Youngest?" Wendy/Skalet's camouflaged eyes widened as if in dismay. "Aren't you eager to learn how I have been?"

"I know how you've been." I let the lip curl up over my right fang and stay there. "Hidden. Safe. While others died."

Wendy/Skalet poured a clear, rosy liquid—serpitay—into each glass. "I see you still haven't learned to conduct yourself appropriately during civilized conversation," she commented, making a tsk-tsk sound with her tongue and teeth. "Sit, Youngest. If you must be insufferably rude and stay this pup, instead of matching form to your elders as you were taught, at least observe the essential courtesies."

I approached obediently enough, watching the growing satisfaction on her face as my paw touched the back of the chair. Smoothly and without hesitation, I continued forward and swept the table clear with both arms. Crystal thudded on dead hides and shattered on stone.

Paul didn't move. He kept his face schooled into a mask of polite attention, doubtless aware of his danger as the closest source of living mass to two web-beings of undetermined temper.

"The courtesies are done," I told her.

Wendy/Skalet—*Skalet*—hadn't moved either, beyond rescuing her glass of serpitay before I could reach it. "I see." A small smile played over lips that didn't belong on the face I remembered. *Was the alteration cosmetic or permanent?*

"I liked your real face better," I said.

A shrug. "A change was advisable."

There was only one thing I wanted to know. "Why?"

Her smile widened. "There are those familiar with—"

I controlled the urge to bite, but the impulse rose up my throat to roughen my voice. "Don't play games with me. You know what I mean. Why did you destroy our lives on Minas XII?"

"So we could have this not so civilized conversation, Esen."

I didn't look at Paul, who had lost so much. I couldn't, given the way memories of Largas narrowed my vision to

Skalet's still-smiling face. "You didn't have to send us running through the night," I growled. "You didn't have to ruin everything—"

"To you, it was necessary, wasn't it?" The interruption came from Paul, who dared lean forward to stare at Skalet. He looked curious, nothing more, to someone who didn't know him better, who didn't know the cost of such control. I wrinkled my snout in clear warning to Skalet.

She merely dipped her head graciously at my Human, as if conceding him a victory. "Of course. Secrecy is essential. I could protect my movements from scrutiny, but yours? You exhibit a contempt for safety, Youngest, such that I'm amazed you've survived this long. That business with the Iftsen?" She pretended to shudder. "As well, you remain woefully predictable. It wasn't difficult to arrange events that would encourage you to act in your own best interest for once." I must have growled, drawing her eyes to me. "Surely you see the efficiency. In one stroke, you were freed from all ties you possessed outside this room and, as a consequence, you traveled secretly, here, to hide. A place where I could follow. As your Human wisely notes, everything was necessary for the safety of us all." She regarded her wine. "Ah, but I forget, you have ambition. What do you care for my old notions of following rules and keeping safe?"

Ambition? There was danger in the word, even if I had no idea what Skalet was talking about. *Games—she'd always played them.* "What ambition do you think I have?"

The velvet voice could become as sharp as any knife. "Do you deny you've tried to turn yourself into one of them?" A wave toward Paul.

I blinked.

"Living among them I could understand," Skalet continued more evenly. "This—bond—with a single Human I was willing to tolerate. He has proved useful and discreet; the species doesn't live long anyway." My growling became a snarl and she waited for me to subside, as if patience had been added to her character over the past years. "I admit,

Youngest, I thought you were doing fairly well under the circumstances. You've even handled that fool Kearn without having to explain his corpse." Her eyebrows, arched and artificial, came together in a frown. I could sense the "but" coming. Skalet had never been one to compliment without criticism.

Sure enough. "But you have shocked me, Youngest."

"I shocked you?" This seemed a bit unreasonable, considering I wasn't the one who'd decided to come back to life. "How?"

"By breeding your Human," she replied matter-of-factly. I did my utmost not to laugh—something Skalet had never taken well—as I wondered what Char Largas would have to say about this interpretation of her whirlwind courtship. *She had,* I recalled, *found innumerable ways to keep a certain Lishcyn busy at the office.*

The impulse died as I lifted my ears and heard that Paul was barely breathing. A quick glance showed me his face had gone chalk white. *Easy,* I wished at him. *Never show Skalet a way to your heart.* "At first," she was saying, "I couldn't imagine what possessed you to complicate an already vulnerable identity by acquiring his offspring. Then, I understood."

"You did," I said numbly.

"Of course. You have never been subtle, no matter how I tried to educate you." *Paul should have laughed at this.* Skalet fixed me with her cold, green eyes. "You've arranged that when this one dies, you'll have more Humans of his genotype and your training. At the same time, you've set up a network of machines to gather information throughout this quadrant. Your ambition is as pathetic as it is obvious."

I felt time slipping back, as if I was trapped in Ersh's kitchen by one of Skalet's lessons on strategy. *Figure it out for yourself, 'tween.* There was no doubt in my mind: Skalet was still a lousy teacher. "I have no ambition, pathetic or otherwise," I assured her, somehow finding the self-control not to shout. *Beyond trying to repair what I could of our lives.* "I don't know what you're talking about—"

"Do you think me senile, Youngest? It's clear you have been attempting to create some obscene ephemeral Web, Esen-alit-Quar. I can only assume you're trying to replace what you lost." Skalet actually managed to look sympathetic. "A doomed, foolish ambition. I saw how this Human's offspring abandoned you as soon as they were old enough. I watched you become so desperate you attempted alliances with any species that came near you, from Ganthor to those ridiculous Feneden. I realized I could no longer leave you to fend for yourself."

I hoped my relief didn't show. If this wasn't some trick—*which was all too likely*—then Skalet hadn't found out about my alliance with Paul's Group, or Rudy. She had, however, been closer to my every move than was even remotely comfortable. I spared an instant to worry about Luara and Tomas.

Then wished I hadn't, as the thought made me look again at Paul. His eyes flinched from mine, like something desperate.

Had he lied to me? If Skalet hadn't been there, if she hadn't begun pushing me back into her way of thinking, I might never have felt that jolt of dread. Now I couldn't help remembering. Paul had said he wouldn't see his children again in order to protect them from his past. *Had it been to protect them from my future instead?* Could he have believed I'd seen the twins as another set of Ragems to befriend, to risk with my secret after he was—after—

"Stop this," I ordered both Skalet and my imagination. "Unlike you, I took responsibility for the web-being who killed our sisters, and for any others who might come to this space. I made a life for myself. What would you have preferred I do? Hide in a hole for a hundred years, hoping for the occasional hiker to talk to himself so I could retain at least some familiarity with the local dialect? If Paul hadn't left his own family, his own Web, for me, that's very likely all I could have done."

"Laudable."

I snapped my teeth together over what I might have said, knowing I was the one with the vulnerable throat. *Because of Paul.* "Your approval means nothing to me," I said evenly. "I presume you don't seek mine." I didn't bother to reproach Skalet for abandoning me for fifty years, as Paul's cousin Rudy had reproached him. *Would Paul understand why?* He'd always had less difficulty comprehending the ways of my species than I, his. Still, would he realize that for a web-being who'd lived millennia, as Skalet had, fifty years was the equivalent of a week apart?

It was still enough time to accomplish very many things, especially if you were in a position of unassailable power such as Skalet enjoyed as S'kal-ru. I followed that thought, believing it was important. "How did you explain your failure to the Kraal? You'd cost them ships—lives."

"And how did you survive?" This from Paul, who'd been there when Skalet had asked for—and taken—most of my mass in order to fight our enemy.

"How?" Skalet steepled her fingers, choosing to answer the Human—a choice implying she had reason to know it was safe to tell him secrets. *It wouldn't be trust.* The hair over my spine, never flat since my arrival, stood straight up. "I left the excess mass as a decoy, deep inside a weapons' room vault I knew would be difficult even for a web-being to penetrate quickly. Then I took a shuttle to rejoin Admiral Mocktap."

I stared at her in disbelief, remembering, perfectly, every slice of her teeth through my flesh. "You fed it my mass?"

She pretended to be surprised by my outrage. "Surely you didn't expect me to risk mine against a superior force. My decoy bought you and your precious Human time to escape, did it not?"

"Decoy—" I couldn't speak for an instant. Then, somehow, I found my voice. "You know what it learned from your—decoy."

Hesitation. I watched her fingers tighten around one another.

"You know," I told her, lowering my tone in pure threat, remembering how Paul and I had arrived too late, how we'd found Ersh's home, my home, destroyed; everything Ersh had been, the source of our Web, entombed in her mountain. *The darkest day of my long life.*

Because Death had assimilated Skalet-memory from her *decoy*, and knew where to go.

"Yes." Oddly subdued for Skalet.

" 'Yes.' " I put both paws on the table and leaned into the face of my Elder, hoping my breath was unpleasant. "Have you dared return to Picco's Moon since?"

Skalet's head dropped forward, as if she studied the painful-looking knot her hands had become. The braids on either side of her face slipped past her shoulders, puddling on the stone table like drying blood. But the voice emanating from that shelter was as calm and cold as ever. "I was reminded of it, lately. And how the past shows us the needs of the present. I maneuvered you here because I need the ability Ersh gave you, Youngest. Give it to me."

I didn't pretend to misunderstand. Skalet must have been on that Kraal ship, must have seen how I'd killed our enemy. She had to know I'd assimilated the secret of traveling through space, a secret only Ersh could have kept hidden in her flesh from the rest of our Web. "No." My sensitive ears caught the echo from Paul's lips, though almost silent. *Don't.*

Skalet's head rose within a flood of red and black. "Why? Is it so dangerous? So painful? Or so valuable only you may own it? I should be the judge, as your Elder. It's too important to risk in your flesh alone." Her voice deepened. "Esenalit-Quar. Will you share it?"

Share. Every part of me ached at the word, knew its grip as a hunger. I panted to dump heat and stay in a form that considered biting a social skill, not a way to rip mass from another and *learn*.

If Skalet felt the longing, she controlled it better than I. *Or did she?*

I realized, as abruptly as the wink of light from crystal, that we were no longer Eldest and Youngest—and had never been equals. "I am Senior Assimilator of the Web of Esen," I told her, reminding myself and Paul that things were not as they had been. "I share only what I choose to share, as Ersh did before me."

But Skalet had waited for my awareness, calculated its arrival precisely; I knew by the satisfied way she relaxed into her chair. *And I'd seen that smile before.* "While I am helpless to conceal anything within my flesh," Skalet admitted, much too calmly. "How unfair, 'tween. Ersh and I had so many—uncomfortable—disagreements which could have been avoided had I your ability; while I truly don't care if you know everything I know."

Never underestimate a Kraal. Skalet, a devoted student of that twisted culture, had taught me that. I saw my danger just in time. I dared not seem a threat to her, not here, not with Paul so close. "I wouldn't—"

"Oh, I couldn't stop you, Senior Assimilator. Or could I?" The smile became a sneer. "What if I ate all of you? I could, you know."

Paul turned an interesting color. I tried to ignore his presence; I hoped Skalet continued to do the same. With an effort, I unwrinkled my snout and finally sat down at her table. *Two could play Kraal games.* "Then you wouldn't get what you want," I stated. "I excised my memories of how to move through space from my mass—which would be another of those things, Eldest, I can do that you can't."

Her eyes flashed to Paul's pendant. *Ersh, she was quick.* "Take it, if you wish," I told her, keeping my voice even. "Assimilate the iota of my web-mass within. It's a message—an introduction—to any of our kind Paul might encounter in the future. You might benefit from the concepts of friendship and trust."

"Irrelevant," Skalet concluded, looking back at me. "So this is how you gained information from Ersh after her death. She left such—messages—behind." She tapped the tabletop lightly. "Which means you are quite right to chide me for neglecting our ancestor, Youngest. I should have returned to her pile of rock well before now. Imagine the opportunity I've wasted following your juvenile exploits, when I could have simply gone to the source."

"Then it isn't you?" I blurted.

A lifted brow. "You really should try to speak more clearly, Esen. 'Isn't me' what?"

I closed my jaw, prepared to be stubborn. Skalet merely turned to Paul. "Well, Human? What more would she like to accuse me of?"

Paul gave me that inscrutable look meaning he either saw an advantage to Skalet knowing, or somehow believed he had no choice but to answer. "Mining Ersh's mountain," he told her.

"So that's how the past found its way home," she said under her breath. I doubted Paul could hear. "But she must have known—why no report?" Skalet's face contorted with rage as I saw my web-kin lose control for the first time in my life, or in Ersh-memory, for that matter. She leaped to her feet, shouting: "How dare she betray me! I'll flay her tattoos from her face! I'll have her misbegotten family annihilated! I'll—"

When she stopped to take a breath, I couldn't help myself—too angry at my own betrayer to be careful. "Don't tell me you trusted an ephemeral."

I should have remembered more about Skalet before daring to taunt her. I felt bone shatter within my snout as the force of her blow drove me from chair to the floor, to land in a mass of broken crystal and serpitay-soaked hides.

Through the confusion of pain and noise, I knew Paul tried to come to my aid. *He mustn't.* Blinking red from the eye that could see, I fumbled for the fallen chair, using it to pull myself up until I could grip the edge of the table with a paw. *A Kraal child knew how to snap a neck.*

A long thin hand under my arm yanked me the rest of the way, shoved me into another chair. "Here." A cold lump of ice was pressed into one of my paws. "Put this on the side before it swells." I tried to throw it back at her, tried to find Paul.

"Do what she says, Esen." His low voice came from the side where I was blind and I sagged with relief. His hands stopped my attempt to turn my head to see him with my good eye, leaving me to watch Skalet until I could no longer blink fast enough to keep the lens clear of blood.

"You endure, Youngest." She sounded pleasantly surprised. *Another lie.* Skalet knew I couldn't cycle through web-form when we were this close. It would incite her to change as well, with Paul's living mass within easy reach.

"No thanks to you," Paul snarled as if he'd been the one born with fangs. I tested with my tongue to be sure I retained both of mine, then winced as he lifted my lip to make his own assessment. "She needs a med-tech, not ice. There's broken bone and cartilage, here and below the eye." *My turn.* I grabbed at him, feeling for damage or a telltale flinch. He caught my paws and held them for an instant before putting them back on the table. "I'm okay, Es. Our gracious hostess didn't smash my face, only yours."

"If anyone should have learned not to arouse my temper, it's your young friend," Skalet informed him with her usual callous disregard for ephemeral notions of morality or behavior. "There's no need for treatment. This is a useless form she wears out of sentimentality. Take her to the bedroom where she can cycle before she bleeds herself dizzy. I've left clothes for you both there."

I expected—and feared—Paul would begin a senseless and potentially dangerous argument. Instead, I felt his arms go beneath my knees and behind my back, sliding me gently off the chair and against his body before he stood. Crystal snapped beneath his feet as he adjusted to my weight. Then, with infinite care, my Human web-kin carried me away from my true web-kin.

When did we become, I thought through waves of pain, *another of those ironies Ersh would have enjoyed?*

Otherwhere

SHE replaced the incense by the glow of the spent stick's embers. The chest's smooth black lacquer was centuries old, rumored to predate the arrival of the Kraal in this sector of space; its complex designs of powdered gems and blood had been inlaid over generations. Affiliations were recorded here as well as scored in flesh.

Her hands stroked the doors as she drew them closed, a caress that reset ancient traps and loaded poisons. The family of Pa-Admiral Mocktap had never been careless.

With two exceptions.

Fragrant smoke curled its way to freedom through the nostrils of the sleepless dragons lying atop the chest, having bathed the canister holding ashes from Sybil-ru, the first Mocktap to reach the rank of admiral. Ashes and a name some families would have tossed aside, bending their history into a more palatable shape.

The present-day Admiral Mocktap valued both as reminders. Sybil-ru's carelessness hadn't been arranging the theft from the crypt of the extinct House of Kraslakor. That had been a political maneuver—an apparently unsuccessful one, given the artifacts had never been used to gain status. They'd simply vanished.

No, Sybil-ru's carelessness had been to traffic in a

new poison without verifying the antidote in her possession was the real one, something that became embarrassingly obvious when she died from it herself.

Turning on lamps almost as old as the chest, Mocktap went to her desk. It was home to an incongruously modern comp system. She'd tossed a veil over it, a priceless antique in the subtle golds and reds of a master weaver—an heirloom, last worn by the First Daughter of the House of Kraslakor, on the day of her assassination.

More recently, the veil had been offered as a bribe to her own affiliates, who'd been checking on the known associates of Rudy Lefebvre, Human and otherwise. *Ervickian slime.*

Information had eventually spilled from the one mouth they'd left working. *Valuable information, to one who understood.* Nothing useful about Lefebvre; their working relationship had ended badly, to the Human's credit, no doubt. But to counter their obvious and pain-filled disappointment, the Ervickian had offered the veil, then crates bursting with treasure, then a mountain on Picco's Moon.

She'd sent her affiliates, who found the mountain had a secret of its own: traces of a refined substance, previously unknown to Kraal science. She'd sent additional staff to control the source, then collect more in order to determine its properties. The House of Mocktap hadn't claimed the glory of recovering the Kraslakor Artifacts, despite the pleased and curious rumblings through every affiliation. Let those bored with made-up feuds find a new one more to their taste. *There was more power in secrets.*

Using tongs, Mocktap lifted the filmy fabric and dropped it in a container beside the desk. The poison still impregnating every thread caused paralysis within a second. Death took much longer. *After all, she'd want to talk to anyone interested in her private files.*

The Botharan, Lefebvre, had copies of a select few—sufficient to start him moving in the direction she chose, begin thinking as she wished. She'd given the overzealous fool, Cristoffen, more than his share of information and almost lost control of him—a mistake she would not make again. At least Cristoffen's theatrics had attracted Lefebvre's attention at the right time. She was confident Lefebvre would have no difficulty obtaining whatever he needed from Cristoffen and that buffoon, Kearn. *Perhaps he would kill them for her in the process.*

And once Lefebvre learned the full truth about Paul, Esolesy-ki, and their pathetic band of spies? When he knew about the Other?

He would be the assassin's blade in her hand, honed and ready for use.

Mocktap ran her tongue over her lips. A dangerous and cunning individual. *With a body promising stamina as well as bruising strength.* Had she been younger, with fewer affiliations to serve, she might have kept Lefebvre another few hours, or days. There were drugs one added to the serpitay that produced *effective* reactions. If they both survived, she'd consider it for their next meeting. *She wasn't that old.*

How old was her closest affiliate and mentor, the ascetic S'kal-ru?

That question had been the key. How old? S'kal-ru showed almost no signs of aging, or allowed none, shaving her head and eyebrows, dressing either for battle or in styles that were so out of fashion they'd be a joke on anyone else.

Not that anyone laughed at S'kal-ru.

Not that S'kal-ru laughed either. Mocktap scowled, confounded by an affiliate who had no appetites, no pleasures she'd been able to discern during years of hunting for weakness. A passion for the past: the most obscure detail could come out of that bald, ugly head, always correct. Perfectionism: S'kal-ru was proficient in all aspects of war, from hand-to-hand to arcane technology, and expected the same of her affiliates. If her lack of friendly vices hadn't made her such uncomfortable company, S'kal-ru's talents could have centered her in a maze of high-status temporary alliances—her bloodline a prize for the usually deadly game of courtship. That she chose otherwise had made her the courier of choice for three noble Houses: entrusted with their policy, authorized to make decisions on the battlefield, ranks etched into her skin to command instant and complete obedience from any affiliated Kraal.

Hers was a voice of power.

A voice of lies. Pa-Admiral Mocktap pressed her lips together, as if summoning courage, then called up her files, patiently obeying requests for her identity and purpose, providing the layers of code that protected its contents from a pair of eyes far more dangerous than Rudy Lefebvre's. She wouldn't have dared unlock her files, even on her own ship, in her own cabin, if she didn't know those eyes were both distracted and safely distant.

S'kal-ru's eyes. *The traitor.*

As Sybil-ru, Mocktap knew herself a failure of her lineage, the next so-careless as to swear affiliation to one who meant ruin to her House. S'kal-ru's attention, that of a proven courier, had been flattering; her reputation as a tactician—as adept at system-wide warfare as the greeting table with its etiquette of poison and lies—beyond question. Who wouldn't have gravitated to such a potent combination of independent wealth and old affiliation?

Who wouldn't have gloried in success after success?

Then, the battle where everything changed, where ships were lost under her command to error and an unbelievably powerful biological weapon. Despicable,

cowardly orders from S'kal-ru to destroy the only prototype rather than attempt its acquisition for the Kraal,
losing their only chance for an outcome that wasn't ab-
ject failure.

S'kal-ru had made sure Mocktap's career survived
that stain, even flourished during years of supposedly
hunting the creators of that weapon—but at the cost of
neglecting other affiliations. There were assassination
attempts, credit difficulties, the withdrawal of alliances.
Forced closer and closer to S'kal-ru for her very life,
Mocktap found herself playing incomprehensible
games that had nothing to do with movement within the
Kraal hierarchy or status. Nothing to do with success.
The most recent, the harrowing of the Lishcyn out of
the Fringe, had ended with the creature's escape and
the shaming of Mocktap's elite troops. S'kal-ru's inex-
plicable disappearance had left her responsible. As a
direct consequence, the admiral had changed her locks
and now prepared her own food.

The closer your allies, the less you dared trust them.
Mocktap's affiliates had spied on S'kal-ru from the beginning of their relationship; it was expected, though
they never reported anything but that admirable lack of
weakness—suspicious of itself. No one should be that
perfect. *No one was.* Following the disastrous battle,
Mocktap's self-preserving curiosity had turned into a
drive for vengeance, and she hunted S'kal-ru's secrets
alone, with a tireless patience fueled by the pointless,
inglorious deaths of thirteen thousand, five hundred,
and nine. The complements of three cruisers; the
cream of affiliates from the House of Mocktap. Her
blood, wasted.

But Mocktap had found nothing to refute any of
S'kal-ru's claims from that day, nothing to anchor her
suspicion that her mentor knew more than she revealed, until that fateful afternoon when she'd explored
the family chest, driven by some need to connect with

the earlier failure of her House, Sybil-ru. She'd found someone else.

Sybil-ru's ashes weren't the only ones bathing in fresh incense tonight. Among the tiny canisters of Mocktaps Great and Glorious, Mocktap had discovered one for Uriel-ro, a young nephew, thrice removed, of no recorded accomplishment or affiliation. *A nothing.* Yet family records showed how Sybil-ru had insisted his remains be represented here, in the chest that must be carried by the head of their House into every battle, an honorable internment that had taken place two weeks before her own fatal miscalculation.

The incongruity had drawn Mocktap's attention. She'd waited for one of S'kal-ru's frequent trips away before taking Uriel-ro's canister and dumping its contents on a cloth.

No ashes at all. Only a single withered leaf—duras—and an image, cued to project when the canister was breached. Later, Mocktap confirmed her suspicion that only the hands of someone genetically linked to Sybil-ru could have triggered the projection.

At the time, the Kraal could only sit and stare at a perfect replica of S'kal-ru, sealed in that canister before she herself had been born.

Knowing she'd found the true question: *how old was S'kal-ru?*

Mocktap's hands wanted to shake at the memory; she forbade them. She'd had the background of the image analyzed. There was only one place known to the Kraal Confederacy where fist-sized gems lay on the ground: Picco's Moon.

Picco's Moon, where a smuggler had uncovered the Kraslakor Artifacts, the same stolen by Admiral Sybil-ru Mocktap, which he'd sold to the Ervickian. According to the dying creature, the smuggler had claimed the crates must have been hidden on that mountain for over three standard centuries.

She could date it more precisely. Three hundred and forty-three years ago: when the Kraslakor crypt had been breached, its treasures stolen; when Uriel-ro had died, his canister—with its secret— placed in the Mocktap chest; and when, three hundred and forty-three years ago, Sybil-ru had died of her new poison. Duras.

Mocktap half-closed her eyes. Poisons that effective were expensive. Had the artifacts been the price? If so, why just bury them for three hundred years?

Could S'kal-ru be that old?

An update activating within her files interrupted Mocktap's train of thought. She keyed to accept it, reading the confirmation with relief. The weapon worked. The plans for it, and other devices of S'kal-ru's design, had been given to Mocktap's affiliates twenty years ago for the construction of prototypes. They'd had limited success with a force mesh, none with the scanners, but the weapon had showed promise. A small amount of a specific target material, of unknown origin or properties, had been provided. S'kal-ru, however, had ordered the weapon's test postponed without explanation.

Mocktap had found it expedient to ignore those orders. The sample was now so much dust; her staff had no idea how to obtain more or how the weapon had worked at all. *Asking S'kal-ru would be—unwise.* It didn't matter. She had what she needed. Mocktap specified the destinations of the prototypes, then erased the message along with any record of her com signal. She leaned back, shutting down the comp with a stab of one finger, waiting as it hummed through the steps that would protect its secrets.

Picco's Moon. Its mountain had revealed more than strange minerals and stolen heirlooms. Its ownership, though muddied by an expert, had been traced in part to the very Lishcyn S'kal-ru loved to torment, the one she'd claimed possessed some of the biological technology of the weapon which had destroyed Mocktap's ships, including the secret of its flight through space.

Lies don't live alone, Mocktap reminded herself, nodding with satisfaction. She'd been right to look elsewhere, to turn her attention to a growing circle of names: Esen/Esolesy-ki, Paul Ragem/Cameron, Meony-ro, Lionel Kearn and his crew, Janet Chase, an Ervickian named Able Joe, the disbanded crew of a Tly cruiser, Joel Largas and his kin, and the delectable Rudy Lefebvre. With all her skill, she'd probed for the weaknesses in their affiliations, sought there for information. Med reports regarding truth drugs widened her search. Unforeseen conspiracies focused it.

Finally, she'd reexamined the reports stolen from Lionel Kearn, the ones S'kal-ru had ridiculed, and dared believe in shapeshifting monsters.

Only she knew. No one else could be trusted. Mocktap assigned her affiliates different tasks, communicating only through her, never to one another. She took the unprecedented and shameful step of using non-Kraal. Finally, as S'kal-ru left to act on her own, Mocktap had left the safety of Kraal space to do the same, sensing her chance had come.

Time to stop hunting for a "biological weapon" that had never existed. Time to start hunting the creatures that did. The House of Mocktap would no longer be a pawn in this game between S'kal-ru and Esolesy-ki. *The same game her ancestor, Sybil-ru, had played and lost three hundred and forty-three years ago.*

Ever so lightly, careful not to break the skin—yet, Mocktap drew the scalpel-sharp edge of one fingernail across the marks of affiliation binding her to a being who wasn't Kraal, or Human, at all.

How old was S'kal-ru? The question no longer mattered.

She wouldn't be growing any older.

20: Abyss Night

THIS was my birth-form.

I sought Skalet-memory; my own held nothing like this. It helped me look in the mirror in her washroom, kept my blood-soaked paws steady as I used the sealer.

She wasn't taking it from me.

"Esen. Are you all right? Do you need anything?"

Dear Paul thought I'd come in here to cycle and change. He hadn't expected me to be able to stand, much less demand privacy. No wonder he called from the other side of the door.

I grunted something, timing the sound to match the moment when I stopped sealing to pry another shard of cartilage from my nasal passage.

Skalet's washroom had been battle-ready. I'd expected no less, having seen her preference in living quarters before. It contained what I needed to make emergency repairs to this form, including a numbing spray that worked almost too well. My good eye was frozen open and watered constantly, but it wouldn't be much longer before I could cycle.

Paul's patience didn't last that long. I heard him discover I'd locked the door. As I passed the sealer under the swollen shut eye, he came through regardless. Presumably Skalet expected some damage to her suite, given the quality of her care for guests.

"What the—" the Human hurried to my side, then froze, looking over my shoulder into the mirror. I begged him with my eye to leave me in peace, unable to open my mouth to speak. I knew it would be hard, given what he could see. My Lanivarian muzzle was a delicate, complex structure; Skalet's fist had rearranged most of one side. I supposed I should be grateful to still have a head. I'd seen her Human hands drive through slabs of wood following a disagreement with Ersh; I'd foolishly envied her strength.

That had been temper. This? Whether Skalet knew it or not, she'd struck as hard as she had not from anger, but to keep me from this form, to remove the shape that marked me as alien among our former Web. *Even Ersh,* I remembered sadly, staring at my dear Human's face in the mirror instead of my own, *had known this shape, with its reminder of my non-Web birth, unnerved both Skalet and Mixs.*

Another reason I refused to let Skalet take it from me.

"Let me finish," Paul offered, his face grim and set. There was a reddening down one side of his neck, purple toward the base—I assumed more of Skalet's gentle touch. I handed my Human the med kit and sat rather quickly on the bench, happy not to look at the ruin of my beautiful snout any longer.

Temporary ruin, I reminded myself. Nothing that wouldn't heal, with time and care, but I had none of the first and only this rough patchwork of the second. Form-memory was absolute. When I cycled back into this form, my favorite Esen, I'd re-create how I was at this moment. Consciously or not, Skalet had counted on my cycling as soon as possible—to free myself of pain now, at the price of facing pain later.

But I had no intention of cycling until this form was fit to move safely and could survive, if necessary, on its own.

She wasn't in control of me.

Paul pressed something cool into the joint of my jaw. "Try to speak. Carefully."

"Awrhggh." I drew my benumbed tongue back inside my teeth and tried again. "Dahn oou," I managed, relieved to feel my lower jaw capable of fine movement. Not as serious as it looked, then. I let my tail beat against his knees.

Paul cupped his hand along the intact side of my head, leaning over me so he could look into my open eye. "This is the best I can do, Es. It's going to—" He hesitated, then said honestly: "It's going to hurt like hell when the numbness wears off."

I didn't bother telling him that would be the instant I returned to this form, since any nonmetabolized medication, poison, or food wasn't part of form-memory. The sealer, an artificial membrane that bonded instantly to skin, I would remember; that was why Skalet stocked this in her kit, and not other types of bandages.

Pain, I'd learned to survive. *Ersh would have been gratified.*

Standing required Paul's help, but I made it back to the sink under my own power and began to wash my paws. I needed to give the medications as much time to work as I could, but the red stains sickened me. Paul, understanding, grabbed a damp sponge to work most of the drying blood from my shoulder and chest. My skin shuddered wherever he touched it. *I hated wet fur.*

"She's coming," Paul warned, staring toward the bedroom.

Without turning to see if he was right, I released my hold on my injured self and cycled . . .

. . . moisture puddling around what were feet, five-toed, small and tidy, with a broken nail on the smallest toe of the right foot.

None too soon. Paul steadied me as I gasped and staggered with the relief of being whole again. He barely had time to toss a towel over the med kit and bloody sponge, then pick up a comb to press to my hair before impatient footsteps announced Skalet's arrival.

Paul and I looked at her in the mirror, a matched set of pale Human faces, both with hair threatening our eyes, both with expressions that could best be described as "guarded." Though my face was significantly lower, despite my instinctive stretch to my full height. "You could have knocked," I told her, scowling.

As well complain to the Abyss—or Ersh. "So this is the current Human version of Esen-alit-Quar. Finally, some manners." Skalet surveyed me from head to foot, then back again, her face oddly expressionless. "What do you call this self?"

"B–bess." I shivered, starting to feel the chill of the air against this unprotected skin. Fur was more practical.

"Hurry and dress, fool." She paused at the door, eyes turning to Paul. "You need to change as well. Even Prumbins will notice that much blood."

Neither of us so much as blinked until hearing the bedroom door close behind her.

"She's right. There are clothes on the bed."

I stared up at him. "I'm sorry, Paul."

This drew a grim look. "You aren't the one who should be." Before I could say anything else, my Human tousled my hair. "Web-being, dangerous, powerful, unpredictable. I remember the drill: when in doubt, shut up, let you handle her, be careful. Right now," he paused for emphasis, "that means doing what she says."

Reassured, I followed him into a larger room I didn't recognize. *Probably something to do with staggering through with my only working eye barely able to see.* I spun around to take a better look, something this form did with a pleasing light grace. And a tendency, which I quelled under the circumstances, to keep spinning in order to experience an even more pleasing dizziness. "Skalet must have asked Ansky to design it," I concluded, admiring the use of billowing red silk above, beside, and on the bed. The paintings I ascribed to Skalet's taste: no improbable couplings occurred on her walls, only desert landscapes with starry skies, beautiful and barren.

"Es. Can we talk here?"

I didn't feel like spinning any longer. "It doesn't matter," I told him. "We have no secrets left. But I doubt she'd bother listening. Skalet wouldn't care to hear us become upset or angry or start to Yell At The Top Of Our Lungs!" For a small form, this one could put out a remarkable volume when motivated.

"Very mature." But his eyes remembered smiling.

"I can be," I told him quietly, resting my fingers on a dry patch of his sleeve. The once-handsome blue shirt was dark with drying blood. *Mine, at least.* "Skalet was responsible for what happened—no one else. I'm sorry I doubted your choice of—companions—in the past. You were right all along."

Something eased in his face. "Can I get that in writing?"

"Not likely." His Human levity covered a bone-deep worry, one I thought I understood. I hadn't let him warn the Group or Rudy. It was logical, in Human terms, for him to now consider Skalet a threat to them and his family. "All she wanted was us, here, Paul," I began, hoping to reassure him. "I believe that. I know Skalet. She would consider it inefficient to pay attention to anyone or anything outside her own scheming. It's of no particular interest to her that she's turned Joel and his family against us. It was a tactic to bring us here and will be our problem, not hers, if we're foolish enough to try and reclaim that life. Her not caring, Paul, is the best protection any of your friends, our friends," I corrected, "could have."

Paul studied my face. I hoped whatever he could read of its Human structure and expression reinforced the message I wanted him to understand. *They were safe; we weren't.*

"If you say so, Old Blob," he said finally. "I've seen the results of her caring, that's for sure." My Human pulled off his bloodstained shirt with a grimace and threw it to one side.

Two piles of brown clothing were hiding amid the red bedcovers. Paul started to toss me a set, then stopped, examining them. "Hasn't she seen your Human self before?" he asked, as if puzzled.

"Not for years. But she'd know how I'd appear, my approximate age," I explained. "Why? Don't they look right?"

He held up a shirt that wouldn't pass over my head. I frowned. "It's not like Skalet to be wrong."

"Maybe she wasn't. These aren't new." Paul started looking around the room as I rummaged through the clothing for what might fit. "Ah." A satisfied sound as he pulled a carrysack from behind the bed. It had been forced open.

"The Humans on the Busfish," I guessed. "She sat with that family in order to steal their luggage."

"And ident." He held up a chit. "The Quinn family from Adamershome. My guess? Skalet followed us here to Prumbinat, but didn't have the time or means to bring what she needed to leave again. Which implies she's acting on her own. No squads in black armor, hiding in the closet."

I crammed my lower half into a wrap-style skirt that likely was supposed to cover the ankles of its wearer, but came to my knees. There was no option but to take the undershirt from Paul's pile to cover my top half. And most of my lower half again. At least every item of clothing was the same dull brown. I hunted for footwear. "They've served their purpose," I said, reluctant to remind him. "Skalet wouldn't risk our secret. Beside, she doesn't need help."

"No. She doesn't."

Odd how the Human voice could instill so much meaning into so few words: bitterness, frustration, resignation. I stopped and looked at Paul. He was sitting on the edge of the bed—a somewhat awkward position, given the slippery nature of the bedcover and the softness of the mattress. I watched him pull on the heavy brown sweater I'd left him, saw him put the pendant underneath, against his skin.

Something wasn't right.

Paul felt my gaze and grew still as he looked up at me, his hands coming to rest on his thighs. "Esen. What is it?"

They'd lunched together. Skalet, as Wendy, had introduced my dearest friend to Erpic soup.

There was no such thing as coincidence.

This face must have revealed something to him, because even as I knew, and whirled to run for the door, Paul was in motion. He put himself in my way, held me by the arms as I raged at him. "Let me go! You don't understand! She's poisoned you—"

He wouldn't let go. "I know."

"What do you mean, 'you know'?" I whispered, suddenly unable to move. *The dry corridor... their time alone... she'd planned it in order to tell him?* I stared into his face. His willing answers to her questions, his sitting so quietly at the table when I arrived. It made terrible sense now. "We have to get the antidote," I said, trying to twist free and seriously tempted to kick. "Skalet! Give it to me!" I shouted, just in case I'd been wrong and she was eavesdropping.

"Stop and think, Esen. Please." The desperation in his eyes, more than his grip, made me subside. Paul's hands tightened on my arms as if making sure he had my attention. "The antidote won't be here, if she's telling the truth. Why risk our finding it? She said what she gave me is slow-acting. She wants to hold this over us for days, maybe weeks. Time is on our side. And," this almost too lightly, "it could all be a lie."

My feet felt as though they were sinking into the floor, as if I were web-mass and helpless to prevent my being assimilated by the clearfoil. "It isn't a lie."

"No," he agreed with a heavy sigh. "I don't think it is." Paul loosened his grip, rubbing my arms gently where he'd taken hold of me, as if to erase the memory of our struggle. "She said you'd appreciate the irony. I didn't bother telling her I could as well." A hollow laugh. "After all, you told me how Skalet originally tried to steal duras plants from Ersh and you'd stopped her."

Oh, I appreciated it, I told myself bitterly. But not for so innocent a reason. I hadn't told Paul a Human had died when I'd recklessly interfered with Skalet's plans, those 343 years and a smattering of days ago. Now, poison from the same source was killing another Human, cell by cell, because I'd again blundered in the way of Skalet's scheming. Not just any Human—my friend, here only because of me.

Skalet understood the value of guilt and fear in others. *She just didn't feel them herself.*

Otherwhere

"CRISTOFFEN'S." Timri laid her hand on the cabin door, as if loathe to let Rudy go through it. Her dark eyes puzzled at him. "Are you sure you want to do this before seeing Kearn?"

"I want to make a full report—which includes what our friend might have in here," Rudy said smoothly. "I trust you'll let me know if you see Cristoffen coming home early?"

"No problem. Even in a proper shipcity, he'll call up to the bridge to request permission to enter the ship. Drives Resdick nuts."

"Perfect." Timri stepped to the side. Rudy didn't move.

"If you were anyone else, Rudy Lefebvre—" she began doubtfully. At his broad smile, she frowned, then nodded. "Have it your way. I'll be on the bridge."

Rudy waited until he heard the lift doors closing behind her. After a final glance to be sure the corridor was empty, he took out what he needed to unlock Cristoffen's cabin. Habit alone made him press his ear to the door first.

A sound.

Moving quickly and quietly, Rudy unlocked the door control, then exchanged his tools for a stunner. He used his thumb to key the weapon to wide dispersal, a setting that wouldn't produce unconsciousness in an adult Human, but should drop anyone inside to their knees. *If that person wasn't wearing a Kraal assassin shield.* In that case, he'd drop as well.

Lips pulled back from his teeth, Rudy slapped the door control and pulled the trigger the instant he could fit the nose of the stunner through the opening door. When there was no backlash, he followed his shot inside the cabin with a quick stride, closing the door behind him. Back against the wall, he scanned the room.

Then Rudy whistled under his breath. "Seems I'm not the only one curious about our Michael," he muttered, eyes searching for the source of the sound that had alerted him. It wasn't easy. Clothes were strewn about the deck. Every piece of furniture had been dismantled, and not carefully. The bed had been sliced apart, its jelly core now runnels of melting purple. Sheets of plas might have been dropped by a whirlwind.

Amateurs, Rudy complained to himself, even as a groan and clatter of falling shoes drew his attention to what remained of Cristoffen's closet. He jumped over the jelly and grabbed the being trying to regain his feet, hauling him clear of the rubble.

"Leee—goofme—I'm yourrr superr—superiorrr—Rud—y?"

"Kearn?" Rudy switched his hold from one able to snap a neck to something that helped steady the other.

"Wasssssa do?" Kearn's pupils were dilated with alarm as he reeled back and forth. "Waasssa do tomee?"

"Stun," Rudy informed him. "Zapped the voluntary muscles. It'll pass. You should sit down." Before he could look for an intact chair, Kearn obediently folded and sank to the floor, smearing the puddle of mattress jelly.

Rudy crouched so Kearn could see his face. "While you wait, think of a reason I shouldn't kill you."

The alarm faded to understanding, then something

like desperation. Kearn's head rolled from side to side as he tried to form words. "Es–Esen—no answer. Noanswerme! Here!" One arm jerked up and around spasmodically. "Why noanswerme—must be here! Find—Rud–y!"

Esen? Rudy's hands shot out and took Kearn by the shoulders to keep him still. He resisted the temptation to shake loose the answers he needed. *It might satisfy his impatience. It wouldn't help.* "Concentrate on breathing. Slow, steady. Don't keep trying to talk. You can't make any sense yet."

"Keep—look!"

Rudy nodded, understanding that much at least. "Fine. I'll keep looking."

Kearn's search hadn't been amateurish, Rudy judged, it had been frantic. The other hadn't known what he was hunting for—that much was obvious from the attention given to potential hiding places of any size, from the mattress to boxes of readers. As Rudy poked through the resulting mess, he kept glancing at Kearn, waiting for the tremors to stop shaking the Project Leader's limbs. Questions were piling up faster than answers. What was so important Kearn had ransacked his assistant's room the moment Cristoffen was safely off the ship? Had he sent Timri following Cristoffen to watch him—or to keep her out of the way?

Aha. The only object Kearn hadn't ripped apart, perhaps because it was under an avalanche of once-tidy reports. Rudy nudged it clear with one finger.

An envelope, no bigger than his hand, as yet unopened. Plain, bearing Cristoffen's name and a Sacrissee delivery glyph.

"Care—careful."

Startled, Rudy looked at Kearn. "It's a little late for that, don't you think?"

A shake of the head, more controlled, though Kearn remained hunched and shivering. "Kraal—tech."

Rudy pursed his lips grimly. "There's always that," he said, more to himself than Kearn. The Kraal had added Botharis to their confederacy five times during the last sixty years, bloodless shifts of government no more inconvenient at the local level than a change in tax rates and the occasional curfew. Their hardware, however, had been a more lasting problem. As a patroller, Rudy had dealt with more than his share of obsolete but functional Kraal military tech—some abandoned in fields to become a threat to livestock, most sold to those on the fringe of the law.

Every item came with at least one booby trap, to catch the uninformed.

The envelope could definitely wait.

Instead, Rudy scoured the room, methodically but without wasting time. He'd done enough work on Michael Cristoffen to be unsurprised by what had been relatively Spartan quarters. It had been a wild shot; there would be no secrets here.

Or were there? He stooped to retrieve a small book, its cover a plain black until the light caught its silver tracery of broken shells, ruined feathers, and wide-eyed skulls. He wiped a streak of jelly from the dainty, macabre thing and held it where Kearn could see. "Did he keep this by the bed?" he asked. At Kearn's nod, Rudy opened it.

Not a book. A notebook of—he counted—sixteen pages, each filled with a language Rudy didn't recognize. Handwritten. He'd seen samples of Cristoffen's writing; it stayed between the lines, free of independent flourishes. These strokes strayed in and out of patterns, bold and lovely, the script of someone who viewed words as art. "Do you know what this is?" He held the open book in front of Kearn.

Kearn managed to lean closer, staring at the pages. "Can't—be," he said, eyes wide. One hand reached up; Rudy brought the book to meet it. Kearn felt the page and ran his shaking fingers over the words. "Can't be," he repeated, more strongly, as if the denial helped him fight off the stun.

"Can't be what?"

He took the book in both hands. "This—is new. The writing—old. Too old." His throat worked as he swallowed; he rose to his knees, holding the book up to Rudy. "I've seen—this. Lecture on extinct languages. Human. This script is Naskhi. Dates two—three thousand years before our species left its home system."

Rudy shrugged, mildly disappointed. *So much for his clue.* "Feel up to walking?" he asked.

Somehow, through the remnants of stun disorientation, Kearn managed to look offended. "You don't unnn–understand." He lurched to his feet with Rudy's help, still clutching the small book. "This—impossible. The lettering—Naskhi. The words are Kraal."

Rudy put the impossible book and the unopened package on Kearn's desk, while Kearn leaned against his office wall, as if the trip up the lift had sapped all of his energy. *Unless it was guilt, being caught rummaging through a junior officer's belongings.* "What were you planning to tell Cristoffen about his room?" he asked, rather curious.

Kearn rubbed one hand over his scalp. "It doesn't matter. The main thing is you're here. If here is anywhere safe." He tapped one ear, then waved his hand around the room.

His meaning was obvious, even if nothing else seemed to be. Kearn used to record conversations throughout the ship himself; for all Rudy knew, he still did. As for outside eavesdroppers? Timri had been in charge of ensuring Kearn's office was clean; it was a convenient way to install devices of her own, to listen for Paul. Did Kearn know and want to prevent her hearing what was said today? Or did he fear someone else?

"Why" didn't matter, Rudy decided grimly. Privacy suited him even more if Kearn were guilty. "Nice to be back," he said, his voice deliberately cheerful. He unbuttoned his shirt and began pulling components from pockets in the vest he wore underneath. "It's been too long since I was on a Commonwealth ship." Two components snicked together forming a tube. "The *Russ'* looks good."

Kearn watched, his back against the wall. His voice had lost its stun-slur, but didn't quite manage casual. "F–funding has helped. Resdick is getting a new translight com at our next layover."

"Having problems with the existing equipment?" Rudy added the third and final component, then switched on the detector.

For some reason, this drew a small smile. "A recent one, yes."

Rudy walked around the office, eyes on the detector, then stopped at the chair behind the desk. Not there, but nearby. He checked the drawers. *Ah.* One precise stab with a pen destroyed the tiny transmitter hidden inside.

"We're clear," he pronounced. "And I'm ready for some answers."

"As am I," Kearn said heavily. He walked over to his chair and sat, closing his eyes briefly as if to stop the room from spinning. "Thank you for not killing me, Rudy Lefebvre, although I confess it feels as though you tried."

"Day's young." Rudy sat on the desk, staring down at the other Human, noticing but not understanding the lack of uniform, the fitter body, the worn expression. "What's going on, Kearn? I came here—well, I came convinced you were behind Cristoffen."

"Behind?" Kearn repeated bitterly. "Goes nicely with

'last to know' and 'blind fool,' doesn't it? I'd thought I'd found someone to help me with my work, maybe even carry on. Instead, I found a monster."

Rudy frowned. "I thought your work was monster-hunting."

"My work is finding the truth." Kearn straightened as he spoke. "I'm not the Fenedens' Shifter Hunter. Not anymore."

"But your Cristoffen has other ideas—"

"You were following him, weren't you?" Kearn didn't wait for an answer, going on almost eagerly. "I knew you couldn't be here in answer to my messages, not so soon."

"You sent for me?" The puzzle pieces weren't just falling apart, Rudy decided, they were assuming new shapes and multiplying out of control. "Why?"

"I need your help," the other said simply. "Cristoffen is being controlled by a Kraal. He's already caused the death of a—friend of Paul Ragem's. He's obsessed with Esen, with what he sees as the threat of her kind. He'd do anything to find her. Anything!" Kearn's face seemed to crumple. "I've tried to reach her—to warn her. She promised to answer me. But there's been nothing."

"What did you say?" Rudy asked, feeling numb.

"Cristoffen is a murderer!"

"Not that." Rudy found himself standing, looming over the smaller Human. "What did you say about Esen? You said 'you called her,'" he said, repeating the incredible.

"Yes. 'If you ever need me, I will come.' That's what Esen told me. I sent her a message as soon as Timri could get me a secure com, a warning about Cristoffen. But there's been no answer."

"Called her how?"

"I left a message at Cameron & Ki. I'm not a blithering idiot." Whatever Kearn saw on Rudy's face brought a faint color to his own. "Despite what I admit has been substantial evidence to the contrary. Your lies and evasions were well-intentioned, necessary, in fact. I don't dispute being their enemy." Then Kearn looked rather wistful, and Rudy wasn't sure he spoke to him, or to a memory. "But only an idiot refuses a new, better paradigm. Whether you choose to believe me or not, Rudy, I've known exactly where to find Esen-alit-Quar and her friend, Paul Ragem, since Esen surprised the hell out of me in that closet."

"You were hallucinating—"

"Which you had me believing until," almost a smile, "she told me I wasn't."

Rudy expressed his reaction with several choice and colorful phrases, ending with: "She'd better hope Paul never finds out."

"Indeed." The two looked at one another in an instant of perfect understanding.

Rudy suddenly understood how Kearn must have felt, facing that crisis of belief. He faced one now. Did he keep his suspicion, treat this new version of Kearn as he had the old? Or had he a chance to gain an unexpected ally, a powerful one, with the capabilities of a starship and the authority of the Commonwealth?

Had Esen been foolish? Rudy wondered abruptly. *Or had she been the wisest of them all?*

As if he sensed Rudy's doubts and needed to answer them, Kearn said, "It wasn't easy." He broke off and rubbed his forehead, his hand trembling. "You deserve to know that. When Esen contacted me the second time, and I finally believed it was her, my first reaction was to be terrified. One reason, I suppose, I was so quick to accept Cristoffen. You'd left. The rest of the crew—Timri—there was no one I could trust to tell me the truth. But I had to have it. I had to know, Rudy, if I'd been wrong. So I hunted it for myself."

"Where?"

Kearn took his hand from his forehead, frowned at it, then pointed at the shelves and stacks of abstracts. "In here," he said. He tapped his head once more. "Here. I spent months examining everything I knew— or thought I knew—using a new hypothesis. There is variation in every species, in every group of individuals. I asked myself: what if there had been two creatures like Esen, fifty years ago, with the difference that only one of them had acted in a way we'd call evil? It was a difficult question. I was—and am afraid of her abilities."

"I had a nightmare or two when I found out," Rudy said, returning honesty for honesty. "Not that Esen deserved them."

Kearn's eyes grew haunted. "Nightmares. Yes." He blinked and went on more briskly. "I should never have let mine twist my work, blind me to what I could have found within my own research. I grew angry at myself for wasting time. I accepted the hypothesis and expanded it. If there was an 'evil' 'shifter, could there be a good one? What if Esen had been trying to help us, acting against this evil one of her kind? The folklore I'd collected supported the concept; it fit the evidence from the attacks. And," Kearn almost smiled, "it finally made sense of Paul—what he'd done and sacrificed. I think that's what convinced me, in the end."

"You aren't the only one," Rudy said ruefully. He studied Kearn's face and saw nothing but a tired openness, a relief he found he shared. Acting on impulse, he stood and offered his hand.

Kearn copied the gesture without hesitation, their hands meeting in a firm grip.

"I don't suppose you have anything drinkable on board," the former captain of the *Russ'* said lightly as he sat back down. "I think I could use it."

Now Kearn did smile. "For some reason, I developed a taste for brandy after you left." He looted one cupboard for glasses and a drawer for a bottle. Hurrying back to the desk, he poured them each a drink, then lifted his own glass. "A toast, Rudy. To Paul."

"To Paul," Rudy echoed, then raised his eyebrow. "Any reason in particular?"

"For recognizing goodness, regardless of its shape." Kearn gave a short, self-conscious laugh. "And for knowing when not to follow my orders."

21: Abyss Morning; Surface Dawn

I'D BEEN ready to confront my web-kin and battle for Paul's life. At the very least, I'd been ready to tell her exactly what I thought of her behavior in as many languages as had profanity, and could be expressed using only a larynx, tongue, lips, and two arms. *And scowling.* I'd planned to avoid foot stamping, given I'd found no shoes that fit.

Of course, being so prepared, it shouldn't have surprised me to find Skalet had left while Paul and I were dressing in our stolen clothing.

"She's locked us in," Paul said, coming back to me. He looked more relieved than concerned, something I understood. Skalet was uncomfortable company at her best.

"And left a note," I told him, pointing to a piece of parchment that looked as old as me—and probably was, knowing how rarely Skalet came down to the Abyss. The parchment was stabbed to the stone of the tabletop by a long, delicate pin. Skalet-memory contained far too much detail of how such a pin, if inserted into critical points, could inconspicuously cause convulsions or death in a depressing number of species. *It was,* as if I cared, *easily hidden in hair or clothing.* I couldn't bring myself to touch it.

Paul might not be intimately familiar with a Kraal assassin's pin, but he wisely chose to read the note where it was, rather than touch anything Skalet might have booby-trapped. " 'We leave in three hours. Rest or not, as you wish.' " He checked his chrono. "Not the Busfish, then."

"No."

He walked to the nearest wall and rapped it with his knuckles. "Can you get through this?"

"No." Though I smiled at the suggestion. Humans could take anything for granted.

Paul sighed and rolled his eyes at me. "Esen, is that 'no' as in 'can't' or 'no' as in 'won't'?"

"Both." I stood beside him, pressing my smaller Human hands flat against the opaqued wall. Instead of its usual varied pastel tones, this clearfoil was dark and shot through with pearlescent streaks, like a semiprecious stone. It chilled my palms, so I rubbed them against the fabric of my skirt. "She must have activated a transmitter in here to set the clearfoil. It can't listen to me."

"And the 'won't?' "

I peered up at him sideways, through wisps of hair that had needed cutting my last time in this form. "There's no need for a lecture. Skalet wants me Human, so Human I'll be. For now."

Paul's finger looped the hair behind my ear, letting me see the unhappy look on his face. "I wish you weren't."

Ah. I hunted for what to say, knowing, as he did, that this was another trap Skalet had laid—as potentially deadly as the poison. "Try to feel otherwise," I advised him. "You understand the difference between your purely Human reaction to this form and the reality of me. Skalet doesn't know you. She expects your parental instincts to cloud your judgment, to interfere with our partnership." I stuck my tongue out at him and he forced a smile. "It gives us an advantage."

"Maybe." Paul traced my cheek and shook his head, making entirely too much sense.

"Keep thinking: 'Old Blob,' " I suggested. "Meanwhile, let's see if there's anything to eat around here."

"That you'd trust?" An incredulous look.

I shrugged, already looking around. "Skalet doesn't believe in wasted effort. You've been dosed and she can hardly poison this form if she wants me to stay in it." I was careful where I stepped. Skalet had made no effort to clear the floor of crystal shards. I was sure she'd think I deserved to cut myself, having made the mess in the first place. But having no intention of needing more time with the med kit, I took the smallest of the animal pelts from the floor and began using it as a broom to push the shards into a corner.

As for resting? I might not fear poison, but I wasn't closing my eyes.

"Wake up, Es."

So much for that resolution, I grumbled to myself later, but obeyed the voice. "Is she back?" I asked, rubbing the sleep from my eyes. It was still dark. *No, I was under something, something soft.* I must have burrowed beneath the blankets like my Lishcyn-self into the grass of my box. It was my Human's fault. *Lie down for a few minutes, Esen,* I repeated to myself. He must have known this form would fall asleep.

"Of course I'm back, Youngest. What's the matter with you? Human, is she exceptionally slow to become conscious in this form?"

"I don't know," I heard Paul say. "I've never seen her sleep—this way—before. But exhausted Human children do sleep soundly." The blanket lifted. I squinted up at Paul, seeing Skalet past his shoulder. She was wearing clothing that matched ours, brown and plain, though hers fit. Her hair was missing.

That was a surprise. I crawled into the open and yawned at my web-kin. "Where's your hair?"

"My— If this is a game, Youngest, I tire of it." She glared at me. "Get her ready."

When Skalet turned her back to leave the bedroom, I winked at Paul.

*   *   *

I'd puzzled over how Skalet meant to return to the surface, if not via the Busfish. The Prumbins insisted on living transports to Nirvana. How became clear the moment Paul and I followed Skalet through her air lock. Besides the door to the dry corridor, it had a floor hatch, well-concealed, leading into a very old Kraal submersible.

The submersible was docked under her suite at the Happy House, away from any eyes but the beady, non-image-forming ones of wall crawlers. Still, its mere presence demonstrated a distinct lack of respect for the Prumbins' notions of paradise on the part of both this web-kin and Mixs.

And, I told myself, *a willful carelessness for the sake of convenience.* Ersh must have been furious when she swallowed this memory. One of those uncomfortable discussions had likely ensued. *Skalet the careless.* It was something to keep in mind.

"Strap in."

Paul and I took the bench seats along each side, obeying Skalet and pulling the harnesses over our shoulders—another sign of the age of this craft. I trusted, for Paul's sake, that she'd had it tested for seaworthiness in the last century.

I found myself studying the back of Skalet's head, watching her hands as she worked the controls with an economy of motion few true Humans could match. The interior lights dimmed to a rose-glow as she activated the viewports, the color washing away the foreign cream of her skin; shadows repainted her tattoos. For the first time, I saw her as I knew her, as I hadn't since that terrible day on the *Trium Set.*

When I thought she'd died.

Moisture prickled my eyes and spilled down one cheek. Surprised, I wiped it away, then stared at my damp fingers.

"Esen?" Whisper-soft.

I shook my head, dismissing Paul's concern. There was nothing wrong with me beyond this form's disconcerting ability to feel.

A form the emotionless Skalet wore more than any other. That contradiction kept me from paying full attention as the antique submersible sank below the lowermost buildings along the Brim, then leveled off to move along the Abyss, though normally I'd be fascinated by the life clinging to its walls.

Think for yourself, Esen, I could hear Ersh say. I did my best. After being Lishcyn for fifty years, I'd gained a firm and completely irrational belief that almost any problem could be resolved by shopping. Skalet had been Human much longer, a form I'd begun to understand, thanks to Paul. So what would her behavior today mean, if truly tainted by that form?

She'd sent me away when her identity was first exposed. *To avoid my emotional overreaction—or her own?* When we'd been together, she'd lost control, badly enough to damage me. Having done so, she'd left, returning only when necessary to leave the Abyss. *Remorse?*

If I'd learned anything from my time with Skalet, it was the danger of trying to second-guess her motives. *Were my own any clearer?* The ache in my flesh to reconnect with my own kind couldn't be trusted. The drive to assimilate new knowledge, to share my own, was an instinct waiting to betray me.

None of this mattered, I decided. What did was that Skalet wanted the ability to move through space, something I couldn't permit any web-being, let alone one who played at war.

I closed my eyes on the past and leaned back.

"This is where it gets interesting," Skalet informed us as we stood looking toward the shoreline. Prumbinat's Port City of Gathergo tumbled over the low hills, no more than a series of dark, boxlike outlines. Flashes in the distance marked where starships came and went. Our goal. I licked salt spray from my lips, gauging the amount of time until sunrise by the lack of stars on the eastern horizon.

"I trust you have a plan?" Paul asked her, raising his voice slightly to be heard over the distant crash of surf. He kept his arm wrapped tightly around my waist, his other hand gripping the side of the vessel. The wind whipped his hair and mine. Skalet, having taken hers off, was immune.

She'd brought us to the surface outside the channel used by the Busfish, a precaution against collision as well as detection by the Prumbin authorities. You'd think a living transport would be better able to avoid accidents, but a Busfish tended to aim itself at anything smaller, in reasonable expectation of swallowing it. The safest tactic was not to get in front of one at any time. After surfacing, Skalet had blown off the roof, turning the submersible into a permanent and ungainly boat, limiting our options to one.

I hadn't been surprised.

"Let me tell you a story, " Skalet said, leaning easily against the side of the craft as if she relished its unpredictable rocking. "The Quinn family, having come into an inheritance through a tedious and complicated relationship you don't need to know, celebrate with an extravagant vacation—having learned of the mystical Nirvana Abyss from an acquaintance. Alas, like most Humans, they find the reality of paradise too damp for their taste and choose to leave on the last transport. They plan to change the passage they'd booked—back to the dreary and utterly unremarkable planet of Adamershome—for a visit to Picco's Moon to partake of its famed jewelry shops." One arm waved at the ocean around us. "Sadly, the Quinns are about to have an unfortunate experience with their Busfish, very soon now, being swept from its mouth before docking is complete. Everyone will be most gratified by their survival."

I stared out at what now seemed a very distant, surf-ravaged shoreline. "You can't be serious." The water between was a living darkness, heaving up and down, foaming like a mouth. And I knew what lay beneath all too well. *More mouths.*

Paul didn't bother arguing. "Did you steal their suits?" I brightened. Full environment suits were as good as being in a submersible, as long as one avoided the aforementioned very large mouths.

"Yours is stowed below with mine, Human." A gleam of white teeth in the dark. "But the one belonging to the Quinns' offspring is too small for you, Youngest. A pity. I suggest you scavenge from it what you can for protection."

I elbowed Paul in the rib cage before he could erupt in protest. *It would do no good.* I knew that tone from long ago.

Skalet was enjoying herself.

With Paul's silent and disapproving help, and the arrival of predawn light, I was able to free a set of goggles and rig a belt of the suit material that would hold a knife. I'd tried Skalet's own suit. If it hadn't been so frustrating staring at the fabric inside the chest area while Paul fought to readjust the suit beyond its limits, it would have been funny.

I had allowed myself one comment, midway through the suit demolition. "You could have simply bought three suits, the right size."

"And justified it how?" Skalet had countered. "Souvenirs? If you bother to remember, Youngest, the Prumbin track suits arriving and leaving, not individuals. It's the easiest way to know if they've lost another tourist to the locals."

Her reminder had triggered a thought that kept me silent for several moments, prompting a curious look from Paul. It wasn't something I thought he'd understand, even if I'd felt comfortable talking about the distinction between Web and non-Web in front of Skalet.

I'd known since my second bite of Ersh that web-beings were unique among living intelligences, having evolved in space rather than on a single piece of orbiting rock. It was a more fundamental distinction, to me, than our extended life span. I still had great difficulty grasping the attachment other species felt to their place of origin, or their equally strong drive to escape it.

Now, Skalet had inadvertently given me a new difference

to absorb. We were the only beings who didn't have to trust a suit or ship with our existence. A web-being could cycle and survive in any environment. My Human-self feared the swim to shore; my web-self, the true Esen, was in no danger. *Not that my present brain found that sufficient reassurance.*

I no longer believed I was close to understanding ephemerals. Paul's risk-taking as a younger being had been alarming enough. To find all species but ours so determined to explore a different world, to meet a different kind of being in its own habitat, that they willingly entrusted their short lives to valves, tubes, and fabric? *Where did they obtain such courage?* I wondered if the Prumbins had deliberately created a paradise where such risk had to be accepted and overcome.

If so, web-beings didn't belong there.

At last we were ready. Skalet had begun glowering at me, as if I were delaying on purpose. I didn't bother denying it. My Human-self was in no hurry to leap into the water. As if the Cosmic Gods had decided to pay attention, the waves had grown, each with white foam now slithering down its muscular shoulder. At close range, they lifted the submersible sharply from back to front. In both directions along the coast, they hurled in endless rows toward shore, in a hurry to pummel and drown any land creature they could catch.

Skalet consulted her chrono. "Any time now," she said. Paul tugged the filament he'd insisted link us together in a final check and she lifted a brow. "If we become separated," she warned, "as is likely, wait near the entrance to the ship-city. Without drawing attention." As this last part seemed directed at me and Paul had the audacity to nod, I ignored them both.

Just as well. I was the first to spot the fin, with its telltale antennae and other hardware. "There it is—the Busfish!" I announced, my voice annoyingly higher-pitched than usual.

I steeled myself to jump over the side, since Skalet's plan

relied on us washing to shore shortly after the Busfish docked, then saw Skalet's hand reach for the controls. Before I could do more than shout: "Paul!" the submersible obeyed her commands and split along its remaining seams, fragmenting beneath our feet.

Entering the ocean after the boat was something of an anticlimax.

Otherwhere

"THE situation is under control, Pa-Admiral."

Mocktap braced one booted foot on a boulder near the rim of the mountaintop and surveyed the orange-stained wasteland that was Picco's Moon, doing her best to breathe slowly. It was hard enough to maintain the illusion of strength without this thin air robbing her lungs. Still, she could see why S'kal-ru had chosen this peak as her hiding place. It was as admirably defensible as it was hideous. "Under control," she echoed. "Do you have any idea how ludicrous that sounds, Hubbar-ro?"

The Kraal beside her sighed. "I do, Pa-Admiral. Your affiliates seem disconcertingly optimistic under the circumstances."

Hubbar-ro had been a find she'd gladly attached to her personal staff: talented, ambitious, well-bred, and affiliated. A scoutship captain assigned to S'kal-ru through mutual affiliations within the House of Highbury, he was the only surviving Kraal of rank, besides herself, to have spoken to Paul Ragem and his companion, the creature S'kal-ru had introduced as having affiliations of tenth degree reliability. Nimal-ket. A remarkably lively Ket, given the record of her death Mocktap had unearthed on Ket-Prime.

Hubbar-ro knew only that she, a Kraal of high rank and noble House, had taken an interest in his career and had been properly grateful ever since. Both he and his family had sworn affiliation to the House of Mocktap, several proving their commitment by personal sacrifice in battle. Mocktap trusted Hubbar-ro as much as any of her staff. *And as little.*

"They were successful in dissuading Tumblers from approaching the site," he ventured. "There have been no further incursions."

Mocktap frowned and straightened by pushing her boot against the boulder. She took a moment to tug her battle gear into better alignment before saying: "Rock-based life. Slow and stubborn. You can talk to it until you run out of air, and never be sure it heard a word you said. Ask any trader. I'd be happier if my oh-so-vigilant affiliates had remembered they were dealing with quartz, not carbon. What about the shipcity?"

"The reports we received on our arrival this morning are confusing at best, Admiral. There's a great deal of starship traffic, docked as well as insystem waiting for room on the landing fields. For the most part, the ships are privately owned commercials. I've heard conflicting stories about Tumbler activity. The latest claimed they'd rolled back into the nearest valleys. If you wish, I can take an aircar and verify what's happening."

She glanced at his eager, handsome face, noting wryly that the years had touched it very little, except to add a rakish scar along one cheek and begin what would be a distinguished jowl in another few decades. Hubbar-ro was fonder of the table than dueling practice.

They would know him on sight: S'kal-ru, Paul—Esen. *Nimal-Ket, indeed.*

"No," she said, adding before he could argue: "Pick someone who still has something to prove. After you finish showing me what we have here."

"Certainly," he said, trying not to show his pleasure. "This way, please, Admiral. The lab's been moved into a structure embedded into the cliffside, damaged but sufficiently intact. It's down this staircase. They have the mineral samples there."

Mocktap pursed her lips then shook her head. "Later. I want to inspect our defensive capabilities." She didn't quite smile. "And offensive."

There would be no errors this time, S'kal-ru.

22: Ocean Morning

I FOUGHT nature for pride's sake—my nature, not Prumbinat's ocean—battling the urge to cycle into a form that could swim by instinct, instead struggling to implement memories of useful arm and leg movements before more water went up my nose. Warm water, though, warmer than the air. It had felt very pleasant before I'd sunk below the surface and realized I'd have to work at not staying there.

Before I could panic, or cycle, or most likely both, something pulled me up. I broke through a reflection of goggled faces against an almost blue sky and took a grateful gasp of air.

Which turned into a choking cough as the next wave tried to go down my throat.

"Close your mouth, Youngest."

I obeyed, hoping the goggles translated my glare at my web-kin. Destroying our only vehicle? *She'd done it,* I assured myself, *so we'd have no other choice but to follow her strategy.*

Paul was holding me against his suit, its buoyancy enough for us both. His attention was on the fin now approaching at speed. At first, it was the only thing I could see other than the moving walls of water on all sides and the three of us, bobbing up and down. Then, I realized there were larger waves at intervals. At the top of one of those, I could see the shore. It was significantly closer. Though I couldn't detect any lateral movement, the waves must be pushing us in the right direction.

I began to think this wasn't such a bad plan, which should have made me ready for the worst.

But I don't think any of us were ready for the appearance of a second fin, and a third, and a fourth. I stopped counting. *A school of wild Busfish!* They must have been attracted to their domesticated cousin. Untimely pheromones were always an issue in traffic safety.

We were moving even as these and other nonessential details insisted on parading through my head. Paul and Skalet were swimming across the pattern of waves, their movements a reassuring synchrony of power and skill, except Paul was also towing me. I finally got my arms digging through the water in a way that worked with, not against, the kicking of my legs.

It wasn't enough.

The open mouth of a tame Busfish was an impressive sight at dockside. The open mouth of an approaching wild individual engulfed the sky as it prepared to engulf us.

Given that I wasn't a tasty little Oieta any longer, it seemed remarkably unfair.

The ocean exploded around me. I grabbed for Paul, somehow having hands despite every instinct to abandon them, which would be to abandon him. We clung to one another, on my part with every expectation of being swallowed before my next breath—which was going to seriously complicate the immediate future. I thought furiously. My Human had a suit, which bought us time until the digestive enzymes went to work on its seals.

Then I stared into the gaping mouth, noting helplessly that it did indeed have large, functional tooth ridges both top and bottom. Enzymes were unlikely to be an issue after all.

It turned . . . blue.

Not the blue of sky or tormented ocean.

Web-blue.

Skalet!

Not daring to move, holding form, I clung to Paul as my web-kin assimilated the Busfish.

I knew there were more fins approaching, that this wasn't going to be enough to save him. I knew her choices. There were only so many sentient aquatics, unless Skalet had discovered and assimilated a new species since I'd last tasted her flesh. I knew she would cycle and escape, choose self-preservation . . . as she had before.

I should have known not to second-guess her.

Skalet's blue winked into a mountain of gray-black flesh, scars traced white by barnacles and other hitchhikers. She was easily a third larger than the Busfish. She must have assimilated mass from plankton as well. The other fins sank below the surface as the locals took the route of discretion and conceded their prey to the massive Refinne, a being not of their world.

Nor of the surface!

"No!" I shouted, choking as water splashed into my mouth, watching in horror as Skalet's sides expanded violently, then as suddenly collapsed inward. Her swim bladders had exploded, their contents no longer compressed by the depths of the ocean. "Hurry!" I urged, trying to swim to her as if somehow I could poke her into cycling faster, then I stopped, bobbing up with the waves as she convulsed and rolled on one side, her huge beautiful eyes turning milky and dull—blinded by light this form had never evolved to witness.

A wink of blue . . .

And the ocean was empty of giants.

"Over here, Es."

I swam to where Paul's arm showed above the water. As if the universe had tired of abusing me and mine, the waves were starting to subside into swells rather than minor mountains. I was still breathing hard by the time I reached him and seriously considering a change of form.

"She's alive."

"You sound surprised," I panted, helping Paul pull Skalet's Human-self over so her respiratory organs could obtain air. He increased the buoyancy of his suit to support us both and I settled myself against him, regarding my web-kin soberly as she coughed and sputtered. "The only reason she isn't giving orders already is because she's swallowed more than her share of ocean. Give her time."

"She saved our lives, Esen."

I let my legs float up, my toes becoming tiny pink archipelagos kissed by the now fully risen sun. "Who put us at risk?"

The answer to that question decided to speak for herself, though in a thready voice. "The plan—remains feasible. Paul has the ident. Covers the three of us."

Paul, was it? I spat salt from my mouth, unsettled by a polite Skalet. *To be fair,* I reminded myself, *she'd recently blown up.* She'd also lost a magnificent form to memory. I wondered if any Prumbin had seen Skalet's Refinne-self; if so, she'd added another chapter to the legend Ersh had begun.

Now she was Kraal. Whatever disguise she'd applied to her skin, to alter the structure of her face and the color of her eyes, hadn't been part of form-memory. The person lapped at by the ocean along Paul's other side, held safely in the curve of his arm despite all she'd done, was the Skalet of my memory. Her tattoos splashed like so much red-and-black paint from where neck met shoulder to the top of her shaved head.

This time, I bothered to read them, her memories informing me of the House names and bloody histories behind every whorl and sequence, the links she'd forged with lies. Skalet knew what I was doing and lifted her chin to show me her newest markings. Not full affiliation—there were subtle modifications that made this more an acceptance of service, with connotations of mutual interest. "Mocktap," I acknowledged. "So your admiral survived the loss of her ships."

"A momentary reprieve," she answered. As if suddenly realizing her dependence on another ephemeral, she pushed away from Paul to tread water for herself. "The good admiral has recently become—inconsiderate—of her affiliation."

"To you. Why?"

"I don't recall inviting you to question my life, Youngest."

"I don't recall inviting you to meddle in mine—"

Before I could finish, I found myself looking at Skalet's outraged face through the clarity of seawater. Up again, but before either of us could do more than sputter, Paul said calmly, but firmly: "Save it for dry land, Fems. Unless you'd prefer to wait for the next Busfish?"

The look of outrage on Skalet's face was the best thing I'd seen in days.

Otherwhere

THE office of Project Leader Kearn contained two worried Humans, a nondescript envelope and a black book, and a diminishing bottle of brandy. *What it didn't contain*, Rudy thought glumly, *were answers.*

"So that's all of it. Thanks to your codes and my ingenuity, we've Port Authority reports of attacks on their warehouse—and home," Rudy grimaced. It hadn't been pleasant reading, though it could have been worse. "No reports of fatalities. Paul and Es disappeared from the map sometime before Cristoffen had his fatal meeting," Rudy said, then sighed. "I hope of their own accord, to safety, but there's no way to be sure."

"Paul is resourceful."

The remark, coming from Kearn, felt strange. Rudy supposed it would for a while, until he grew accustomed to being on the same side as his former antagonist. "Oh, he's that," Rudy agreed. "But it will be difficult to get any answers. There's the Largas family involved—you know that history. They've shut down any other source of information I'd dare approach. Maybe they're at fault. At first, I thought it was Cristoffen—" He didn't bother admitting he'd also thought it had been Kearn.

Kearn shook his head. "I've kept the ship—and him—well away from the Fringe. And there's nothing left in the data banks to lead him to Minas XII. I'm sure Timri looked after that."

"Good." Rudy paused, then smiled ruefully. "Esen told me not to worry about Cristoffen—that you'd handle him. I couldn't understand why at the time."

Kearn's face darkened. "I didn't handle him well enough. Had I known about Paul's extended family before this—Cristoffen has a damn list!—I might have prevented one tragedy. Are you part of—no," he said quickly, holding up one hand before Rudy could answer. "I know more than I should already. These aren't safe times for any of us, not with Kraal involved."

"More than you know." Rudy told Kearn about his meeting with Sybil. When he finished, the Project Leader shook his head.

"What's the connection?" he said thoughtfully. "The Kraal are the key. I feel it." Kearn counted off on his fingers. "There's the one you suspect on Minas XII, this Meony-ro. The Kraal who contacted me forty years ago. The Kraal who is now leading our Cristoffen by the nose. Your 'Sybil.' And this enemy she wants you to find."

"Five," Rudy nodded.

"Or are there? If we discount Meony-ro—since he isn't in a place to act freely—there are four. My contact with the Kraal," Kearn seemed to hunt for words, then said, "differed in style from what I've learned of Cristoffen's. A pair, interested in Esen."

"There's another pair," Rudy offered. "Sybil and her enemy."

Kearn steepled his fingers and nodded. "So. What else do we know about the Kraal?"

"They're self-destructive lunatics." Rudy had moved to the chair; now he lifted his feet to Kearn's desk, careful not to disturb either book or envelope. "Lunatics who spend far too much time learning how to kill each other."

"Each other. Yes. That's significant, Rudy. Kraal feuds are always internal. They rarely travel outside their own space. When they must, they do so in groups and never keep households on alien worlds. Important, yes," Kearn stretched out the words as though checking their flavor. "I find it highly improbable there could be four separate Kraal engaged with outsiders. We are dealing with two individuals—I'm sure of it. Sybil and her enemy. Both of whom are interested in Kearn's Folly."

Rudy regarded Kearn with new respect. How had he worked with this being for years and never seen this side of him? *Then again*, he thought honestly, *he hadn't bothered to look, believing, like the rest, that Kearn was nothing more than a joke.* "Which one is which? There's no way to know."

"We can speculate. Something has changed to make Sybil need your help to find her enemy." He put down his glass too quickly, his face stricken. "Rudy. You don't suppose—could Esen become Human? Could she be the Kraal in your image?"

Rudy smiled into his glass. "She can be Human," he acknowledged. "But not that one. There's nothing Kraal about Es."

"Good, good." Kearn wiped his forehead and scalp before taking a drink. "That would have made things much too confusing. I've so many questions about her as it is—not now, I know." He paused. "But the timing— I still believe there's some link here. Trouble for Esen and Paul on Minas XII, then the incident with Cristoffen, then Sybil hires you to find her enemy. An enemy no longer in Kraal-controlled space, or she wouldn't need you. It's as if a battle is being waged, with Esen at its core. But why?" He looked a little embarrassed. "Surely the Kraal don't believe the rumor about a biological weapon any longer."

"Sybil didn't mention it. I had the feeling she was

after blood, not secrets." There was that other complication. Rudy came to a decision. He reached under his shirt and tugged the scorched data cube from its hiding place. "Cristoffen brought this to his meeting with Duda. He baited him with it, saying it contained information about—" he took a steadying breath, "—about another of Esen's kind, living in this part of space. That if Duda and the rest of the Group knew about this being, they wouldn't be helping Esen."

Kearn stared at the tiny thing almost hungrily. "Were you able to read any of it?"

"Not yet, not with the equipment I had available. You might have better luck." Rudy put it down beside the envelope and book, lining the three items in a row. "It could be a Kraal fabrication. It might be misinterpreted information or material related to the real monster—the evil one you mentioned. Or—" he paused suggestively.

"Or it could be exactly what Cristoffen claims."

"You don't seem surprised."

Kearn glanced up from the data cube. "Why would I be? Esen is a living being. She had to come from somewhere; there have to be others of her kind there at least. My discussions with other academics suggest there have been many contacts over the years, given the number of folktales about 'shifters. Why would Esen be the only one?"

There was no point in secrets, not now, Rudy told himself, although he winced at Paul's probable reaction to what he was about to reveal. But Kearn's obsession might mean he actually knew more than any of them, maybe enough to help if he had all the pieces. "Esen believes herself to be," he explained. "Her species—she calls herself a Web-being—isn't from this sector of space. The only others living here were members of her family, six altogether. All but Esen died as a result of that same monster you hunted. Esen told me it was a member of her species, but mindless—

driven by instinct to hunt them for food and killing any other intelligent life it encountered during its pursuit. She called it 'Death.'"

Kearn's eyes might have been riveted on his, but Rudy thought the other Human was looking inward, adding this information to other pieces, watching it rearrange what he knew into new shapes. He didn't interrupt.

Finally, Kearn pursed his lips and gave a quick nod. "Well, if there is a second web-being involved in all this, it isn't a predator. I think we'd know that by now. 'Death' wasn't subtle."

"Agreed. But if there is one, is it Sybil's enemy or someone else? Or is this a ruse to enlist Cristoffen, to help the Kraal find the real thing—Esen? Or— We don't even know the right questions," Rudy growled in frustration.

"We might have the answers and not know it," Kearn said calmly. "Leave the cube with me. I must examine what Sybil gave you—and I want to look into this book immediately. Can you open the envelope without blowing up my ship?"

"Of course," Rudy told him, pretending to be offended.

"Let's do it before Cristoffen returns. I'll have someone from the crew seal up his room so he doesn't find the mess before we have a chance to talk to him. For what good it will do." This last seemed to come from bitter experience.

"He probably doesn't know much, but there should be something in his comp from Sybil. We should have a look at whatever Timri pulled from his files."

"Yes, yes. You know, we missed lunch. I'm sure of it. There isn't time to waste, but I have some crackers . . ."

Rudy's eyes narrowed. He watched as Kearn bustled over to a cupboard, glass still in one hand. *Some-*

thing isn't tracking, he told himself. "Timri has searched his comp, hasn't she?"

"She's been busy. I've asked her to check Cristoffen's messages using my codes and arrange for him not to receive any more. Which I assume explains the envelope." Kearn seemed to be having difficulty opening the cupboard. "We don't need her to be further involved. That's why I wanted you here. You have the expertise—"

"Yes, but two—"

"No." Having found his box, Kearn slammed the cupboard shut with unnecessary force. "Cristoffen's friends are too dangerous. I won't take chances with the Kraal. I don't want you saying a word to Timri. Not one. Why do you think I had you remove her—" he stopped, but it was too late.

Well, well. Rudy put his hands behind his head and leaned back to study his former commander's flushed face. "The only people in danger from Cristoffen or his 'friends' are the ones on his list—or those who should be," he observed dryly, then shook his head in wonder. "How long have you known, Lionel?"

Kearn seemed to sag. "That she spies on me for Paul? Since that day I overheard you both. That she's part of this group of his?" Kearn tossed the box of crackers on the table and the brandy left in his glass down his throat. "I didn't know it existed until Cristoffen showed me that abominable list. At least he believes Paul dead." His voice became husky. "I had no idea I'd driven Paul to anything so desperate. I knew he'd put his life on the line, but not that he'd convinced others to join him. It's what Timri would do, risk everything for a cause. I can't let her come to the attention of the Kraal—"

There were two doors into Kearn's office. Rudy's feet thudded to the floor as the one leading to the bedroom burst open, then he relaxed. *This,* he decided, *was going to be entertaining.* Timri's fury looked remarkably self-righteous for someone who'd taken the ultimate low-tech route to eavesdropping. Kearn had some explaining to do.

But Kearn, who'd been startled enough to drop his glass, was staring behind Rudy. Rudy whipped around in his chair to see Cristoffen standing in the now-open door to the corridor, the weapon in his hand aimed at Timri.

Before Rudy did more than tense, stuffy, nervous, ever-so-foolish Kearn—whom Rudy had misjudged at least twice today, not to mention innumerable times during their years together—stepped into the weapon's path.

Cristoffen fired.

23: Shoreline Afternoon

"IT'S not open to discussion."

Ersh. I glared at my web-kin even as I wondered if there'd ever been a more ridiculous argument—or place for one.

Not in any memory I'd assimilated, that was certain. Bad enough the three of us were roped together, but Paul was floating on his back looking like a rotting corpse about to explode, while Skalet and I hung in the water, our arms draped across his chest for support.

"We cycle, swim to cover—there have to be some rocks or barges in the harbor we can use for shelter. We rejoin Paul on the shore." Something nibbled my toes and I drew up my feet, doing my utmost to avoid looking into the water. "There's definitely mass to spare in here," I added somewhat breathlessly.

The warm, sun-bright waves of Prumbinat's ocean were carrying us inexorably toward her shore. From the look on Skalet's face, it was more likely those waves would switch direction than that she'd change her mind. *Not just her face*, I thought, wincing inwardly at the pain she must have endured to gain that set of three scars, parallel and deep, running from shoulder to breast on her right side. Ceremonial marks, made with a dueling claw. She must have stayed Human while they were inflicted, Human while they healed—carefully anointed to produce the maximum amount of scar tissue—and, as adamantly, continued to refuse to be anything but Human now.

Nor, she insisted, should I.

It didn't seem to be penetrating her bald skull that her preference meant two of us without means to stay afloat while fighting the line of breakers between us and shore, with only Paul immune from the peril of swallowing seawater until forced to cycle into something that could breathe it.

"I have an idea," Paul informed us. Skalet looked startled, as though she'd forgotten our tiny green raft had a living core. Understandable, since the goggles had darkened to protect his eyes, leaving no external clues. I was surprised only that he'd waited so long to intervene, being somewhat used to my Human taking charge when our plans—altered—unexpectedly.

Paul's idea involved more technology than biology. *Given what had got us into the water in the first place, that was probably just as well.* He had me use the small knife from my belt—something that occasioned squirming over him and sinking all three of us for a moment—to reset the servo propulsion system originally intended to retrieve his suit, and presumably its occupant, from the Abyss. With the right timing, a lack of Busfish in our path, and some luck—my personal contribution to the plan, though I didn't tell Skalet—he felt the system should provide enough thrust to push the three of us through the worst of the surf and into calmer water.

I trusted Paul, who'd sounded confident. Mind you, he sounded confident whenever trying to convince me of anything I doubted, including his recent proposal to visit the Ycl.

Skalet had no reason to trust Paul or accept his plan. I expected her to argue—or at least express various dour opinions on our chances—while we waited to drift closer. Instead, she submerged herself so that only the arm holding onto Paul's suit, and her face, showed above the surface. I presumed this was to protect her skin from the sun. I'd experienced a severe reddening of the tip of my nose in this form once before and understood such caution.

There had been freckles.

"Make sure you're both secured," Paul said after a few moments of stoic breathing, birdcalls, and the slapping of water against suit and skin. "It won't be long. Our speed's picked up."

Judicious kicking kept us centered in the main channel leading to Gathergo, following the churning wake left by the Busfish. As we passed between the first set of tall yellow warn-offs—a somewhat pointless precaution since the surf made it impossible to see the warnings unless aimed straight at them—I could spot the Busfish's fin drooping beside the wharf, framed by rows of tethered Carcows. The beasts were waiting to pull long, segmented carts jammed with those passengers opting for quaint and unforgettable over convenient and odor-free. I hoped, as I spat salt water, that my companions were planning on the latter. I was all in favor of trying a mode of transport that wouldn't want to eat me. *Once we were on land.* Something my Human-self anticipated greatly.

It felt as though dry land was farther away than ever, despite the way the second set of warn-offs sped past our little flotilla of Humanity faster than the first. The channel was narrowing as it approached landfall, waves from the open ocean now funneling between massive break walls. Those walls of tumbled rock and coral, painted a predictable yellow, were part of the Prumbins' ongoing efforts to keep their Drossy herds from making landfall where they shouldn't, and from grazing on what the Prumbins would prefer to eat themselves. Not to mention walk on what they shouldn't and leave what they shouldn't behind.

There was, I thought, *a lot to be said for Rigellian sheep.* Beginning with their being too small to accidentally sit on their shepherd.

Not that this was the optimum moment to ponder agriculture. The three of us were tied together with the filament originally intended to keep me tethered to Paul. The lack of slack wasn't a problem, since we wanted to be as hydrodynamic as possible once the propulsion unit was engaged. What was a problem was the way Skalet and I had to gasp for breath between drenchings. Supposedly Paul was doing his best to be a stable life raft, but at times I thought he was deliberately testing the lungs of this form by tumbling down the leeside of each wave.

All too soon, we approached the narrowest point, where the pent-up waves heaved into a tortured landscape of white-capped mountains, with the added bonus of a significant undertow grabbing any foot dangling too low. This maelstrom approach suited the Busfish and Drossy, giving the huge creatures a necessary boost over the submerged sandbar that had originally protected this part of the coast. The Prumbins had considered dredging a channel, but leaving the sandbar as an obstacle had proved the only way to slow down approaching Busfish. Always a concern.

So this was it. I took a deep breath, holding it and Paul as Skalet set off the propulsion system. I lost the breath immediately as my view of the waves ahead became much too intimate, an alarming blur of froth and blue-green as we plunged straight through. The tie around my waist dragged me along, but the water's force tore at my grip on Paul. My left hand came loose.

A hand clamped over my right wrist, holding it firmly against Paul's suit as we kept moving forward.

Ersh knows how I avoided cycling. The urge didn't come from our apparently suicidal passage through the channel, although it should have. No, what risked my self-control was the feel of Skalet's hand performing such a—Human— act.

We were in daylight again, so quickly I felt disoriented. The waves were tamed back into long, gentle swells, their power diluted as they spread the width of the harbor. Our momentum kept us moving on the crest of one, right on target.

"We're clear. We made it." I saw no reason for Paul to

sound as though he was gasping for air, since I was the one with seawater burning her sinus cavities.

Skalet, who'd been looking ahead, said, "Wait." Something hit my leg. Her foot. She was kicking to slow us down.

Obviously, there was something not quite right with my web-kin. I hauled myself on top of Paul's suit to see what she was doing. "Getting to shore was the idea—"

"Not there. Not anymore." Her breathing was ragged as she put more and more effort into altering our course.

"What's happening?" this from Paul, who was stuck on his back and facing the way we'd come.

"Give me the knife."

"Not until you—"

"Then you cut him free of the suit, fool, so he can swim! Hurry!" Skalet began to swim in earnest, awkwardly, pulling the rest of us using the line around her waist.

There were many things that made me stop and think about my actions. That snap of command in Skalet's familiar voice wasn't one of them. I began slicing the fabric of Paul's suit with frantic haste. *What had she seen in that glimpse landward?*

My Human helped, ripping loose the fasteners and tossing aside the goggles. I cut free the line binding us together before Skalet could tow him underwater. With a final struggle, Paul pulled himself out of the suit, which sank as he released it. He ducked his head below the surface, washing what appeared to be lines of dried sweat from his face and hair. Then we both relaxed, treading water, preoccupied by the sight of Skalet's thin white arms appearing and disappearing as she swam steadily away, parallel to the beach.

We turned to look at each other, I for one delighted to see a face instead of goggled and distorted eyes. A tired face, that nonetheless smiled at me. "Are you all right?"

"Ask me again on dry land." As if that had been a signal, Paul and I looked toward shore.

There should have been something ludicrous, almost

harmless, about a group dressed in black uniforms moving among colorful tourists on a tropical beach. *There wasn't.*

"If those are Kraal," I protested, "why is Skalet avoiding them?"

"Does it matter?" Paul asked grimly. "You can't swim much longer."

I spat out a mouthful of water. "I'll cycle and tow you," I offered, already preparing to leave this form, with its tired legs and tendency to sink.

"No."

"You, too?" I sputtered in disgust. "There's mass everywhere—"

"Esen, she has a reason for staying Human—for wanting you to do the same. Let's not second-guess her or the Kraal." Paul, as at home in water as any primate could be, took off his footwear and tucked them in the belt of his pants. Then he rolled over on his stomach, looking as comfortable as if he'd been on a mattress. "Hold onto my shoulders. Careful not to—" I eased up and Paul resurfaced. "—push down," he continued.

"Thaddaway," I offered helpfully, as my Human steed's arms began to dig into the Prumbinat Ocean with a reassuringly steady rhythm.

Although there was nothing reassuring about following Skalet as she fled her adopted culture.

Otherwhere

THERE was a Port City on Picco's Moon, consisting of a necklace of prefabricated aircar and tug hangers loosely arranged around a trio of buildings on stilts. The stilts served the dual purpose of allowing passing Tumblers to ignore the existence of the buildings—which had somehow been built over one of their most commonly used roadways—and made it feasible to host meetings between Tumblers and nonmineral beings on the ground floor, had such meetings ever been held.

The two larger buildings belonged to Crawdad's Sanitation Ltd.: one was the windowless and heavily guarded warehouse where the officially sanctioned collection of ritual leavings, from the ground floor and other, more secret locations, were sorted for buyers offworld. The other possessed windows that were usually curtained against Picco's lurid orange and contained luxurious living accommodations for those doing the guarding, collecting, and sorting. The top three floors were devoted to sanitation inspectors and their vehicles, since locating new deposits of ritual leavings was a chancy thing that depended on patterns of Tumbler movement.

The shipcity itself was an open and reasonably busy one, the Tumblers unable to comprehend why a sanitation company would want a monopoly on shipping. So Crawdad's was forced to welcome independent brokers interested in bidding on smaller or damaged stones. In the spirit of making the best of things, the sanitation company did open a bar for spacers, justly infamous for the dilution and cost of its drinks.

The third building held the maintenance personnel and equipment required to keep starships—and spacers—moving. Unlike other remote and bleak postings, there was a long list of applicants for even the most menial tasks here, individuals drawn by rumors of easy wealth. One of the most popular was that you could sell the soles of your boots—and accumulated gem dust—for a small fortune. As Crawdad's owned the boots and all rights to any dust, debris, or dirt—however faceted and valuable—newcomers learned to be grateful for the percentage of sales Crawdad's granted each worker. Or became poachers.

There was law, of a sort, on Picco's Moon, if you counted a Port Authority that divided its time and resources between resolving docking disputes, rescuing and prosecuting crashed gem poachers, or acting as local guides so entrepreneurs and traders didn't wander into one of the local and quite toxic Tumbler garden spots. No one was fond of cleaning up the result, especially Tumblers.

Chief Constable Alphonsus Lundrigan could have been in charge of Picco's Moon's Port Authority since the just past Eclipse or since alien ships first landed. Few Tumblers were able to identify separate species let alone individual members. If asked, however, Tumbler Elders would have chimed themselves pleased, overall, with the efforts of the flesh-burdened to keep their own out of the way. Before recent events, that is.

Tumblers, it turned out, were not so different from nonmineral beings. At the first sign of serious trouble, they were quite capable of finding out who was in charge and who should be responsible.

The only problem, Alphonsus grumbled to himself, *was he was neither.*

The shipcity had grown since he'd last stood at this viewport. As it had last night, and the preceding true day. And the ones before those. The docking tug operators were becoming adept at packing them in. It was easier since no one seemed in any rush to leave. There were ships on every scrap of properly level pavement, including what had been tug lanes. Now, from where he stood, the entire winding expanse of the Literiai Plateau was a maze of starships. If he squinted through the port from the side, it could almost be a forest.

A forest the Tumblers wanted removed.

Maybe. Or maybe they were encouraging more trade—the visitations seem to suggest that. Everyone knew the day had to come when the Tumblers realized they didn't need to pay Crawdad's Sanitation to clean up the Port City.

They'd sent him messages, brought daily by a delegate who, in most un-Tumbler fashion, asked for him by name. Long, convoluted messages. Messages that were longer than most books he'd ever read. None of them actually referred to the starships. None of them, that he could tell, were complaints. Some were quite entertaining, in a cryptic way.

Yesterday, they stopped. Alphonsus didn't know what that meant either.

But it didn't take an alien culture specialist to know this haphazard flood of uninvited ships was unpopular with one group. Alphonsus grinned to himself. Naomi Crawdad and her company suits were burning up the com lately as well. Since the rush, a Tumbler couldn't drop a glittering bundle without a horde of spacers ready to pick it up.

Not that there'd been a Tumbler here since yesterday's chime-along—or whatever you'd call it when an impressive group of twenty Tumblers lined up to chime a single chord for most of the afternoon, right in front of the only shipcity access not plugged by a starship. Alphonsus' grin widened. Crawdad's futile effort to cordon off the deposits had almost precipitated a riot.

It wasn't that he disapproved of the company's legal and exclusive contract; he simply enjoyed seeing someone else grab the big ones for a change.

A polite cough signaled that his second-in-command, an older Moderan named Bris, had managed to sneak up on him again. *Having padded feet was cheating.* "What is it?" Alphonsus asked, turning his back on the viewport.

"Sir." Bris had stopped a safe distance away, although he was really quite adept at not spitting when vocalizing sibilants. His soft snarls were translated into comspeak through the implant in his throat. "We've a translight com for you. It's Joel Largas of Largas Freight. He says—well, you'll want to hear this for yourself."

Alphonsus stiffened. *Was this it? The trouble he'd been waiting for?* He hadn't slept a full night this week, not since that warning arrived—or, more accurately, since he'd flashed a coded message to Paul Cameron and it had been reflected back, an indication the host receiver was nonfunctional and the backups hadn't been engaged.

Paul had promised the system was foolproof, that he'd be able to compensate from any location with a translight com.

In his lengthy career, on worlds and stations where he'd investigated crimes that turned stolen boots and incomprehensible chiming into ways to mark time until retirement, Alphonsus had learned the simplest explanation for someone failing to make contact as expected.

They couldn't.

The person who might know was waiting. Alphonsus tried not to appear to hurry to the com room, the heart of any Port Authority. Picco's Moon boasted better equipment than its traffic required, by way of obligatory donations from Crawdad's Sanitation Ltd. Much of the equipment sat unused, however, because Tumblers funded the staffing. Since none of Alphonsus' predecessors had been able to clearly convey the need for increasing numbers of staff, they'd been unable to increase that funding from the amount requested before Alphonsus was born.

The lack of staff hadn't been critical until this week, when he'd had to assign search and rescue personnel to sit the coms along with the regulars, or risk ships coming in on the same landing vectors. Right now, it looked deceptively peaceful; the staff looked half asleep. A few waved a greeting. Most were leaning on one or both elbows, staring into their displays. Cups of sombay paraded across every surface, some steaming, most cold.

At least they only had to deal with local traffic on actual approach, Alphonsus thought with relief. Innermost of three Port Cities in the Xir System, their responsibility was confined by Picco's orbit and included only this Moon suitable for landing. Outsystem traffic routed through Port Authority on Nerri, the most distant of Xir's worlds, into Xir Prime, then was further sorted insystem as it passed Port Authority on Szhenna, a popular stop for methane breathers seeking a spa experience.

Alphonsus decided against having the call transferred to his office, however much he'd prefer privacy. Privacy implied something to hide, not a safe thought to raise when it was true. "Station 4, please," he asked quietly, hearing Bris echo the request as he took the empty chair. When the green light flashed, he pressed the button to accept. "Port Authority, Picco's Moon. Lundrigan, here."

"Phonse, when are you going to retire?" The friendly, familiar greeting, as if nothing was wrong. He'd know Joel Largas' rich voice anywhere.

"When they raise my pension," he replied, as always. "What can I do for you, Joel?"

"Get me down there, Phonse. Your people are telling me to park in orbit. My captains are telling me there's some kind of rush—that Tumblers are throwing gems at them. What's going on?"

"If I knew, I'd tell you. But you know I can't mess with the docking priors. We've got—" Alphonsus snagged the daily report from Bris' paw and read the line in red "—thirteen ahead of you. And Largas Freight has, last I looked, six ships already docked. I'm not playing favorites. They'd lynch me!" Given the passions he'd witnessed for himself the last few days, that wasn't necessarily exaggeration.

"I can't tell you everything on an open com. Trust me, Phonse, you want me down there, now. The criminals responsible for the attacks on Minas XII—I've reason to know they are already on Picco's Moon or coming your way." A pause. "You know me, Alphonsus. You know I wouldn't be here—wouldn't be asking this—if it wasn't a matter of life or death. I've kin on those ships. Including my grandchildren."

"I know." The *Largas Legend* had finned down two days ago, Tomas and Luara Largas being sent to pay the courtesy call and docking fee. Tomas, all grown-up and looking more like his grandfather every day; Luara with their father's eyes and disconcerting attentiveness. Without a clear idea what had happened, Alphonsus hadn't dared ask if they knew why Paul wasn't answering. "Give me a moment. Lundrigan out."

Alphonsus drummed his fingers once on the console, then lifted two in a signal. Bris leaned closer. "The evac pad's still clear?" he asked.

"You can't be serious."

"We don't want criminals roaming about, do we? Let's get him down, hear what he has to say. He can keep his engines live—lift out of the way if we need the pad. Make it happen, Bris." Alphonsus surrendered his chair to the other, whose subvocal snarl didn't need translation.

Alphonsus walked toward his office, preoccupied by the dreadful conviction he knew exactly which criminals Joel planned to expose to him. He was halfway across the com room floor when the com-tech at station nine turned and said: "Sir! Sir, we have Ganthor."

The head of Picco's Moon Port Authority stopped in his tracks. "Say again?" he asked weakly. The entire room went silent. Everyone listened. Out the corner of his eye, he saw Bris rising from his chair, the hair on his shoulders and back fully erect so the Moderan looked half again his normal size.

The com-tech's voice was amazingly professional, all things considered. "I repeat, sir. We have Ganthor on approach."

"You're sure?"

"Yessir. It's hard to be wrong about them, sir." An understandable edge to the last "sir."

"Do we have them on scan?" Alphonsus demanded, moving toward the scan-tech as he spoke, meeting Bris so they loomed together over the unfortunate being. "Hurry up! What's the word from outsystem?"

Voices began to overlap, properly calm, informative voices, now that he'd put them to work. "Szhenna reports fifty heavy cruisers incoming on the elliptic." "Nerri confirms a group of fifty. Now they report a second fleet upward of seventy. They're still scanning."

"I have them, sir. It's hard to count them while

they're bunched. Sir. Szhenna confirms. The Ganthor aren't responding to hails. They're just—coming."

Alphonsus put one hand on the scan-tech's shoulder, half reassurance, half to keep himself steady. *He was a Port Jelly, not a general.*

"Maybe they heard about the gem rush," someone ventured, provoking a few nervous chuckles.

"Let's not make assumptions," Alphonsus said, straightening. "Cilla, send a squeal set for one-day translight, coded for Commonwealth military vessels. Tell them our situation. Make sure they know we have significant civilian traffic on the ground and no way to clear landing space. Warden, Lerya, Joe. I want those ships out of orbit and any inbound fools turned around now. Send them to Szhenna if you have to. Who's linked to Nerri?"

"Me, sir."

Dravis. Her voice wasn't as steady as the rest, but that could have been feathers over her implant. "Advise Nerri to shut down this system if they haven't already. No incoming traffic. Get that confirmed by Havaline. Don't take some groggy 'tech's word for it."

That drew another, easier set of laughs. They were settling into the work, relying on him.

"Yes, sir."

"And someone go down to crew quarters and wake up Mason and Trit. I want them to go out and find a Tumbler who knows what's happening. Now."

The Chief Constable took a deep, steadying breath through his nose and let it out again, then nodded to himself. They'd done what they could about the near future—that left dealing with the now. "Bris?" he said firmly. "Let's find out what Largas wants and get him off that evac pad. We might need it."

24: Shipcity Afternoon

FOR once, I wasn't the one who'd misjudged a form's capabilities and had to suffer the consequences. Though my pleasure in Skalet's current misery was probably both ephemeral and childish, I couldn't bring myself to feel any guilt at all. In fact, I thought Ersh would have enjoyed it, too.

I was, however, a little puzzled by its cause. Finally, after testing the cold rain curtaining our shelter with my fingers for the third time, and imagining Skalet crouched just beyond sight in the deluge, I had to ask Paul. "Do you know why she won't come in here with us?"

We sat shoulder to shoulder, so I knew he could hear me over the storm. Still, his answer was slow in coming. "I'd know if she were Human," he said at last, in that tone of voice he used when hoping to avoid further questions.

Not that it worked. I was a firm believer in questions, and their answers. His reply was not satisfactory at all. "She is not Human," I pointed out. "I see no reason why she can't come in out of the rain." Skalet didn't have the excuse of needing to dump heat—her cycle into the Refinne and back would have taken care of that excess quite nicely. *Which meant,* "She could become chilled," I told him. Not that it was much warmer inside our tiny cavelike shelter, given we sat on cracked pavement, protected by a portion of collapsed wall.

For some reason, Paul sighed deeply at this, then moved as far from me as possible. Intermittent bursts of lightning helped me see that he was pulling off his clothing. As a being of superior judgment, I clutched mine tighter to me and prepared to protest this behavior.

But the next flash revealed I was alone. *Paul?* I waited three breaths, then, just as I shouted: "Paul!" a figure dove through the rain to crouch next to me. I reached out in the dark, touching chilled, wet flesh, feeling the shudders coursing through muscle as the body tried to warm itself. "That was pointless," I started to say, then realized the breathing beside me wasn't his.

Flash. Skalet, a glimmer of rain-slicked white. She had clothing in her hands and was struggling to put it on. *Paul's clothes.* Several possibilities passed through my mind, none of which completely fit the events. I pulled up my knees and curled into a morose ball to await enlightenment.

Once Skalet finished squirming, she gave a low whistle. Another figure dove into our shelter—as wet and almost as cold—and shoved against my other side, pushing me into my web-kin. She didn't complain, likely because I was by far the warmest thing in our now overcrowded cave.

Was, being the operative word, as Paul tucked himself into my shoulder and his chill began to steal heat from that part of me as well. From the feel of them, they'd divided the clothing so neither had adequate protection from the weather. Both were soaking wet.

I decided against further questions, given the unlikelihood of a sensible answer from either of them until the storm ended. *If,* I grumbled to myself, trying to reclaim at least some room for my shoulders, *I received one even then.*

I certainly didn't expect one from Skalet, even if she was responsible for our huddling here to wait out the monsoon which had taken the place of sunset. Paul had the Quinn family's ident. Skalet and I knew the codes to release funds to any of a hundred other suitable identities for this planet. We could have been dry and warm by now. *With supper.*

But no. We were waiting for dawn and hiding in rubble, the remains of a row of buildings near the shipcity. From the way the pavement shuddered periodically, structures built to withstand hurricane winds had succumbed to the arrival of massive docking tugs and other paraphernalia of modern transport. Though I recalled from Ansky-memory that Carcows could do significant damage to cobblestone, if allowed to follow the same route too often.

Useless facts. I hunched into a tighter ball of discomfort, wishing I had the Human ability to pick and choose what to remember. Like Ersh, I could isolate selected memories into specific portions of my mass and completely remove them from my body—a dreadful process requiring a significant period of mourning, and occasionally fudge, even when I knew my missing portions were in the kitchen cryofreezer.

There should be an easier way. Whenever I complained, Paul was fond of telling me that facts, seemingly useless or otherwise, belonged in libraries, collected and organized for anyone to use. *A dangerous concept.*

Paul and his library, I sighed to myself, relaxing into the growing warmth along both sides as the larger Human forms beside me began giving back what they'd taken. It was a dream my friend clung to as fiercely as he protected my secret; a dream fed every time I answered a question about another species or taught him another language; a dream my secret made impossible.

Web-beings don't dream. But we sleep as appropriate to our formsake's. As I drifted toward unconsciousness, I found myself imagining Paul's library as he'd described it to me in loving detail late one night, long ago. There had probably been wine involved. The building would be low, white, and welcoming, with a shipcity of its own formed by visitors. There'd be a park close by, large enough for a Lanivarian to run, delightfully wild and dark at its edges. At its core would be gardens, each suited to a different species so those who wanted a scent of home could find it, while explorers could sniff or otherwise sample a dozen planets in a stroll.

Inside, there would be comfy chairs for any being who chose to visit. I'd added this to the vision; Paul had smiled.

Then he'd talked about rooms for scholarship and debate, space for those inclined to stay, and transcription halls for those who wished only to come and collect what they wanted.

As long as they came in person and left knowledge in return.

I smiled sleepily. *My Human web-kin.* A library of language and culture, where users had to contribute. Open to all species. Skalet had feared I was forming an ephemeral Web. *What would she think of Paul's dream?*

The being in question moved uneasily, making a small, unhappy sound in his sleep. I made sure my elbow, rather small and sharp, wasn't in his ribs, not worrying about Skalet's comfort as I readjusted myself. *If she wanted to sleep,* I told myself, *she could cycle into a Skenkran and hang from the ceiling.*

I knew I was being petty. For one thing, an adult Skenkran couldn't fit without folding in half. My mood had something to do with losing the urge to sleep between imagining Paul's future and being aware of Paul's present—both ruined by my web-kin.

How had Skalet known to follow us here? That was the easy question. Of the ships available to us on Minas XII, only one had had a destination a web-being would choose for hiding. It wouldn't surprise me to learn she'd arranged for that freighter to stop at Minas XII on its way to Prumbinat. Skalet was no believer in luck.

Why wait until now? Harder to answer. I might have assumed it had something to do with Picco's Moon and what was happening there, except for her reaction to that news. I poked my neat Human tongue into an intact cheek, remembering all too well. As for one of Skalet's affiliates betraying her? Again, if she'd only just discovered that, it couldn't be why she'd sought me out. There was something else, something she was hiding.

I was seriously tempted to cycle and bite her to find out.

*   *   *

Hunger woke me, hunger and snoring. I could ignore the first, and did for a while, closing my eyes tightly against the dark, promising my stomach sustenance when the sun returned. But the second?

I had no idea if it was the positions they'd both curled into, the seawater they'd likely inhaled, or some peculiarity of exhausted, damp Humanity, but I was being assaulted in stereo. Mind you, Paul's snore was an almost hypnotic rumble. That alone I might have endured. But Skalet? There was nothing endurable about an erratic whistling sound interspersed with a most undignified snort.

Besides, it was high time I started things moving in a direction of my choice, not hers.

They'd probably considered me safely boxed in between them. Obviously, neither remembered the flexibility and stealth of a young Human. It was the work of three whistle/snorts for me to extricate myself from my elders and slip out of the shelter.

The rain had stopped, replaced by a soft, warm breeze redolent of wet Carcows and compost. The fronds of the trees scratched against one another and the tree trunks, making a hissing sound as though we were still by the shore. *And I was dry!* I looked up at the starry sky, lifted my arms above my head, and spun a couple of times for the sheer joy of it. *Very quietly.* Paul had frequently demonstrated an uncanny ability to hear the tiniest noises I might make, even if he'd been fast asleep. I didn't doubt my combat-trained web-sister could do the same.

Then I tiptoed away, my bare feet making no noise at all on the cobblestones, heading for the glow at the end of this street that marked an intersection with the living part of Gathergo, the part that led to the shipcity.

It was time for me to start acting like the Senior Assimilator of the Web of Esen.

Including finding something to eat, I promised my now hopefully gurgling stomach.

Otherwhere

RUDY couldn't tell who looked more flabbergasted: Timri, frozen in the act of grabbing for Kearn; Kearn, hands half-raised as if to protect himself; or Cristoffen, staring down at a weapon that had fired a flash of searing blue . . . and done nothing.

Before Kearn's bemused assistant found something else to fire, Rudy shoved him up against the wall, using his broad forearm to pin him there while he tore the weapon from unresisting fingers and tossed it to the floor. "Don't move," he ground out, not taking his eyes from Cristoffen's. "Lionel," he called. "You all right?"

"Did you lose your mind?" this from Timri, although it wasn't clear to Rudy if she was berating Cristoffen for trying to kill her or Kearn for trying to protect her. Likely both, he thought.

"Captain Lefebvre?" Cristoffen bleated past Rudy's arm, though he wisely remained still. His eyes had opened wide, their pupils dilated. "What are you doing here? Do you have any idea what's going on? You should be helping me—"

Rudy considered playing along and then shuddered. *Lie to the Kraal with this hothead at his side?* "I don't think so," he growled, all the while quickly checking Cristoffen for other weapons. None. *An unprepared hothead at that.* He pushed his captive toward a chair. "Sit and be grateful I didn't snap your neck."

"Lionel!" Answering one question, Timri had by this

time taken hold of Kearn by one shoulder and was shaking him. "What were you thinking?"

"Not now, Timri," Kearn insisted. He pulled free, then walked over to his desk chair and sat down, for all the world as if preparing to give another of his stuffy lectures on proper crew deportment. He even steepled his hands on the desk. They were shaking, but he did it. "I think you have some explaining to do, Ensign. Starting with whatever that was you tried to use against—a fellow member of this crew."

It was *one of his lectures.* Rudy did his best not to smile.

Timri had already picked up the weapon, passing it to Rudy without a word, her troubled gaze never leaving Kearn. Rudy lifted the crude, stubby thing so he could examine it and still keep an eye on Cristoffen. There was a trigger and a handle suited to a Human hand, but where the muzzle would be on a conventional blaster, the metal opened into a wide mouth. It looked designed to make bubbles, not cause death—a harmlessness Rudy didn't believe for a moment, despite the lack of effect on Kearn. He took advantage of everyone's preoccupation with Cristoffen to tuck the thing inside his shirt.

"But—" Cristoffen was groping to understand and not doing particularly well. "Why did you get in the way, Project Leader? I could have—"

"Killed me?" At the other's mute nod, Kearn went on: "Fortunately for both of us, weapons seem to misfire around you. However, I think I deserve to know why, don't you?"

"My cabin—someone broke into it—I came here to warn you—it had to be her. But—" Cristoffen stared at the objects on the table in front of him. "It was you, Project Leader?"

"Hey, I helped," Rudy said, easing closer in case Cristoffen tried anything. "And while we have your attention, Michael, why don't you open your mail? And, carefully, if you don't mind?"

Cristoffen glanced up, his face suddenly fearful. "And then? When you don't need me anymore?"

"We don't need you now, you murderous little worm—"

"I will have no more violence," Kearn admonished Timri sharply, then turned back to Cristoffen. "Now, Ensign. I want you to follow Captain Lefebvre's orders. He's in command of the *Russ'* now." Rudy cooperated by doing his best to look as though this wasn't a complete shock. "We have reason to believe the Kraal feeding you information—and this weapon—is in the pay of the Esen Monster. That's why we searched your room—looking for evidence. She's been using you to identify and remove the very Humans who have been spying on the creature for signs of the pending invasion. You've been working for the enemy."

You old fraud, Rudy thought admiringly.

Cristoffen's lips parted and his pupils dilated. "How do I know you are telling me the truth?"

Kearn patted the book on the table. "Do you know what this is, Mr. Cristoffen?"

"It was a gift. It came with the shield. I couldn't decipher the language. I assumed it was a code the Kraal would explain later, when I needed it. I was told to keep it in my quarters."

"This is not a gift," Kearn said very gently. Sweat gleamed on his forehead, but he leaned toward the Human who had just tried to kill him. "This is your death warrant. It's a Kraal assassin's mark, to be retrieved as proof by the one who kills you. If you want to know if I'm telling you the truth? That envelope, Ensign, will contain a message. That message will concern a final task the Kraal will ask of you. After you do it, you will be killed."

Assassin's mark? Rudy glanced at Timri, who shook

her head very slightly. So she didn't know if Kearn was making this up either.

Cristoffen didn't share their doubts. His eyes fixed on Kearn as though the other was his sole point of reference in an unsettled universe, his right hand reaching to draw the envelope across the table. Only when it began to fall over the edge did he look down and use both hands to hold it. "I'm supposed to bite it open," he said faintly. "Or the message self-destructs."

"You do know they love to use poison," Rudy said before he could stop himself. Still it seemed a shame to lose Cristoffen before opening his mail. "Try spitting on it, instead."

"Unless you prefer chewing," Timri added unhelpfully.

"Comp-tech." Kearn didn't look at her. "Go to the bridge and inform the captain that there's been a change in command. Pass along my regrets, but he's to collect his gear and remain on Sacriss XIII until another Commonwealth ship is in the area. Assure him we will make sure that is soon, and he'll receive full pay in the interim. Then, have Resdick notify Port Authority to hold a tug at our disposal." When she didn't move, he finally looked up. There was something in his eyes that was almost pain, an unfamiliar grimness to his mouth. "Timri. I'd like you off the *Russ'*, too. No, don't bother protesting, I know better than to ask. But do this much for me."

Timri's face might have been carved of stone. "So I won't know what's in the envelope. Rudy, tell him this isn't right."

Rudy crossed his arms and shook his head. "It is. I could argue that one of us should be on the other side of the door, in case this is a trap for more than just Cristoffen here, but I won't bother. Just trust us. You don't want to know more about the Kraal than necessary."

She gave Kearn another hard look. "Go," he said, very gently. "Please."

When the door closed behind her, Rudy made sure it was locked. Then he moved Kearn from his desk with a sharp nod to the corner of the office. "So you aren't distracted," he told a now-ashen Cristoffen. "Now. Go ahead."

"I can't. My m—mouth is dry."

Kearn disappeared into his bedroom, then returned with a glass of water. "Try this."

It would have been funny, Rudy thought as they watched Cristoffen's efforts to spit on the end of the envelope, *if you didn't know the Kraal.*

"That's all I—oh!" The exclamation came as the first tiny droplets contacted the envelope and immediately turned bright orange, then black. At the same time, one side of the envelope began to bubble and hiss. Cristoffen dropped it on the table and backed away until he hit the wall.

"Wait," Rudy cautioned. The outer material gradually dissolved away to reveal the contents of the envelope: a single sheet of ordinary-looking plas, coated in a silvery dust. So it had been rigged. *Not with poison*, he realized with an inner chill. *This Kraal liked to make a statement.* The dust was all that remained of microscopic darts embedded throughout the envelope, the type able to burrow through clothing and into skin, through flesh and into vital organs. Not a pleasant or swift way to die.

When the reaction appeared over, Rudy used a pen to nudge the sheet until the dust slipped off the words, then read: " 'Bring the item from Sacriss XIII to Picco's Moon as quickly as possible. Someone will meet you at the shipcity. Be sure to bring the book I left in your care. I require it now.' Well. No fuss with codes and cryptic meaning—"

"She's going to kill me!" Cristoffen interrupted,

pressing himself flat to the wall. "You were right, Project Leader! That's an assassin's mark and she's going to have me killed on Picco's Moon."

"Who's going to have you killed?" Kearn snapped. "We can't protect you if we don't know."

"I never saw her face!" the distraught ensign cried. "I don't know her real name! She called herself Sybil. That's all I know. You have to keep me safe. Please. You never know what they look like, where they'll be. They could be anyone. You have to . . . please . . ." his pleas faded to mumbling.

Rudy understood the pity in Kearn's face, even if he didn't share it. But then, Kearn hadn't seen Cristoffen enjoy the death he'd caused. "I'll take Mr. Cristoffen to his new quarters," he volunteered.

"Get crew to help you. And check on the bridge, Captain," Kearn said. "I don't want any delays. You know the course."

"Aye, sir," Rudy said. Taking the unresisting Cristoffen by one arm, he began to leave. Then, on impulse, he turned and gave a seemingly casual salute.

The first he'd given Kearn and meant.

25: Shipcity Night

ONE has certain expectations when prowling the streets of an unfamiliar shipcity after dusk and storm. Garbage, vermin, and puddles come to mind. But Gathergo itself, like the Prumbins, tended to a clean shabbiness, even during Hops Fest. As I walked along the still-damp cobblestones, definitely wishing for sandals, I could hear music from my left, toward the Port City itself. To my right were the dark fronts of warehouses and trader offices, closed for the night—possibly for the week, depending on how much each business relied on sober Prumbins. No vermin or garbage in sight. Though my feet found enough puddles to make up the difference.

Straight ahead, cobblestones turned to pavement. I'd seen my share of shipcities and most were busy, exciting places reached by temporary roadways filled with beings in a hurry, dodging machines and each other. The roadways led to rows of starships, ephemeral buildings that came and went in the arms of docking tugs, the tugs in turn having their own roadways and traffic jams. Beyond all that, the field where starships could use their own wings to fly.

Shipcities were wonderful, I sighed, *to an Esen with a boarding pass and luggage*. Esens without either, I'd noticed, tended to encounter unpleasantries such as guards, locked ports, and highly unsuitable accommodations. *There was a great deal to be said for traveling first class*. Something I doubted Paul or Skalet intended.

I didn't have much time before one or both awoke and

started the tedious process of planning what to say to me when they found me, so I walked a little faster. Though my mouth watered at the thought of the Hops Fest and the charming, food-packed booths which would line every street in the city itself, my present self might be conspicuous. In the shipcity, however, I would have no trouble pretending to be just another Human child. Independent Traders referred, usually affectionately but not always, to their offspring as "ramp rats" for good reason.

I reached the end of the street and stopped. *So much for this plan,* I thought with disgust.

Rain-wet pavement, laced with its own puddles, reflected the starlight. A piece of plas, caught by the onshore breeze, tumbled past my feet; a small invertebrate clattered after it, perhaps as hungry as I was. A smattering of lights in the distance marked what I hoped might be larger freighters, still fin-down. Then I realized their even height meant I was looking at parked tugs.

The shipcity was empty—deserted. *Why?*

I might have stood there, gaping, for a significant length of time—given the unappealing alternative of returning empty-stomached and shipless to my web-kin, followed by the requisite explanation and inevitable scolding—but a sound from the dark caught my attention.

Music, but from the shadowed edge of the shipcity warehouses, not Gathergo itself. And not any music. The whisper-soft, soulful wail of a kythen was as out of place here and now as a barefoot Human-seeming child.

Ersh knew, I'd come here alone in an attempt to be responsible. *And get a little time away from the others to think,* I admitted honestly. Responsible meant walking back to our shelter. *Thinking for myself?* That meant following those notes from the dark, which seemed to sink deeper into my body than any sound should.

The musician, as I'd surmised, was a Grigari. I found him squatting peacefully on the lowermost of a staggered group of crates, two pairs of feet and two tails dangling over the side of his chosen perch, his third, prehensile tail looped over an upper crate, perhaps for stability—although the species' ability to climb would make a primate take up swimming. As I approached, he continued to blow into his kythen, long-fingered hands stroking the keys and hovering over holes, supporting the long, thin instrument with his remaining two feet. The bell at the end was pointed down, muting the sound—an indication this musician played for himself, not the street.

He knew I was there. His magnificent mane was spread to collect sensory information about me: odor, temperature, other radiations. Its stripes were black and white in the dark, as were the patterns on its soft leather scales. In daylight, the dark portions of mane and hide would be revealed as some vivid, warning color: purple perhaps, with green and blue. Not that the species was poisonous; they were, in Ersh's terms, show-offs.

And talented ones. I half-closed my eyes, recognizing the piece he played now. Chariss Sonata #12. One of my favorites. It ended all too soon.

When he stopped, I thanked him in his own language. "An unanticipated delight, Serg Kythen."

"I am no master player, Small One," he replied, but seemed pleased. "You may have my name, since you did me the courtesy of listening. Z'ndraa."

"Bess."

"Are you acting within custom for your kind, Bess, to be out here alone? Did your parents send you searching for beer? It is that way." The tip of his left-most tail pointed vaguely toward Gathergo.

"No." *Although the thought had potential.* I hugged my knees, putting my chin on top of them, and considered his first question. The night breeze ruffled the now-dry edges of the oversized shirt I wore, but didn't chill my skin. It went off to look for starships. "I am often alone," I decided.

"Ah. Different ways. I am not, usually, a seeker of solitude. My music likes an audience."

"Then why are you here?"

He blew a trill like a laugh through the kythen. "The Prumbins have filled the streets with their music. It is a fine and cheerful tuning, well-suited to dancing and the drinking of beer. However, my poor kythen cannot compete. To hear myself, I had to find this place alone. Which had an audience after all! I am pleased, Small Bess."

"It's just 'Bess.' " I informed him, lifting my chin. "I am not small."

"Ah! My mistake. So you are a wanderer, Not-Small Bess?"

"No." Then, as he waited patiently, a shadow in a shadow. "Yes," I said, hearing the bitterness in my own voice. For no reason except that he listened, I kept going: "I'm supposed to be. It's the nature of my kind, to roam throughout space."

"You do not wish this life?"

"I thought I could be different and made a home. It's gone now. I don't know why. I don't know how to get it back—or if I'm supposed to even try. I don't know what will happen to me or those I care about—" I sighed and realized I'd been babbling nonsense. "I'm sorry, Z'ndraa. Please excuse me, I—"

"Ah," he said a third time, but now with satisfaction. "Do not be sorry, Not-Small Bess. You have shown me a song. I will call it 'Saturne's Dream.' Why Saturne? My muse, whom I appease with truth."

Instead of playing, the Grigari put down his kythen and whirled around, climbing the wall above the crates where he turned to hang head down. Then, he began to sing, his voice soft and deep:

> *"you dream of another self*
> *a soul to mend beyond the fear*
> *of tomorrow the star in the shell*
> *that remains of all that was dear*
> *just a lonely heart caught by summer*

a late butterfly in amber
torn apart by an unresolved dream
a quiet oh so quiet scream
breaking under the need for answers
out of silence pleading for understanding
within and without always a wanderer
found forever in questioning"

The song ended. Without saying another word, Z'ndraa flowed gracefully back down to his crate, picked up his kythen, and began to play another sonata.

None of my memories held the song he sang for me; they couldn't, since Z'ndraa had composed it as he sang, based on what he heard me say and sensed about me through his mane. It was a singular honor. The Grigari believed compositions inspired by chance encounters revealed inner truths to both musician and listener. I couldn't know what truths Z'ndraa found for himself in the song; I chose to avoid searching for my own, at least tonight, feeling unresolved enough. I stood and walked away from the musician and the deserted shipcity, accepting the unlooked-for gift with the thoughtful silence he expected.

I was greeted with silence as well. Mind you, that probably had more to do with Paul's and Skalet's reaction to finding bags filling the space that had been filled with Esen when they'd both fallen asleep. *Some moments in life*, I decided, *were worth remembering in exact detail.*

Skalet and Paul squinted at me over the dim light of the glow I'd embedded in a crack. I waited until I saw them exchange a look and Paul begin to open his mouth, before saying calmly: "I bought new clothes. There's food as well." Except for the portion now comforting my stomach.

I hadn't been the only one hungry, judging by the speed with which they reached for the bags. Over a roll of warm, meat-filled pastry, Skalet gazed at me doubtfully. "Bought?" she asked.

"Bought. I found a busy currency dealer and pretended my parents had sent me with their credit code to retrieve chits for the beer tent."

There was a pregnant silence, then Paul chuckled. "Nice parents," he said, pulling out the clothes. I grinned and reached for mine.

Skalet was less easily impressed, of course. "Were you followed?"

"Hopefully," I informed my web-kin, reasonably sure my grin had turned other than friendly.

She tensed, looking past me into the darkness. "What do you mean?"

"The talk in Gathergo tonight isn't about this year's hops—it's about the Gem Rush on Picco's Moon. It seems the only starship on Prumbinat that hasn't already left belongs to your old friends, the Kraal. And you're going to get it for us."

Seeing Skalet speechless twice in the same day went a long way toward keeping my back straight and my hands steady. But Paul's eyes on mine were worried.

He had a right to be. If independents from here were rushing to Picco's Moon, ships from Largas Freight would as well.

I hugged my new clothes and walked outside to find room to change. It didn't matter. Skalet wanted to go to Picco's Moon and so did I.

It was time to go home.

And, as the singer had told me, find some answers.

Otherwhere

THE flesh-burdened were incapable of understanding. The Tumblers withdrew to their valleys in frustration, satisfied they had made the correct decision.

Almost satisfied. There were debates and questions. One Elder expressed concern about the prompt departure of the Ganthor once the mercenaries had removed the other species. They had no wish to replace one soft problem with another. A message was crafted to alleviate that concern. It was a brilliant document, over five hundred pages in length, and all agreed it covered every possible argument.

The Ganthor Matriarch in charge of the first and second invasion waves gave the message to her Seconds to pass along to accounting. It obviously dealt with how to most quickly obtain full compensation after the fact. There were pleased ::!!:: throughout her Herd at this sign their new clients were so thoughtful.

Another Elder broached the distasteful topic of environmental contamination. A few had to leave the debate, too revulsed by the thought of fragmented soft-flesh. Three Tumblers had sturdy enough constitutions to draft a second message to the Ganthor, a message they decided must also be provided to the flesh-burdened at the Port City as well as those on Ershia's Mountain. It included gruesome details on how the battle scenes were to be thoroughly cleansed of any remains or liquids that might have originated within a living thing—one of the authors of the message having a very sturdy constitution and a rare imagination for a crystal being.

The Ganthor Matriarch divided the message into what she viewed as separate mission requirements and provided one to each of the Herds under her command.

Alphonsus Lundrigan sent his copy to Crawdad's Sanitation Ltd.

Admiral Mocktap laughed and tossed it aside.

26: Shipcity Night; Scoutship Day

"PUT those away."

I had to admit, it was pleasant seeing someone else on the receiving end of Skalet's searing contempt.

Whispers of: "Your Eminence" multiplied through the dark. There had to be a dozen of them I hadn't seen. Fingertips flew to cheeks as weapons were dropped. "We had no idea you were already here."

The Kraal, true to my prediction, had caught up to us before my web-kin had had time to do more than take turns scowling at me as they each dressed. The black-garbed troops were quite exceptional at skulking about in the dark. If I hadn't been expecting them, I might have been shocked by the seemingly magical appearance of all those blaster rifles, pointed our way.

Previously pointed our way, I noted with gratification. Now, they were somewhat sheepishly threatening the pavement. The three leading Kraal, who'd dropped to one knee in order to see who they were shooting at under the rubble, pulled off their hoods. Two males and a female, tattooed with affiliations I couldn't read in the light of the glow alone.

Skalet, more practiced, had no problem. "Ordin. Mocktap. Shecca." As she spoke, she pushed her way out of our shelter, forcing the Kraal to scramble out of her way. Paul and I followed. Once outside, she brought the glow in her hand closer to her face, an unnecessary emphasis of the marks that commanded their utter obedience. Ordin was a House bound to Bract, one of the three major Houses for which S'kal-ru spoke as Courier. Mocktap, owing personal subservience to S'kal-ru herself. Shecca, more problematic, but bearing a whorl of commitments to Ordin and so drawn into that affiliation as long as S'kal-ru was of higher rank.

I missed the Ganthor. *With them, a little shoving gave you a place in society.* Firm shoving, with bruises and the risk of broken furniture, but as everyone in the Herd usually joined in there weren't hard feelings.

"Detail your mission. Now." Skalet was letting her hard feelings show. The poor Kraal, already intimidated by flushing an irate noble instead of terrorized little me, crouched even lower.

I didn't think they needed to know her fury was at me. Skalet wasn't fond of being backed into a corner.

"Standard pursuit and locate, Eminence," replied the taller of the two males who had first seen Skalet. "One of the ships leaving Minas XII came here. The watch commander decided we should break orbit and search for the target on foot. Our team was assigned Gathergo—there are others at the remaining Port Cities. It was my decision to follow the child. Her purchases and secrecy implied she was supplying a fugitive."

"Such—initiative." The way the word came out Skalet's mouth made me start to worry if we'd get on the ship without blood on the sand.

The Kraal stiffened. "If we have interfered unknowingly with Your Eminence's plans, please allow me, Ordin-ru, to take responsibility for my commander and troops." He paused, but Skalet declined to respond. Drops of sweat on his forehead gleamed in the glow's light. Kraal apologies could be accepted or rejected in various unpleasant and permanent ways. He was a brave being. "We should have followed our original orders and waited in orbit. Obviously, you were better able to recover the target." At that, his eyes slid to Paul, who was standing beside me.

Target? Before I could open my mouth, Paul squeezed my hand in warning. I looked up to see his face had assumed a look of bland innocence.

The moment teetered on what was going on in those Kraal heads. They'd found S'kal-ru with their "target," under questionable circumstances. I dare say most non-Kraal Humans would jump to certain conclusions, prime among them a shift in loyalty. However, Kraal were accustomed to their leaders acting covertly and independent of the apparent chain of command. They would, I presumed, wait to see if this was a brilliant coup by Her Eminence, or a mistake worthy of assassination.

I missed the Ganthor even more.

Skalet knew better than to let them think too much. "Irrelevant. Your search of this city has ended, Ordin-ru," she told him, an impatient snap to her beautiful voice. "Notify your ship to prepare for immediate launch upon our return. I will bring with me two items of personal luggage which will not be described or recorded in any manner. Is this clear?"

Not a murmur. There were, I decided, some advantages to Kraal. "Does your 'luggage' require any special handling, Your Eminence?"

"Not at present. Ooof!"

The swift kick I gave her ankle was worth the way their weapons swung from rest to ready.

"Luggage," indeed.

The Kraal ship had been tucked on the far side of the line of docking tugs, fin-down where they could safely launch without having to be moved to the field itself—although Port Authority would doubtless attempt to fine them for such behavior. Not to mention the probability of needing new paint on the nearest tugs. Debts that would be paid, among others, Skalet assured me, by Pa-Admiral Mocktap.

"Shouldn't you wait until we are off one of her ships?" Paul commented. Skalet had demanded and received all of the officers' quarters on the *Octos Ra*, giving us two decks and eight cabins of private luxury at our disposal.

Including the captain's. Skalet had been in luck again, since Captain Arzul-ro was not only an affiliate, but member of another House for which S'kal-ru spoke as Courier. He'd been overjoyed to have such an illustrious guest, professing an earnest and likely sincere desire to die in her service.

"Her ship?" I repeated. "Hardly."

"Paul is right, Youngest," Skalet said absently. She was busy at the captain's desk, using his comp to see what had been happening during her time in the Abyss. She hadn't wasted time getting back into uniform, although Captain Arzul-ro had apparently been traumatized by the lack of something suitable to offer. I began to wonder how long Arzul-ro had been stuck on this scoutship. "I don't want to underestimate Mocktap's affiliations on board. We should be safe from some methods of assassination simply by having these two decks. Others we'll have to deal with as they come." There was distressing amount of anticipation in her voice.

"Which is why you didn't want to be greeted by Kraal at the dock."

"One can't tell affiliation from that distance, Youngest. You know that. I was hardly going to risk a confrontation without such knowledge. As for your little stunt—"

I interrupted: "Got us a ship, heading for Picco's Moon."

Skalet swiveled her chair to face me, a lean figure in unrelieved black, her strong thin hands pressed together heel to fingertip, as though in prayer. There was nothing of the supplicant in her harsh: "Where you will take me to what I seek."

"Give Paul the antidote."

She shook her head. "Always in a hurry, Esen-alit-Quar.

Still, it's as well the *Octos Ra* is a fast little ship." Her hands separated, palms up as if offering me something, then her left hand turned over. "The duras has already begun to damage every cell in his body. Nothing irreparable—yet. But in another couple of days?"

My Human heart seemed to beat too quickly. I didn't dare look at Paul, didn't dare think of what was happening to him. "Skalet. Please. I promise. You know I keep my word."

"That was when you were Youngest, and trembled at the thought of Ersh's displeasure. But you're Senior Assimilator of the Web of Esen now," she mocked.

"Skalet, please?"

"Easy, Es," from Paul. "I feel fine. Don't antagonize her—"

"Listen to your wise, vulnerable friend, Esen-alit-Quar." Her wicked smile warned me even as she said: "Still, a child your age should keep busy, or she'll get into trouble. Let me offer you a game to while away the time, Youngest. One or more of these officers will employ duras. It's still very popular among the upper classes of Kraal society. You might just find a vial of antidote in one of the cabins. I give you leave to hunt to your heart's content."

"Paul—"

"He stays with me. To protect him from traps. Not to mention that there could be an assassin or two. You'll be fine, I'm sure. You did pay attention to my teachings, I trust."

I gave myself one more look at Paul, who appeared torn between launching himself at Skalet's throat or trying to stop me from leaving. Something in my expression must have reassured him. His fists opened and he settled back in his chair. "Yours? No," I told her with immense satisfaction. "You were a lousy teacher."

Then I left.

*   *   *

Opulence became boring very quickly. My Ket-self would have enjoyed visiting cabin after cabin, running those sensitive fingers over carved wooden doors and luxurious upholstery. Well, to be honest, my Ket-self was also inordinately fond of plumbing fixtures.

As Bess, I was impatient with what seemed nothing but distraction. Which it was, in a sense. Stuffing their quarters with expensive furnishings allowed each Kraal officer to create a bewildering maze for eyes as well as feet. There was nothing standard, no repeating pattern from one room to the next to help a searcher locate secrets.

A lie. There was a commonality. Every cabin contained a shelf of duras plants, their tough stubby leaves a promise of death as well as mass. Skalet's plan had succeeded to the point of obscenity.

Two days.

I didn't bother being polite. When it was faster to walk over a sofa than move around it, I climbed over priceless embroidery and left footprints in rare fur. I did bother being careful whenever I opened a drawer or other hiding place. I might have living mass at hand and so could cycle to remove poison from this body, but it wouldn't help if some paranoid Kraal had rigged a cupboard door with explosives or—

Or something more specific. The thought stopped my examination of a truly obsessive collection of cosmetics.

Ersh. What if this wasn't some internal rivalry? What if Skalet's newly discovered enemy knew what she was?

It could be. Mocktap had history with our kind—not just relatively recent events, either. I had no trouble remembering every detail of Skalet's misadventure on Ersh's mountain, including that name on the lips of Uriel-ro.

I should keep searching, despite the probability that any valuable toxins and antidotes likely left with the cabin's displaced resident.

I should, but . . . *Ersh.*

Cosmetics forgotten, I turned and ran out of the cabin, heading for my web-kin.

I'd been forced to buy sandals with tiny metal strips on the toes. The resulting sound on cobblestones was considered charming by Prumbins. It had likely helped every Kraal in Gathergo follow me. But I could move as quietly as thought over the plush carpeting the corridors of the officers' deck. For that reason, I wasn't surprised, at first, when no one called out a greeting as I walked in the door to the captain's cabin.

At second glance, I was alone. No sign of Paul. No sign of Skalet.

I fought to calm myself as I hurried through the various rooms. No sign of struggle. No blindingly obvious message left to warn me. They hadn't been kidnapped.

But no message left to inform me either.

A stroll around the ship? Unlikely. No, I told myself bitterly, this was some plan of Skalet's moved into action by my convenient absence.

She'd made a fool of me again.

Instead of Ersh's "voice," I seemed to hear Paul's suddenly. *When in doubt, don't.* While this was his favorite expression in regard to my desire to experiment with the menu at a new restaurant—being the one responsible for getting my Lishcyn-self home afterward—I knew he felt it was something I could apply more broadly. *There had*, I admitted to myself, *been times when acting without all the facts had had less than stellar results.*

This was Skalet's chosen environment. This was Paul's true form. Each had a vested interest in the other's survival until we were off this ship. If the two of them couldn't handle potential assassins and Kraal politics, no one could.

Relieved, for the moment, of responsibility for my elders, I finally paid attention to myself. My mouth had a foul taste and my skin itched from dried salt. There was sand where there shouldn't be. *Surely this hair wasn't supposed to be stiff.*

So, while the rest of the universe conspired, plotted, and generally readied itself to cause me more grief, I treated my Human-self to a well-deserved bubble bath, without Busfish, in the gilded marble tub belonging to the captain of the *Octos Ra*.

Otherwhere

THE strong upsweep ended with a flourish. Not flamboyance—a statement. *This handwriting*, Kearn thought, *said as much about the author as the words.* Confidence. Determination. An attention to detail verging on obsessive. They were all there.

The words? He stretched, feeling and dismissing the complaints from his neck and lower back from hours spent hunched over his desk. Perhaps he'd been a little obsessive himself, to want every word translated. But there'd been no page he dared ignore. The key, some revelation, could be in front of him, waiting for him to recognize it.

Rudy had tested the pages for biological tracers, proving the book had been in the possession of Sybil's enemy.

Kearn allowed himself a moment of satisfaction. The translation was complete—his contribution, his expertise. *Now they knew why.*

"You haven't slept."

He glanced up to find his office door ajar, Timri standing in the opening. "You never knock," he said mildly, smiling.

Timri didn't smile back, but then, it wasn't an expression she used often. She was prone to seriousness, the fine lines edging her mouth and eyes those of concentration, not mirth. Right now, they were deeper than usual. "Rudy's still complaining you didn't give him his old cabin back."

"It's yours now," Kearn pointed out. "How's the crew taking the switch in command?"

"As you'd expect. They can't imagine you doing something as bizarre as pulling in a civilian, so there's a rumor Rudy has been working undercover as a freighter captain to catch smugglers. I think he probably started it." She hesitated, then came to sit in the chair across from his desk. "About the cabin. Rudy says you play favorites. Why would he say that, Lionel?"

"I have no idea." Kearn felt his cheeks warming and hastily put his hand on the book. "You came at a good moment. I just finished the translation. We've imaged the pages, taken all the samples Rudy can imagine. It can be returned."

"To this Sybil. Cristoffen's Kraal contact." Timri narrowed her eyes. "I hope you aren't suggesting we let him go through with this meeting. Beyond the fact that he can't be trusted—he's a wreck. He'd throw up on her boots."

"I really shouldn't have lied to the poor boy," Kearn shook his head. "Being shot at must have jarred loose my morals."

"That's what I came to talk to you about, Lionel. I haven't had a chance to—"

Kearn shook his head. "No. There's no need."

Timri scowled. "There's every need. Shut up and let me thank you for saving my life."

He fussed with sheets, managing to send several to the floor by accident. As he bent to pick them up, he mumbled: "I didn't save it. The weapon didn't work."

"That doesn't change what you tried to do."

Kearn replaced the dropped sheets, patting them into alignment with their mates on his desk, putting others on top and patting those. "I happened to see him first, that's all. Either of you would have done the same. A reflex."

A slender hand pressed on top of his, trapping it on top of the pile of notes. He met her eyes reluctantly. "Lionel. You knew I was a member of Paul's Group. You knew I've spied on you since coming on board— lied to you. Yet you put yourself between someone who believed in you, and me, who didn't." There was the beginning of anger in her voice; she hated puzzles.

Her hand was warm and strong. He'd thought it would be. "You heard what I told Rudy."

"That you've come to your senses about Esen and Paul? I heard." Timri withdrew her hand; his felt suddenly cold. "Puts me out of a job," she added lightly, "if you weren't lying."

"Lying?"

"Relax," the corner of her mouth lifted. "You've always been a terrible liar, Lionel. Your face goes all red. You sweat. You even stammer if it's going to be a really big lie."

"I d–do not—" Kearn began, then blushed furiously as he stumbled over the words. "Rank insubordination," he complained weakly.

"So kick me off the ship at Picco's Moon." The moment of humor faded, replaced by a look he knew very well indeed: obstinance. "I want to know why you let me keep spying on you. I want to know why you stepped in front of Cristoffen's weapon. In all our years on this ship, no matter what ridiculous thing you've done, I've understood why, Lionel. Now I don't."

Kearn let his eyes travel over her face, lingering on the perplexed creases above her eyebrows, savoring the line of cheekbone and jaw. He closed his eyes briefly to keep it all.

Then opened them, and abandoned fantasy. "My reasons are my own, Comp-tech," he said briskly, despite feeling as if he stood in front of Cristoffen again and stared into the muzzle of his own death. "If you have a problem with not knowing, I suggest you consider a transfer. I will provide a message of recommendation, of course."

"A transfer? I was joking, Lionel."

"I'm not." Somehow, Kearn found the strength to keep his eyes on hers and his voice even. "It's time you considered your own career and life as well as the needs of your—friends. There will be serious repercussions at the end of this—not just because of my putting a civilian in command of a Commonwealth ship. Cristoffen. I don't intend to let him to walk away from what he's done, but we both know I will be held at least partially responsible. And should be."

"You couldn't have known what he was capable of—"

Kearn shook his head at her protest. "I knew he was trouble. I brought him on board thinking I could control him, to protect Esen and Paul. And don't forget that my name is on the orders taking us to Urgia Prime, bringing us here—and who knows what else he's done using my codes." He managed a smile. "It doesn't matter. Not really. I was planning to retire anyway."

"I hadn't thought—" she paused, seeming to look inward. The creases on her forehead gradually eased. "The captain of the *Resolute* offered me a post last month. It's an explorer. When I saw it, I thought it would be a chance to look for web-beings beyond the Fringe." The creases reappeared. "It's ridiculous to talk about things like this now, Lionel. We're in the middle of—"

"It's not ridiculous to look ahead, Timri," Kearn said, wondering if it was lack of sleep or the emptiness of his own future that thickened his voice. He coughed to clear it. "The *Resolute* would be a wonderful opportunity. You've turned down too many offers already. I know."

"Probably more than I do. Seems to me you blocked

most of them to keep me here," she said, but without bitterness. "It's all right. I couldn't have left before. Not while I was, well, before you— This really does change everything, doesn't it?" A note of wonder crept into her voice. "I am free to go."

From the look on her face, she'd already left. Kearn opened the book and riffled pages. "I should get back to this. It isn't long until we reach Xir. Was there anything else, Timri?"

"Get some sleep before you fall over," she suggested, almost jumping from her seat. "And, Lionel—"

"Yes?"

"Thank you. Good night."

The smile of someone who used it rarely was a wonderful, dangerous thing. Kearn knew he'd remember it, always.

Even after she was gone.

Rudy was taking a late supper—or was it breakfast?—when Kearn walked into the otherwise deserted galley, book in hand. "You're up late," the new captain of the *Russell III* commented. "Or is it early? My system's not running on shiptime yet." *Never went to bed, given the purple bruising under those eyes.* "You finished the translation," he guessed, pushing the sombay across the table as Kearn sat to join him.

Kearn nodded and poured himself a cup. "Yes. The bridge told me you were here. I thought you'd want to know as soon as possible."

Rudy waved the hand that wasn't full of toast. "Please. As long as it isn't something that will spoil my appetite."

"It might if you were Sybil."

"Go on."

Kearn placed the book on the table between them, moving his cup a cautious distance away. "As I told you, very few could read this." His tone was tired, but triumphant. "If I hadn't attended that lecture—with a fine luncheon, I might add—and Professor Strasig hadn't kindly shared his data on Naskhi script with me? Plus this is an older style of Kraal. But once I knew the corresponding lettering, it was quite straightforward to decipher." Rudy waited patiently as Kearn carefully turned pages until he reached the beginning. "It starts by listing the founding Kraal Houses. That's not unusual; the culture is obsessed with genealogy. But here they are named in order of their inheritable flaws, with blunt comments on the viability of each line and the most potentially successful alliances. And here." He chose a page near the middle. "This describes a property: hills overlooking a seashore. No location, but everything else you'd need in order to build a substantial estate there, from fortifications to designs for gardens. The rest of the book is filled with notes about materials, personnel, supply lines."

"I don't want to diminish your accomplishment, Lionel," Rudy was forced to say when Kearn finished. "But what do plans for a new house have to do with Sybil hiring me?"

"Not a new house," Kearn corrected, eyes glowing with excitement. "A new House. This is a blueprint for the establishment of a new power within the Kraal."

"That happens?"

Kearn traced a gilded skull on the book's cover with his finger as he spoke. "Often enough to spawn most of their wars. I did some research. There are various methods, almost all involving the destruction of an existing House."

"Why doesn't this surprise me?" Rudy asked grimly.

"The founding of the Lysar is fairly typical. They claim to have won their status through battlefield heroics. True, in a way. They captured the flagship of their own ally and affiliate, the Noitci, killed every member of the family they could find, then made off with the Noitci

Artifacts. A House proves its legitimacy within the Kraal hierarchy by possessing ancestral relics that link it to the time of the founding families. Those relics were in the artifacts—which now belonged to the House of Lysar."

Rudy lowered his cup of sombay so he could regard Kearn through the steam. "Sybil's information included a report on the recovery of the long-lost Kraslakor Artifacts. It meant something to her—or her enemy."

Kearn stared at the book. "We dated the inks. The person writing in this book did so at intervals over the last forty to fifty years. The most recent passage is days old. We can't be talking about the original thief."

"Of course not. The crypt was robbed over three hundred years ago. But a descendant could be carrying on a dream. Not to mention Kraal feuds are passed down bloodlines, aren't they?"

"Yes." Kearn lifted the book. "But it's more than that. Sybil and, presumably, her enemy are pursuing Esen. Why? What could this possibly have to do with her? Do you know anything that might help? Has she told you anything?"

Rudy hesitated, a pause that caught Kearn's attention. The older Human set the book down, and put both hands on top of it. "You find it hard to talk to me about her, don't you?"

That, Rudy thought, *was putting it mildly.* "It's not that I don't trust you now. It's, well, it's a habit, Lionel."

"I understand. Well, let me start with the obvious. Even if she's not a living weapon, Esen possesses attributes any Kraal would value: the ability to camouflage herself, for one. Then there's blood feud—the desire for revenge. The Kraal came out of their first encounter with Esen with flags waving in triumph over an Inhaven colony, but they lost ships. More importantly, they lost the crews of those ships: thousands affiliated to the House of Mocktap. Mocktap is still considered disgraced." Kearn smiled at Rudy's expression. "You didn't know?"

"No. Paul and Esen don't talk about those days. How do you know?"

"The Kraal have academics, my dear Rudy, and they are as prone to gossip as those of any species. The disgrace of a noble House is an irresistible topic."

"So we have an entire House of Kraal who would blame Esen for their misfortune if they knew of her existence." Rudy didn't like where this was leading. "And two Kraal who do know."

"Not to mention Kraal tech developed specifically to affect a being of her nature."

"You think that's what Cristoffen fired at you?" Rudy frowned. "You think it's a weapon designed to be used—on Esen?"

"Or another web-being. Yes, I do."

"Then we must destroy it!" Rudy pulled the weapon from its concealment under his shirt.

Kearn was shaking his head. "It goes with you, along with this book." At Rudy's look of surprise, he gave a weary smile. "You're planning to meet Sybil on Picco's Moon. She expects both. She needs both to deal with her enemy."

Ice seemed to form along Rudy's veins. "Why?"

"Think about it. She gave the book to Cristoffen in order to hide it, here, where her enemy wouldn't find it. Why would she want it back now?"

"She feels ready to confront her enemy." Rudy looked at the ugly weapon in his hand, wishing he could make it disappear. "Because she'll have this. You're saying Sybil believes her enemy is a web-being. Then why worry about the book in the first place?"

"Maybe Sybil began by suspecting something simpler—something Kraal. If she knew her enemy wrote secrets in this book, she'd want to steal it, to find someone to read it for her. This book would confirm her suspicions. A new House would impact on her affiliations. From what I've heard, it could change affiliations across the Confederacy, alter the balance of power—especially if the founder was someone extraordinary."

"But when Sybil kept looking," Rudy went on as Kearn stopped, "she found her enemy was more than extraordinary." He swore softly. "I don't like this, Lionel."

"You'll like it even less when I tell you who we might be dealing with."

Rudy didn't see the triumph he expected. Instead, Kearn looked troubled. "You know? Who?"

"I don't know. I'm taking a wild guess. But fifty years ago, a Kraal named S'kal-ru arranged for Esen, as Nimal-Ket, to leave my ship. Paul left me, too." Kearn hesitated, then put aside all those years of distrust and betrayal, saying: "to help Esen. S'kal-ru's ship was one of those destroyed by the wild web-being; I believed she was dead. It couldn't be confirmed, of course. I couldn't get access to Kraal data banks; difficult people to deal with, Rudy, in every sense. Even my so-called Kraal benefactor." There were patches of color on his pale cheeks. "I'm sure the information I received from that source was only what the Kraal wanted me to know. But what if S'kal-ru was a web-being? What if she didn't die?"

"Can we compare the image I have to one of this S'kal-ru?"

"There isn't one. Not that we can access. Kraal have an almost pathological aversion to images of themselves, particularly if they'll be seen by anyone else. Portraits are made after death, when an individual's affiliations can no longer change."

Rudy shoved his plate aside, no longer hungry. "Do

you know what you're saying, Lionel? Esen believes she's the only one of her kind left. Paul believes that."

"What if they're both wrong, Rudy? What if S'kal-ru, for reasons of her own, faked her own death. Hid herself from Esen. A web-being living as a Kraal." Kearn looked as though he'd seen a ghost. Rudy understood completely.

"And affiliated with Mocktap, the House disgraced in the attack."

"Exactly. What if someone in Mocktap has found out S'kal-ru's secret and designed this weapon to use against her?"

"Sybil."

Kearn nodded. "But what I don't understand is why a web-being would want to found a new Kraal House—"

"Or why she'd hide from Esen," Rudy said grimly. "Or who is responsible for the attacks on Minas XII, if not Largas."

Kearn wrapped his hands around his cup, as if too tired to lift it. "One thing we must remember at all times, Rudy. Not all of these creatures are like Esen. We've seen at least one capable of dreadful things."

"Just like humanity."

"Just like that. But with their abilities?" He shuddered. "I want you to take that weapon. I want you to be ready in case—"

"In case of what?"

Rudy's outrage didn't appear to affect Kearn at all. The older Human looked resolute. "Sybil's enemy might be ours—and Esen's—too."

"I—" The shrill of the com cut off Rudy's protest. He was at the panel in three quick strides. "Lefebvre. What is it, Bridge?"

"We've received an emergency squeal from Picco's Moon, sir. Every available Commonwealth ship is requested, Priority One."

Rudy met Kearn's worried look. "Any indication why?" he asked.

The voice became a little breathless. "They're reporting incoming Ganthor assault vessels, sir."

"Thank you, Bridge," Rudy said calmly. "I'll be right up." He switched off the com. "This puts a twist to it. Any thoughts, Lionel, before I go?"

"Only one. Why is it always Ganthor?"

Rudy was tempted to smile at the plaintive note in Kearn's voice, even though an assault fleet heading anywhere was no laughing matter. "Esen's fond of them," he said.

"I've noticed," Kearn commented wryly. "Get to your bridge, Captain. I'll be in my office. No, I'll be in my bed. Ganthor, indeed."

27: Scoutship Night

"ES. Wake—"

The rest of what Paul tried to tell me couldn't penetrate the cold water suddenly covering my ears. *And face.* I flailed about wildly until my left hand caught hold of the side of the tub, my right gripped some fabric, and I hauled myself upward. "I hate water," I announced firmly, spitting bubbles from my mouth with every word. Paul stood back as I climbed out, shedding more bubbles on the tile floor. "This me hates it, anyway."

He handed me a huge, thick towel monogrammed O.R.— for *Octos Ra*, I assumed, implying Humans needed help remembering what ship they were on. "You'd have been fine if you'd stayed awake," he said unsympathetically. "Hurry up. We've things to talk about."

I peered at him through the folds of the towel as I rubbed bubbles out of my hair. "Where were you all this time?"

"Demonstrating an unexpected talent for mischief." Skalet leaned in the doorway. She'd gained a sidearm and a knife, with a silver-and-gemstone belt to hold both.

Paul actually smiled. In fact, he looked remarkably smug for someone gradually being poisoned. "It was your order, Your Eminence. 'Ignore the luggage; it's my concern only.'"

Skalet narrowed her eyes. "Literal fool. No doubt why Arzul-ro commands a scoutship, at his age."

I was tempted to stamp my foot. "What happened?"

"I leave your Human alone for a few minutes. He breaks

his word to me by leaving as well—then walks on the bridge and uses the translight com as freely as can be without anyone so much as blinking an eye—or contacting me." Skalet seemed more impressed than angry.

Had she known what Paul was capable of doing with access to that level of communication equipment, she would have been more worried than either. I did my best not to look anxious myself.

"Absolute obedience has its pitfalls, doesn't it," Paul said, no longer smiling. "I've tried explaining to you, Skalet. You're better off with willing allies."

"And you'd be better off if you'd never met Esen. Admit it, Human."

The words were colder than the tile under my bare feet.

"There's never been a second I've believed that."

"Really. Should we go into the specifics of what your relationship has cost you?" Her voice was like some dark and bitter wine: "Your family. Your career. Your mate. Your offspring. Your—"

"Enough!" I cried, pushing past Skalet and heading for the bedroom, shivering from more than exhaustion.

"Esen!"

"Let her go." Then Skalet said: "Stop feeling sorry for yourself, Human. For all you think you've lost, she's lost more. And her loss will last aeons after you and your kind are dust."

I turned back, sure I would see the hurt in Paul's face, ready to counter the hateful things Skalet was saying. But he simply looked intent, the way he did when hearing more than words. He took a step closer to Skalet; she straightened and backed one step. He stopped, as if understanding. They were the same height, I noticed, if otherwise as different as two beings could be.

"Her loss," Paul asked very gently, "or yours?"

None of my memories held this look on Skalet's face, a flash of naked pain, as though Paul had laid open some wound she'd thought healed. It was gone so quickly I might have imagined it, except I knew its replacement all too well. Rage.

Paul, however, wasn't an unsuspecting young fool. He avoided her blow with a smooth tilt of his head, staying where he was as if challenging her to strike again. "Tell me I'm wrong," he said.

"Wrong?" Her eyes were still wild, but she lowered her arm. "Of course you're wrong. What do you know of me? What can you know?"

She asks this of a being who wants to visit the Ycl, I thought with a certain sense of fatalism.

"I know you're not Human."

Neither of us had expected the obvious. Skalet looked stunned, then gave a short laugh, turning to me as if inviting me to share her humor. "Your Paul is a remarkably perceptive creature—"

He hadn't finished. "You aren't Human. Which means you don't belong in this form, no matter how hard you try, no matter how many scars or tattoos you sear into this version of yourself." When Skalet did no more than whirl to stare at him, Paul went on, his voice grim, low, and utterly implacable. "You aren't Human, no matter how long you've made yourself stay in this form, no matter how many Human reactions and feelings you've had to learn to deal with. It's not enough. I saw you in the ocean. I've seen Esen explode like that when it's been too long. Have you cycled at all since we last saw your true form, on the *Trium Set*?"

Memory rolled over and showed its scars. "She has. Twice," I breathed, staring at my web-kin. "You were on D'Dsell, weren't you? The Panacian, N'Klet, who helped Kearn hunt us down for the Feneden. That was you. Were–were you the Kraal helping him all along?"

"You talk of what you can't understand, Human," Skalet replied scornfully. "As for you, Youngest? That leap took you long enough. Of course I was N'Klet. You never did appreciate the value of a disguise to our work. And that fool Kearn—you should be grateful I kept him on a leash."

I hugged the towel up around my neck, stepping closer. "Paul was tortured because of you."

"That was your doing," she said callously. "I was dead, remember?"

"And then Paul almost died. You—you planned that, didn't you! You wanted to force me to fly, to show you how it was done. Tell me the truth, Skalet!" She wouldn't answer. I knew it. There was only one way. I released my hold on this form, cycling into web-form and staying there . . .

The web-flesh in Paul's pendant called to me, despite being frozen. The engines of the *Octos Ra* sang to my perception as they bent space around us. I tasted Human on my surface, as well as the remnants of berry-scented bubbles.

And a cluster of molecules that were Human and not, twisted into a shape that wasn't their origin, a source of tantalizing energy. *Share!* I sent, filling the room with the scent of my urgent demand, my need, my hope. My mouth formed, jagged, open, ready.

Share!!!

Nothing.

Share? as if I begged.

I let the scent diffuse and dissipate, trying and failing to comprehend refusal. Finally, I oozed up the concentration gradient to the leaves of the duras plants in the cabin, coating them with my web-mass, coaxing the living cells into more of me. I cycled . . .

And howled: "How dare you refuse me! How could—" Pain lanced through my face and shot up my muzzle . . . my eye was blind . . . before Skalet could mock my agony, I whined and cycled again . . .

Human. Pain-free, except for the tears in my eyes. I blinked, only then seeing my web-kin clearly.

Skalet was huddled on the floor, at the far side of the cabin from me. Paul was kneeling beside her, his hands supporting her shoulders. Her face was turned to the wall and her legs were drawn tightly beneath her body, as if she tried to hide.

Paul looked up at me, his face filled with a compassion I'd never expected to see him show my so-powerful Elder. *Although*, I thought distractedly, *I should know better by now*. It was Skalet who'd changed; my own flesh I didn't understand.

"Aren't you—lonely?" I asked her, feeling the dreadful isolation of this small, humanoid me as never before.

Her head moved slowly, as if she had to fight to look at me. Tears leaked from her eyes as well, a curse of this form, distorting the tattoos on her cheeks. "You had no right to do that to me," she whispered. "I won't cycle. I can't bear it. I can't bear web-form—too alone."

"But I'm here now."

Her lips drew back from her teeth in a snarl; the black and red of the tattoos transformed her face into something malignant. "You? What are you? Not of Her flesh. Some other thing, but not of Her. There is nothing—nothing left of Ersh."

Ersh.

I heard the word and knew it as the tolling of a bell, a single chime built of history and pageant, of garden soil and solar wind, of guilt and penance.

I heard the word and felt it as Skalet must, as the origin, the only boundary, the definition of what we were.

Ersh. I'd been right, those years ago, when I'd despaired that sharing Ersh's secrets made me different from my web-kin, that it would isolate me forever. It was more than my birth from Ansky's flesh that drove Skalet from me. There was more of Ersh in me now than she would ever have, more trust, more secrets.

And she knew it.

I found myself on my knees, helpless to know what to do for Skalet or myself. The Grigari's song came back to haunt me: "a quiet oh so quiet scream."

"There may be—something—on Picco's Moon," Paul offered, possibly aware he was the only one presently able to think clearly.

"A trap," I found myself protesting. "Mocktap will be waiting."

The lines of Skalet's face shifted from despair to a hunter's fix. Paul lifted his hands from her shoulders as she eased back from the wall; he stepped out of her way as she rose to her feet in a single, sinuous motion. "Why do you say that?"

I stayed on my knees, looking up at the two of them. "You taught me there's no such thing as coincidence, Skalet. So try this. You murdered Uriel-ro that day on Picco's Moon. I was there." I ignored the sudden cloud on Paul's face. *He should know I edited the nastier bits from my stories.* "And now you're being betrayed by a descendant of his House, a descendant who has seen a web-being attack her ships, who has had access to everything you've done as a trusted affiliate. Someone is mining Ersh's mountain, Skalet. You said yourself you suspect Mocktap. And lo', a Kraal ship of her affiliation as well as yours conveniently waits for us on Prumbinat, ready to take us to Picco's Moon. You're the military genius. Tell me what you see, if not a trap."

"I see a naked child lecturing her elders. Someone who gives too much credit to ephemerals and not enough to her own kind. No one knows what I am except the two of you."

"That's not entirely true," Paul said.

Since I was naked and had lectured, and knew Paul shared my opinion of the ability of machines to duplicate the abilities of any web-being, that meant he believed someone else did know about Skalet. *Before me?* I found myself furious at the injustice of it. "Who?" I demanded. "Who knows about her?"

"Michael Cristoffen."

"Kearn's lackey?" Skalet sounded incredulous.

"I had a message. Cristoffen was overheard talking about another web-being, one who has been living in this sector of space for some time. This was before he—" Paul paused and sent me a warning look, the kind that meant he had news I wouldn't like. *As if*, I thought with some resentment, *I was enjoying any of this.* "Esen. Cristoffen used Kraal tech to murder someone on Urgia Prime."

I wrapped my arms around my stomach, curling up as if struck. *Zoltan Duda.* It had to be.

"A very productive time on the bridge, Human," Skalet said, her voice almost back to normal. "Now—who did Cristoffen murder?" She stopped to glare at me. "And why are you, Youngest, rolled up in a ball on the floor?"

"When did you forget who you were?" I asked bitterly. The Web of Ersh had marked the loss of ephemeral life. We'd had cleansing ceremonies that lasted days, sometimes weeks. Duration didn't vary by the number lost. If it had, we could never have stopped. No, it was potential we mourned. The brighter that fleeting light, the more we felt its passing. Ersh had taught us the significance of death as well as life.

Zoltan had shown such promise. I knew the source of that message, having asked Rudy to follow Paul's newest recruit. It wasn't that I suspected Zoltan of turning against us. In fact, I'd feared the opposite. He'd cared too much. And now had paid the price.

Skalet had no idea what I meant. We shared the same memories, I realized, but she'd chosen to push those aside, perhaps deeming them of little value in her new life as a Kraal.

Fair enough, I thought, standing slowly. I felt the same about much of what she'd tried to teach me.

"I suggest you concentrate on how Kearn's associate learned of your existence and had an assassin's shield." Paul's voice was rock steady but I wondered if Skalet had learned to read Human faces enough to understand the significance of his pale, set face. *She'd better not push him.*

"I will. But first," her voice became a purr. "Who is this victim that he would be murdered by a shifter hunter—and our little Esen mourn his loss?"

Something hardened around his mouth. "I don't know."

Before I could avoid her, Skalet had me by the arm, her

fingers digging deep in warning. "Answer. This is a very slender bone. I could snap it before you could stop me."

To my relief, Paul didn't blink. "Go ahead. You're the one who likes being Human, not Esen. She'd love an excuse to cycle into something stronger. Wouldn't you, Old Blob?"

Well, I could think of innumerable other reasons I'd prefer over suffering a broken arm or even a pinched one.

"You're lying. This is the form that matters to you—the one of your own kind."

Paul's chuckle was so spontaneous and unexpected, even Skalet had to believe it was genuine. "Bess? I'm actually more fond of the Lishcyn. Then again, I do have a soft spot for her as a Ket. And her Whirtle?" Suddenly, he grew serious and looked down at me. "All your forms matter to me, Esen, including that shy and beautiful teardrop you only let me glimpse. And no one of them matter to me more than you."

I pulled my arm free with a yank, restraining myself from any further juvenile behavior with an effort. *Although I would have loved to stick out my tongue.* "I'm going to get dressed," I told my web-kin. "And I suggest you realize who are your only allies on this ship, S'kal-ru."

Unfortunately, my splendid exit was marred by a knock on the door. I dove for the bedroom, where I could peek around the doorframe without being in the direct line of any projectile. Skalet motioned Paul to follow me, a precaution I heartily approved, before saying: "Enter."

No assassin. It was Captain Arzul-ro himself, breathing so deeply I was sure he'd run here from the bridge. Considering there was a perfectly functional com system, this implied a problem he didn't want to share with his fellow officers and crew.

"Your Eminence." His hands flashed to his cheek tattoos so quickly I wasn't sure it counted as a salute. "Forgive the intrusion, but Nerri Port Authority has closed the Xir System to unauthorized traffic. It's a general broadcast."

"Do they give a reason?"

"Yes, Your Eminence. They have War Hogs insystem. Scans confirm: two Ganthor assault fleets, with battalion carriers and suborbital support capability. Heading for Picco's Moon. May I assume this is part of your schedule of operations?" He was patently hoping it was. No one, especially Kraal, underestimated Ganthor.

Skalet threw me a look that was vintage Ersh. I shrugged and shook my head.

This wasn't my fault.

Otherwhere

"YOU'RE sure I can't get you a drink, Joel? You look as though you could use one." Alphonsus considered his old friend thoughtfully. A drink might not be enough. There were blue-black bruises under his eyes and the skin of his cheeks had taken on a yellow hue. His eyes glittered almost feverishly, unable to settle on anything. Cracks and dried skin competed for space on his lips. Both hair and clothing had gone without washing for too long, as if he no longer cared about his appearance.

Joel Largas should have been in a med box days ago.

His condition, combined with the worried looks the crew of the *Largas Loyal* had given the Chief Constable behind Joel's back, had changed his plan from a brief. "Hello and get that ship launched," to bringing Joel here, to his office, where they could talk. Alphonsus liked his office. It was tidy. He had a plant in each corner and a vid of his first grandchild's school play on one wall. It wasn't the kind of place where old friends looked about to collapse—or Ganthor dropped from the sky. "You've heard we have trouble inbound," Alphonsus said, dropping all ceremony. *Nothing spread faster than bad news—and Joel was always the first to know.*

Joel nodded brusquely. "You've folks anxious to lift out of its way."

"Too late. That window's closed, orders of the Commonwealth. If there're any—unpleasantries—they'd rather it be in space, not here. That means keeping the approaches clear of noncombatants. Reminds me. I've sent a tug to move the 'Loyal so I can get the emergency transport on the pad." The Chief Constable expected some reaction to this, but Joel's face didn't change. Nonplussed, he continued: "Don't worry. I told them to be gentle. I don't know how you keep that old lady running. Means you'll stay fin-down with the rest for a while."

"Suits me. I've business here." Short and sweet—especially from a spacer who hated regulations and orders so much he'd moved his entire family to the Fringe. *What was going on?*

Alphonsus deliberately assumed what his wife of seventy-five years called his "stuffy" face, the one that encouraged the innocent not to waste a minute of his time and the guilty to waste even less. The one that said: prove it. "You talked about criminals. I'm listening."

"I saw them. Kraal elite troops, I swear to you."

The day kept getting better and better. "Damn it, Joel, I have enough going on here without you trying to start an intersystem incident. Your own constables are saying it was an extortionist's efforts to squeeze local business—" The official line from the authorities on Minas XII had the expected arrow pointing to the Dump.

"I saw them, Phonse. Stealth gear, all the latest toys. Kraal all right. They were after Paul Cameron and Esolesy Ki. It's a miracle we escaped."

"I didn't see your name as a witness on any report."

Joel's humorless smile split his lip, and he paused to dab the resulting drop of blood with a corner of his sleeve. "Not wasting my time talking to local jellies. Besides, I was busy helping Paul and Es move to their hiding place. We weren't taking any chances with Kraal around."

Alphonsus did his best to keep his relief to something reasonable. "Where are they?"

"Sorry, Phonse. I trust you, but I promised Paul I wouldn't tell a soul, not even his own children. They plan to stay completely out of touch until it's safe. I've closed down all their business, made sure everything's paid. The staff have gone home." Joel nodded. Once he started, he seemed unable to stop, his head moving with every word. "That's how it is. But I didn't promise I wouldn't do some looking on my own. It isn't right, what's happened. Isn't right."

"So what brought you here?" Alphonsus let a thread of impatience into his tone. It wouldn't do to seem too interested in the affairs of Cameron & Ki, despite his own concern over Paul and Esen.

Given what was overhead, it was easier than he'd thought.

Joel didn't appear hurried. He spoke carefully, enunciating every word as though he'd practiced what he said—or had said it so many times it was now by rote. Alphonsus was used to this from witnesses to a crime. It chilled him from a friend. "The attack came right after Es arranged a flight here on one of our ships. She and Paul were in a hurry. I didn't ask why, but I could tell it was important." The rote slipped a bit. "First time I've—first time I've heard her postpone a shopping trip until on the way home. And her stomachs were growling. All of them. You've met her, right? You know that's not a good sign." The eyes glittered again.

"I haven't had the pleasure of meeting Fem Ki," the Chief Constable said easily. "Only Hom Cameron. Of course, I know both by reputation. Cameron & Ki handles some imports for the Tumblers. Few bother to dabble in that market. Communication issues." *Which had recently gone from amusingly eccentric to danger-*

ously confused. "They've done better than most," he added thoughtfully. "Maybe they had a lead on events here well ahead of anyone else. That could explain their hurry."

"It doesn't explain the destruction of their home and warehouse. But I found something. There was a note on Es' desk about a mining operation on Picco's Moon, an illegal one."

"How did you find that?"

"One of the office staff was looking for clues and brought it to me. That's not important. What is, is that Esolesy Ki is listed as one of the owners of the property where the mining was taking place."

Alphonsus added "official disapproval" to "stuffy." "Did she tell you?"

"I called in some favors."

"I bet you did."

Joel shrugged, then leaned forward, putting his arms on his thighs. "Don't go all rules and regulations on me, Phonse. You and I go back a long way."

"Long enough that you know there are lines I don't cross." Alphonsus snapped, then softened his tone. "Sorry. Tell me why you think these Kraal troops are here."

"You know they are. My captains reported seventeen Kraal ships landing here in the past week." Joel sat back, looking smug.

Alphonsus threw up both hands. "And I've got twenty-one Ervickian ships, three Whirtle heavy freighters, a Heezle yacht full of underage brats, and who-knows-how-many Human ships. If you want the rest of the breakdown by species and preference, I'll call in Bris. He should have it updated by now. It's a free port, Joel, with the locals throwing a fortune in gems at spacers. Of course there are Kraal." He calmed down and put his hands flat on his desk. "And I have over a hundred Ganthor ships on approach. To be honest? Even if you could march in your elite troops and make an eyewitness statement identifying them—oh, and toss in an extradition agreement that works for both the Kraal and Tumblers—I still couldn't deal with it right now. That's the way it is."

"So you won't help me."

"Can't." Alphonsus relaxed and shook his head slowly. "You've already done the best you can for your friends, Joel. They have the right idea. Lie low until this is resolved. It will be. By the authorities. You make sure to give your report to Minas XII when you get back."

"I will. I understand. Thanks for your time, Phonse." Largas stood, using the chair arms to steady himself as he got to his feet. He held out his hand, callused and rough. He might look weak and ill-used. His grip was still strong.

Alphonsus frowned slightly as he shook hands. "You've never given up this fast in your life, Joel Largas. If all my officers weren't busy, I'd lock you up just to ease my mind."

"And your Maggie would have something to say about that."

"True enough. As it is, she'll be mad I didn't get you home for supper. But we're not leaving the com room until, well, until things are resolved." Alphonsus saw Largas to the door, then stopped before opening it. He put his hand on the other's shoulder, feeling bone where there should be muscle. "Listen, Joel. I didn't want to ask. You look like something an Ervickian would spit out. But I have to—I need you."

"Need me?" The bushy eyebrows rose a little, then came together. "You think it isn't a bluff. You think the Ganthor are coming planetside. Why? To fight who? Each other?"

"It doesn't matter. We have two Commonwealth ships on the way. Only two, in range. This had better become a war of words, Joel, because even as innocent bystanders we haven't a hope in hell if it's anything else."

The old spacer's eyes had lost their distant focus, as though the urgency pulled him back from some abyss. His tongue moistened his lips. "Tell me what you need me to do."

"Get the captains ready. Yours. The ones you know are steady. Quietly. Quickly. The ships are a mess out there. I can't send some to the field without causing a panic among the rest. Most are too bottled up to move. But I have to be ready to evacuate as many folks as I can. That means priority one lifts to ships on the outer edges and those squatters on the field. I don't want people to die arguing over property. You've done this before, Joel. You've made it work."

"Fifty plus years ago," with a note of desperation. "I'm old, Phonse. Surely you have someone else."

Alphonsus gripped Joel's other shoulder, looked him in the eye. "There's no one I know who could do this better. There's no one else they'd listen to without wasting time arguing. They know you. I know you. You're fair, you're honest, and tougher than any of them. But more than that. You wouldn't turn away anyone who needed help; you wouldn't abandon your worst enemy. You didn't on Garson's World. You won't here. Can I count on you?"

Did age put the tears in Joel's eyes—or something he didn't understand? Alphonsus waited until Joel nodded, then let go of his shoulders. "I'll do my best," Joel said, his voice growing firmer with each word. "We'll make room on the '*Loyal* for Maggie, and the families of your people here. Send them over when—when you like."

"Thank you."

The door opened as Alphonsus reached for the control. It was Bris, his nose twitching at Largas. With typical Moderan bluntness, he didn't bother with greetings. "You have an urgent incoming on your secure channel, Chief Constable, and I've updates on ship movements insystem of Nerri. The transmission from Mason and Trit is due in five. There are—"

"I can see myself out," Joel said quietly. His big hand rested on Alphonsus' back for a moment. "Take care of us, Phonse."

For the first time, Alphonsus wished he'd taken that cushy security job Maggie's uncle had offered him. Sitting a com desk at a marfle tea plant, confronting hideous dangers like insect infestations and in-laws.

His eyes kept straying to the chair where Joel Largas had sat and lied to him.

The secure call had been Paul. Curt and brief, in his persona as Paul Cameron. Phrases with hidden meanings for those who knew.

"Esolesy Ki's fine, too." *Esen was all right.*

"See you're a little overcrowded down there, Chief Constable. Watch for pickpockets." *A threat to them, already on the ground, here.*

Largas. How much of what he'd said was true? Were the Kraal the threat—or was he?

"Understand your concern and would comply with the warn-off, but our ship carries essential perishables for the Tumblers. We have an off-site landing planned. Don't worry. We know what we're doing." *They knew the situation and were coming to talk to the Tumblers.*

The brightest spot of his day. Mason and Trit hadn't found a Tumbler, let alone talked to one. The beings were staying deep inside their valleys—forbidden turf without an invitation.

He rested his eyes on the vid of his granddaughter, watching her twirl and dance—and bump into her neighbor, both girls consumed by giggles that spread through the rest of the class until all that remained of the original choreography was the finale, when they all bowed together.

There were children in the Port City. More on board the ships locked to the ground.

There were children scattered over the Moon's surface, waiting for the next Eclipse to start their new lives.

If Paul and Esen could do anything to help them, they would. Alphonsus believed that. And he wouldn't let anyone get in their way.

He looked back at the chair and his expression turned to the one his wife had never seen.

Deadly.

28: Scoutship Morning

ESEN-ALIT-QUAR. Esen-alit-Quar.

There should be voices, not the ghosts of memory, to greet me here.

"Bess." Skalet's voice interrupted. "Pay attention."

I tore my attention from the viewscreen, a faint blue afterimage of Picco's vivid orange burned into my eyes, complete with the dark, insignificant spot that marked her living moon. I hadn't expected the sight of two hunks orbiting, however large, to affect me. *Perhaps,* I comforted myself, *it was a consequence of this form.*

If so, Skalet should be staring into space as well, not hovering in front of a Kraal battle display peppered with moving dots.

"That's a lot of Ganthor," I offered helpfully, swallowing hard as Skalet-memory rose up and made sense of what looked random. *Holding patterns. Retreat routes. Invasion formations.*

"Expensive." This dry observation came from Paul. He was sitting, one knee to his chest, on the bench that ringed the upper level of the small bridge. From there, he overlooked the display and us. His skin was startlingly plain among the tattooed Kraal, its paleness emphasized by the black crew uniform Skalet had given him. A Kraal my apparent age would be too young for affiliations, but I caught several of them staring at Paul despite Skalet's orders that we were "luggage" and invisible.

"Expensive—and one-sided," Skalet added almost under

her breath. The bridge crew, each within a force field and locked to his or her station for battle, were following her stalk around the display with their eyes. Trained, but not experienced, I decided, and hoping for news they were on the side with the Ganthor and not otherwise.

I hoped so, too. But as I couldn't imagine any side of anything that could need this many Ganthor, it didn't seem likely.

Skalet, as befitted a Kraal noble, wasn't giving her affiliates any hints. She was, I knew, enjoying their efforts to second-guess her.

"Any further signals?"

"More warn-offs from Port Authority, Your Eminence. They are getting quite vehement about it. Nothing from the Ganthor."

"They aren't talkers." Skalet stopped moving in front of Paul. She tilted her head in question. "And your sources?" She'd let him make one more call once we arrived on the bridge. Monitored, this time.

"You heard Port Authority. They're too busy to shoot us down, if that's what you're worried about. They don't need to, do they?"

"They need our help," I said quietly, unable to avoid daring this much in a room full of strangers.

"One scoutship?" Skalet's laugh was low and rich. She was back in her element again. "What help do you imagine that would be?"

"You know what I mean."

"Do I?" Archly. "Let me tell you the usefulness of this ship, little one. It's going to take us where we need to be, then lift us away again with what we've come to find. Before the Ganthor shatter this miserable rock into dust and memories." She turned away from me and snapped: "Take us down, Captain."

Whatever else you could say about the Kraal, their way of life fostered an ability to follow the most ridiculous orders, when delivered by a superior in whom they had belief.

Arzul-ro didn't even flinch. "Do you have a specific landing site in mind, Your Eminence?" Challenge offered.

"You have the coordinates." Challenge accepted. I took a discreet step away from my web-kin, not being one of those present in battle armor.

The two faced each other, both tall, thin, and dressed in black, both living weapons. Arzul-ro may have thought himself to have the edge in weight and reach. It didn't matter. He lasted five seconds before dropping his eyes from Skalet's and lifting his hands to his tattoos. *Challenge withdrawn.* "Of course, Your Eminence. The admiral awaits you at the mine." The bridge lighting began to dim, replaced by a rise in that of the tactical display and from each control panel. A flurry of orders and directions circled the room. I didn't bother paying attention to either. There was a more pressing issue.

"S'kal-ru, may I have a moment please?" I said calmly, resisting the temptation to either walk up behind her and poke her in the back—unwise when my web-kin was so thoroughly aroused—or to shout—also unwise on a bridge where all but two individuals were armed to the teeth and contemplating Ganthor.

And outnumbered one hundred and thirteen to one. I didn't bother counting the individuals within each ship, since it was unlikely to matter in space, although I was quite sure everyone here was aware that a battalion carrier could hold upward of ten thousand stamping and excited Ganthor plus their gear.

Quite a sight, really. Not to mention the drooling and bumping.

Not that I wanted to see it for myself. Skalet-memory was enough. She'd spent many years as a Ganthor Matriarch on behalf of the Web, and Ersh had made sure I'd assimilated all of them. She was fond of the species herself. As I was—usually.

"What do you want?"

I stepped close enough that our conversation had some

chance of not being overheard by everyone present. "Suits. For Paul at least."

Skalet put her hand against my cheek. An affectionate gesture to those who didn't know better, or who couldn't see the wicked gleam in her eyes. "Dear Bess. Don't worry so—this is the easy part. Now be a good child and keep yourself out of the way."

"Out of—" words failed me.

There was no point attempting to argue. I went up the stairs, noticing absently they were inlaid with freshwater shells from Jylnicia and edged with wood carved into playful waves. Kraal ships abounded with paradoxes.

"I'm to stay out of the way," I informed my Human as he made room for me on the bench, sitting in a position that would be comfortable if its restraint field engaged without warning.

"I heard." Paul's eyes didn't leave the display, now showing the *Octos Ra* as a tiny yellow dot. It looked like a Mendley shrimp heading for a school of Busfish. *A suicidal shrimp.* "S'kal-ru sounds confident," he said, as if hearing my thoughts.

"She always does." I hoped it was loud enough to carry. *"Child,"* was I? *"Dear Bess?"*

I had some idea of what Skalet was planning, or more precisely, I knew what she knew about the Ganthor. It remained to be seen if she knew as much about the Kraal.

"Let's make this a quick approach," Skalet ordered, her lovely voice raised just enough to penetrate every corner of the bridge. "No point wasting time."

The pilot looked to his captain. Arzul-ro spoke up immediately: "Best speed that lets you maneuver around the—"

"No," she countered happily. "Straight ahead. Ignore their ships. If they get in our way, they can move."

Paul was nodding to himself. The Kraal seemed stunned.

"I don't have all day, Captain."

It hung on the moment. I leaned my chin on the rail to watch, reluctantly admiring Skalet's command of Human body language as she stood waiting for them to obey. There was no doubt, no fear in that spine or shoulders. Nothing but confident anticipation on her face. Slowly, she raised one eyebrow.

No coincidence that eyebrow was etched with the affiliation binding her to the House of Arzul and it to her.

Captain Arzul-ro bowed his head slightly and said: "Pilot, take her in."

It took the *Octos Ra* five minutes to reach the outer ring the Ganthor had established, passing close enough to a cruiser that it occluded two viewscreens until the tech adjusted. *No reaction.* Except for the sweat I saw furtively wiped from some brows.

"Steady," Skalet crooned.

Twenty of this form's heartbeats until we passed another; ten to another; then we seemed to pass so many they blurred together. *No reaction.* We disappeared from the display, too close to other, larger ships to be resolved as distinct by the scoutship's device.

I was quite sure we hadn't disappeared from the Ganthor's scanners.

"Keep going," Skalet sang softly. The Kraal were beginning to relax, perhaps believing the Ganthor were letting us through.

I could have corrected that impression. It was more that the Ganthor were too busy rousing themselves into battle frenzy to bother. But this image hardly reassured me, so I didn't think I'd share it with anyone else.

Our brave little dot showed again, almost clear of the waiting fleet. Then, suddenly, a lone ship appeared, moving directly into our path.

Skalet was actually humming under her breath. "Stay on course," she told the pilot.

"But—"

"She'll move—or you'll make her move."

"Yes, Your Eminence." His reply seemed to come through gritted teeth.

Our dots grew closer and closer. Then were one.

Collision alarms tolled. The lighting switched to reserve, plunging portions of the bridge into darkness. The restraint field sucked me into the bench even as I felt Paul take my hand. Skalet stood in the display's glow, her head up and back, smiling. She'd hooked her arm through the railing, in case the grav failed.

"Make it clear to them," she said. "Push harder."

"Yes, Your Eminence!" From the fierce joy in his voice, the Kraal seemed to have caught whatever disease inflicted my web-kin.

There was a gonglike ringing through the hull, then nothing.

The display showed two dots, the yellow one leaving the other behind.

"Three orbits," Skalet said, her voice deep with satisfaction. "Make sure we're not bringing company on our tail, then land. You two—with me."

Otherwhere

TUMBLERS, as befitted a species dependent upon the accumulation of mineral salts for growth, lived within their environment, spending day and night where they could be bathed at any moment by the nourishing mists of their valleys. There were no Tumbler homes or buildings, no shelters. Having never hidden from weather or predators, they needed none. The fruits of their society were etched in stone or traveled as sound. Accident, landslide, or moonquake had been their only enemy, avoided when possible but accepted as part of the cycle of life, until the recent and regrettable behavior of the flesh-burdened.

If concealment was a difficult concept for the average Tumbler to grasp, it proved even harder to accomplish. Remaining motionless and hoping intruders would go away hadn't worked. The flesh-burdened had a disconcerting ability to spot a Tumbler and, worse, would continue to return at random intervals until the Tumbler moved—in which case they would follow until the Tumbler entered one of the sacrosanct valleys.

Wedging oneself into a crack proved distressingly permanent for at least three individuals, who, following a period of mineral accumulation, were unable to extricate themselves.

The Elders were forced to resort to extreme measures. They ordered the ramps into their valleys blocked, and forbade any Tumbler to engage in bliss until the Ganthor had cleansed their Moon of the flesh-burdened. And hopefully any revoltingly organic consequences.

Within the gentle, corrosive mists, an entire species stood and waited to be understood.

While overhead, the Matriarch of the Fleet stomped and waited to be ordered to the attack.

Not that she could wait much longer. One of the reasons Ganthor made such excellent mercenaries was also the reason they made such lousy ones.

Their infamous battle frenzy was a matter of precise timing. Not long enough, and they'd be as likely to bicker among themselves as attack the enemy. Too long?

And nothing could stop them.

29: Orbit Morning

THE antechamber to the bridge was done in whites, shocking to the eye after the dim lighting of the battle bridge. The furniture rose out of the carpeting, its shadows forming a confusion of stark lines and angles along the walls. The only color was the tray of essentials and a blood-red bottle of serpitay on the glossy tabletop, white glasses arranged around it.

For once, Skalet ignored the Kraal niceties. The instant the door closed, she turned to us. "We don't have much time. Here." She took off the belt holding her weapon and knife and pressed them into Paul's hands. "Now. You. What to do with you."

As I was helping myself to a handful of appetizers—this form being constantly famished—I wasn't immediately sure if she was commenting on my manners or something else, and pulled my hand back. "Sorry."

"Not the food, Youngest. Eat if you must. But the orbits give us breathing space and I intend to make the best of it." She watched Paul strapping on the weapon and waved his hands out of her way impatiently, making the final adjustments around his waist herself. She touched one of the compartments on the belt. "The hood is in here. You'll need it to hide your face when you rejoin the others."

I stopped chewing. "What are you planning? A mutiny?"

"Hardly. This crew is mine now. It's what Mocktap might have waiting that we prepare for."

"What about the Ganthor? And who hired them?" My

Human-self's voice had an unfortunate tendency to become shrill. "You know the only beings who could afford this many Ganthor are the Tumblers."

"Or web-beings," added Paul, well aware of the fortune Ersh had amassed for us. *Several, if you counted the fact that she'd invested as a member of every species that valued personal wealth.*

Skalet glared at me. I spread my open hands, after hastily brushing the crumbs from both. "He had to know," I reasoned for her. "We live together. There was shopping."

"If I didn't know you've been appropriately cautious in your spending over the years, Youngest, other than a predilection for tasteless silk, I'd be distinctly—unhappy—with this turn of events. Tell me, Human, is there anything you don't know about us?"

Given the look on Paul's face, the answer wasn't going to improve Skalet's temper. "We don't have time for this," I reminded them. "Did you hire the Ganthor or not?"

Her nostrils flared with distaste. "I wouldn't do anything so flagrantly obvious."

If she'd told me once during our lessons, she'd told me ten thousand times: *Finesse, Esen. Never use a sword when the scratch of a pin will do.* "If it wasn't you, then it had to be the Tumblers."

"Nonsense. They can hardly bear the concept of blood, let alone the idea of it spilling over their Moon."

"Life defends itself." This from Paul. "There was a Tumbler killed on Ersh's mountain. There could have been more since."

"Who would—?" For a split second, Skalet's face seemed oddly vulnerable. I understood. Not only were the Tumblers gentle, fragile creatures—for all their mineral composition—but it was Ersh's chosen form. We'd rarely seen her as anything else.

For a while, I'd wondered if Ersh lived as rock because of me. Surely it helped her endure—or ignore me—for long periods. Tumblers had emotions, primarily the calm, slow sort you'd expect from beings who could converse for a month about microfissures. Another reason Ersh liked the form. *They had,* according to her, *a proper time scale for living.* Their feelings were usually related to their surroundings rather than a reaction to the behavior of others. As a Tumbler in her own home, Ersh tended to feel calm and relaxed. Until something I did happened to change things. *Then,* I remembered nostalgically, *she'd become the only Tumbler on Picco's Moon to have a temper and lose it.*

I shook myself free of memory to hear Paul say: "Then you agree. We have to do something—"

Skalet raised her hand to stop him. "I do not. You think we can make any difference in what's happening here? We'll be lucky to escape ourselves."

"We have to try."

"No, we don't. You see, Youngest? This is ephemeral thinking at its worst." She walked around Paul, who went stiff and angry under this mock-inspection. "Try. Meddle. Change. Affect. Corrupt. These aren't our ways, Human. We don't interfere. We let time pass and nature take its course. We—remember. And we endure."

This would have been more impressive coming from Ersh. I stuffed the remaining appetizers into my pockets for later and scowled at my web-kin. "Looked in a mirror lately, 'S'kal-ru'? You've been meddling with these Humans all along."

"You made a home for yourself, Youngest. Do you begrudge me the same?"

Snick. Just like that, everything became as clear to me as if her flesh were part of mine. "You." I stepped away from the table, feeling my hands form fists. Small, but tight. "You started all this. You were here first. This war is your fault."

"I don't know what you're talking about. I haven't been back to Picco's Moon. I told you that."

"Hired help." This from Paul, never slow to make connections. "You sent your affiliates to dig out the artifacts you'd hidden on the mountain. Why wait until now?"

"Ersh forbade it," I said very quietly.

"Along with this form for two generations," Skalet admitted freely, tracing a path from her throat to her waist with the fingers of one hand. "But when she—left us, it was necessary to make other plans for the future. I watched you, Esen, make a life for yourself. I knew I could do better. I would found a House of my own." She shrugged. "For which I needed the artifacts in my possession. I didn't send miners. I hired a gem smuggler to retrieve them. He told me the cave was empty." Skalet's smile was one to give any being nightmares. I felt sorry for the smuggler. "It was possible. Plausible, in fact. Ersh hadn't been—pleased. She could well have destroyed the crates and their contents three hundred years ago."

"Someone stayed to mine the mountain." The peak, where we'd met to share; Ersh's home, where I'd learned to hold the varied and beautiful forms of living intelligence; the diamond-dust of Tumbler children. I regretted the rich delicacies in my stomach. "To disturb Ersh's rest."

Her eyes were sober. "Esen. I would never have permitted it. I didn't know about the mining until you and Paul told me. I first learned the smuggler had lied to me—that the artifacts still existed—when they appeared on the doorstep of an obscure little museum on Signat, the homeworld for Conell and Bract, my most powerful affiliates. No House claimed credit for their recovery. Clearly a Kraal move; potentially one against me. What could I do then? I'd lost control of the game, or it had new players. It was time to pay attention to another."

"Me." I glanced at Paul. He was leaning against the table, arms folded across his chest, that intent look on his face.

"You, indeed." Skalet's smile faded. "My failure to obtain the artifacts was—inefficient. It conceivably put this form at risk, if my link to them—if my past—had been exposed. It was time to obtain what you had, Youngest, in order to protect myself. The ability of web-form to move through space. Ersh's secret."

"Which you don't have yet," Paul stated. "And now someone—Mocktap—stands in your way. Interesting, isn't it?"

Skalet's attention was a dangerous thing to draw. I'd practiced for years to avoid it. *Mind you, my motivation had been to limit the number of boring problems she could assign me.* She considered my Human now, as if weighing his future value against the impertinence of his question. "How did you know it was Mocktap?" I asked to divert her.

It was scarcely more comfortable having her glare down at me. Still, she answered. "I needed to learn what had happened on Picco's Moon. Not all the artifacts had reappeared. But I didn't dare go myself. I ordered my most trusted affiliate—see, I admit my folly, Youngest, will you?—to check several mountains, including Ersh's, for any activity. A training exercise. I know the capabilities of my people, Esen. If there'd been an empty ration tube on the mountain, they'd have found it. Mocktap's report said they found nothing. She lied. And 'lies don't live alone.'" The last seemed a quote, but the source wasn't in my memory. Her face became pensive. "Only we do, Esen-alit-Quar."

Two maudlin web-beings, I thought, remembering my conversation with the Grigari musician. *Ersh.* I shook my head and didn't bother to argue. Although I was sorely tempted to point out that for once I hadn't been the one whose planning went awry. Only the consequences facing us made me say, instead: "We might not be alone or otherwise, if we can't resolve all of this. I hope you've thought of that."

"I do have a plan, Youngest." Skalet sounded offended that I might doubt her or its outcome. *Perhaps we shared blind optimism as a fault.* "You and Paul will jump from the *Octos Ra* on approach, then make your way to the mountain peak in time to meet me. While I deal with my—problem— you will find what I want from Ersh. I'll arrange for the Kraal to evacuate, with us on board."

"Jump?" I squealed, over Paul's fierce, "What about the Ganthor?"

Skalet's eyes gleamed. "And there is a small matter of a hand weapon Mocktap likely possesses. It's effective against us, my dear web-kin. Try not to get in her sights."

That silenced us, as I was sure she intended.

Then, I held out my hand, palm up.

"What's this?" she asked.

"I want Paul's antidote. Before you get in her sights or the Ganthor attack." I had to look up to meet her eyes. "You are welcome to risk your own life, Skalet. I won't have you risk his. I promise you will have what Ersh remembered for us."

The black and red of her tattoos blurred her expressions, but I thought I saw a touch of respect. Without looking away from me, Skalet gestured Paul to her side. "I have your word, Esen-alit-Quar?"

"Esen!" I didn't look at him.

"You have my word."

Skalet smiled. Before either of us knew what she intended, she turned to Paul. Taking his head in her hands, she drew his face to hers, holding it there so she could press her mouth against his in a long, involved kiss that had nothing to do with passion.

I should have guessed she'd built her own immunity to the duras poison for more reasons than self-protection. *Still*, I decided, squeezing my eyes shut, *there were some sights that could scar a young and impressionable mind forever.*

Not to mention I had to start building this form's courage before leaping out of a descending scoutship onto terrain even the Tumblers called "precipitous."

And, I thought numbly, find a way to stop the Ganthor from attacking this world.

Giving Skalet the secret of flight while avoiding the Kraal seemed the least of my problems at the moment.

Otherwhere

IF Timri hadn't spotted him following Cristoffen, Rudy thought, he wouldn't have made it on to the *Russell III*. If Kearn hadn't convinced him he was an ally, he wouldn't be standing on the orange-touched pavement of the Literiai Plateau this afternoon, one hand on the pitted ramp of a tramp freighter, waiting for a ride.

And if they didn't all die here, in the next few hours, he would be surprised.

Because no one was being allowed to land on Picco's Moon except Commonwealth military, and of those close enough, only the *Russ'* had been already on its way when the squeal from Port Authority came through. *With what was on the other side of that bright orange sky, the smart move would have been to turn around*, Rudy grimaced to himself.

At least Kearn hadn't panicked, though two of the crew had turned green and run from the bridge when they'd seen what ringed their destination. In fact, he'd commented that he hadn't been aware the Ganthor had that many serviceable ships in this sector, before sitting down to watch Rudy handle the approach down the lane the Ganthor had left to the shipcity. It closed behind them. The other Commonwealth ship was sitting in orbit around Szhenna, her captain's most potentially useful function to keep other ships from straying into a battle zone.

Which left them.

At the request of a haggard Chief Constable Alphonsus Lundrigan, Kearn had tried clickspeak, in hopes the Matriarch of the Fleet would respond to that, since she hadn't to comspeak. *No reaction*. The fleet was ready and it was waiting.

For what? Payment? A coded signal? The arrival of a real foe?

None of them knew, but suspense was likely better than the alternative.

Cristoffen's contact with the Kraal hadn't shown yet. Rudy couldn't imagine being more conspicuous, and found it hard to resist the impulse to stand in the shadow of the ramp. He wore a Commonwealth uniform, complete with the formal cloak Timri had assured him Cristoffen wore on every possible occasion. As if that weren't enough to single him out, despite the tightest ship packing job Rudy had seen outside a scrap yard, there were few other figures outside. All but his own moved quickly and furtively. He'd been informed there weren't even people on the ships surrounding him. In a rare show of cooperation—or the recovery of the common sense they'd lost to join the Gem Rush— they'd voluntarily moved into starships on the periphery.

Ships that could take off, if the Ganthor let them. *He should be on the* Russ', Rudy chafed. *Doing something about* this *situation*. The damn Kraal could wait for Armageddon with the rest of them. Kearn hadn't agreed, believing there might be a connection.

"Rudy? Is that you?"

Recognition sent a jolt of adrenaline through every part of his body. As he turned in the direction of the voice, Rudy deliberately eased the muscles of his face, smiling that smile that invited others to underestimate him. "Meony-ro. Fancy meeting you here."

The Kraal was slightly older than Paul, and solidly built. He hadn't lost the fitness of years of military service—not to Rudy's eye. His face usually, as Esen aptly put it, resembled crumbled brickwork or a clown's mask, depending on his liquid intake. Now, however, it was alight with what seemed to be relief, spots of color on each cheek. The orange reflection from Picco emphasized the faint scars where tattoos had been. "I was on my way to the *Russell III*—to see if there was news about Hom Cameron. We aren't getting any com feeds to the ships. I came with Hom Largas—Joel Largas," he added, as though something in Rudy's face prompted an explanation, then frowned. "When did you rejoin the Commonwealth? Hom Largas will be disappointed."

"It's temporary," Rudy said easily. "I'm filling in for Michael Cristoffen—making a delivery for him, in fact."

Meony-ro looked blank. "I don't know the name. Should I? Is he the new captain?"

The wash of relief Rudy felt probably showed on his face, but he didn't care. "Probably not. It's good to see you."

"And you. Have you heard anything about Hom Cameron or Fem Ki?"

Timri might know more by now. She was meeting with Alphonsus. Rudy hadn't dared delay, assuming the Kraal would be watching for the *Russell III* to land. "Nothing yet. Miserable business. Was anyone hurt in the attacks?" He leaned back on the ramp, keeping a casual eye on the surrounding area. "I don't have many details."

"Not for want of trying. Their home was obliterated. Professional and neat. The front half of the warehouse remained standing long enough for the employees in there to get clear. I'd say the only injury was Hom Largas."

"Joel?"

"He was with Hom Cameron and Fem Ki when they were attacked in her greenhouse. They escaped together. Joel helped them get away, but he was shaken up and hasn't recovered. We couldn't stop him coming here, trying to find who did it. Now he's helping with the evacuation. I think Silv is going to turn gray watching."

There was a dark spot in the sky. An aircar approaching. "Here's my ride," Rudy said quickly. "Give my best to Joel. Tell him I'll stop by when I'm back."

Meony-ro turned and squinted at the sky, then looked at Rudy. "Rudy? That can't be for you. That's a Kraal ship."

Two Port Authority aircars whizzed by overhead, aimed at the intruder. They met and hovered together at the edge of the shipcity. Rudy had no doubt the Kraal would have whatever clearance and documents would be required, but it gave him some breathing space. "I don't have time to explain," Rudy said. "You'll have to trust me. Now get of sight before they arrive." He gave Meony-ro a gentle shove.

The Kraal slid smoothly to one side, somehow ending up with his arm around Rudy's neck before the Botharan could compensate. "I don't think so."

"Combat reflexes," Rudy commented.

"I've never tried to hide my training."

"No. Only your affiliation." The arm loosened and Meony-ro turned Rudy so they were face-to-face.

"Hom Largas said Kraal troops attacked them. I had nothing to do with it," Meony-ro said angrily, his voice flat and hard. "I owe blood-debt to Paul Cameron. I would never betray that."

"Not for an older one?"

"I owe no Kraal loyalty."

"What about Pa-Admiral Mocktap?"

For a second Rudy thought he'd gone too far, that Meony-ro would attack him in earnest. Then the Kraal eased from that brink—slightly—but his eyes held a promise of violence. "Her least of all."

Keeping perfectly still, Rudy said carefully: "Paul is

my cousin as well as my friend. If you know anything about Mocktap, anything at all—it could help him."

"What do you need to know?"

"What does she look like? What is she like?"

The Kraal's nostrils flared and there was a sheen to his skin, though the air was thin and chill. "Dark as night's underbelly; tattooed in ice; too old to bear off-spring, too young to retire. A noble," his lips twisted as though the word left a foul taste. "What is she like? As any noble, it is her role to command and her role to bestow guilt and blame where she sees fit." Meony-ro flicked the fingers of both hands against his cheeks, hard enough to leave a mark. "Ours is to obey the one and accept the other, unless we have the luxury of other affiliations which would support us in a dispute."

"You were her affiliate."

"Of her House alone. I wanted no more than Mocktap. So, why am I here, Rudy, instead of at her side?" The Kraal paused to check that the Kraal aircar was still delayed by the others. "I was senior gunner on the *Septos Pa*; my brother, captain of the *Octos Ank*. Proud of our posts and affiliation. Then—there came a day, a battle, when all that changed. Pa-Admiral Mocktap ordered me to fire and—" he stopped, as if this was where he wanted the story to end.

"Tell me what happened, Meony-ro," Rudy urged quietly. "It might be important."

"I obeyed, as always, without question. But our target dodged the nightshade's bolts. To this day, I don't know how—or what it was. Monster, weapon. It doesn't matter. Mocktap chose me to accept the blame for the result and stripped me of my affiliation. It was her right." He spat the word.

"Because you missed?"

"Because I didn't." Meony-ro's eyes seemed to burn into Rudy's. "My display didn't show the *Octos Ank* in the line of fire. Mocktap's did, but she was so afraid of what we fought that she ordered me to fire anyway, killing my brother—thousands more. I refused to clear her conscience with my death and ran from Kraal space. But I—it was hard to live with myself after that. Paul—Hom Cameron—found me in the Dump and—" He pressed his lips together.

The aircar was moving again, its escorts heading back to the perimeter. Rudy drew Meony-ro farther into the shadows. "What would the name 'Sybil' mean to Mocktap?"

"An ancestor of her House. Rudy, why are you asking me all this? Was Mocktap responsible for the attacks? Is she here?" He looked wildly at the approaching aircar. "Is that her affiliate?"

"I hope so, or we'll never find out. Listen. Go to the *Russ'* as you planned. Say I sent you. Ask to speak to Project Leader Kearn in private. Tell him what you've told me about Mocktap and anything else you can think of."

The Kraal, a shape in shadow, seemed to be studying Rudy. Then: "Hom Cameron told me to trust you, Rudy. And you've been a friend to me as well. I accept our affiliation." He bent and tucked himself out of sight, under the ramp. Rudy heard his whisper as the aircar descended. "Watch for her hands, Rudy. The nails of one are poisoned; the others are razor-sharp."

Wonderful, Rudy thought, putting on his best smile for the two hooded, black-garbed, and highly-armed Kraal now examining him from the door of the aircar. *Just wonderful.*

The Kraal didn't ask for identification or codes. They simply helped him on board the well-appointed craft with a courtesy that would have been warmer if it hadn't been for their faces being concealed. The hoods were, Rudy knew, the accepted way to preserve the privacy of the House and affiliations. Particularly if the wearers planned to commit a crime. Once he was seated, they left without delay. Rudy presumed Port Authority was glad to be rid of extraneous air traffic on a day when it could well start raining Ganthor assault vehicles.

They flew low and fast, which suited him. There was something about Picco's Moon that suited the Kraal, he thought, watching the landscape rip and fold itself. Covered in riches the locals disdained; inhospitable, yet carved by deep valleys that were, by all accounts, rich with life; and that unsettling orange that betrayed all color but black. He looked up at Picco, forming the horizon and half of the sky, and wondered how many Ganthor ships he'd spot with a telescope.

The mountain of all their speculation and wondering appeared to be disappointingly typical. Just another in a line of jagged peaks that weren't tall enough to condense the scant moisture from the atmosphere and gain snowy caps. He pressed his face to the viewport, looking for any sign of life. As if sensing his curiosity, the pilot veered away then approached from the northern side.

Two Kraal ships, scout class, were suspended on a thirty-degree portion of slope by their boarding grapples—an interesting, if challenging way to deal with a lack of suitable landing space. A talus of debris started from a long gouge in the surface, presumably the mine. Halfway down the slope was a ledge finished into a landing pad large enough for an aircar, the cliff face beside it carved with a series of openings like windows. Rudy automatically memorized the position and significance of each feature.

Then, he saw what didn't belong. A narrow stairway wound up the mountain from the landing pad to the top of the peak, its steps so shallow a Tumbler could roll up them, its center worn into ruts. The peak itself, now that it had his attention, was flatter than it should be.

What had eroded it? There was almost no rain here. It hadn't been a machine.

Rudy's mouth went dry as he remembered ancient ruins on other worlds, temples whose stone was worn by the passage of countless worshipers. But Tumblers didn't build steps. Their paths were wide and smooth, glittering with ritual leavings until poachers found them. There were several on this slope. Others in the distance.

How long did it take for footsteps alone to wear a staircase up a mountain and flatten its top?

And whose feet had it been?

Rudy focused on his image of Esen as Bess, her bright Human eyes and friendly smile, fighting back the fear that she was far more alien than he could ever have imagined.

They took him to the cliffside house, for that's what it must have been, Rudy discovered, as he stepped through a ruined door into what had been a kitchen.

Before a battle had raged in it. The Kraal had done some rough housekeeping, shoveling the debris of blackened cupboards and servos into one corner, topping it with the splinters of what had been a wooden table and chairs. Unremarkable stuff, until you realized there had never been a green plant or tree on Picco's Moon. Time hadn't paid attention; there was little in the way of dust or loose stone. Moisture collected in the valleys; there was no damage here from water or rot.

There were other rooms leading into the mountain from this one. He didn't bother exploring. He was expected, from the look of the camp table set with exquisite porcelains and crystal and the two chairs.

His hostess entered from another room as if summoned by the thought. Gone were the silks, replaced by battle armor and a sidearm. Her hair, silver white, was cropped close to her skull, carved away from the tattoos that marched past one ear in a smooth, sensual curve. She smiled warmly. "My dear Rudy."

"Sybil." He inclined his head. "You aren't surprised to see me."

"Of course not. Some refreshment before we begin. I insist."

Rudy waved off the attendant who'd appeared behind him, intent on removing his cloak. "I've no wish to seem impolite to such a gracious and powerful hostess as Pa-Admiral Mocktap, but under the present circumstances?" He gave her his most charming smile. "I suggest we not delay our business."

"Admiral?" Her eyes actually twinkled. Sybil seemed inordinately pleased; with him or herself? "You see? I'm not surprised at all. Call me Sybil. I like the way it sounds in your mouth." She made a girlish pout, an unnerving expression among her tattoos and wrinkled skin. "Such a shame we are being rushed. War hogs are always a nuisance. I had such excellent plans for our visit. Another time, perhaps?" Without waiting for an answer, she sat in one of the chairs and beckoned him to the other. A nod removed the attendant. "Sit. What have you brought me?"

Rudy moved his hands slowly and carefully to bring out the strange weapon and the handwritten book, quite sure the wrong gesture in this room would find him piled in the corner with the ruined table. He put both on the table, between the place settings. She made a small sound of satisfaction. "Excellent. Best of all, they've arrived with you. You do know what these are." Her hand rested on his before he could withdraw it, the nails strong, red, and perfectly shaped.

Poison or blade?

Rudy had known the risks in coming here. Kearn had wanted him outfitted with tracers and listening devices. Those would have been found during his trip in the aircar, with him likely dumped from just the right height to break most of his bones, but not all.

He was on his own. So Rudy gently pulled his hand free and used it to point to each of the objects. "A weapon against Kearn's Monster and S'kal-ru's plan to establish a House."

"Bravo!" She seemed as pleased as if he'd been one of her own, not a for-hire. "I knew you'd figure it out. There was another I'd had in mind for this in the beginning. Well-motivated, highly recommended. You know her, I believe. Janet Chase? Had issues with being this close to the Fringe—something about a price on her head. You, on the other hand, have all that lovely respectability. Arriving on a Commonwealth ship, no less. I chose well."

"Compliments don't pay my fee, Sybil," Rudy commented.

"Very true. Don't worry. I've already transferred a very handsome amount to an account under the name Rudy Leslie on Urgia Prime. If it's not enough—well, you are most welcome to come and see me for more. In the meantime," Sybil gathered up the book as if it were treasure, "this stays with me. Insurance, you might say, against further surprises. While this," Sybil nudged the weapon toward him, "is for you."

Rudy didn't bother hiding his surprise. "Why?"

"To finish your assignment. You didn't think I'd waste your talent, do you? I expect you to kill her for me."

"Kearn's Monster?"

"Mine. S'kal-ru. Oh, surely you knew. You put all the rest together—and so easily, too." Sybil leaned forward, her eyes glittering and dark. "S'kal-ru—and Esolesy Ki, Kearn's Esen. So much more than they seem. Creatures of mystery and power, playing games with the rest of us. How long? How long have we been their pawns, Rudy? S'kal-ru cheated my ancestor 343 years ago and looks younger than I. How much older can she be?"

Rudy didn't touch the weapon. "You are entitled to your beliefs, Sybil. I for one have a problem wrapping my head around the idea of shapeshifting beings that live for hundreds of years—"

"What if it's thousands of years. Tens of thousands. What if they've toyed with us all along? Kearn found legends older than our first steps offworld. How old are they?"

She'd found his nightmare and brought it to the surface, held it out to him as if in offering. Rudy couldn't stop the shiver that ran along his spine. He knew the Kraal saw it and understood. It was in her smile.

And next words. "You saw the stairs. Come. See the rest."

"The Ganthor—"

"Are not attacking yet. Come, Rudy, and see the truth."

He couldn't stop himself from following, despite feeling as though every step might take him farther from Esen and closer to something else. Something terrifying.

House? The humble entrance and kitchen had been a lie. Huge portions of the mountain had been hollowed out. There was a wide corridor behind one door, punching back into the rock, but Sybil first led him to each side of it, through layers of curved rooms, only the first still scorched and damaged. Behind those were others, their contents a mix of still-intact furniture. Only some pieces were suited to a humanoid form, and even those varied in age and style as if an unorganized antique collector had used the rooms for storage. There were closets bursting with fabrics, some fashioned into recognizable clothing, some styles he'd never seen.

Like Esen's secret closet on Minas XII.

Then, back into the corridor, where Sybil waved him ahead through a large, wide doorway. "We've used part for our work here. The rest is as we found it."

Rudy squinted as he entered, surprised by brightness in what was, after all, a cave. The vaultlike expanse stretched as far as he could see. To his immediate right, a group of Kraal ignored his presence, tending a cluster of machines. Above, light beamed down from a combination of fixtures and through what appeared to be inset gems. They were what they appeared, Rudy realized as he saw other Kraal on ladders, busy prying loose the treasure.

Ahead and to the left, stone had been coaxed into a confusion of platforms and channels, interconnected, solid as the mountain itself. He walked forward, running his hand along the unfinished rock, trying to puzzle it out. The platforms ranged from knee-to-shoulder height, none shading another. Then Rudy's fingers touched softness. He looked down and saw the platform beside him was filled with dust-dry soil, coated in a layer of desiccated leaves. They all were, he saw.

A greenhouse. *Like Esen's.*

Complete with a prosaic jumble of pots and tools by the doorway.

"One last thing, my dear Rudy." Sybil was standing near the machines. "A surprise the mountain itself had for us." She nodded toward a pile of rock. "We've found a substance within the surface strata of the peak. My scientists have no explanation for its existence and are only beginning to discover its properties. They tell me," this with an almost bored sigh, "it could be a previously unknown form of matter, with great potential. I let them deal with such things."

She gestured to one of her affiliates, who brought over a flask of brilliant blue. Rudy started and almost backed away. He knew the color. *Like Esen's,* the flash of blue he'd learned to watch for as she cycled.

Sybil stepped close to him. Her fingers, tipped with death, captured his collar to hold him still as she brought her lips to his ear. Her breath was hot. "Familiar, Rudy? I, too, have seen this color. As it ripped apart my ships."

Rudy had enough presence of mind left to keep silent. *Paul. He had to talk to Paul.* Esen's Human face was slipping away from him . . .

"We are the ones who know the truth, Rudy. We're the ones who have to act."

Sybil released her hold. Handing the flask back to her affiliate, she led the way back to the outer room, her boots making crisp sounds on the stone. Once there, she sat and he sank slowly into the other chair.

"There are two of these beings who have made themselves part of our affairs," Sybil said without preamble, her voice sharp and brisk as though this had become a briefing. "My feud is with S'kal-ru. She, in turn, has been battling with the other, Kearn's Esen. The attacks on Minas XII, the affair with the Tly and Feneden—I see you know of what I speak." This, as Rudy's head shot up and he felt himself flush with the memory of shame and anger. The Tly had used truth drugs to expose what he knew, how he hunted for Paul; they'd tortured his cousin almost to death.

"Those were her doing?" he demanded.

"In part. She professed herself 'interested' in how Esen would react."

Rudy slapped his hand down on the table, rattling the porcelain. "'Interested!'"

Sybil smiled faintly. "I would seek direct affiliation with Esen if I could. She would be a formidable ally. Perhaps S'kal-ru fears this and has already dealt with her rival once and for all. It was her intent to execute Paul Ragem and put Esen in a position where she would have to reveal valuable secrets. They were able to escape the first trap. I have received no word yet if they escaped the second." Her smile widened. "But it may not matter."

"How can you—"

"Because we have S'kal-ru. She's on the ship I sent to bring her here, docked to this mountain, awaiting only my invitation to join us. She will be looking for a threat from me. You, on the other hand, are the starred piece, the random element in our game. Are you ready, Rudy Lefebvre, to meet her for yourself?"

Rudy's fingers closed over the weapon on the table. "Yes."

30: Mountainside Afternoon

"YOUR elbow's in my eye."

"Shush! No, it isn't."

As I should be the one to know, being bottommost of this tangle of limbs and ejection gear, I thought it highly unreasonable of Paul to argue. As I started to protest further, his elbow disappeared and his hand took its place. *Over my mouth.*

He tasted of grit and sweat. I didn't care, frozen into a heart-thudding caution. *Had we been seen?*

I'd always hated Skalet's plans. Today, more than ever. *Jump from the scoutship, indeed.*

Still, the jumping part had been more fun than I'd expected. The ship had swung low and wide on its approach, passing over the Edianti Valley. I'd gazed down, feeling unexpectedly moved. Then we'd been tossed out the door.

The Kraal, predictably, had developed remarkable technology for getting personnel—usually armed to the teeth—into dangerous territory. The packs they'd strapped to our backs boasted preset thrusters, programmed with the desired landing coordinates. In case there were any issues concerning altitude, elevation, and the competency of the programmer, the packs also contained an antigrav unit. Ours kicked on at about the moment I was sure there were such issues to worry about. The rest of the descent was a gentle fall.

Until Paul had slipped and rolled down the slope, taking my legs out from under me and propelling the two of us into this fortunately shallow crevice.

His hand lifted away slowly. "We're clear." My heart settled in my chest.

My Human climbed out first. I didn't bothering complaining that my shoulder wasn't a step, too busy following behind. My Human-self was quite good at rock climbing, or rather boulder scrabbling, I realized as Paul helped me to my feet.

We'd landed on a scree of uniformly small and loose fragments.

Mine tailings.

I bent down and touched the rock with my fingertips, moisture clouding my vision. *Ersh.*

"Esen. We have to move." As he spoke, Paul tugged the ejection pack from my shoulders, then tossed it into the crevice to join his.

I blinked, rubbing the tears from my cheeks and managing to smear a good amount of dust over my face in the process. This form had its disadvantages. Not that I had much choice until I found a source of living mass.

"This way," I said, pointing upslope. With the exception of the loose rock, I knew every part of this terrain as well as I knew the lines on these fingers. *Well*, I thought practically, running my eyes over what remained familiar, *at least those parts that hadn't seen a moonquake for fifty years.*

We clung to shadows I knew, slipping up shortcuts that felt oddly different to Human feet. Steeper, higher. *Perhaps paws were bouncier.* I could tell Paul was impressed, if not surprised, by my ability to sneak around my own home. I didn't think he needed to know most of my practice had been hiding from Skalet.

The move with the Ganthor had served my web-kin well. The crew of the *Octos Ra* were hers now, beyond doubt. They wouldn't reveal Paul's and my presence—or absence. More significantly, their switch in affiliation priority could potentially spread through the ranks of Mocktap's elite troops, especially if Mocktap herself could be publicly disgraced. That part of Skalet's plan made some sense. The part that had Paul and I leaping out of the *Octos Ra* and trying to avoid Kraal traps and armed guards lacked something important, in my opinion. *Our safety.*

So far, so good, however. Which I supposed would make Skalet insufferably proud of her scheming.

We were about halfway to our goal when I held up my hand to stop Paul. "Wait," I told him, straining to make sense of a shadow where I didn't remember one. Then, most alarmingly, it moved. But not toward us. Up the slope.

With a regrettable lack of consultation, my Human was moving, too, in pursuit. I wasn't sure if he'd seen more of the figure than I, or feared we'd been discovered. I hesitated, unsure if it was more dangerous to attempt to help or to stay where I was, my hands gripping the cold hardness of unforgiving rock.

Ersh.

As if the thought of her had been a trigger, I found myself helpless under a surge of memory that wasn't mine . . .

. . . so alone. Always alone. Guilt the keeper; shame the prison. *Safety is in hiding.* Should have remembered.

Climb. Must climb the slope. *Caution.*

Pain! Shocks into fire with every step and slip. Fire burns in emptiness, fire remembers the shape of an arm and a hand, four fingers and a thumb. *Lost forever.*

Like the children. The chimes of distress and confusion from the gentle ones had drawn Ersh down the mountain. The calls of those who had never needed to defend their own, who had never seen those of flesh. Who had not known what to do.

Follow the Rules. Match form to form. Safety is being the same. Cycle to Human-form. Steal the children back, while the poachers are numb with drink and sleep.

Caught! Trapped! Attacked! Run for safety. *Pain! Pain!* Hold form . . . hold form . . . hold form. *Mustn't be seen as different. Pain!*

Safety was being hidden. The knowledge makes move-

ment possible, imperative. No one follows. She's left confusion and guilt behind, carries her own. The Tumbler children
are scattered again, glittering in the harsh light of Eclipse.

Pain! Cradle the ruined end, seared closed. The emptiness remembers fire. It always will . . .

. . . I gasped clear of the past, finding myself cradling my
right arm as though mine had been amputated by blaster fire,
not Ersh's, weeping with her anguish, her anger for the
Tumblers.

"Esen! What's happened? Are you hurt?" Urgent ques-
tions, yet from a distance. Footsteps and the rattle of stone.
I shook my head to reassure my worried Human, although
Ersh-memory still burned along my nerves.

The sounds of someone falling brought me fully into the
here-and-now. I focused my eyes on Paul as he hauled that
someone up and back from me, to his feet. "Answer me,
Esen!" Paul panted.

"It wasn't my arm," I assured us both. "Yes. I'm fine. But
who—?"

Paul jerked his captive around to face me. "Look who I
found spying for the Kraal," he said, in that voice I could
never recognize as his, the one promising dark and deadly
things.

"Lionel?" The battered and very worried-looking Human
blinked owlishly at me, semi-suspended in a grip I suspected
was much tighter than it needed to be. "Paul, let him go."
When Paul simply stared at me as though I'd lost my mind,
I scrambled up beside them both and tugged at his arm. It
felt like metal. "Let him go. You're hurting him."

"That's the general idea," Paul growled. "Stop it, Bess."

Ersh. "It's Lionel, not the Kraal. He's here to help us.
Aren't you, Lionel?"

"Esen?" Kearn croaked. "Is this you?"

I ignored the now-apoplectic expression on Paul's face.
"Of course this is me. What do you think?" I did a quick
pirouette, careful not to trip.

"Thank g–goodness, you're all right. And you're—this you—why, I never dreamed you'd be—c-cute." This with quite commendable enthusiasm, under the circumstances.

Paul let out a string of highly expressive, if implausible adjectives—none of which included "cute"—ending with my name and a profound sigh. Then: "What have you been up to now?"

Lionel craned his head to look at Paul. I smiled, knowing there would be dimples. *Cute dimples.* "Making friends, Paul."

I was reasonably sure being this happy with frenzied Ganthor above and my untrustworthy web-kin ahead—not to mention everything else Kearn told us in hurried, desperate bursts as we climbed—was likely to call down the notice of the Cosmic Gods. But I didn't care.

I'd restored part of Paul's Web.

And, from the look of him, Lionel Kearn had restored himself. Each time I glanced around, he was keeping up—not easy on a steep slope scored by cracks and tumbled with rock. Even more surprising was the strength in his voice as he talked about difficult and dangerous things.

Those things should have wiped the smile from my face and joy from my heart, but couldn't. There was a rightness to seeing the two Humans together, even if they'd never been friends. Kearn knew Paul Ragem and that knowing linked Paul to his past, his real past, again.

And Rudy was here!

I could be forgiven for skipping a bit.

"Careful, Es." Paul's admonishment from behind was hushed but kind. He hadn't said anything to Kearn that wasn't a prompt for information or demand for more detail. I thought it likely both Humans had too much they wanted to say, and knew it would have to wait.

The only good news was that Rudy Lefebvre was on Picco's Moon. Paul might worry about his cousin being in harm's way, but not about his ability to cause some of his own. My grin faded slightly. I wasn't looking forward to trying to explain Skalet's recent behavior to the hot-tempered Human. It was something I might leave to Paul, who seemed to have reached his own accommodation with the nature of my web-kin.

Rudy was here, now, meeting Mocktap—explaining why Paul had caught Kearn on the mountainside. Kearn had been too worried, in the end, to let Rudy come alone. He'd followed the Kraal aircar, counting on their preoccupation with Rudy and the Ganthor overhead to let him approach safely. *It was probably*, I decided with pride, *the dumbest and bravest thing Lionel had ever done in his life.*

Paul had been silent for a moment after hearing this. Then he'd put his hand on Kearn's shoulder. *Perhaps*, I'd thought smugly, *he'd start to regret some of those colorful adjectives he'd used for me.*

What hadn't been good news, in any way, were the stakes. Joel Largas had followed us, on one of many ships crewed by friends. Worse, the *Largas Legend* was already fin-down. With Tomas and Luara.

Of those who lived here? I knew Paul thought about Phonse and Maggie; he cherished their friendship. I hadn't met Alphonsus Lundrigan myself, having been reluctant to come back here for many reasons, but knew he was another of those guarding my secret. Now, he was guarding this tiny world.

I lost the urge to skip. *Add to the total all of the other innocents trapped here, with their friendships and family.*

"Here." I told them at last. "Here" was the spot I knew Skalet had had in mind. It had a view of the landing pad and front of the house, but was conveniently shielded from any window by boulders. *Unless one had attractive but inconveniently tall ears.*

The Kraal presence became suddenly and sickeningly obvious, from the nine armored figures stationed around the broad ledge, to the aircar, to the tracks their machines had scored in the stone, to and from the doorway.

Two guards stood beside the door.

Ersh's door.

My door. I found myself growing more angry than melancholy. The Kraal didn't belong here. This had been our home.

The guards were alert, but not paying any more attention to the downslope than any other direction. *Maybe we'd done it,* I thought hopefully, having not bothered to discuss with Paul my gamble that the Kraal wouldn't bother setting automatics to watch portions of the mountainside too steep for Tumblers. I glanced at Paul and almost jumped. He'd pulled on his hood, erasing his face, and had become a perfect match for any of the guards posted ahead of us.

He motioned me closer. "I want you to stay here," he said very quietly. "With Lionel."

What was he up to? Skalet's plan had called for Paul to stay here, too. She wouldn't find it reasonable for Paul to substitute Kearn for himself. I didn't either. I shook my head at him vigorously, brushing back the hair that landed in my eyes.

"Esen. I have to get that weapon—the one Skalet warned us about." The hood was maddening, but I didn't need to see his face to know it was set and stubborn. "And Rudy could be in there. Stay out of the way until I'm sure it's safe."

"You can't pass for one of them," I protested, trying to avoid sounding hysterical. *It was close.* "They'll know—"

"Look!" This from Lionel.

We peered around the boulder in cautious unison. I had an almost irresistible urge to giggle and bit my lip to quell it.

Three Kraal were walking down the staircase, one with the ease of long practice.

Skalet.

There were subtle changes among the Kraal in front of us, the automatic response to look alert and efficient for authority, the self-preserving instinct to be on guard around an individual who might be a target for assassination—or be preparing to conduct one of her own. Skalet reveled in it; I could see the satisfaction in her eyes even from here.

It was easier still as she kept coming in our direction.

Paul, Lionel, and I ducked as one. Paul yanked off his hood, presumably to better glare at me. Lionel went pastier than usual.

It was easiest of all when Skalet leaned on the boulder and gazed down at me, her elbows on the stone. I looked up at her, remembering exactly why I'd always hated her plans.

They'd always involved embarrassing me.

Otherwhere

"NO change, Chief Constable."

Alphonsus ignored the tremor in the voice. *Half exhaustion, half apprehension.* The wait was taking its toll on everyone.

Maybe not everyone. He glanced at the Human sitting with the off-shift com-techs, offering sombay and a moment of conversation, and smiled to himself. *Joel Largas might have spent that week in a med box.* Alphonsus had known many beings who coped valiantly with emergencies; he'd known a very special few who rose to them like this, gaining and giving strength as the situation worsened. Joel had already accomplished the impossible, moving even the most stubborn, knuckle-brained spacers into the evacuation ships. Now, he was here, seemingly inexhaustible—ostensibly to be the eyes and ears of the ship-bound; in reality, finding another place to help.

No matter what was going on between Joel, Paul, and Esen, Alphonsus was grateful.

"Keep me posted," he told the scan-tech calmly, as if this was an ordinary day, and collected Bris with a look.

Back in his office, Alphonsus closed the door before turning to his second-in-command. "It can't be much longer, Bris. We have to be ready. As ready as we can be."

"Do you want me to issue hand weapons?"

The Chief Constable tugged a brown, wrinkled leaf from one of his plants, then looked around in vain for a place to put it. He tucked it in a pocket. "We'd look like combatants. Project Leader Kearn didn't recommend it."

"We're combatants already, whether we want to be or not," the Moderan spat. Bris was too civilized an individual to seek battle unless there was a mating opportunity involved; that didn't mean he was passive about the prospect. "Your Cultural Expert said the messages from the Tumblers could be interpreted as hostile," he pointed out. "We're the only ones here they could be angry at!"

"Maybe not." Alphonsus plucked another dead leaf and stuffed that with the first, hoping he remembered to clean his pockets before going home—if he went home. "There's the illegal operation on that mountain—the mine." In a way, that report had marked the start of it all.

"What difference does that make? After all our years here," Bris argued, "have you known a single Tumbler who could tell you and me apart? How can you expect them to distinguish between a group of miners and the rest of us? They'll send the Ganthor against everyone."

"And you think issuing weapons will make any difference?"

Bris hesitated, then his fur gradually subsided from its outraged halo behind his ears. "No."

Alphonsus nodded. "Nor do I." He ran his hands along the plant's lush new growth, admiring its softness. "Make sure all nonessential personnel get to their transports and stay there. Stand by to squeal the launch alert to all ships. We'll wait."

"How long, sir?"

How long did it take a Ganthor to pass the point of sanity?

"As long as we can," he told Bris. "As long as we can."

31: Mountain Afternoon

"THINGS change."

Skalet's cryptic excuse, whispered in my ear as we were marched into our own house by invaders, suited more than her revealing our presence to the mortified Kraal guards. I was reasonably sure we would have been shot and dragged away on the principle that a mistake covered up hadn't happened, if she hadn't immediately taken charge. Since it was her fault we were discovered, I wasn't inclined to be grateful.

Things change. Paul and I had last seen Ersh's home after her struggle with Death. The kitchen looked tidier, thanks to the Kraal's deft use of a shovel. I didn't see my favorite jacket. I'd left it behind; it should have been here. The Tumblers would have respected Ershia's home, however strange to their ways.

Skalet took my hand in hers. In a Human this might have been a gesture of protectiveness; from her, it was a reminder of her intention to hold me to my word. *Or was it her Human-self's reach for comfort?* I felt her temperature soar to fever range as she dumped energy to hold form. I was surprised mine was under control. *Perhaps her attacks on us had been valuable practice,* I thought bitterly.

We were first to enter Ersh's house, but not the last. Paul and Kearn came behind us, behind them came the two from the *Octos Ra* who had accompanied Skalet, and, behind them, more Kraal until the last arrivals couldn't fit inside.

All had removed their hoods, perhaps anticipating a crisis of affiliation.

"Take us to the Pa-Admiral," she told the lone attendant waiting inside. The Kraal touched fingertips to cheeks and turned to lead the way down the main hall.

To the greenhouse! I must have balked. Skalet gave my hand a sharp tug to move me forward.

Thirty-three steps for this me. Twenty-seven for my Lanivarian-self, although I'd done it once in a mere sixteen bounds—using all four feet and being highly motivated to escape the kitchen. *Not that the fire had been completely my fault.* Ten tumbles for Ersh. I would hear her coming and count them down. Ten, nine, eight . . . ending with her crystalline self collecting and refracting the light.

There was light, still, in this place that had been our only source of living mass on Picco's Moon. Light, but nothing else I knew.

For I had no memory of it looking like this. *It never had.* Ersh had started her plants within a low-ceilinged crevice at the back of the cave she'd made her home. From that start, it had always contained green and growing things, always smelled of moisture, soil, the fine aroma of living decay, even as the walls themselves were carved farther and farther back, leaving portions of themselves as new platforms, even as the ceiling was chipped higher and higher, with Tumbler children planted between the fixtures.

Now the platforms held dust and most of the children had been stolen.

Skalet wasn't moving. I wasn't sure she breathed until I heard a tiny gasp. I squeezed her hand as tightly as I could, all too aware we weren't alone and that memories of Ersh or home weren't going to help us now. We'd been—expected.

Pa-Admiral Mocktap. I knew her face, even if she wouldn't know this one of mine. We'd sat on the bridge of the *Trium Set* together, those years ago, attempting to defeat a web-being with Human technology.

She knew Paul's. I saw the recognition in her eyes as they

slid past Skalet. A slight widening of surprise as she saw Kearn.

Rudy Lefebvre. I wanted to feel reassured by the sight of his face, but it wasn't familiar. He stood at attention beside the chair where Mocktap sat enthroned, dressed in a formal Commonwealth uniform, and only his lack of tattoos made him look other than Kraal. His face was pale and set into hard lines, as though he faced an unpleasant but necessary task. He didn't look at me or Paul or Kearn. His eyes never left Skalet.

Kraal. The rest of the room was filled with black-garbed figures—tattooed with allegiances to Mocktap as well as other House names—as well as their machines; the former ominously intent on us, the latter droning busily to themselves.

"Welcome, Your Eminence," Mocktap said. "You honor us with your presence." Her eyes locked on mine for a moment, and she frowned as if unsure what I was. Or sure, but confused why I was here. *Either,* I thought with a chill, *implied she knew too much.*

I might have imagined Skalet's dismay at our surroundings. Her voice was controlled and level, with a nice touch of irritation. "If so, where are your manners, Mocktap? I see no serpitay. I hear no respect. You delayed this meeting."

"My apologies, Your Eminence. There were matters to attend to—matters pertaining to your arrival." There was a small table flanking her other side, with two cloth-covered objects on it. Mocktap lifted the cover from one, revealing a black-and-gold-bound book. "Including this. I believe I've found something you lost. Interesting reading, S'kal-ru."

Skalet's temperature rose so quickly I thought she'd explode, so I pressed my foot against hers. Otherwise, I did my utmost to seem exactly as I looked: young, harmless, and above all, Human.

As a disguise, it had the benefit of being true—at the moment.

"Fool." That one word, in Skalet's rich, throaty voice, echoed around the chamber. A few Kraal looked worried.

"How so?" Mocktap leaned back, crossing her booted feet. *Overconfident,* I added to myself. "Surely not because I know a traitor and confront her with proof. Or is it my see-ing advantage for my House and taking it that so offends my mentor?"

"Fool. How many times more before you become a lia-bility to your affiliates, Mocktap? Saying this once will do: killing Tumblers without understanding their nature. Your carelessness has brought a Ganthor battle fleet and will very shortly eradicate what remains of Mocktap along with what-ever 'advantage' you think you've found." Skalet's skin cooled against mine as she spoke, despite the heat of her words. "As for that book and its contents?" She smiled. "When did it become treachery to raise my value to my af-filiates? To strive for a House of my own? If so, then most here are descended from traitors."

Mocktap surged to her feet. The Kraal nearest her put their hands to their weapons but I judged it too early to tell why. "Did you think you could—" an almost imperceptible hesitation and a glance at me, as if my presence made her change what she planned to say at the last possible instant, "—you could plot to abandon us, to strip power from your former affiliations? Undermine my command?"

"Do you actually believe you command here?" The scorn was vintage Skalet.

Mocktap took a step closer, away from her chair and Rudy. It wasn't by accident that this put her in the brightest spot of light. I'd noticed a trend to theatrics in all Kraal, in-cluding my web-kin. "These are my affiliates, S'kal-ru, not yours."

Skalet opened her fingers, releasing my hand. I didn't move, beyond easing my hand to my side—not wanting to draw further attention to myself or, more importantly, draw attention from Skalet. We had no other way to win, besides words.

I refused to consider the alternative, not with the only living mass within reach walking on two feet and having a desire to live another day.

"Affiliation is earned, not claimed." S'kal-ru turned as she spoke. "It is deserved, not taken." She moved slowly, making sure to catch and hold the eyes of each Kraal in the room. Then she stopped, facing Mocktap again. "I should think the answer to that is quite clear."

"Do you deny dropping off these—these spies!—before landing?"

Skalet smiled. "My valued informants? Considering you'd ordered them shot on sight, of course I did. Hubbarro?"

Another face familiar to my Ket-self. He stepped forward as though giving a report, not looking at Mocktap. "I was made aware of Her Eminence's concern for their safety in the event of any confusion. She informed us where to watch for their arrival."

Ersh. I would have given anything to be able to kick Skalet's shin.

As if I'd said this out loud, I suddenly had Mocktap's attention. "You—you—" her finger stabbed at me. "You now affiliate with your own Enemy against us all?"

"My niece?" I felt Kearn's hands grip my shoulders as he spoke up, a tight hold as if he needed the support. I spared a moment to be amazed he dared touch me, a web-being, let alone attract the interest of over a hundred potentially hostile Kraal. *This particular me did seem very reassuring to Humans,* I concluded, although I worried about the potential complications of having another avowed uncle. I looked at the first to claim that title, Rudy, but his eyes remained in their disquieting fix on Skalet.

Kearn was still talking, in his fussiest, most worried voice. "Fem S'kal-ru promised me safe passage for her off this Moon. There are G-Ganthor, you realize. I really don't think there's time for all this talking." This drew grim nods from more than a few.

When neither crew member of the *Octos Ra* volunteered that I'd arrived with Paul, not Lionel, I took an easier breath. Skalet had been right about their loyalty, at least.

Mocktap must have sensed her support slipping away, but there was no sign in her bearing. Kraal nobles acquired that erect, confident stance early—or didn't make it past puberty. "Niece?" she repeated, with a scornful laugh that utterly failed to measure up to my web-kin's standards. "Hom Kearn. There's no need for pretence here. You are safe from them, with me. I promise you. Now. We both know this isn't your niece—or a child at all. Tell them."

He kept his hands where they were; I could feel their trembling and admired him even more. "I think I should know my own—"

"Yes! You should! This 'child' isn't Human. Nor is S'kal-ru! If anyone should know that, it should be you, Kearn. You've hunted them for years! They are monsters! Shapeshifters!"

There are some laughs that are so rich and full, you can't help but smile to hear them. Such a laugh came from my web-kin, surrounded by enemies and the evidence of our own mortality. I felt a chill run down my spine.

"Not Human?" Skalet raised her arm and ripped the fabric of her sleeve. Taking her knife, she used the tip of its blade to draw a fine line of red down the skin of her forearm. "Quite the disguise," she said, some of that laugh still in her voice.

The Kraal were convinced. It wasn't a movement away from Mocktap's side of the room so much as a shift of body weight, as each decided the more probable target should violence erupt.

Mocktap wasn't done. "You were here," she shouted. "Here! Three hundred and forty-three years ago, to hide what my ancestor Sybil-ro gave you. In payment, you killed one of my House and poisoned her." There were mutters now, ranging from incredulous to impatient. Mocktap must have sensed she'd lost them, for she suddenly whirled and grabbed what had been on the table, holding it up. "This is what we found here. This is what you are!"

If the mutterings grew louder, I didn't hear them. Nothing mattered but the flask in her hand and its brilliant blue contents. I felt Skalet tense herself to move, knew her hunger matched mine. Perhaps it was greater, since this was *Ersh*. But Skalet's needs no longer mattered, only mine. My flesh burned to cycle and acquire the web-mass before me. I dimly heard Kearn's yelp of surprise as his hands left me. I . . .

There was only one other being in that room who knew what might happen—what was happening—although how a Human made the leap of understanding to grasp that Skalet and I could no longer control ourselves even Paul couldn't explain later. But he didn't hesitate. The knife he threw glanced against Mocktap's arm, startling her into dropping the flask. It fell to the floor, smashing open, blue splashing in broad arcs across the floor . . .

. . . where it sank into the stone, until nothing remained but fragments of plas.

I think Skalet would have killed him, if she hadn't been busy defending herself from Mocktap. The Kraal had leaped forward even as the flask shattered, her own knife in hand and a look of fury on her face.

Confusion and shouting erupted from all sides. Black-garbed figures blocked my view and I did my best to plunge through them, only to be grabbed from behind and held. "Are you trying to get killed?" Paul accused, not letting go. "Let her handle it."

Calm descended, and silence. *Too quickly,* I worried, but then, these were Kraal. The situation hadn't been resolved, not yet, or they would be touching their tattoos to vow affiliation to one leader. Instead, they backed away, leaving room around the two rivals.

Skalet was standing. I sagged a little with relief, even though I'd been sure my web-kin could handle one aging admiral. Mocktap lay at her feet, propped up on an elbow, teeth drawn away from her lips in a snarl. I was surprised she still lived. Skalet must have had a reason; it wouldn't be mercy.

Then I noticed my web-kin was staring at the floor. She was standing where the flask had broken open. No blue remained. I could have told her it was hopeless, having tried to taste Ersh in stone before.

A drop of red cratered the dust at her feet.

Another.

I pulled free of Paul and moved to where I could see Skalet from the front. Her own knife was in her hand. Why was another hilt protruding from her waist? Even as I tried to find a way through to reach her, she straightened and looked right at me, then above me to the Kraal. "To whom are you affiliated?"

A roar of "S'kal-ru! S'kal-ru!" went up immediately, fingers lifting to tattoos.

When they paused for breath, Mocktap said, loudly and clearly: "Rudy."

Rudy Lefebvre, who'd been like a statue through all of this, moved quickly enough now. He took two steps to find a clear line of sight and raised an odd-looking weapon, aiming it at Skalet. She dropped her knife to the floor then. Pressing one hand around the hilt in her flesh, she straightened, as if daring him to fire.

The room seemed to fill with insects as every Kraal powered up his or her weapon, bringing it to bear on Rudy.

Looking back on the moment, I might have acted a little impulsively. But I'd had more than enough of tall, black-garbed figures getting in my way. So it made perfect sense to me to duck between the nearest set of long legs and dash to my web-kin.

Skalet, in her own way as wise about my idea of sensible behavior as Paul, simply grabbed me by the neck with her free hand as I arrived and gave me a shove in the direction of my momentum, so I skidded along the floor well out of range.

And on my face.

I rolled over to glare at her. She raised a brow in dismissal, then returned to the new threat. "Rudy Lefebvre. I hadn't realized you were an affiliate of—this."

"I'm not."

"Don't tell me you believe this story about monsters?" Skalet asked, her voice its usual blend of magic and steel. I could see the cost as blood coated her fingers like a glove, soaking into the black of her clothing.

"I believe you tried to harm my friends. I believe you tried to have Paul killed at least once, maybe more than that."

Well, I thought without surprise, *so much for the Human's first impression of Skalet.*

"A misunderstanding." This from Paul, who'd worked his way through the crowd with a little more dignity than I. Kearn, I was glad to see, had stayed behind the first row of Kraal. "Stand down, Rudy. We've other problems right now."

As if he hadn't heard, Rudy's eyes flickered to me, then back to Skalet. "How old are you?" he asked quite desperately.

The question puzzled the Kraal and brought a smile to Mocktap's face.

I climbed to my feet and brushed dust from the front of my clothes, wishing, not for the first time, to be anything more impressive. *How Skalet could stand this form, I couldn't begin to fathom.* "I am, Rudy Lefebvre," I told him impatiently but kindly, "exactly as old as you see me, as is S'kal-ru. If that worries you for some reason, I suggest we sit down and discuss it like reasonable a—" *The word "adult" just didn't work.* "—beings. Later and hopefully with supper, because no one's fed me anything but appetizers today and I shall probably faint soon."

Something slowly eased in his face. "I'd forgotten what you looked like," he said, making no sense at all.

Or too much. "Put that away," I suggested, understanding

Paul's look of dismay and sharing the emotion. *This isn't what I am, Rudy,* I wanted to tell him. Now was not the time. "We have to talk to the Ganthor and Tumblers. You know we can do it. Let us try to settle this before anyone is hurt. Think about the beings at the shipcity, those here. The Tumblers."

The nasty thing lowered until it pointed at the floor. The Kraal nearest Rudy snatched the weapon from his hand and he didn't protest.

"Ah, Rudy. You had so much potential." This from Mocktap, who'd wisely remained on the floor given the significant number of Kraal gun sights steadied on her. "Still, if you want something dead—" a weapon identical to the one taken from Rudy appeared in her hand, like some conjurer's trick "—kill it yourself."

Skalet lifted her arms away from her body, in a gesture of surrender. Blood dripped from her right hand. "And you think you can kill me with that toy?" she asked. I thought I heard a faint huskiness in her voice. "Explain to my affiliates, Pa-Admiral. I'm sure you have their complete attention."

Mocktap's eyes gleamed as she eased to her feet, weapon locked on Skalet. "A new toy, of your own design, S'kal-ru. You should enjoy the irony of being destroyed by it. In case you wonder, I had a second prototype made at the same time as the first. You taught me that. Always have a backup plan." She laughed. "This is exactly that. A weapon to kill a monster."

"So kill me with it," Skalet said. The Kraal were so quiet her words must have carried to the back of the room.

If this was her plan, it was the worst yet. But before I could do more than start to protest, Mocktap's eyes narrowed and she fired.

Never be vulnerable—unless it's to your advantage. Mocktap should have remembered that teaching of Skalet's, too. For there was nothing but surprise on her face as it tumbled to the floor, most of the rest of Pa-Admiral Mocktap having disappeared in a contained backlash of energy.

Skalet would have followed, except that Paul was there to take her weight as she collapsed.

"Let the child approach."

Child. I forced a smile on my face that likely had no dimples whatsoever as the Kraal hovering around Skalet moved out of my way. They'd pushed Paul aside to take care of Her Eminence and were now bickering over which of them deserved the honor of carrying her to her ship. And which ship she'd take.

That wasn't part of my plan.

"Privacy, if you would be so kind, S'kal-ru," I asked politely, standing beside the platform where they'd laid her, cushioned by bits and pieces of battle gear.

Skalet took one look at me, then waved the Kraal away. They hovered unhappily. Paul was watching me, from where he'd stood to talk urgently with Rudy and Kearn. "Do you have what I want, Youngest?"

"Order the Kraal to the Port City. All of them."

She was pale, with sweat beading her tattoos. Shock, I thought, callously calculating the time she had left in this form without medical help. "Why?"

"You know why. They're the only troops on Picco's Moon. Kearn's told me there are spacers trapped in their ships. Your newly devoted affiliates can be of use there if the Ganthor do attack, perhaps hold them back long enough for an evacuation." She started to shake her head. "Listen to me, Skalet," I said fiercely. "You used these Humans. You owe them a chance to survive. The Ganthor will shoot down their ships before they can get to orbit."

Her eyes closed and opened. *Agreement.* Then, weakly: "I'll go with them. The ship—med-techs. I need—this form needs—"

"No," I said coldly.

She stared at me, her pupils dilated. "What are you saying—this form—I'll die—"

"You won't die," I told my web-kin. Then I told her the rest of my plan.

"I take it back. There's a lot to be said for blind obedience." Paul stood in the doorway, watching the two scoutships slip from the mountain and head to the Port City. All the Kraal were on board and accounted for, except for three small patrols Mocktap had sent to discourage Tumblers from curiosity. We'd decided they could take their chances. "Alphonsus is expecting our new friends. He sounded surprised, but grateful."

"Any word about the Ganthor?" Kearn asked.

"Nothing. But no news is good news."

"They can't delay forever. It has to come soon," I muttered to myself. Louder. "Are you two sure you want to watch this?" Rudy hadn't wanted to see it. He'd helped bring in the duras plants from the *Octos Ra,* but now waited by the aircar. *We would,* I thought, worried about this among so much else, *have to talk.*

Paul frowned at me. "If you think I'll let you near her alone—?"

"Don't—don't underestimate the Youngest," Skalet wheezed from the hall. The two Humans rushed to help her reach a chair. "I did." She looked half-dead.

"At least I wasn't the one to make a weapon against web-flesh," I accused. We'd made sure the one Mocktap had given Rudy had been retrieved from the Kraal. Its pieces were now so much slag. I think Paul had enjoyed doing that.

"There was a time it seemed—advisable."

I picked up an armload of duras and shook off the soil from their roots. Our eyes locked together over their leaves. Hers glittered with pain and determination. "I do this for Ersh—" Skalet paused for breath, "—because she wanted a home as badly as either of us—and this form, this species, was her choice. They deserve my help. Not your ephemeral web-kin, your 'friends,' or these strangers. Not you, Esen-alit-Quar."

The name echoed in the kitchen, becoming the tap of a spoon as Ansky cooked, an argument between Mixs and Skalet, Lesy's giggle. Then a low, resonant—and unexpected—chime, followed, as usual, by a bellow of *Esen*!

I saw Skalet remembering. "When this is over, wait for me on the peak where we have shared before, web-kin. I will be there. You have my word," I promised, laying the plants on her knees then stepping back. "Good luck."

Her next breath seemed too labored, and the hilt embedded in her fleshed jerked, as if the knife tried to dig itself deeper. Then, S'kal-ru and the duras winked together into the blue of web-form. There was scarcely time for me to hear Kearn's gasp before the blue became sapphire and diamond . . .

And Skalet became Tumbler.

She didn't bother with conversation or delay. One moment she was standing on the ruin of a chair, the next Paul and a somewhat numb-looking Kearn were dodging out of her way as she leaned forward to tumble out the door.

"My turn," I said with relief, reaching for another plant.

Paul coughed. I eyed him suspiciously. He returned an innocent but meaningful look. "You aren't planning to be Ganthor, are you?" he asked.

"You can be Ganthor," Kearn echoed in a delighted singsong, his eyes glowing. "Ganthor. This is amazing. Amazing!"

"She can," Paul confirmed. "And our Esen is a very fine Ganthor. But—"

"But what?" I glowered.

"You aren't exactly—it's not going to impress the Matriarch of a battle fleet if our representative is—well—cute."

There were several conceivable replies to this. I chose to be mature and civil, which meant using none of them. "I wasn't going to be Ganthor anyway," I informed him haughtily.

It was Esolesy Ki who left Ersh's mountain with three Humans in a Kraal aircar, a somewhat testy, very hungry, and anxious Esolesy Ki. We were off to save Picco's Moon from the Ganthor. I had a plan.

A plan that depended on what I knew and how well I could use it. Unfortunately, the consequences of failure weren't usually so high. I struggled to stay confident, and keep my stomachs—and form—under control.

Being naked, I thought glumly, *didn't help.*

Otherwhere

THE path was known. The mission clear. It was only the why that eluded Skalet. Why had she listened to the Youngest? Why had she tossed aside her newly confirmed affiliates and their technology to become this vulnerable being, alone and exposed?

Why had she let Esen rob her of herself?

The thought eased her tumble to a stop. *Herself?* This was herself as much as any form. *Wasn't it?*

Perhaps the Youngest sought revenge for the damage to her own favored form—her so-called birth-form. She couldn't understand that birth came in the severing of mass, in the struggle to take as much as possible, yet escape the origin. No, not escape, to become another of the One, a moon to its planet, forever in orbit. Safe.

What remained of Ersh lay within this rock.

Instead of grief and loss, Skalet suddenly found that—appropriate. A Tumbler included the inorganic in the cycle of life, found rightness in Ersh's decision. Her Human-self could not have understood, would never have felt this peace.

Had she been S'kal-ru too long? Could the Youngest have been right to insist on this form?

Skalet chimed discontent. *Unacceptable.*

A pebble shifted, knocked another loose, and became a tinkling of stones rolling down a slope. Pebbles shifted and stones rolled all the time.

Again. Closer. Pebbles didn't shift at regular intervals.

Click. Slither. As if refined metal brushed against rock.

Skalet tumbled forward, her angle of descent easily anticipating the next switchback in the path. Once around its bend, she stopped, rising up to stand against the hard, eternal comfort of Ersh's mountain.

All Tumblers were good at waiting. Her pursuers would be aware of that. They'd know Tumblers were peaceful creatures, unable to defend themselves with other than long-winded rhetoric and futile chimes of dismay. They'd know how easy it was to shatter a helpless Tumbler into dust.

Skalet lifted her hands, gemlike fingers at the ready. If this form had had a mouth, she would have been smiling.

Time to teach them something new.

Skalet reached the entrance to the Edianti Valley, noticing the new landslide marring the smooth rampway. It didn't matter; her goal was higher, on the heights. Picco's reflected light was failing, losing not to night, but to the brilliant wash of sunlight as this side of the Moon turned away. Fortunate timing, as the way to the sounding stones was perilous enough by the light of true day. Skirting the crumbling valley edge would be impossible in the dark.

The stones, twinned and shaped as much by nature as the craft of Tumbler, leaned against one another, as if already sharing secrets. Skalet pressed her back to the nearest, looking out over the mist. It rose from the valley like too much stuffing from a crate, those it protected and nourished deep within its folds. Out of sight—but not beyond hearing.

She began to talk to them.

*   *   *

Tumblers listened to one of their own. A stranger—by the timbre of the voice, an Elder, a wise one.

A hermit, perhaps, like Ershia the Immutable. There was a rhythm suggesting similarity; a confidence that resonated with those who'd climbed her Mountain.

The message was accepted, considered, shared.

There were two kinds of flesh-burdened: those who had been and those who would come. Past and Future.

Tumblers chimed with comprehension. They felt the orbit of Picco and their Moon. They understood the passing of time.

Those who had been? They were dangerous. They had been cleansed from the Mountain. They had been cleansed from the Moon and its skies.

Tumblers felt a deep relief. Many, impatient for bliss, rolled to the rampways and began clearing the rubble.

Those who would come? They would be mannerly and live in the Port City, conducting business at all times in a way to protect Tumblers.

Tumblers experienced a sense of order restored and expressed their gratitude to the mysterious Elder as a chorus of chimes that gradually spread from valley to valley.

The Elders who had arranged for the Ganthor chimed happily to themselves, secure in the knowledge that they no longer had to deal with the flesh-burdened "who had been."

Skalet listened to the varied responses and would have shaken her head, had she possessed one. *You were right, Youngest,* she admitted to herself, ruefully aware Esen would taste this from their sharing to come.

If she dared.

Fear was irrelevant. She must possess the ability to move through space, to be independent of all other life. That was the key, to never have to depend on others, to never have them abandon you.

As Ersh had abandoned her.

Skalet rolled a little faster. The Youngest would deal with the Ganthor and return. The sooner they could exchange mass and leave this place, the better.

And with any luck, she'd find more flesh-burdened along the way.

Otherwhere

THE Fleet grew dangerously impatient. The only word from the Moon had been messages from the Specified Adversary—obvious attempts to subvert their contract. The Matriarch had ignored them.

She wasn't to be trifled with.

The battle frenzy always started with the weak and expendable ones, the outer ring of the Herd. With luck, battle could be won without more than culling the unfit, leaving the rest scarred and experienced. It took time for the frenzy to spread deep into the Herd, to reach the Seconds and Matriarch within each ship. Longest of all for it to reach her.

She'd done her best to stay aloof and delay. This wasn't an ordinary situation. They'd detected no massing of troops, no clusters of starships. The surface scans showed no weapon emplacements other than a pitiful set of cannons on a mountain. Ganthor weren't hired killers. They were hired mayhem.

But against what?

If it hadn't been for the price offered, she would have ordered the Fleet home long before this. Instead, she'd let them sit here, waiting for signs of a real enemy. The arrival of the Commonwealth, the Kraal, had held promise. But their ships could only have been couriers, of no value as opponents.

She'd waited too long.

The Matriarch of the Fleet snorted hot, blood-streaked mucus from her nostrils, feeling the urge to attack rippling through her muscles, the drive to defend the Herd pumping hormones and courage throughout her body.

Time's up, she told the small orange-and-black dot on her viewscreen.

32: Port Authority Night

RUDY flew us fast and straight to the Port City. I knew the trip well, having done it in various forms. It would have been nostalgic, except for what waited for us.

And what we brought. I found myself studying my companions. Paul sat beside me, slouched and resting. He still wore Kraal battle gear, stained—again—with blood, although this time it was Skalet's. There was no doubt he was aware of who waited for us, but I knew he focused on what we had to do to the exclusion of personal concerns. *Stop the Ganthor.*

Kearn kept turning to look at me with so much curiosity brimming in his eyes I couldn't imagine how he contained himself. Once, as if overwhelmed, he'd reached back and touched the scales of my arm. I'd lifted my lip to show him my tusk, with its charming inlay, and he'd smiled back.

And Rudy. I sighed, hearing the unhappy gurgling of my empty stomachs. He spoke only when necessary, appearing intent on our flight, though the aircar had perfectly adequate automatics.

I didn't need to know what Mocktap had told him. What mattered was that only Paul knew the truth of me and accepted it.

I'd heard the surprising news about Joel Largas—that he'd kept our secret to himself. I thought I could guess why. Like Mocktap, he knew the worst thing would be to be disbelieved, to have his own kin scoff at his ravings. I didn't dare believe it marked a change in heart.

I'd seen his face.

My Human heard me sigh again. Without a word, even though he couldn't know which of many possibilities troubled me, he rubbed the scaleless spot under my chin in mute understanding.

I'd expected to be whisked in a side door, secret and safe, to where Alphonsus would have arranged for a com system. There, in private, I'd do what I could to stop the Ganthor.

I could never, in a thousand life spans, I thought with some horror, *have imagined this.*

The area beneath the Port Authority building, between its stilts, was packed with spacers and other beings. *Who should have been safely on their ships!* It was irresponsible. It was disorganized. It was disruptive. It was . . .

"A hero's welcome," Rudy observed dryly as he shut the aircar door behind us.

Paul gripped my left arm with both hands, correctly assuming my first instinct after this bizarre announcement would be to run. Kearn wiped his forehead, probably half worried about the size of the crowd and half enjoying it. Rudy had slipped into captain mode, his face a professional mask.

I was—my scales became so swollen I wondered if I could move.

"It's all right, Es," Paul said softly as the crowd noticed our arrival and began chanting "Cameron & Ki! Cameron & Ki!" counterpointed by some doggerel in Ervickian that had something to do with juice and two straws.

All I could think of was how very glad I was that Skalet was roaming the mountainside, because she would never have let me live this down.

Stay hidden, stay safe, indeed.

"Steady, Esen. Head for the door. Keep it natural. Show some tusk."

"Keep it—Paul?" This last a plaintive call as I was surrounded by well-wishers of several species, strangers and friends.

Being taller than most, I could see the same thing happening to Paul and our other companions.

Through the hugging, and despite the unintentioned imprisonment of my poor feet under spacer boots, I managed to push my way to the ramp leading up to the building itself. There was a cleared space at the base, centered around an irate Moderan with his hair standing straight out in full threat. Even giddy Humans comprehended that type of body language.

When I was close enough, he called out: "I'm Bris, second-in-command. Come this way, please, Fem Ki."

"Trying—" I assured him, smiling at the happy faces on all sides. Finally, I squirted into the open and almost toppled into Paul, who'd done the same. No sign of Kearn or Rudy, but I presumed they'd fight their way through eventually. "Lead the way," I urged Bris.

"What's the occasion?" Paul asked as we half-ran up the ramp.

A snarl and spit. "While we appreciated the arrival of the Kraal, these fools took the sight of military personnel deploying around the shipcity as a sign that all was now under control. When word spread that you two were responsible, they left their ships to make this ridiculous display. How did you get Kraal elite troops here anyway?"

"Long story," I said, puffing along behind the two of them. *Less fudge and more time running,* I promised this form. My empty stomachs weren't sympathetic. I'd have to fill at least two of them soon or be useless.

We passed through three sets of security doors, each held open by anxious-looking beings in Port Authority uniforms. The implied urgency wasn't reassuring at all.

Bris took us straight into the com room, where grim-faced personnel didn't look away from their screens. Not all were so engaged. "Hom Cameron!"

Meony-ro? Before I could pick my jaw up from my chest,

he'd trapped Paul in some kind of hold. Then I blinked and realized it was a hug. Paul looked at me with a "don't ask me" expression, but cooperatively patted the other Human on his back.

I rehinged my jaw and found myself meeting the cold, hard stare of Joel Largas.

Having released Paul, Meony-ro came up to me, holding out a bag. I heard something about clothing and took it in my hand.

Joel had aged a decade since the greenhouse. I wanted to weep, knowing it was my doing.

My Human was suddenly at my side, as he was always. The two of us confronted the one who'd been like a father, without a word, likely mystifying everyone around us.

Alphonsus broke the silence. "There's no time for reunions," he said gruffly. "The Ganthor have started forming up for descent. If there's anything you can do, Fem Ki, it has to be now."

I looked straight into Joel's dark-rimmed eyes. "If that's all right with you?" I asked.

Joel took a step back and to the side, leaving me a clear path into the room. I hurried forward, but when Paul tried to follow, Joel stepped in his way, stopping him with a hand to his chest. "Paul can wait with me."

I tilted one ear toward the scan station, hearing the soft bleeps as moving ships announced their presence to traffic control. "You can all wait with Joel," I told them. "In the other room. I only need one secure com station. Which one?"

No one moved, as if I'd paralyzed them. I clacked my teeth together with annoyance. "Chief Constable. I have something to tell the Matriarch which should stop all this. Only the Matriarch. Now if you wish to delay me until my intervention is impossible—?"

Alphonsus knew I was more than a naked Lishcyn trader, holding her new clothes in a bag. His staff, obviously worn-out and close to panic, probably thought I was some lunatic off a ship.

Paul knew me best of all. "Es can do this, if you let her." There was no doubt in his voice.

"Let's go." When they didn't move, Alphonsus raised his voice into a cracked shout. "Move it! Go! The first station to your left, Fem Ki. It's already tied to the Ganthor Matriarch's ship. Not that she's responded to us."

"Thank you," I said sincerely and went to it, waiting as the com-tech abandoned her seat with a reluctance I was quite sure the others shared.

Paul made himself last to leave the room. As he closed the door, he whispered what he knew my ears alone could hear.

"Get it done, Old Blob."

You can't escape biology.

One of Ersh's favorite sayings. It came to mind as I emptied the sombay from one of the cups near the com station, then rapped it against the console. The sound was too high. I stuffed a crumpled sheet of plas inside. *Tap Tap.* Much better.

I located the control to send my signal to the Ganthor, then sought Ansky-memory. My birth-mother, the one who loved ritual and legend. She'd been the one to add this to our Web, those many years ago.

For the Ganthor were herbivores, with a herd social structure ingrained in their behavior long before they'd become an intelligent, space-faring species. It made them formidable mercenaries, who stayed together to defend the Herd, to the death if need be. Behavior well-suited to protect against being flanked by a predator. Keep it in sight, stay together, stay strong. *Charge, trample, and mutilate.* It worked for them.

It gave them a weakness. They needed to see their enemy. More precisely, they needed to know their enemy *could* be seen. Ganthor made up stories to frighten their young into staying close to the Herd—much like other mammalian species. But their stories featured an invisible, creeping foe, one able to slip within the outer ring of any Herd, to lurk inside a home, to strike down any Ganthor at whim, then be gone.

They called it the *Herd Wraith.* Ansky had witnessed for herself the effect of these stories on Ganthor. They would become uneasy, prone to milling about as if in search of what they couldn't see.

I didn't expect that reaction from trained mercenaries. But I thought it gave me a way to communicate with the Matriarch that others might not have.

Scent would have helped convey the mood, but I was reasonably sure the ships were so full of battle pheromones that any smell I provided would go unnoticed. Activating the com, I clicked *Danger to Herd* with my thick-nailed fingertip on the countertop, then used the cup to rap a *!!* stamp of emphasis.

A long moment of silence. Then: *Specify*

I didn't let myself feel relief. If they were talking, it was likely because the situation above was close to out of control. *Situation misleads* I clicked. *Herd Wraith*!!*

Repeat

*!!*Herd Wraith*!!*

Another pause. Then: *Fleet Matriarch*Specify reference*

I had her attention. This was where it remained to be seen if the Ganthor wanted a way out, or the Matriarch was herself too close to complete frenzy to see what I offered. *Kraal subterfuge*Weapon test*Observers deployed*!!* Danger to the Herd*!!*

Another silence, in which I wished for fingers delicate enough to cross in Paul's gesture for luck.

Client status

*Satisfied*Kraal exposed*Apology without penalty*Full payment ready*Provide account* I reached over to the next console and waited.

A stream of numbers flashed across the screen. I accepted the account number and bill for the Fleet, and, with a growl of disbelief from my empty stomachs, transferred forty-three percent of the wealth accrued by Ersh's Web over two hundred years of varied and successful Carasian mining portfolios. Ansky had received some excellent tips while in the pool.

Gratified The Matriarch acknowledged what she saw on her screen. *Standing down* Then, as if clickspeak could transmit humor, *Herd Wraith??*

I put down the cup gently, so she wouldn't hear it, feeling my hearts restarting. *Mutual understanding* I explained. *Clarity*

Clarity she echoed. Then, what I didn't expect: *Herd friend*

I'd been right. The Ganthor, or at least their Matriarch, hadn't been fooled. She'd known something was wrong the moment they'd arrived, but had no way to honorably withdraw without the Tumblers' consent. Any attempt to ask for that consent would have been frustrated by the difficulty of communicating directly with the Tumblers and the Tumblers' fear of the flesh-burdened. She'd been trapped.

Meanwhile, the Tumblers had continued to communicate a great many things. From what I'd been told, very little of it had conveyed its intended meaning to the nonmineral.

Herd friend I sent back, then ended the connection.

You can't escape biology, I thought, then shuddered at how very close we'd all come to disaster because of it. Had the Ganthor landed and slaughtered innocents, the repercussions would have reached to the homeworlds of every spacer here—as world war. As for the Tumblers? A Ganthor landing in force would have destroyed countless Tumbler children as well as shattering the bodies of any adults within range.

And, on a personal note, I would have lost my family. *Again.*

Clarity I clicked against the console. *Mutual understanding*

I listened to the words and finally knew what I, Esen-alit-Quar, had to do.

But first, I had to deal with Skalet and her wish for flight.

Otherwhere

A TUMBLER rolled its way along a mountaintop. This was perfectly normal behavior for a life-form made from an aggregation of compatible crystals, if not a perfectly normal mountain.

This mountain was Her.

Knowing herself alone, Skalet chimed a familiar chord, the one she'd heard each time the Youngest snuck up to Ersh and struck her with a hammer. She'd never understood why Esen dared; she'd never understood why Ersh allowed it.

Until today, when she'd taken orders from the Youngest. Skalet tilted back to observe the sky. No Ganthor drop pods. No assault vehicles. Esen-alit-Quar had succeeded.

What potential. Ersh had seen it from the beginning. Esen-alit-Quar wasn't simply different from the others of their Web.

She would be as Ersh, one day. The source and repository of knowledge for a new Web, deciding what to share in flesh and what to keep hidden. And, like Ersh, Esen would make those decisions based on her own Rules.

Skalet rolled around the scar in the mountain and found her favorite place to wait. The Kraal valued leaders. S'kal-ru had tasted that ephemeral notion of power, been trapped into a longing for it. She'd been wrong.

Ersh hadn't ruled her Web nor, one day, would Esen. They were something both simpler and far more potent. *And annoying,* Skalet added—honest with herself.

A conscience.

33: Port Authority Night

"I HAVE to go."

"Because you gave your word. I was there, Esen."

I ran the forks of my tongue over my tusks to check they were squeaky clean. The quarters Alphonsus had loaned us had included a small, but most welcome 'fresher. "Then why are you arguing with me?"

Paul threw up his hands. He looked himself again, albeit a tired self. There'd been time to clean up and dress, but I think what had most improved his appearance was being Paul Cameron again. Neither of us had talked to Joel Largas yet—that worthy had retired to his ship—but so far, life seemed to be reassuringly back to normal. *And without Ganthor,* I told myself, inclined to feel smug. Paul had even, to my great satisfaction, spoken to his offspring over the com. They'd been charmingly relieved to know we were all right, although busy prepping for launch. It seemed every spacer was anxious to lift as soon as tugs could move their ships into position. The Gem Rush was evidently over.

A first step, I thought to myself.

Our own celebration had been a quiet one. Most of the staff had been awake so long they'd fallen asleep over their first beer, although the last time I'd looked, Meony-ro was still holding court with the few left. Before he'd gone home, I'd overheard the Chief Constable virtually threatening a person named Naomi into promising more free drinks when everyone was awake again. Humans could be so odd.

My Human wasn't being odd. On the contrary, he was

demonstrating a fine grasp of reality. "Esen, you can't let Skalet have what she wants."

I showed a cheerful tusk. "Oh, but I plan to." Then I relented, seeing him run one hand through his hair, as he did when I was being particularly frustrating. "She doesn't know what that is, Paul," I assured him.

"And you do?"

"We'll find out." I checked the fall of my new outfit. It wasn't silk, but did cover the required areas. And the yellow wasn't a bad choice, given the orange lighting. *No bag or hand light,* I fussed. Paul, of course, wasn't worrying about something so trivial. "I promised," I insisted, noticing his frown hadn't left.

"You can't trust her."

Typically Human. "Trust isn't required," I told him. "Although if you want to talk about trust, she did give you the antidote to the duras."

He turned an interesting color. "Don't remind me."

I tilted my head. "I thought Humans enjoyed kissing. I've seen you do so many times, with different partners. Did you not enjoy Skalet's?"

The color deepened. "You ask the worst—Es—" Words seemed to fail him, then suddenly Paul relaxed and grinned at me. "You're trying to change the subject."

"Perhaps." Then I showed both tusks. "But I admit to curiosity."

"You?" Paul laughed. "Which means I won't hear the end of it until I answer." He tapped me lightly under the chin. "Let's say it's not like shaking hands, Old Blob. There's an emotional context involved which can be very pleasant—or otherwise." His fingers drifted to his lower lip. "Skalet's? Was—otherwise."

"Good. I didn't enjoy watching either."

Another tap, even softer. "I know, Esen. Did I tell you how brave you've been?"

"No," I said happily, "but feel free to—"

A knock on the door interrupted my encouragement,

which was probably as well. *Compliments,* I'd noticed, *often ended with a discussion of what I could have done better.* I went to answer it.

"Wait." All the ease gone from his face, Paul waved me to one side and reached for the weapon he'd left lying on the pile of Kraal clothing. He held his finger to his lips when I would have protested. "Come in," he called.

The door opened. The night-lighting in the hallway showed me no more than a silhouette. Human-sized.

Having adaptable eyes, Paul recognized our visitor and tossed the weapon aside with a glad: "Rudy! Welcome. I thought you'd be down in the bar with Meony-ro, helping him drink to the end of Mocktap."

I backed away until I felt the wall behind me.

Rudy wore spacer coveralls, presumably from the *Russell III.* There was a slight lurch to his steps as he accepted the invitation and walked into the room. Paul put one arm around his cousin's shoulders. "I can't tell you how glad we . . ."

Paul had seen me.

So had Rudy. His face lost its smile and became troubled. "Hello, Es," he said, no slur to the words. *Not drunk then.* A being with something on his mind.

I was reasonably sure I knew what it was.

Paul seemed at a loss. He took his arm from Rudy, then looked from one of us to the other with almost comical suspicion. "Something I should know?" he asked, the words deliberately light.

When Rudy didn't answer, I did. "Your cousin finally noticed I'm not 'Bess.'" There was a note of hurt in my voice I could no more prevent than I could settle my third stomach. I shunted its contents to the safer fourth. "He no longer believes I am his friend—your friend. Why do you think I wanted Mocktap's weapon destroyed?"

"What?" If he'd been Lishcyn, I would have expected to see Rudy's jaw on his chest. "No—that's not true!"

"Ah." Paul schooled his expression into the attentive,

noncommittal one he used when negotiating for Cameron & Ki—or when he had reason to believe I'd hidden fudge—and gazed at both of us in turn.

"He was planning to kill Skalet," I said, glaring down my snout. "He listened to that Kraal. Ask him what he thinks of my kind."

Suddenly, Rudy looked as angry as I felt. "It's one thing to be told you're almost six hundred years old and quite another to see a staircase worn down by footsteps! Footsteps! Do you know how long that takes? How long someone must have lived there?"

Actually, I did, but something in Paul's face warned me against reciting facts at the moment. "So I'm on the—young—side of the family," I said instead, unwilling to leave the wall just yet. I knew Rudy too well not to fear him, if he'd become my enemy. "That doesn't mean we're a threat. That doesn't mean you should—"

"Es. Calm down. Explain to Rudy. Tell him about the mountain."

I was tempted to burp something unpleasant, but Paul stopped me with that look. "It's where I grew up," I said grudgingly. "Ersh's home. I told you she was the first of our kind in this section of space. She lived a very long time, but you won't find records of her. Like all of us, she stayed out of sight. The rest of our web-kin would come to visit, share what they'd learned, then leave again. The mountaintop was Ersh's favorite gathering place. She," I swallowed, "she liked the view."

I didn't think it would help to add how she'd also thrown me off her mountain to bring out my web-nature, or how she viewed my subsequent terror of the sheer cliff as an aid to faster assimilation. "The room where you and the Kraal waited for us was our greenhouse. The material Mocktap had refined into the flask—" I couldn't find the words and looked at Paul.

He understood. "Ersh died by spreading herself throughout the stone of that mountain, Rudy. The blue substance was part of her body, stolen from its grave." Rudy sat down rather suddenly and Paul took the seat across from him. "Not some secret weapon," my Human went on gently. "Not some new and powerful material. The remains of Skalet's and Esen's—mother. Now do you understand why we had to come to Picco's Moon? Why all this mattered so much we couldn't stay away?"

Rudy rubbed his hand over his face, then looked up at me. "I thought—I thought I was handling it all, that I understood. Then Sybil—Mocktap—told me about S'kal-ru, how she'd played this game with her family for centuries, how she did the same with you. I saw the staircase—guessed how old your kind could become. It was as though you were playing with all of us—like—"

"—blob-shaped gods?" I offered helpfully.

"Something like that."

Paul's lips quirked and I flopped one ear at him. "Skalet's unique," I told Rudy, taking a cautious step from the wall. "She chose the Kraal form to explore their obsession with strategy—those games. But as much as our true nature dictates how we appear in each form, each form has an effect on who we are. After a time, I believe she began to think as a Kraal. I," I added soberly, "do not. Do you understand?"

"I think so. I'm trying. But, Esen, please believe me. I didn't come here because I had any doubts about you. You're my friend—my family. I can handle your—unique abilities. I came because—" It was Rudy's turn to halt and look at Paul helplessly, then back to me. "I almost killed your—your sister."

I blinked.

"Can you forgive me?"

For a being who could resolve a conflict among Ganthor, Tumblers, and Humans—plus a variety of others—I could be remarkably obtuse when it came to my own friends. Of course Rudy had been anxious about how I'd react. I felt all my stomachs settle, along with the universe in general.

But, of course, a Human in full confession mode never knew when to stop. "And, Paul, can you forgive me?"

Paul didn't ask, "for what?" No, he turned his full attention on me, and said in that firm, "there will likely be consequences" voice he and Ersh did so well: "Esen?"

"Rudy did me a small—favor," I admitted.

The Human in question nodded. I wondered if he had had a little too much to drink tonight after all. "She was concerned you were too gullible—that Group of yours. I could understand why. I mean. Really, Paul. To trust all those people with Esen's secret?"

"So you spied on them for Esen."

"Well. Yes." Rudy looked apprehensive. I would have been as well, except the smile spreading across Paul's face was nothing short of beatific.

Ersh. "You knew," I accused him. "All along."

"What sort of conspirator would I be, if I couldn't keep track of the two of you?" Paul said comfortably, ignoring Rudy's frown and the grumbling of my stomach.

"Why let me think I was—that we were—"

"Because," his smile faded, "I recruited the best people I could find to help us—to help you in the future, Esen. But there was no point unless you trusted them. How could you, unless you checked them for yourself, without me? And it was worthwhile," he said very grimly, "given what Rudy learned about Zoltan and some of the others."

Needless to say, his approval was better than being scolded, if puzzling. "You knew I asked Rudy to spy on your friends," in case Paul had missed the essential detail. "And you're happy?"

"Impatient, might be the better word. I've been waiting for some time."

"For what?"

Rudy, as befitted a member of the same species, understood first. "For you to act on your own."

"I do that all the time," I said rather huffily.

"Not against Paul," Rudy countered, nodding as if this made perfect sense.

I glowered at both of them.

My Human smiled back, looking vastly content. "Consider it a consequence of my Human parenting instinct, Old Blob. I needed to be sure you'd think for yourself, even if it meant you'd refuse to take something I told you for granted. There'll be no new members of the Group, Esen, unless you pick them. And no more surprises for your own good either."

I began to sense the possibilities. "So you'll listen to me."

"I'll always listen." Paul raised one eyebrow. "I won't always agree."

Fair enough. I showed both tusks. "True day starts in half an hour, gentlemen. I'd like to be on the mountain by then."

Where someone who always planned surprises for me waited.

Otherwhere

"I KNOW you're there."

Startled, Kearn slipped at the edge of the rock cut. The voice spoke comspeak, but was made of bells. He looked in vain for its source, his hand light sending its beam coursing over strange shapes and producing irregular shadows that moved across his view as if alive. And waiting to pounce. "Is that Fem Skalet?" he whispered.

"Kearn?" the voice grew startled as well. "Are you alone?"

"Yes, yes." Kearn relaxed as his light found the Tumbler, squinting up through the reflections. Then he saw where the crystal wasn't gleaming. Something on the hands and arms ate the light, something dark.

Skalet lifted one long hand, as if to show him. "Fools' blood."

"I—" he decided he didn't really want to know. "Esen was able to send the Ganthor away. She didn't tell us how . . ." He left room for her to answer. When she didn't, he shone the light to find a safe path for his feet, feeling the darkness press on every side, and went closer.

Bells could toll in warning. "Why are you here, Kearn? Do you think to kill a monster?"

"No. I have something of yours. I wanted to bring it back to you, before you left." He halted to pull the book from his pocket, then played the light over the gilded bones and scales of its cover.

Bells could tinkle with laughter. "You came here, in the dark, to bring my book to me? Why?"

"I—I read it, Fem Skalet. You have lovely handwriting, by the way. The other you," Kearn fumbled for whatever terminology a web-being might prefer, then settled for: "S'kal-ru."

"A scholar. I'm impressed." A pause. "The book isn't necessary. Esen and I. Did you know we never forget? Not a molecule, a whisper, a sunrise."

"No. I didn't know. I guessed. Hypothesized. To remember each form, there had to be a mechanism. There—"

"We are memory." Another pause. "Still, I should like the book. Thank you for its return."

Kearn found himself as close as he dared, and found a boulder on which to sit. He set the light down, so it splashed against another rock and back over them both, then drew his coat more tightly around his shoulders against the chill night air. "It was fascinating to read. I gained valuable insights into the Kraal—"

"And into a web-being?"

Caution, not warning. He went on before his courage failed. It almost had twice before: when leaving the *Russell III* and when landing here. *But this was his only chance.* "I believe so. I have so many questions. I—" Then, the truth poured out, as if the dark made it safer. "They'll take my ship away. My research funds. But I thought, if I could talk to you for a while, I'd know enough."

"You can talk to Esen all you like. I'm sure the Youngest would be pleased to reveal all manner of secrets for the asking. Why come here? To me?"

"This." Kearn patted the book. "This—this is how I am. I put pieces together, fill in every detail. Reading it,

I thought we were alike in that. And—" he hesitated. "I don't wish to cause offense, Fem Skalet, but . . ."

"Go on."

"This was written by an adult."

Definitely a laugh. "Do tell Esen you said so. I can see her face now. Whichever one she's wearing." A chime as the Tumbler moved, seemed to look up. "She'll come soon—when true day restores safe passage. When our business is done, I don't plan to return." A minor chord. "Like you, Lionel Kearn, I find myself at a loss for a future."

He lifted the book. "Your House?"

"Events here have made me—conspicuous—among the Kraal. It is not conducive to establishing a home. Or safe, for that matter. I can wait."

Kearn licked his lips, tasting acrid dust. "How long? How long can you wait? Another two generations? Three?"

"You do have questions." Another minor chord.

He closed his eyes briefly. "My apologies, Fem Skalet. My enthusiasm gets the better of me."

"Your enthusiasm—your passion—kept you searching when no one else believed. I valued it then. I value it now." A pause. Then, "How long before the Kraal settle? What do you know of the House of Bryll, and its conflict with . . ."

Kearn leaned forward, intent on the magic of that voice.

34: Mountain Dawn

ESEN-ALIT-QUAR! Esen-alit-Quar!

I'd always hear their voices on this mountain, I thought as I took the last three steps to the top. The Kraal had left enough scars on the peak; I'd asked Rudy to land the aircar on the pad below. He and Paul followed me now.

"Skalet!" I called, walking to the place where I'd always walked.

She appeared, but not alone. Kearn, of all beings, walked beside her as she tumbled toward us. I gave my jaw a strong push to keep it in place. "You're late, Youngest."

Some things never changed, I thought.

Paul, who knew what to expect, had warned Rudy. They both looked concerned, if for different reasons. Rudy had resolved to learn more about the "non-Bess" me, and worried about what that might be.

Paul? He worried about me. I could see it in the way he stayed calm and reassuring, helping me remove my new clothes before I could cycle and leave their molecules as a fashionable stencil on the ground.

Paul, Rudy, Kearn. Skalet and me. The mountain. *Some part of me found it fitting that we were again six.*

The rest of me knew exactly what Ersh would have said about the presence of the Humans and winced.

Skalet tumbled to her accustomed place and waited. Paul and Rudy, without knowing, took positions where Mixs and Ansky would be. Kearn was closer to Skalet than Lesy ever stood, but on that side. The place for Ersh remained empty.

"Where is what you promised me, Youngest?" She held up one bloodstained hand. I found it didn't trouble me, this once, that Skalet had fought and likely killed. The Tumblers had been without a champion.

I nodded at Paul. He held up a cryosac, opening its mouth to show a brilliant blue, then closing it again.

Skalet leaned toward him, as if to roll. "Wait." I told her. "I have something to say to you first."

"Why should I listen?"

"Because Paul has his thumb on a control that will heat and destroy what's in his hand."

She chimed amusement, then settled back. "Very well. Say what you wish."

"Not like this," I told her, then cycled . . . moving through web-form too quickly to change my mind . . .

. . . until the cold thin air burned its way into every part of my damaged muzzle. My good eye watered as I braced my feet. I heard Rudy gasp and Paul's snapped order for him to stay still. He'd known I planned this. The Web of Ersh met in their preferred forms. It was her Rule.

Skalet didn't hesitate. Crystal blurred and flashed blue, then . . .

. . . fierce eyes surrounded by black-and-red tattoos met mine. She dropped to her knees, naked, the knife gone. The wound fountained blood until Kearn gave Skalet his gloves to press over it, then it merely welled out and over, puddling in the diamond dust. He wrapped his coat around her shoulders, then stood back, shivering.

I spoke even as Kearn cared for her, knowing her time in this form was short, feeling my own form grow weak. "You never asked why Ersh shared with me alone, Skalet. It was because I was the only one who could protect the rest of you from her secrets. Things about her and her beginnings. Things that changed me forever." I tasted blood as my wound reopened. "It was no gift. It was a penalty of my different beginning she used to spare you—all of you.

"I am the Senior Assimilator of our Web, Skalet," I continued, taking an unsteady step into the center of our circle. "If you would now share what Ersh chose not to give you, I will provide it. But you will no longer be who you are. And you will lose the Ersh you remember."

Her hand plunged down to grip the stone. Not to brace herself, but as if asking a question. "I want to—fly."

From somewhere, I found the strength to look down at my trembling web-kin and tell her the truth. "No. You want the Ersh you knew. I can give that much, Skalet. If you trust me."

I saw the answer in her eyes even as she cycled to save herself . . . I did the same . . .

. . . sensing the perfection of her teardrop shape, beyond it the throbbing heart that was Picco's gravity, courted by the echo of her Moon, beyond that the singing spin of stars and atoms . . .

Share . . . I released the message to the winds, offering my flesh.

Feeling Skalet's jagged teeth rip through me as proof I was again as I was meant to be . . .

Tearing free bites of Skalet-mass, to replace what I'd lost. Assimilating her memories into mine . . .

. . . as proof I was no longer alone.

Humans were perhaps the most adaptable species to ever develop self-consciousness. I had further evidence, if I needed any, when I found duras plants conveniently nearby when I was ready to cycle from web-form into something that could sit in an aircar.

Comfortably Lishcyn again, I looked for Skalet, finding a magnificent Moderan lifting its fangs at me—an expression of happiness. But her memories in mine were like shattered crystal, edged in grief and need. I found I had to push away the emotion in order to assimilate the rest.

Most I knew, or guessed. Her life within the Kraal hierarchy had become a desperate struggle to be Human, to fit in and succeed. She'd done her best, but I could have told her being Human wasn't as easy as slipping into that flesh. Memories of her manipulation of Kearn were overlapped by their conversation of this morning, colored by a new and rather perplexed respect.

She'd feared Death, that another mindless web-being might attack us, and planned weapons to defeat it. But she'd been Kraal enough to assume her worst enemy would be her closest ally, and made the design include a trap keyed to Mocktap. Rudy could have killed her. She'd believed he would.

Her impressions of me ranged from infuriating to embarrassing, but, like Kearn, I'd earned something approximating respect.

I thought I'd keep her impression of Paul to myself.

What I'd shared kept Skalet quiet as well, on the trip back, although she'd had an implant grown into her throat to utter comspeak. I knew what she was assimilating.

Memories of Ersh. I'd had hundreds of years living with her, while Skalet collected information on other species for the Web. I gave every minute of them back—including the ones where I was in trouble.

It seemed only fair.

We were, in the end, family.

There was a balcony attached to the Port Authority cafeteria, for those who didn't mind the looming presence of Picco. I stood there, watching the shipcity disassemble and move itself back into space—one more amazement in a day I wouldn't forget, even if I could.

"I thought I'd find you here." Paul rested his elbows on the rail. "Any sign of a Tumbler? Alphonsus tells me the sanitation workers are getting worried. Something about pensions."

I pointed to a glint of light on the horizon. "They're out there. Should I tell Alphonsus they believe he's been replaced? That everyone here is—new?"

Paul's laugh was low and contagious. I bent my ear to enjoy it. "Will it matter?"

"I suppose not." I curled my lip. "But I do like the irony."

We became silent to watch the lift of two freighters, paired flame until one peeled away from the other.

"Speaking of irony, you did notice that Skalet managed to steal the bag of bits, I trust? In spite of your talk with her about the value of not-knowing."

My other lip curled over a tusk and stayed there. "I noticed," I said contentedly.

"Rudy offered to hunt for them while she's in *Russ'* med box." At my look, Paul chuckled. "Don't worry. I told him not to bother. But she's not going to be happy when she finds out they are your bits, not Ersh's."

"Or she will." The bits were something of a gift. Paul and I had accumulated a fair amount of information on other species during our time at Cameron & Ki. I thought Skalet would appreciate it. *Eventually.* I'd also included something of Paul's. That, I expected to hear about.

"You were never going to show her how to fly, were you?"

I glanced at the silver pendant hanging from his neck, watching it catch the light and return it as flashes of orange. "How could I?" I said, turning back to the view. "You know I excised that mass. When they destroyed our home, they destroyed our cryounit. Not that Skalet would have believed it."

Mind you, I thought, *she'd have been right.* The pendant still held its message introducing Paul to another web-being, but since our last trial together, it had held more. I looked on it as my conscience, that my greatest and most dangerous temptation rested out of reach, just over Paul's heart.

"So what now, Old Blob?" Paul twisted around to put his spine against the railing and looked up at me. "Apparently we are clear to go back to the export business—if the Largas family hasn't offended too many customers with suspicious questions about our whereabouts. Meony-ro even managed to get those knives appraised for you."

"And Joel?"

"Yes, Joel." Paul bent his head so I couldn't see his face. "He's never said a word about us. Even now, he talks to me as if nothing's happened. But it has. I don't know what to say, Esen."

"I do," I said gently, bending down so I could look him in the eyes. As a result, I went off my center of gravity and had to grab the railing for balance. "I do," I repeated, deciding erect was safer.

Paul pushed his hair from his eyes and gazed at me fondly. "And what is that?"

"That I owe Joel Largas a home free of his nightmare, even if he is willing to accept me back."

"You're sure?"

I watched another starship seek its future.

"It's time to make a fresh start," I told my web-kin.

Otherwhere

IT WAS standing room only at the Circle Club, which was fine for those species who'd never developed an interest in chairs. Rudy made his way around a few, careful of feet, tails, and other, more sensitive appendages. Friday nights were busy ones, in the Dump.

A couple of questions gave him directions to the back; spacers knew where to find each other. Rudy eased by a waiter balancing a huge bowl of cream-drenched pyati, then spotted his goal.

He hesitated. His visit to Minas XII had been a quiet one. Paul and Esen had wanted some personal belongings from their office. He'd offered to pack them up and arrange shipping, not really thinking what it would be like to come back. Then, the message from Silv to meet here.

At first, Rudy had ignored it. But there were few things more boring than sitting in a passenger compartment waiting for a transport to lift, especially if you were used to being on the bridge of a ship like the *Russ'*. The bridge would be full of strangers, now. They were all gone. Timri had taken a new post; Kearn had retired; even Resdick was apparently off on his own. Cristoffen? He hadn't stood trial after all, having come to believe everyone around him was a monster. Rudy could almost feel sorry for him.

Plus, he'd had enough of his own company. So here he was, avoiding being trampled by customers with larger feet—or none—and wondering if it was too late to head to the bar and blend in with the crowd.

It was. "Rudy! Over here!"

He found a smile and wore it as he went to the table where Silv was waving, because Silv wasn't alone, or with his crew. He sat with Joel Largas.

Worse, the moment Rudy sat down, Silv got to his feet and hurried away.

Amazing, Rudy thought, *how suddenly too-intimate a table in a busy bar could become.*

"Joel. You look well."

The old spacer signaled the waiter, then regarded Rudy. "Seen you look better. What happened with the Commonwealth ship?"

"My reinstatement hadn't been approved by anyone but the Project Leader. They didn't look too kindly on his ignoring the chain of command."

"You're too good a captain to waste because of protocol."

Rudy took the glass of beer that arrived and poured a third down the back of his throat. "Thanks. They didn't think so."

"I do. You can have a ship with Largas Freight. Just say the word."

The Botharan stared into his glass for a moment, then looked up. "Not without the truth between us, Joel," he said heavily. "Whatever you've decided to tell everyone else—even if it's what you've been telling yourself—it isn't going to work with me."

Joel's eyes were bright under his bushy eyebrows. "No, I didn't think it would. The truth?" He tossed back a shot of something amber, and followed it with a pour of beer himself. "I drove away two friends as dear to me as any son and daughter could be."

"You thought you had reason."

"Yes. I did. And I would have killed them if I'd had the chance. I was sure they planned to do the same to me. In fact, Rudy," Joel leaned forward, his face gone pale, "I thought they did. Last thing I remembered was them arguing about what to do with me, then Paul's face—" Joel closed his eyes.

Rudy traced a circle on the table. He knew what Joel meant. He'd seen Paul defend Esen.

"I wasn't dead. I woke up in bed. My own," the spacer continued, his voice growing unsteady. "Might have been a bad dream, but the entire family was crowding around, worried and all talking at once. Paul and Es had brought me home. They could have been—should have been—running from the Kraal. Why, I asked myself, would they do that? You know, don't you, Rudy?"

Rudy helped himself to a shot, then nodded. "Because they were the same people you'd always cared about. What you found out didn't change them. It changed you."

Joel pressed both hands flat on the tabletop. "Changed me? Changed me for the worse. I thought— terrible things, Rudy. Horrible things. I couldn't sleep or eat. I didn't dare tell a soul. Who would believe me without proof? Then, when Char called translight, frantic and ready to turn her ship around—I made up a lie that they were safe and hiding. How could I tell the truth then? I did what I could to track them down. All the while my family thought I was some kind of hero, risking my health." His eyes filled with moisture. "A hero, when I was trying to hunt down my own friends."

"You were a hero, on Picco's Moon. The Chief Constable told me what you did."

"You know who saved us all."

Rudy leaned forward. "Tell me. Say it."

Joel's lips worked, but no sound came out.

"Who, Joel?"

"Esolesy Ki." The older Human shuddered and took a quick drink. "Es. The Esen Monster."

"Bess," Rudy added.

Joel looked stunned. "Your—niece?"

"Didn't you wonder what she was doing in the Dump, being held at gunpoint by that Tly maniac, Logan? Esen went after him herself, trying to keep Paul out of trouble. She—" Rudy found himself grinning, "—she has a tendency to miscalculate sometimes. She means well."

"Es and those damn leaves—" Joel stopped, and wiped his eyes. "They need a new ventilation system in here." He stared at Rudy, looking suddenly lost. "Why haven't they come home? They have to know I've kept their secret. I will keep it."

"For one thing, you scared them off the planet. You're a formidable enemy, Joel Largas. And now? They don't want to upset you any more than they have. Esen tends to worry about such things."

"I've survived a war and seventeen marriage contracts. I don't upset that easily. Rudy, I want to understand how I could have been so wrong. I need to." Joel's voice became husky and thick. "I want to see them. I want to be able to look them in the eyes and not be afraid."

So. "Let me tell you a story about a blue blob, a dungeon, and a young alien language specialist named Paul," Rudy began. Then he smiled, a wide, honestly happy smile. "And after that, you can tell me about my new ship."

35: Barn Afternoon

THERE were worlds where vegetation crowded the sky and others where you had to dig in sand up to your shoulders, if you had them, to find something to bite. And, more rarely, there were worlds like this one. I patted the turf with my paw and drew fragrant, lively air through my healed nostrils. A world like a greenhouse, welcoming and rich, where the life of a thousand other worlds could thrive. I put my chin on my shoulder to look up at Paul. "What do you think?"

He hadn't smiled since I'd told him our destination, remaining the next best thing to grim throughout the trip. I'd have worn out my cheerfulness on him days ago, if I hadn't had so much stored up.

My good mood, I decided unrepentantly, *was probably making him worse.*

This world liked him, too. A breeze was playing with his hair, and trying to interest his lips in a smile. The warm sun had already taken off his jacket, which was lying on top of the belongings I'd insisted we pack for our excursion. Some seeds were hanging on to his pants, hoping for a ride.

"What do I think? That you arranged all this to torture me for something. Care to tell me what?"

There was real pain in his voice and I relented. Standing up, I put one paw on Paul's shoulder and used the other to draw an imaginary line. "I bought it. All of it. From there to," I squinted against glare from the lake below, "there."

"Esen. You know where this is— Pardon?"

I let my tongue hang out with glee. My muzzle had distressingly bare patches—and the meds suspected the new fur could grow in dappled—but some clever use of cosmetics helped disguise that and protected the new skin from the sun. "I know exactly where we are, Paul. Botharis. Your homeworld. That's the farm where you attempted to fly. That's the farm where Rudy grew up. That's the road to the—"

"Shut up, Fangface, and tell me what you did."

"Bought it. All of it."

Paul seemed unable to find even the unlikely adjectives he used on occasion. "We shouldn't be here," he gasped finally. "We can't stay here."

"Why?" I asked.

"Because—"

When he appeared stuck on the word, I went on: "In case you are wondering, the title is registered to Paul Antoni Ragem Cameron and me, Esen-alit-Quar."

He pressed his hands to his eyes. I wasn't sure if this was to hide from me or avoid the lovely view. "Esen. Did sharing with Skalet cause you to lose some part of your mind?"

I poked him gently in the stomach. "Silly Human. I checked all this with Lionel and Rudy. There's no reason we can't use those names. The Botharan government has changed seven times at the planetary level since your family lived here. Fifteen times locally. There are no continuous records worth considering. And, best of all, Botharis is presently very loosely affiliated with the Kraal Confederacy, for now anyway. So Skalet can come and visit, but there shouldn't be any occupation. She didn't think so, anyway. She'll let us know."

Paul sat down rather abruptly. I dropped on my stomach

beside him. "You're planning to live here?" he asked numbly.

"Well, I'm a little more ambitious than that. See that barn? The white one?"

A touch of asperity. "I know my family's barn, Esen."

"Just checking." I put my chin on my paws, wiggling my nose to discourage an adventurous insect. "What you don't know," I told my Human, "is what's inside. Rudy moved in the system you'd given him. He has another on Minas XII now."

"You've been busy." That suspicious voice.

My tail beat down the grass. "Oh, it gets better. Want to know what happens next week?"

"I'm not sure." But he'd gone from numb to thoughtful. *At any moment,* I thought happily, *there'd be curious.* Sure enough. "What happens next week?"

"The servos and contractors arrive. I shop for comfy chairs. And gardeners. Everything is lovely, but we do need some landscaping around the new building."

For a peace-loving being, Paul could move very quickly. He had me by the scruff of the neck before I could blink, his nose almost touching mine. I gave it a quick lick. "The short and highly informative version, Es," he demanded, giving me a shake.

"Your library."

"But—" Paul sank back down, his hands trailing along my fur. "I thought you hated the idea."

"Skalet hated it. She's getting better. I worried about it. That's not hating."

"And you aren't worried now?"

I sat up, resisting the urge to scratch away a freeloader. It was a moment for dignity. *Never easy in this form.*

"What happened—what almost happened—on Picco's Moon could have been avoided if there was a dictionary of the Tumbler language and customs. Or the Ganthor. Ideally both. The problem didn't need a shapeshifter to solve it. It needed understanding. I decided you were right. That what

I know, what we learn, is better shared. And not just with my annoying web-kin." I gave him a chance to say something. He seemed paralyzed, except for something shiny about his eyes. "This will also let me keep watch for any more web-beings. Lionel is coming to help. We can continue to process incoming information as before. Expand that. All in the open."

"In the open. Esen, you said it yourself. Safety is being hidden. You can't risk revealing what you are—"

I shook from my mane to my tail, setting free a cloud of hair and grass bits to sparkle in the air. "Not for a moment. But, isn't this a better way? To be hidden in sight, free to be who we choose, do what we wish? To be ourselves?"

Paul looked at me, then out over the fields. "It's a wonderful dream, Esen. You know I want this, believe in this. If we could—" his breath seemed to catch in his throat. Then, "It's too dangerous."

"Tried safe. Didn't like it. Dark and soggy—remember?"

"Esen."

"You wanted me to act for myself," I reminded him. "I have. So my question for you is a simple one. Will you help me?"

I thought I'd seen every expression of his dear face, but I'd never seen such achingly vulnerable joy, as if he'd protected himself so long against it, it threatened to overwhelm him. "There's a lot to do," I warned, gruffly.

Paul took a deep breath, then let it out slowly. He did it again. "We'll need architects," he said almost calmly. "Permits. I realize funds aren't an issue, but there's—" I could see the ideas starting to take hold in his eyes and held up one paw.

"So the answer is yes?"

Paul dug his fingers behind my left ear, unerringly finding the perfect spot, and said: "Yes."

*   *   *

I stayed on the hilltop, watching Paul pace out his library—a task he couldn't complete before the sun went down, but that didn't seem to matter. He was so full of joy I wondered that his feet touched the ground at all.

I tucked this moment into my private memories, the part of Esen that would never be shared, but always be treasured. *We'd both,* I thought, *recovered something of our pasts.*

Who would have dreamed it could lead us to our future?

Julie E. Czerneda

Web Shifters

"A great adventure following an engaging character across a divertingly varied series of worlds."—*Locus*

Esen is a shapeshifter, one of the last of an ancient race. Only one Human knows her true nature—but those who suspect are determined to destroy her!

BEHOLDER'S EYE
0-88677-818-2
CHANGING VISION
0-88677-815-8

Also by Julie E. Czerneda:

IN THE COMPANY OF OTHERS
0-88677-999-7
"An exhilarating science fiction thriller"—
Romantic Times

To Order Call: 1-800-788-6262

Julie E. Czerneda

THE TRADE PACT UNIVERSE

"Space adventure mixes with romance...a heck of a lot of fun." —*Locus*

Sira holds the answer to the survival of her species, the Clan, within the multi-species Trade Pact. But it will take a Human's courage to show her the way.

A THOUSAND WORDS FOR STRANGER
0- 88677-769-0

TIES OF POWER
0-88677-850-6

TO TRADE THE STARS
0-7564-0075-9

To Order Call: 1-800-788-6262

DAW 12

CJ Cherryh

Classic Series in New Omnibus Editions

THE DREAMING TREE
Contains the complete duology *The Dreamstone* and
The Tree of Swords and Jewels.   0-88677-782-8

THE FADED SUN TRILOGY
Contains the complete novels *Kesrith*, *Shon'jir*, and
Kutath.   0-88677-836-0

THE MORGAINE SAGA
Contains the complete novels *Gate of Ivrel*, *Well of
Shiuan*, and *Fires of Azeroth.*   0-88677-877-8

THE CHANUR SAGA
Contains the complete novels *The Pride of Chanur*,
Chanur's Venture and *The Kif Strike Back.*
    0-88677-930-8

ALTERNATE REALITIES
Contains the complete novels *Port Eterntiy*, *Voyager in
Night*, and *Wave Without a Shore*   0-88677-946-4

To Order Call: 1-800-788-6262

DAW 9